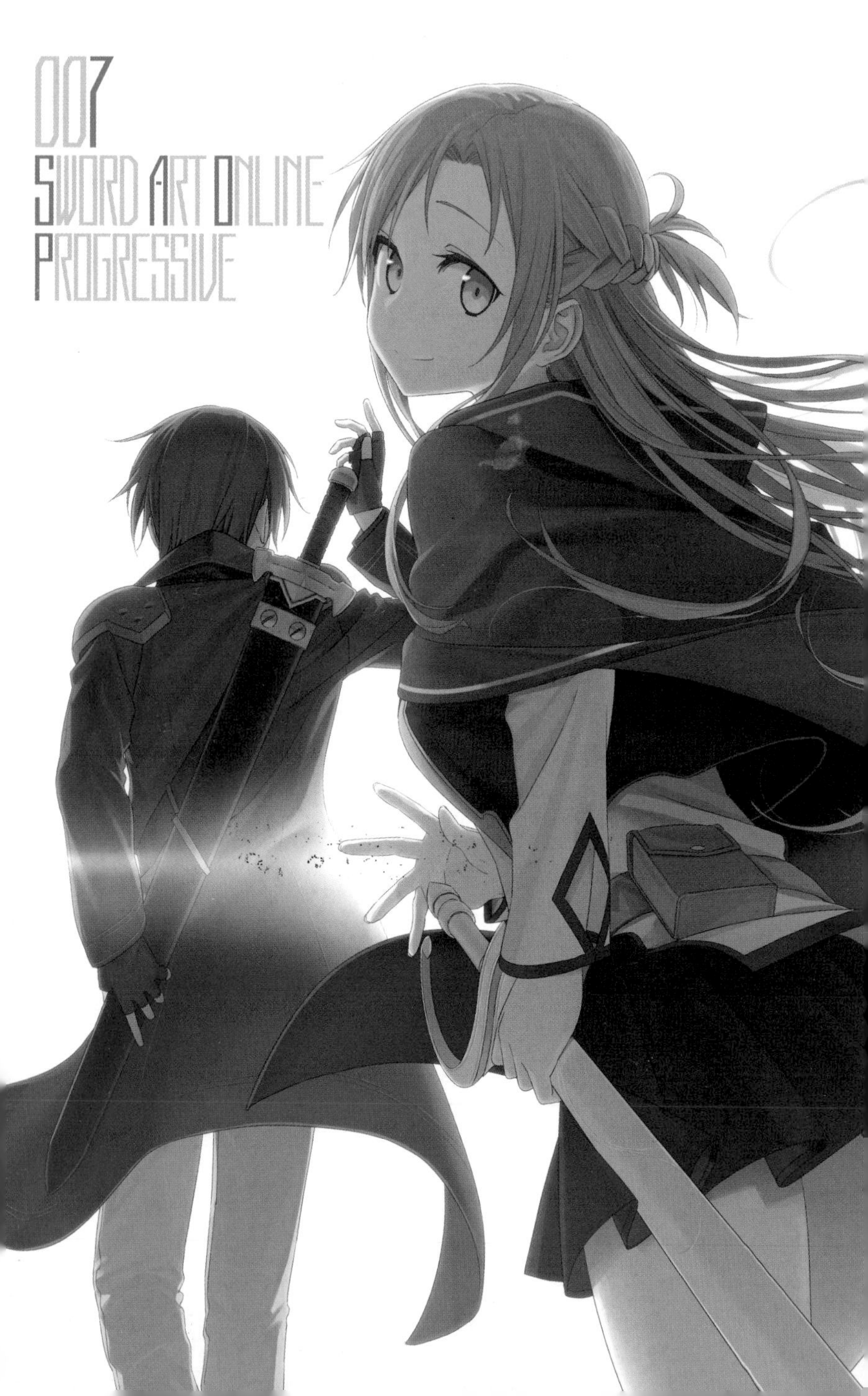
007
SWORD ART ONLINE
PROGRESSIVE

SWORD ART ONLINE PROGRESSIVE 007

CONTENTS

ART: KISEKI HIMURA
ORIGINAL STORY: REKI KAWAHARA
CHARACTER DESIGN: abec

#037: First Strike

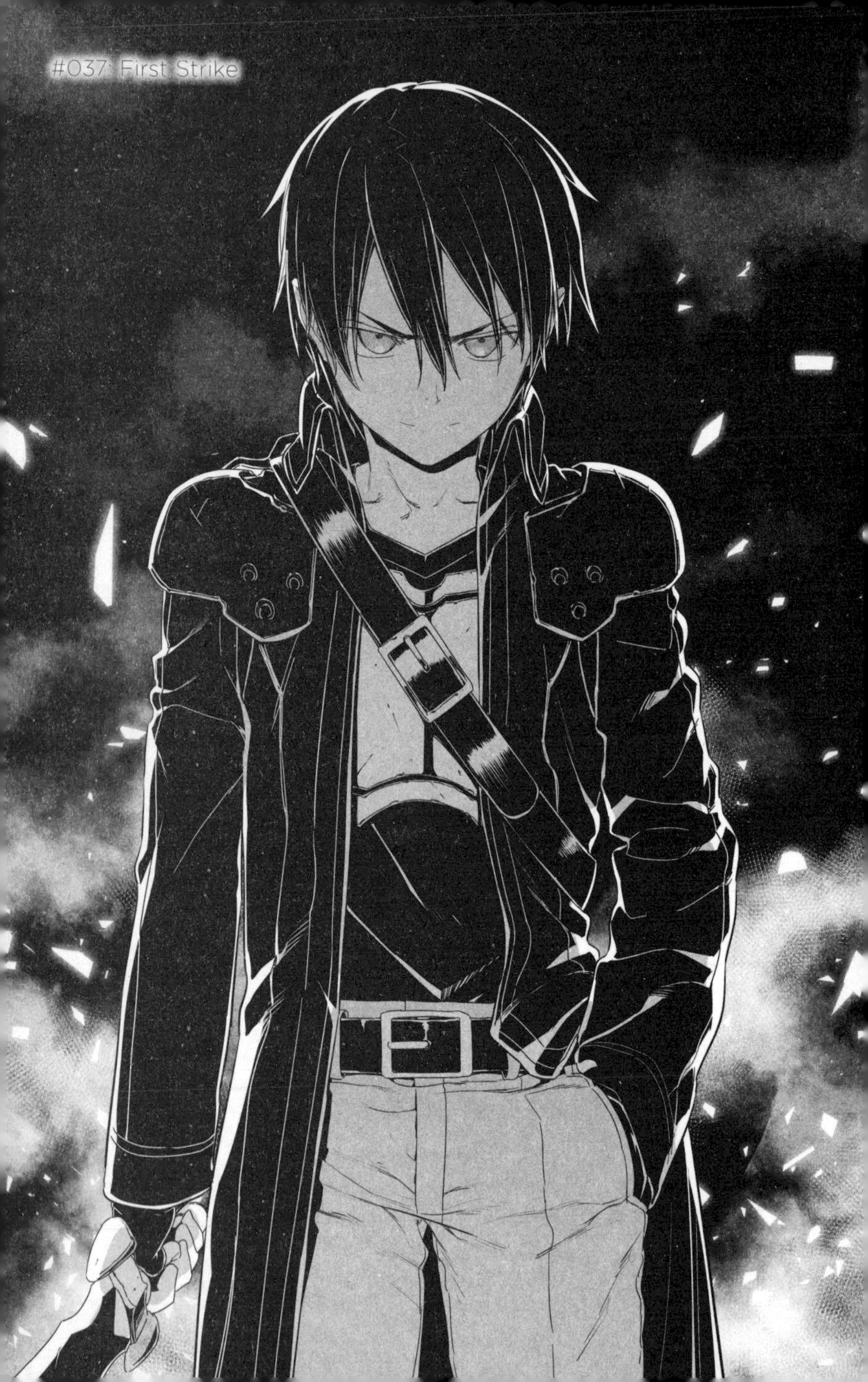

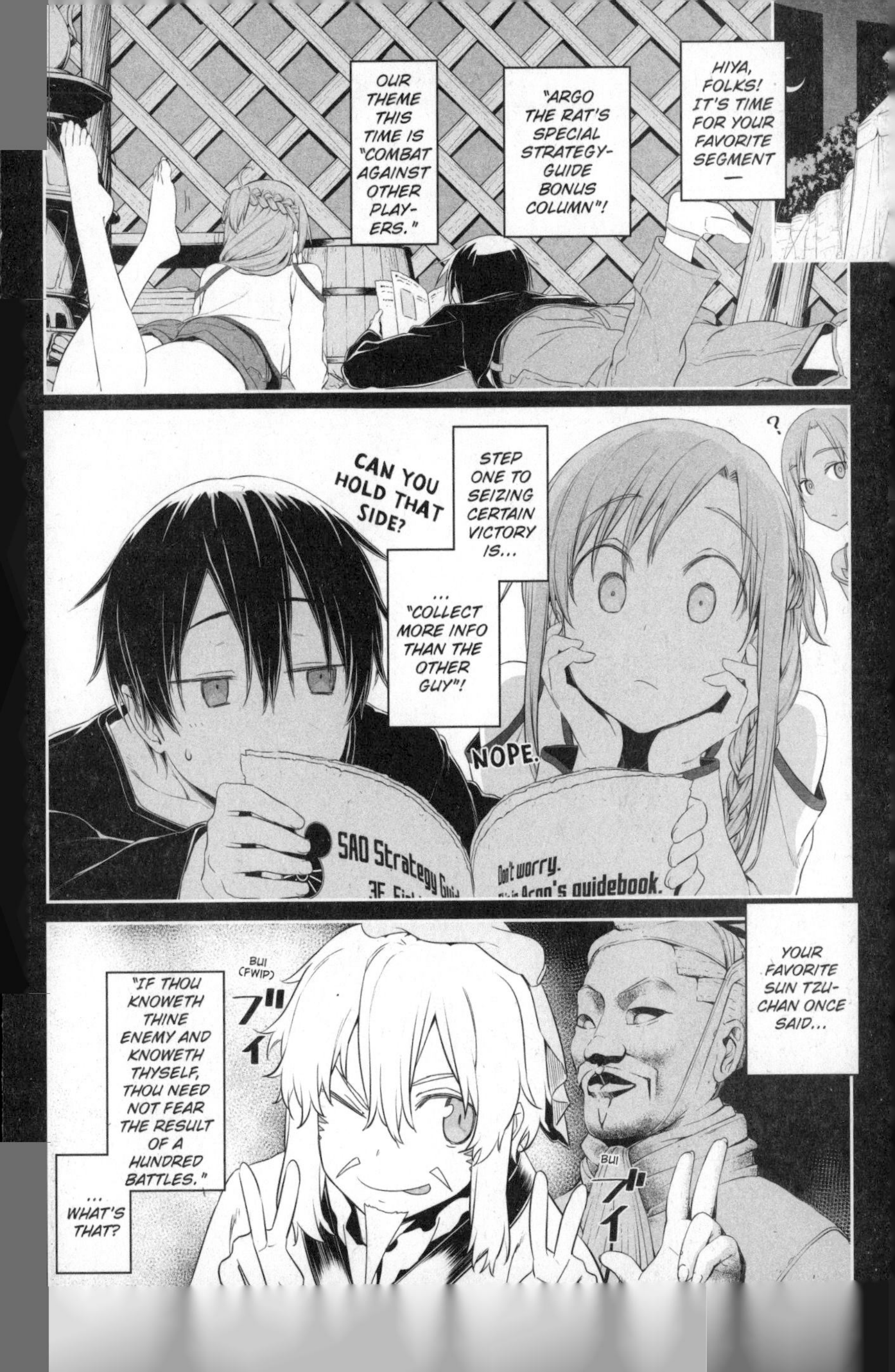
HIYA, FOLKS! IT'S TIME FOR YOUR FAVORITE SEGMENT—
"ARGO THE RAT'S SPECIAL STRATEGY-GUIDE BONUS COLUMN"!
OUR THEME THIS TIME IS "COMBAT AGAINST OTHER PLAYERS."
?
STEP ONE TO SEIZING CERTAIN VICTORY IS...
... "COLLECT MORE INFO THAN THE OTHER GUY"!
CAN YOU HOLD THAT SIDE?
NOPE.
SAO Strategy
Don't worry.
Argo's guidebook.
YOUR FAVORITE SUN TZU-CHAN ONCE SAID...
BUI
ブイ
BUI (FWIP)
ブイ
"IF THOU KNOWETH THINE ENEMY AND KNOWETH THYSELF, THOU NEED NOT FEAR THE RESULT OF A HUNDRED BATTLES."
... WHAT'S THAT?

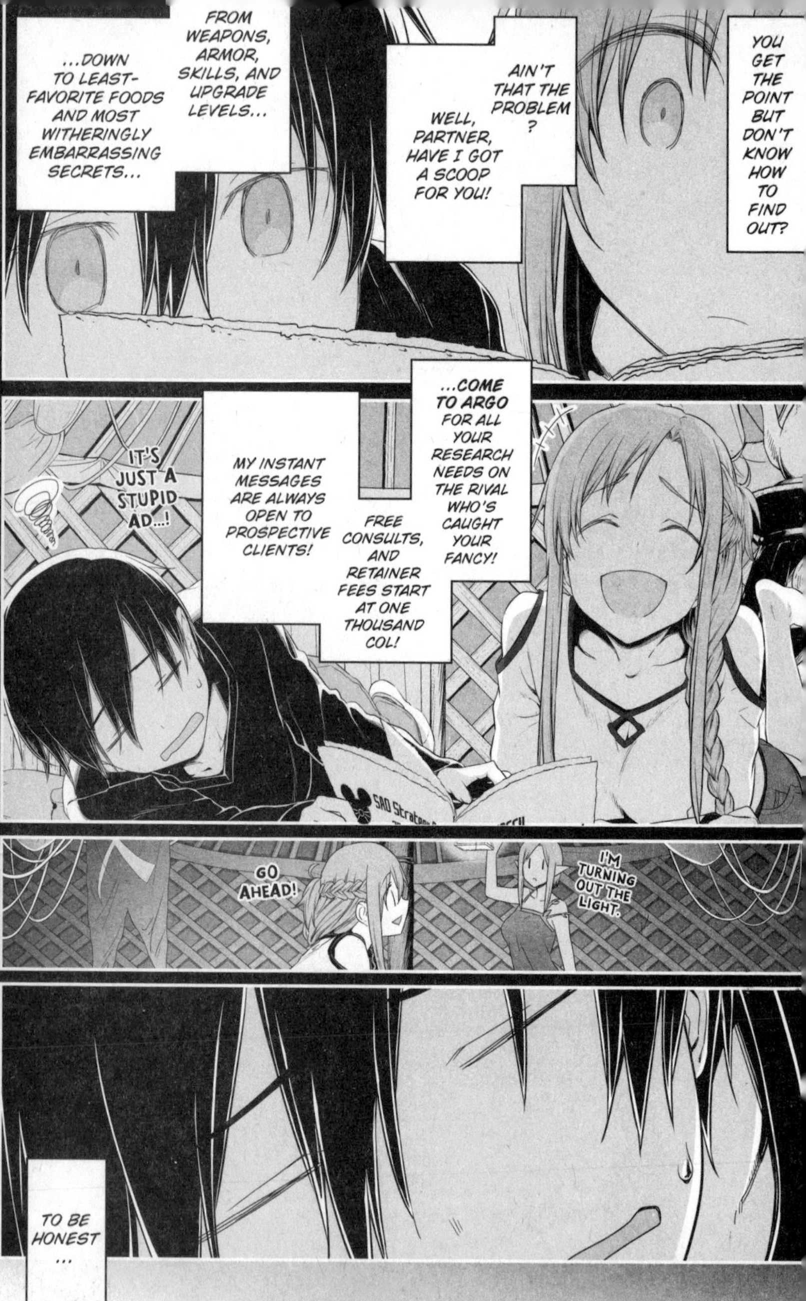
YOU GET THE POINT BUT DON'T KNOW HOW TO FIND OUT?
AIN'T THAT THE PROBLEM?
WELL, PARTNER, HAVE I GOT A SCOOP FOR YOU!
FROM WEAPONS, ARMOR, SKILLS, AND UPGRADE LEVELS...
...DOWN TO LEAST-FAVORITE FOODS AND MOST WITHERINGLY EMBARRASSING SECRETS...
...COME TO ARGO FOR ALL YOUR RESEARCH NEEDS ON THE RIVAL WHO'S CAUGHT YOUR FANCY!
FREE CONSULTS, AND RETAINER FEES START AT ONE THOUSAND COL!
MY INSTANT MESSAGES ARE ALWAYS OPEN TO PROSPECTIVE CLIENTS!
IT'S JUST A STUPID AD...!
I'M TURNING OUT THE LIGHT.
GO AHEAD!
TO BE HONEST...

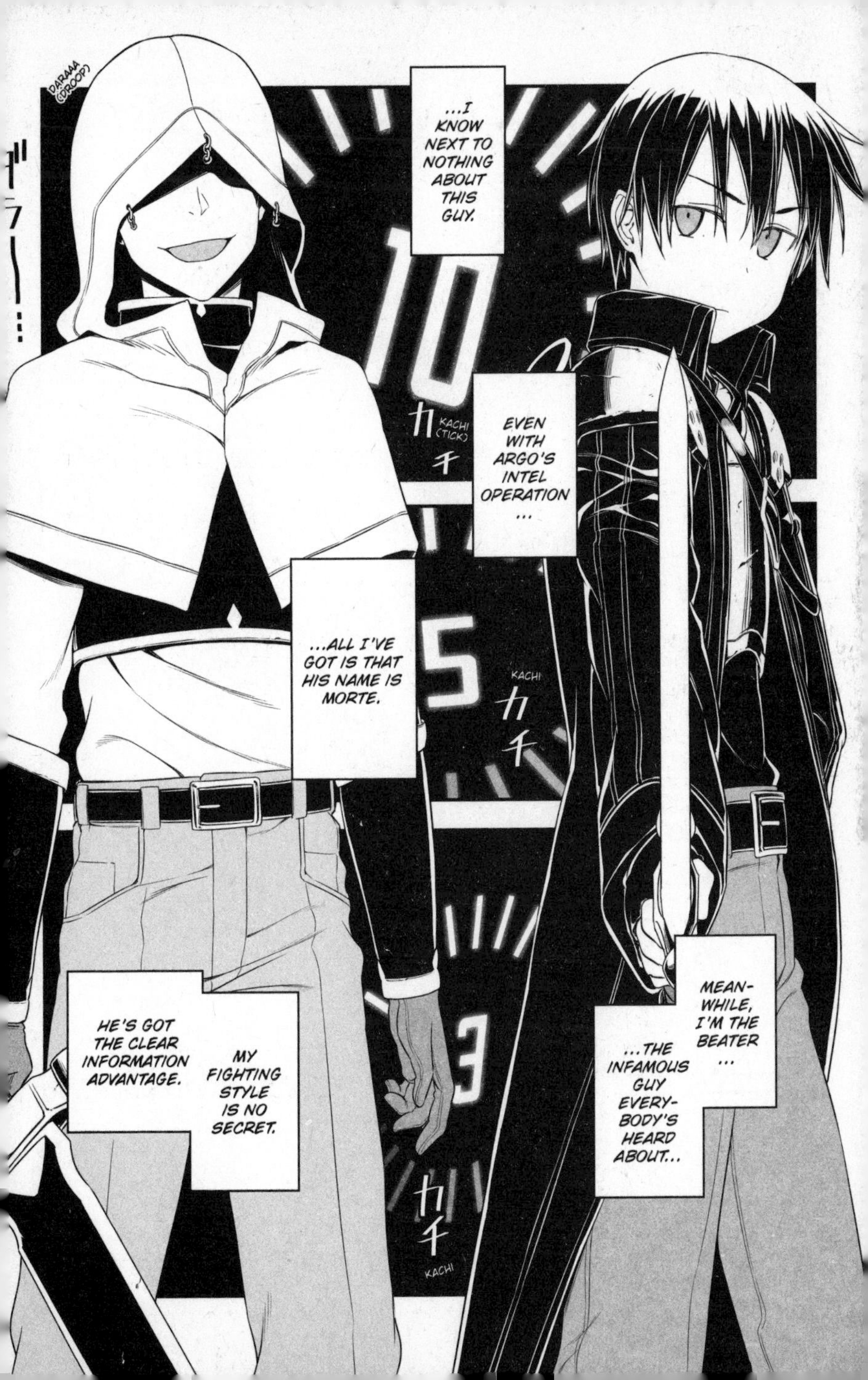
...I KNOW NEXT TO NOTHING ABOUT THIS GUY.
10
KACHI (TICK)
EVEN WITH ARGO'S INTEL OPERATION...
DARAAA (DROOP)
5
KACHI
...ALL I'VE GOT IS THAT HIS NAME IS MORTE.
MEAN-WHILE, I'M THE BEATER...
...THE INFAMOUS GUY EVERY-BODY'S HEARD ABOUT...
3
KACHI
MY FIGHTING STYLE IS NO SECRET.
HE'S GOT THE CLEAR INFORMATION ADVANTAGE.

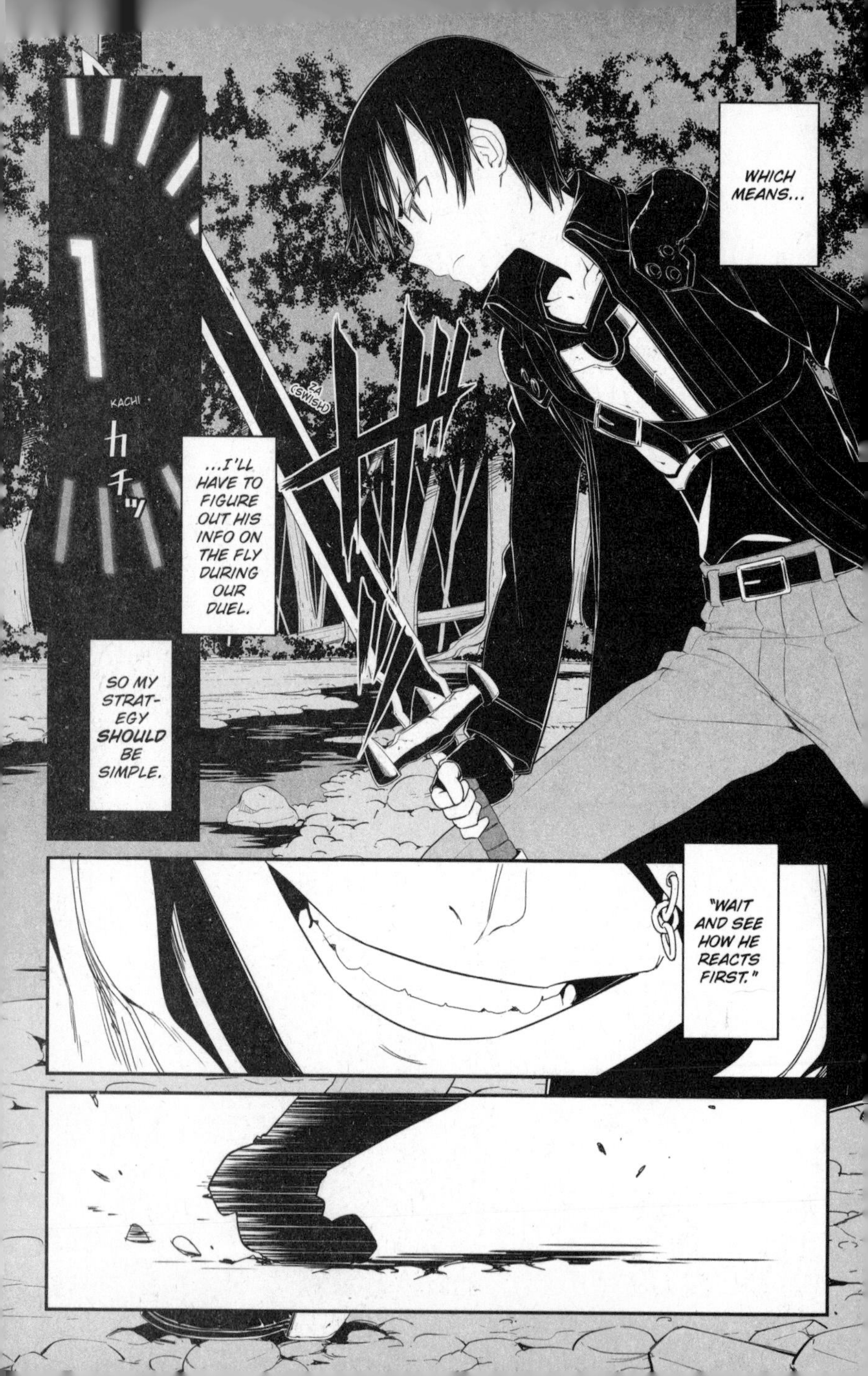
WHICH MEANS...
ZA (SWISH)
...I'LL HAVE TO FIGURE OUT HIS INFO ON THE FLY DURING OUR DUEL.
KACHI
カチッ
SO MY STRAT-EGY SHOULD BE SIMPLE.
"WAIT AND SEE HOW HE REACTS FIRST."

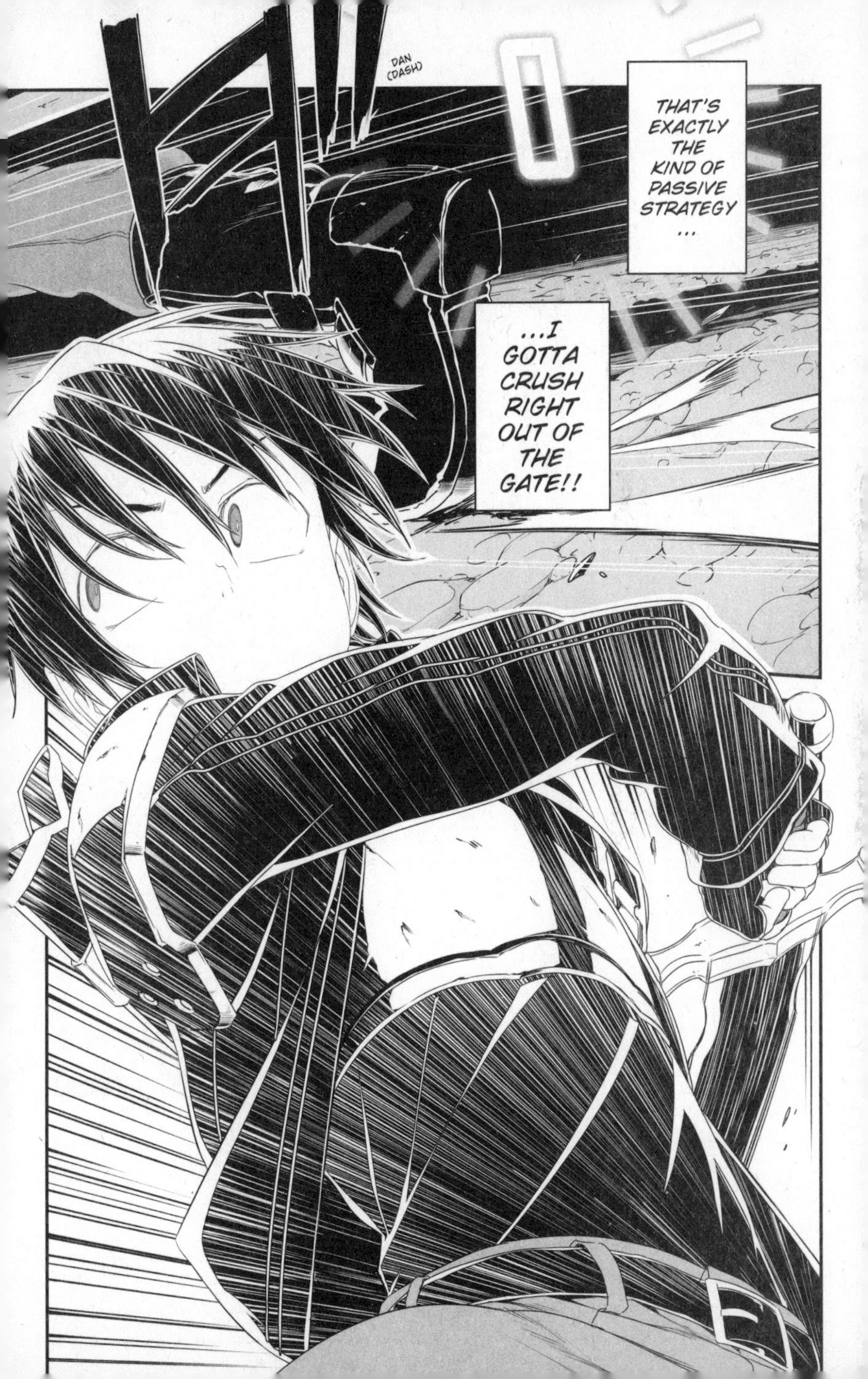
DAN (DASH)
THAT'S EXACTLY THE KIND OF PASSIVE STRATEGY ...
...I GOTTA CRUSH RIGHT OUT OF THE GATE!!

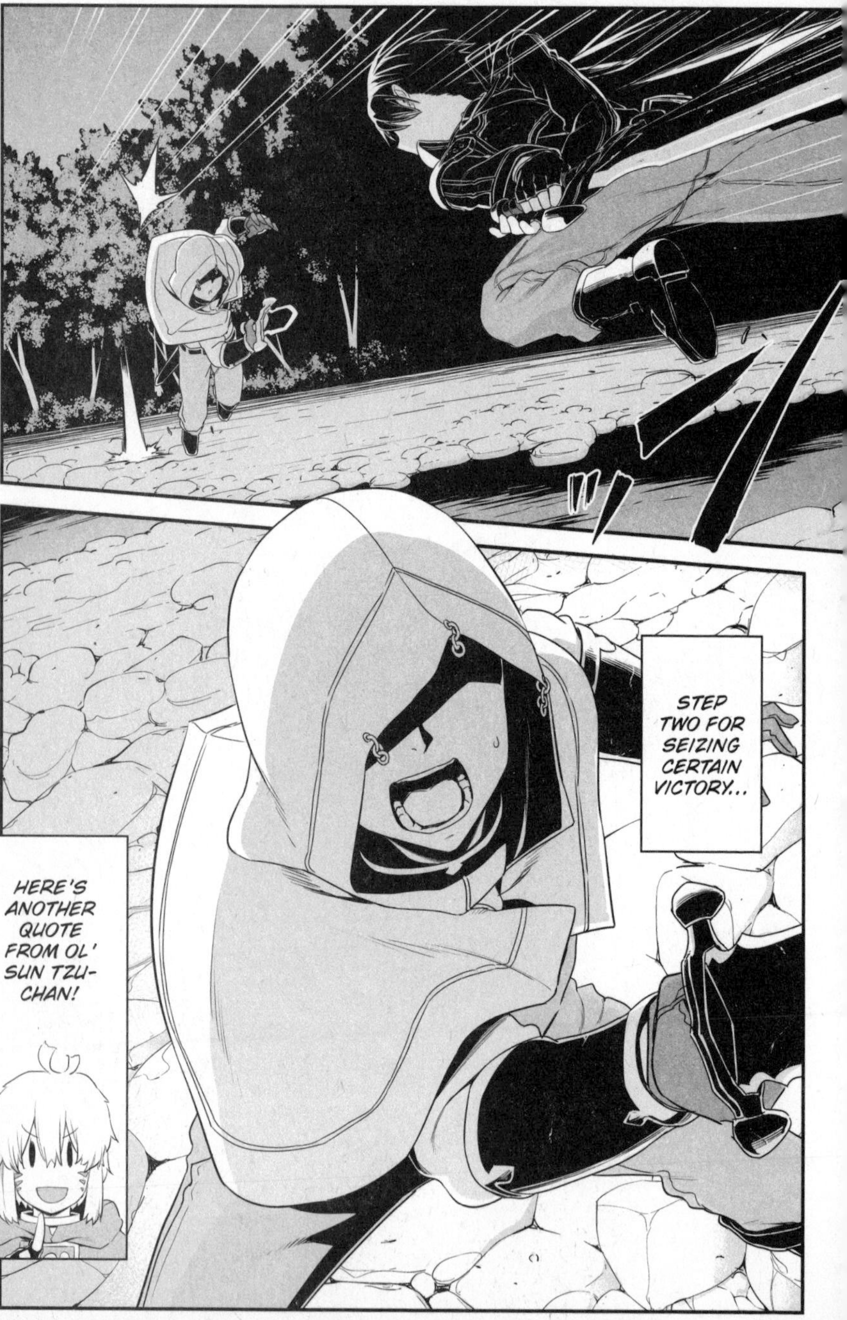
STEP TWO FOR SEIZING CERTAIN VICTORY...
HERE'S ANOTHER QUOTE FROM OL' SUN TZU-CHAN!

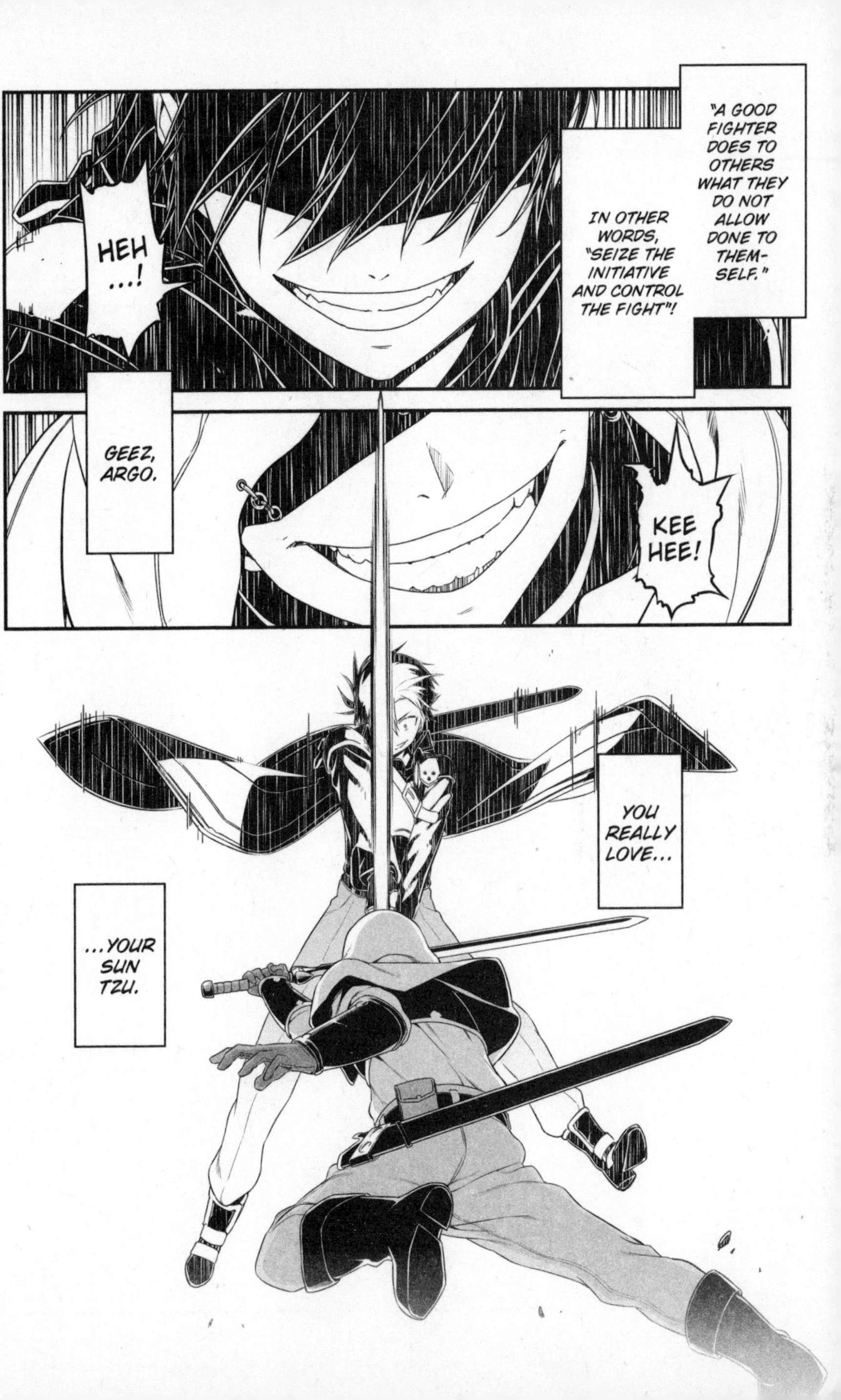
"A GOOD FIGHTER DOES TO OTHERS WHAT THEY DO NOT ALLOW DONE TO THEM-SELF."
IN OTHER WORDS, "SEIZE THE INITIATIVE AND CONTROL THE FIGHT"!
HEH ...!
KEE HEE!
GEEZ, ARGO.
YOU REALLY LOVE...
...YOUR SUN TZU.

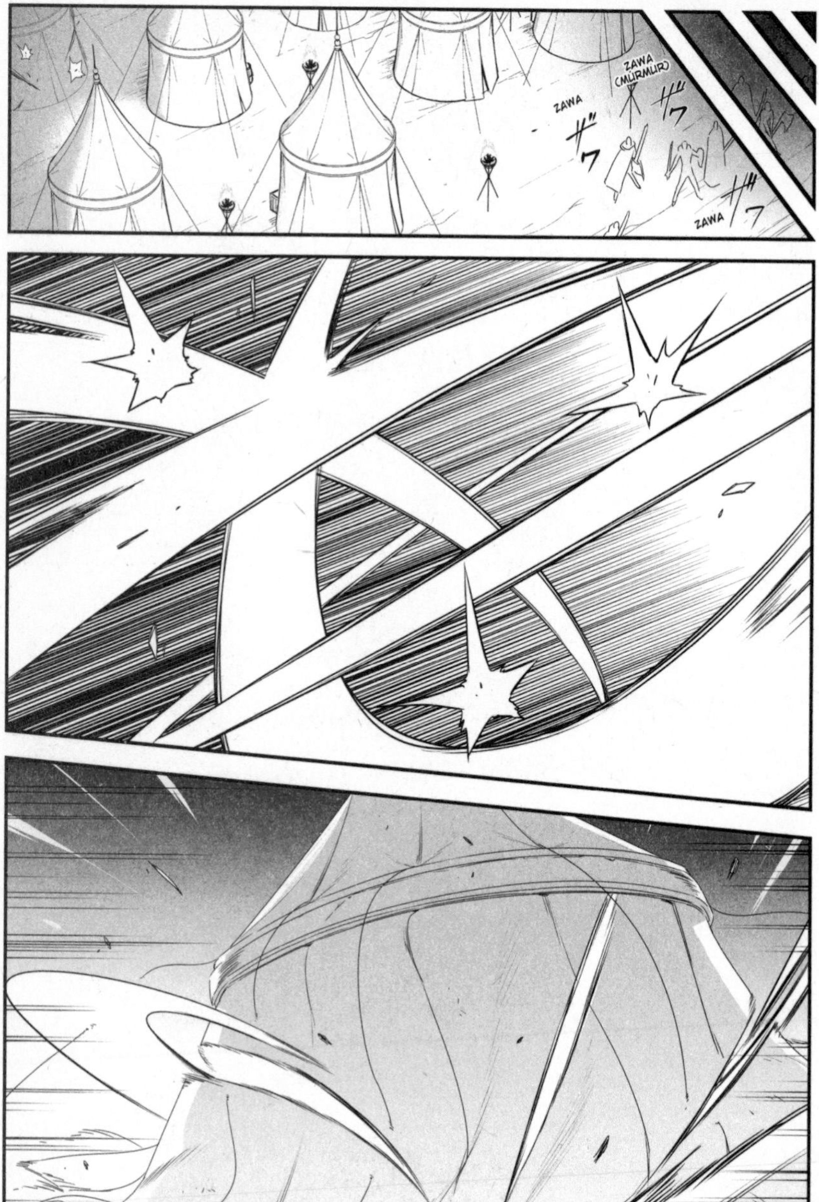
ZAWA (MURMUR)
ザワ
ZAWA
ザワ
ZAWA
ザワ

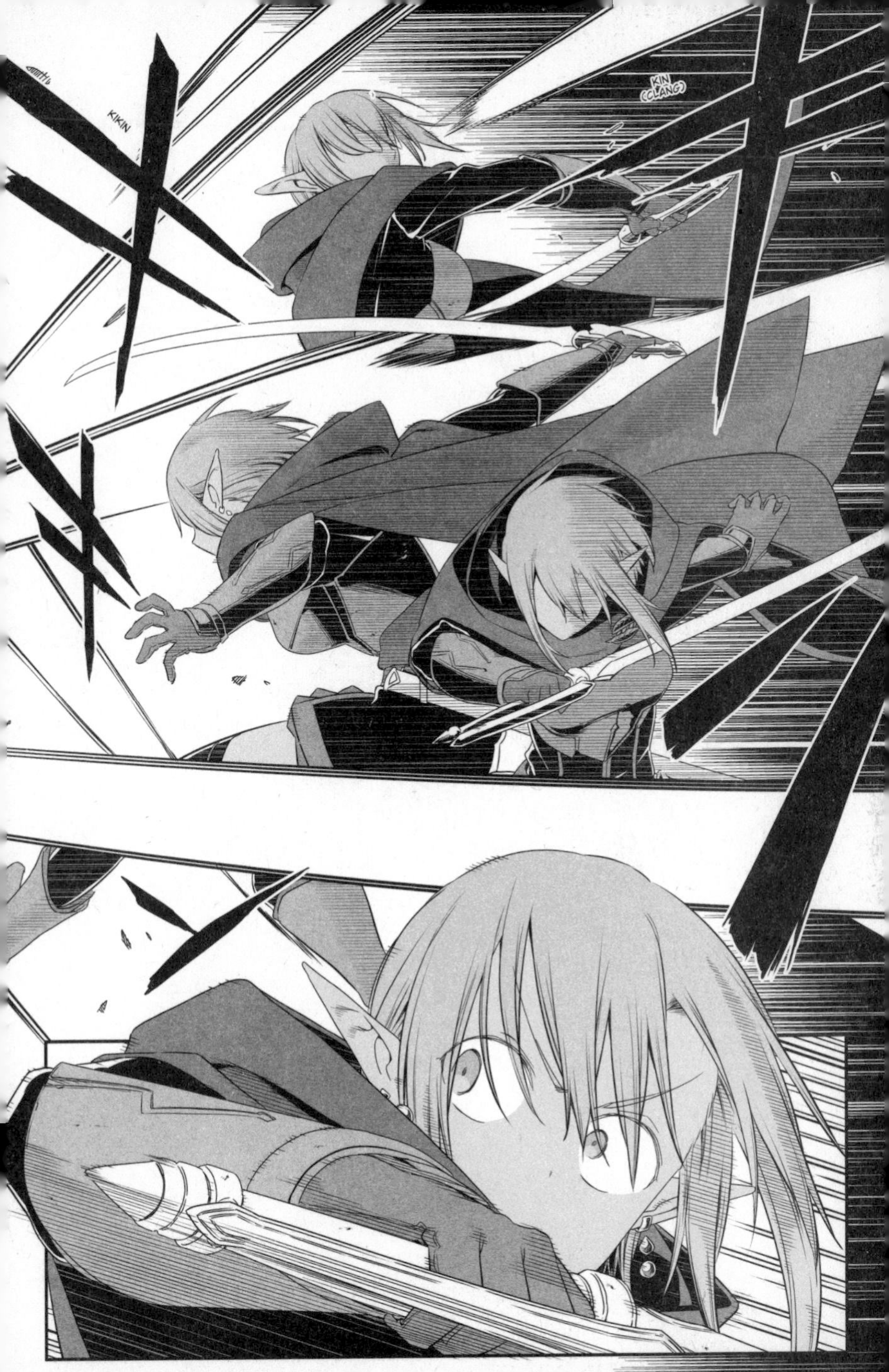
KIN (CLANG)
KIKIN

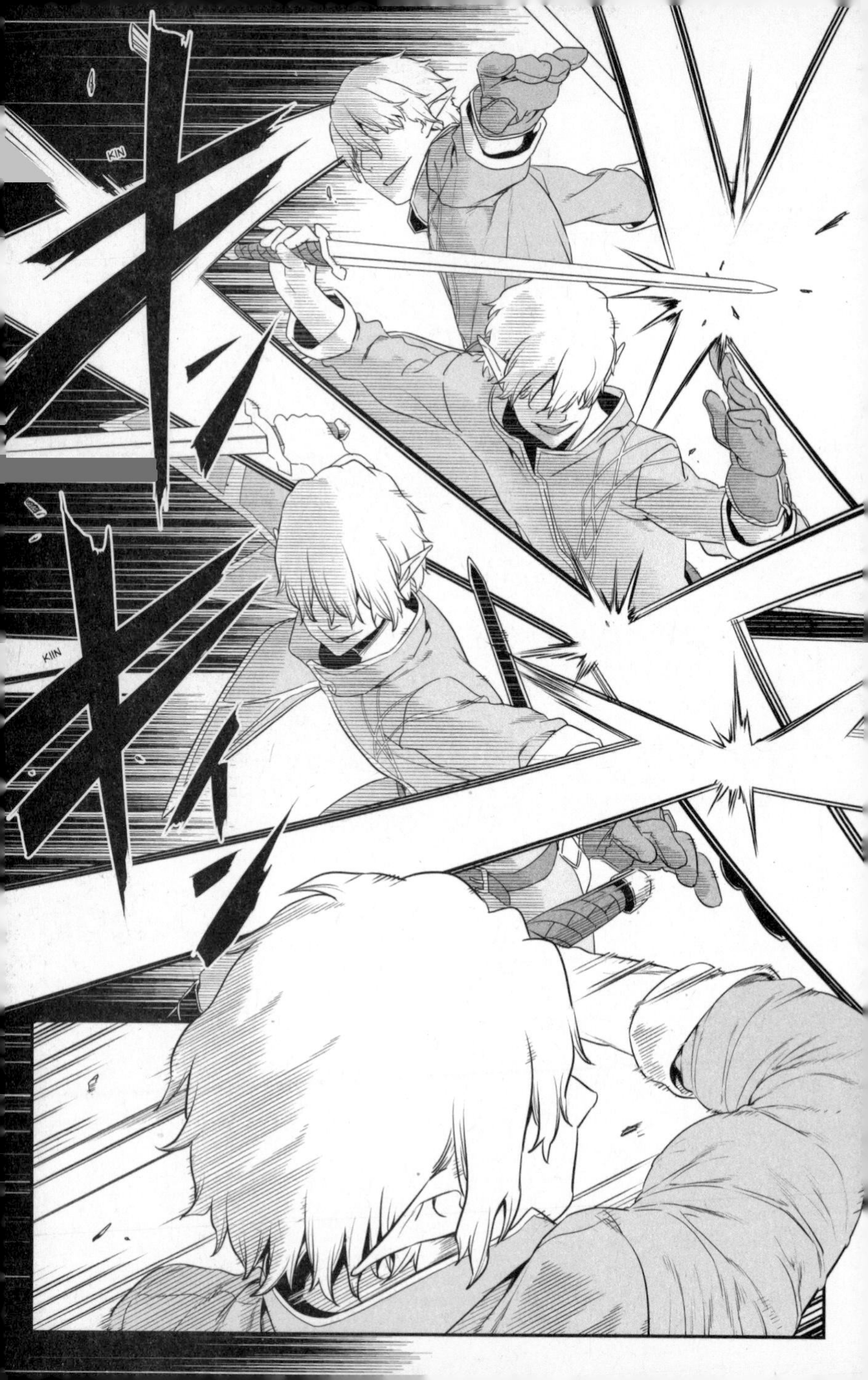
KIN
KIIN

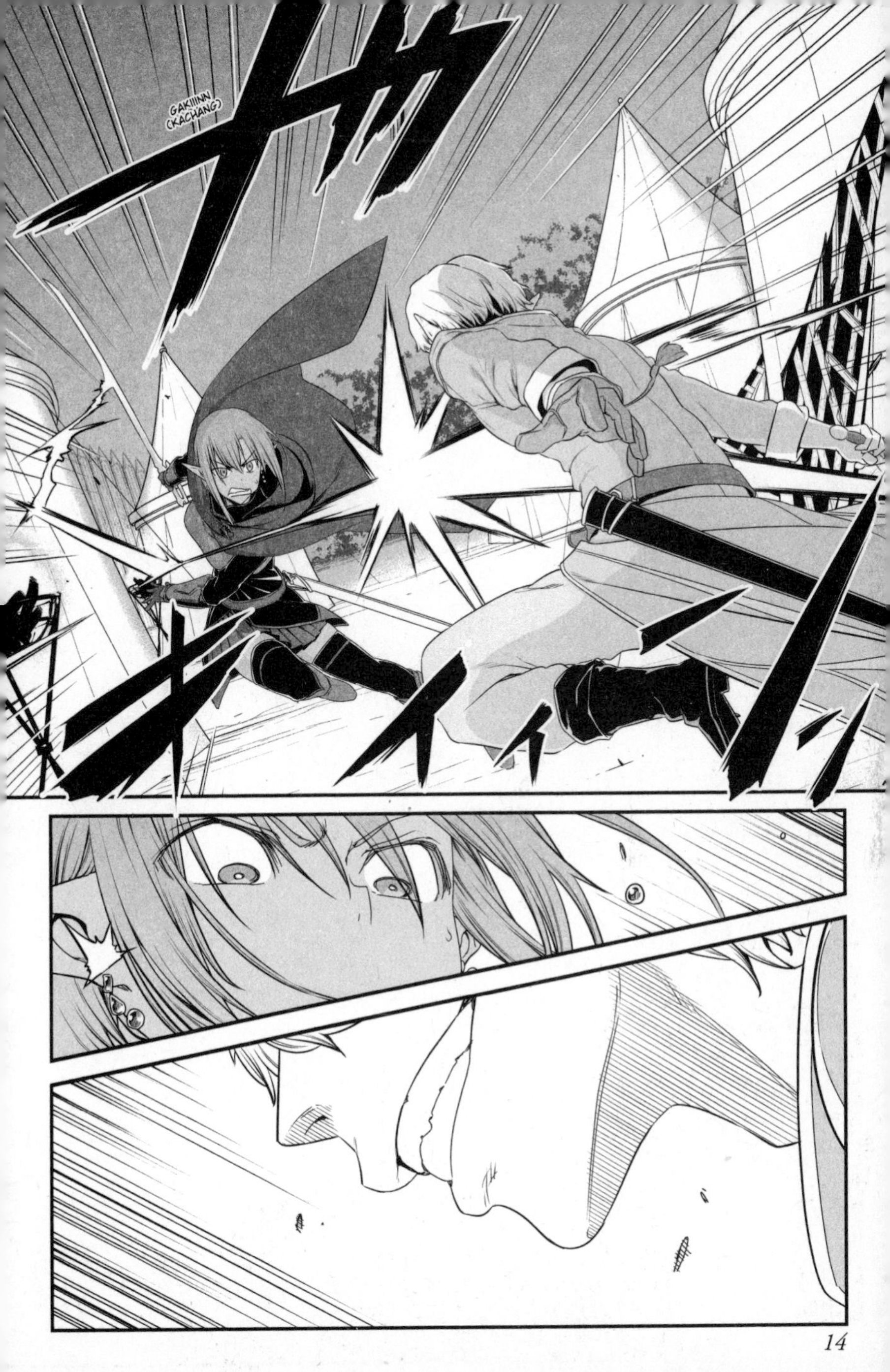
GAKIIINN (KACHANG)

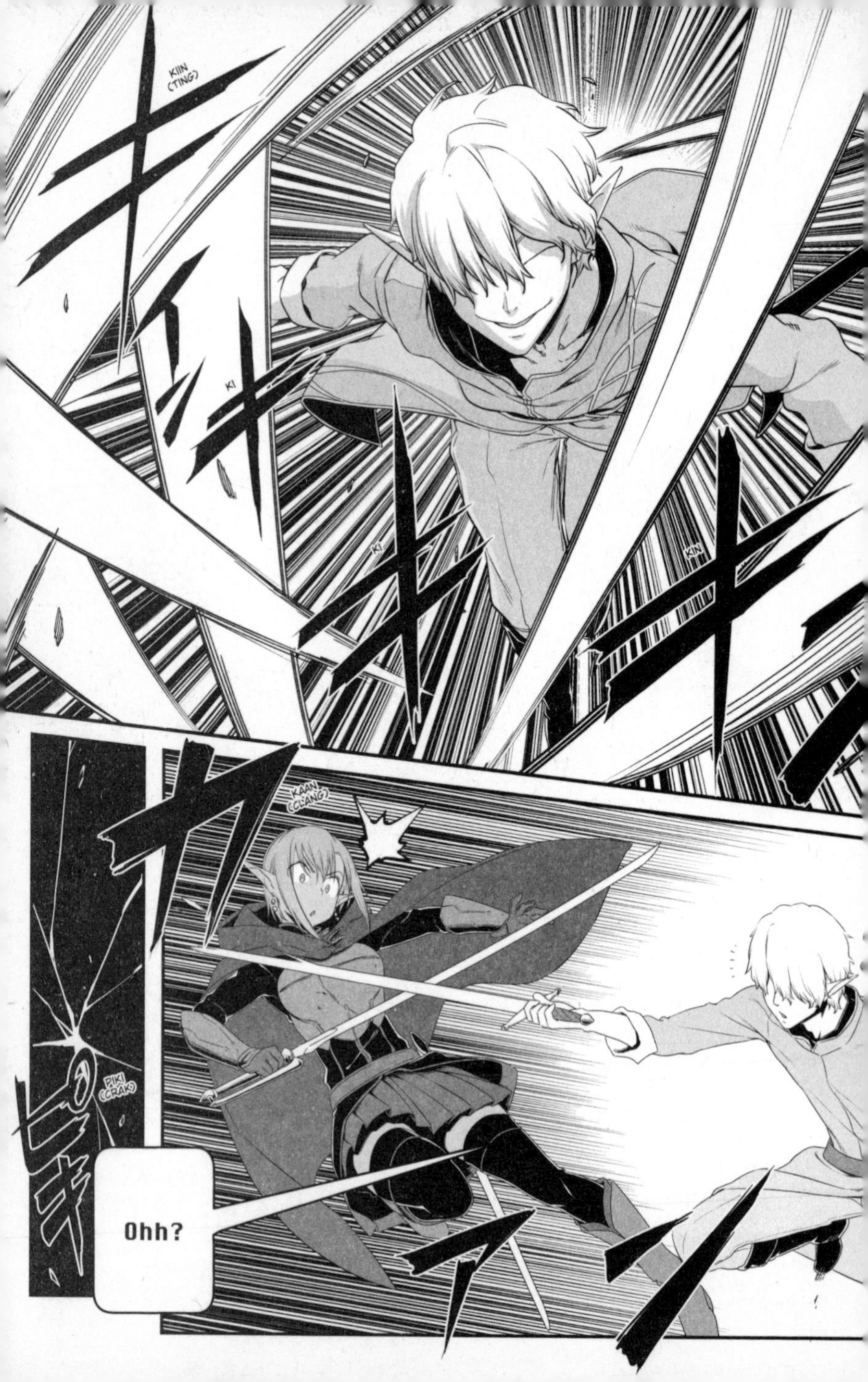
KIIN (TING)
KI
KI
KIN
KAAN (CLANG)
PIKI (CRAK)
Ohh?

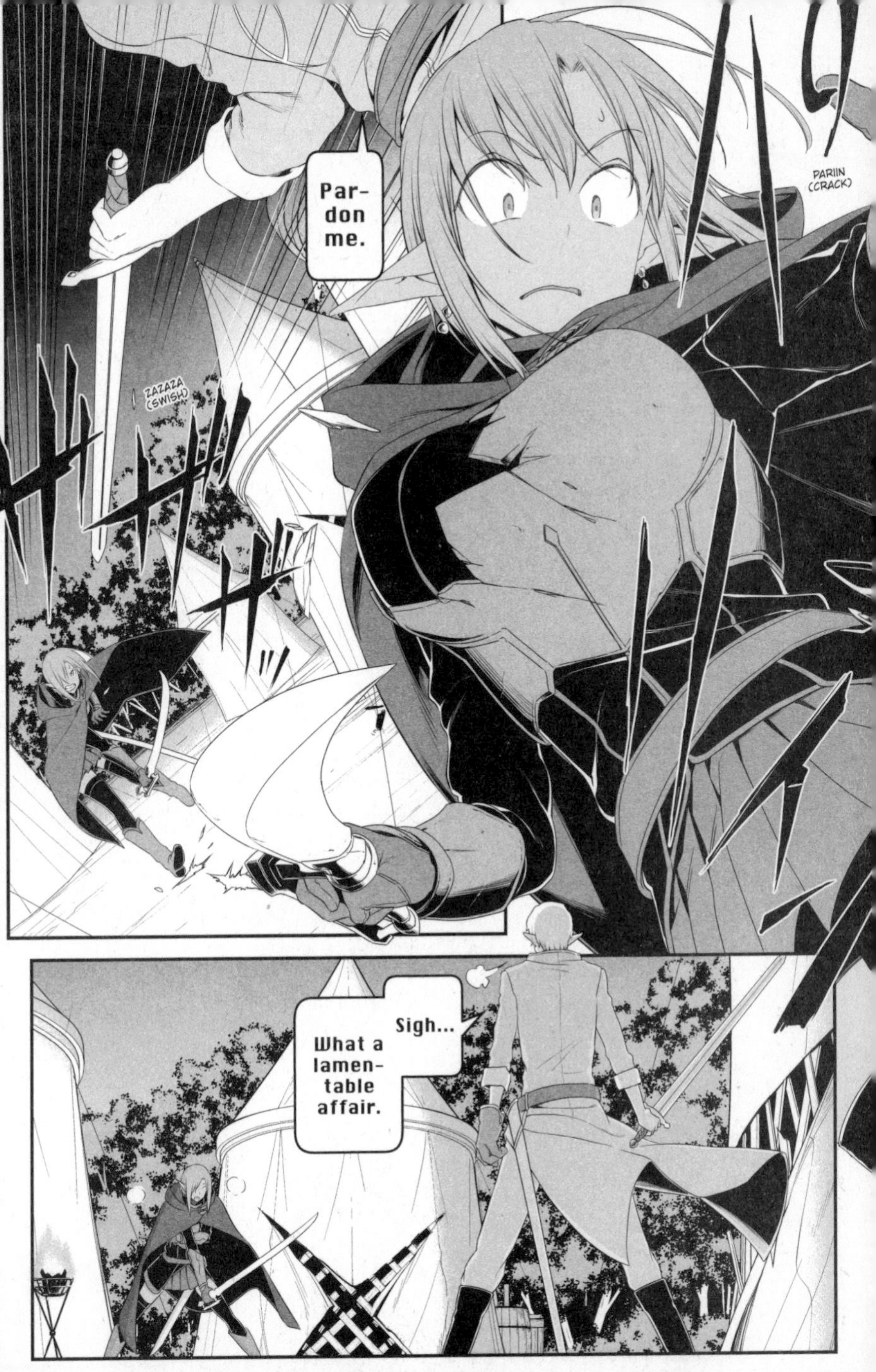
PARIIN (CRACK)
Par-don me.
ZAZAZA (SWISH)
Sigh...
What a lamen-table affair.

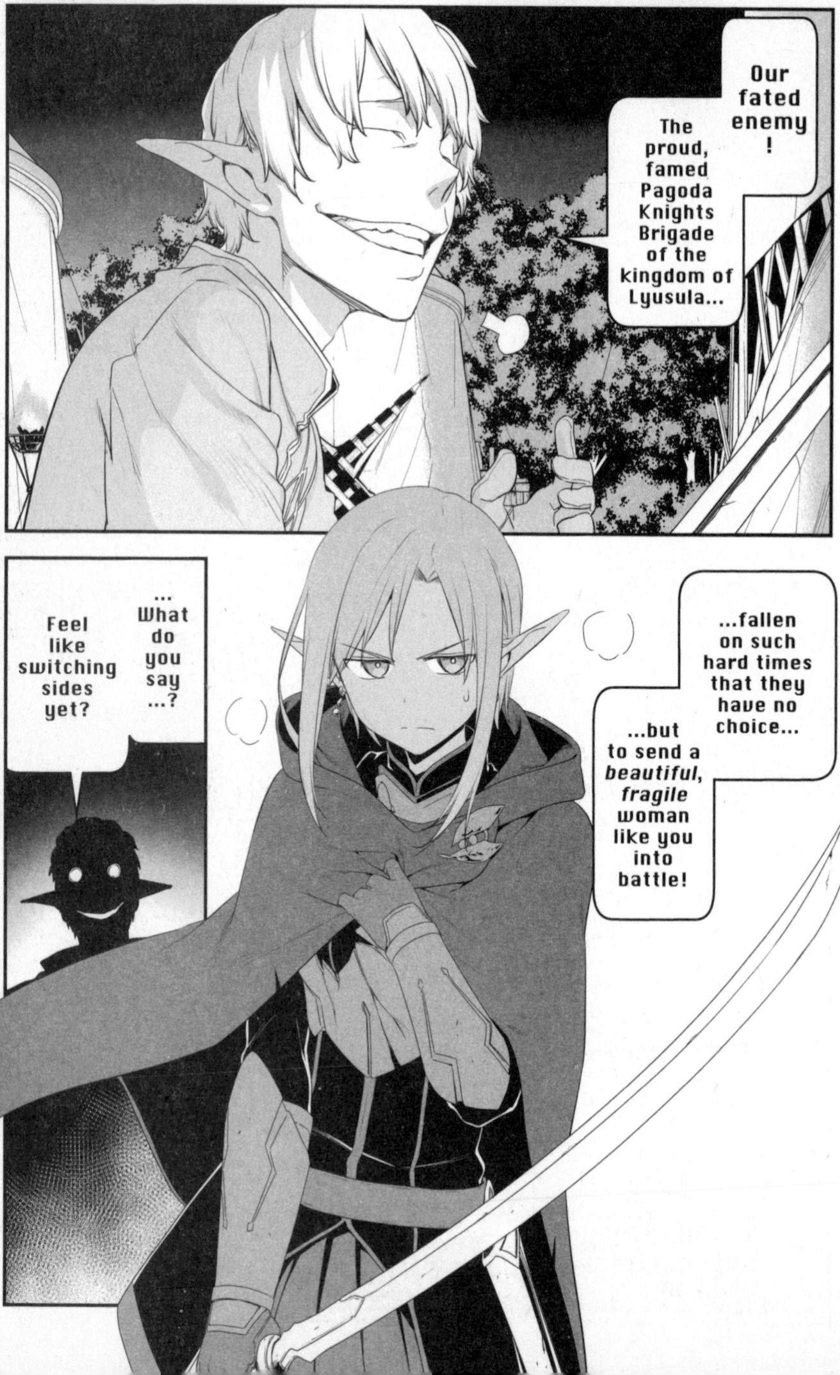
Our fated enemy!
The proud, famed Pagoda Knights Brigade of the kingdom of Lyusula...
...fallen on such hard times that they have no choice...
...but to send a *beautiful*, *fragile* woman like you into battle!
...What do you say...?
Feel like switching sides yet?

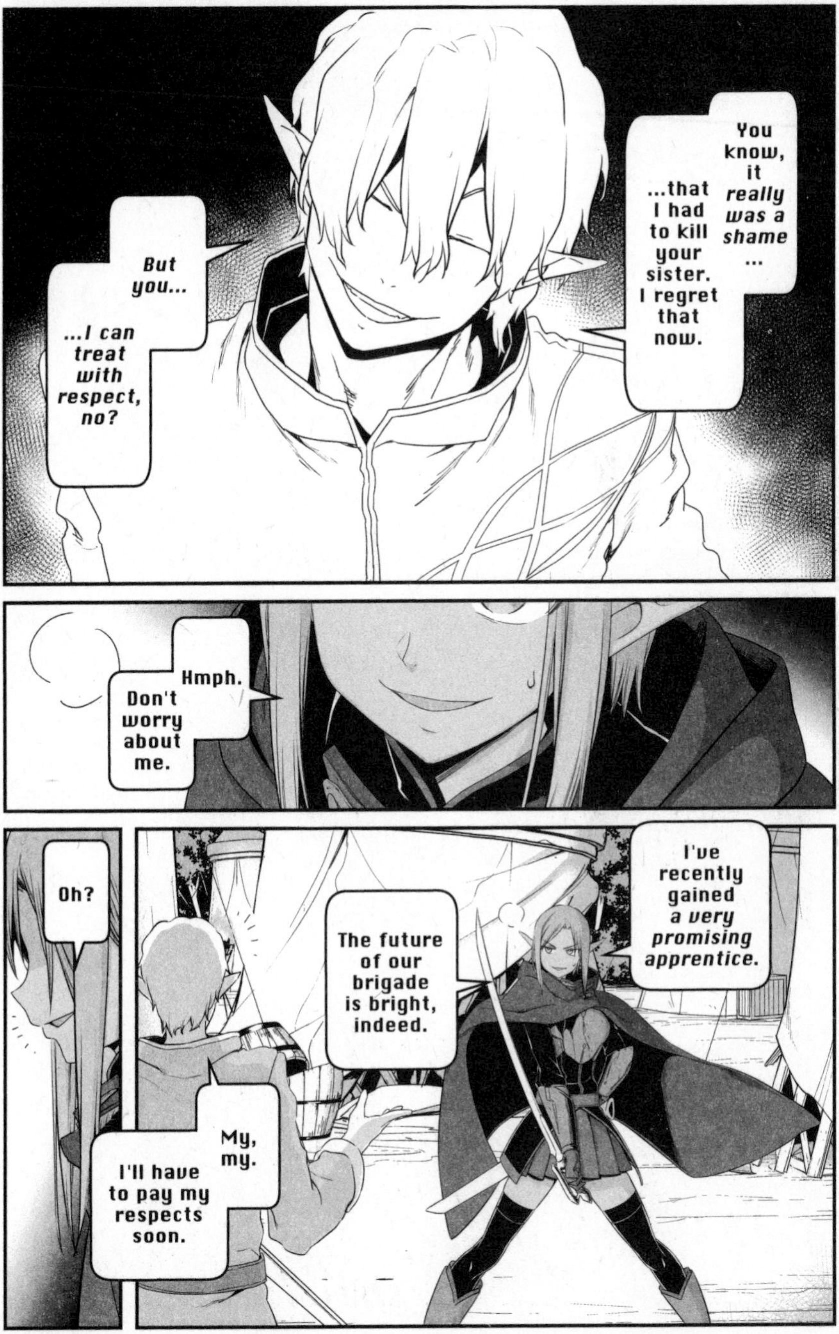
You know, it *really was a shame* ...
...that I had to kill your sister. I regret that now.
But you...
...I can treat with respect, no?
Hmph. Don't worry about me.
I've recently gained *a very promising apprentice.*
The future of our brigade is bright, indeed.
My, my.
I'll have to pay my respects soon.
Oh?

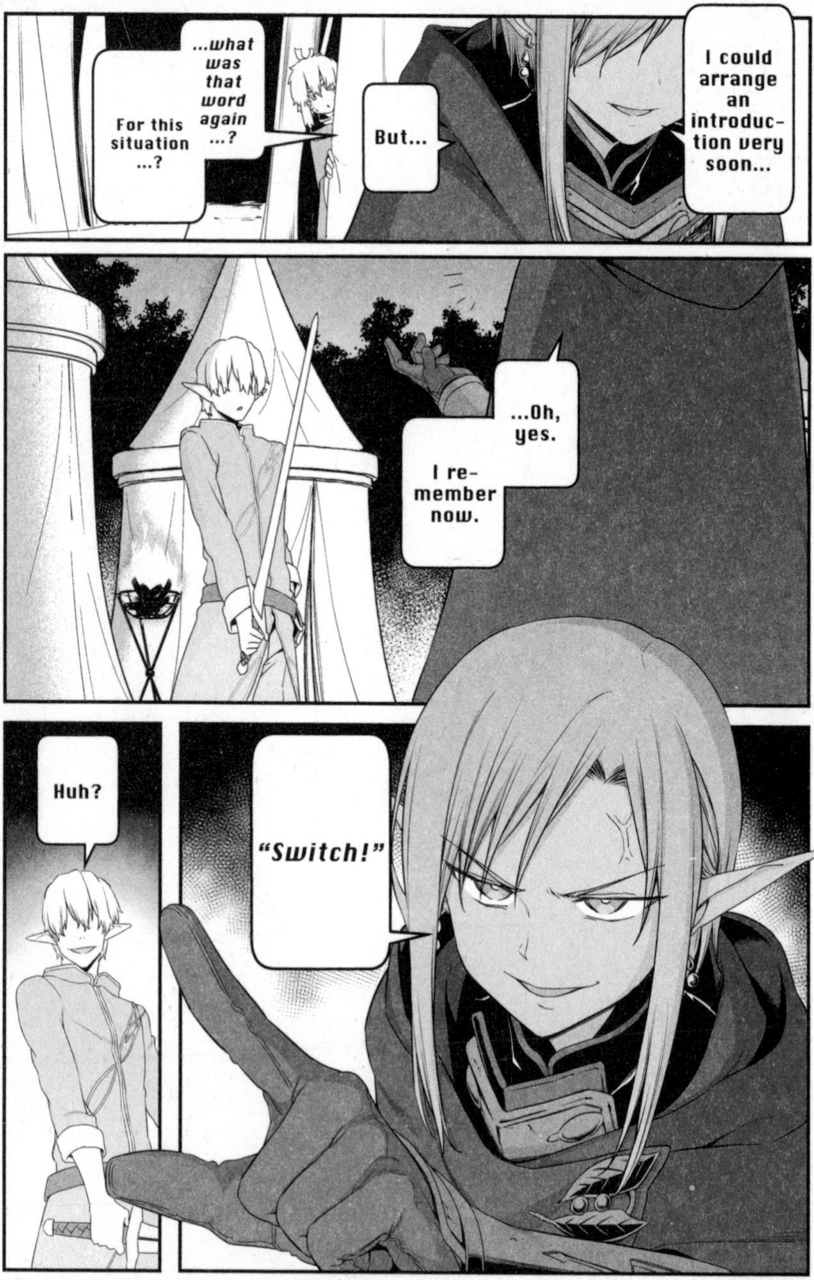
I could arrange an introduction very soon...
But...
...what was that word again...?
For this situation...?
...Oh, yes.
I remember now.
"Switch!"
Huh?

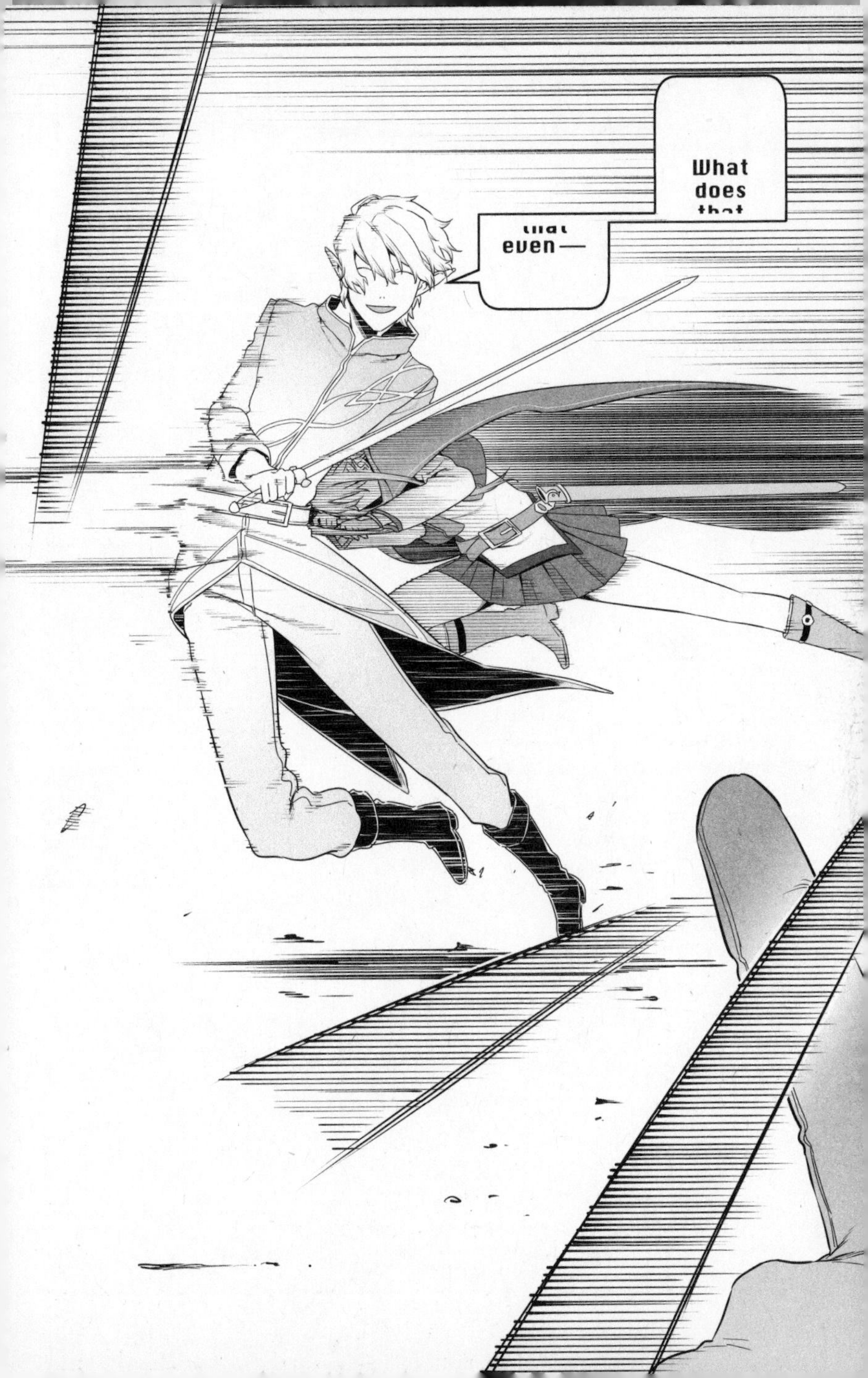
What does
even—

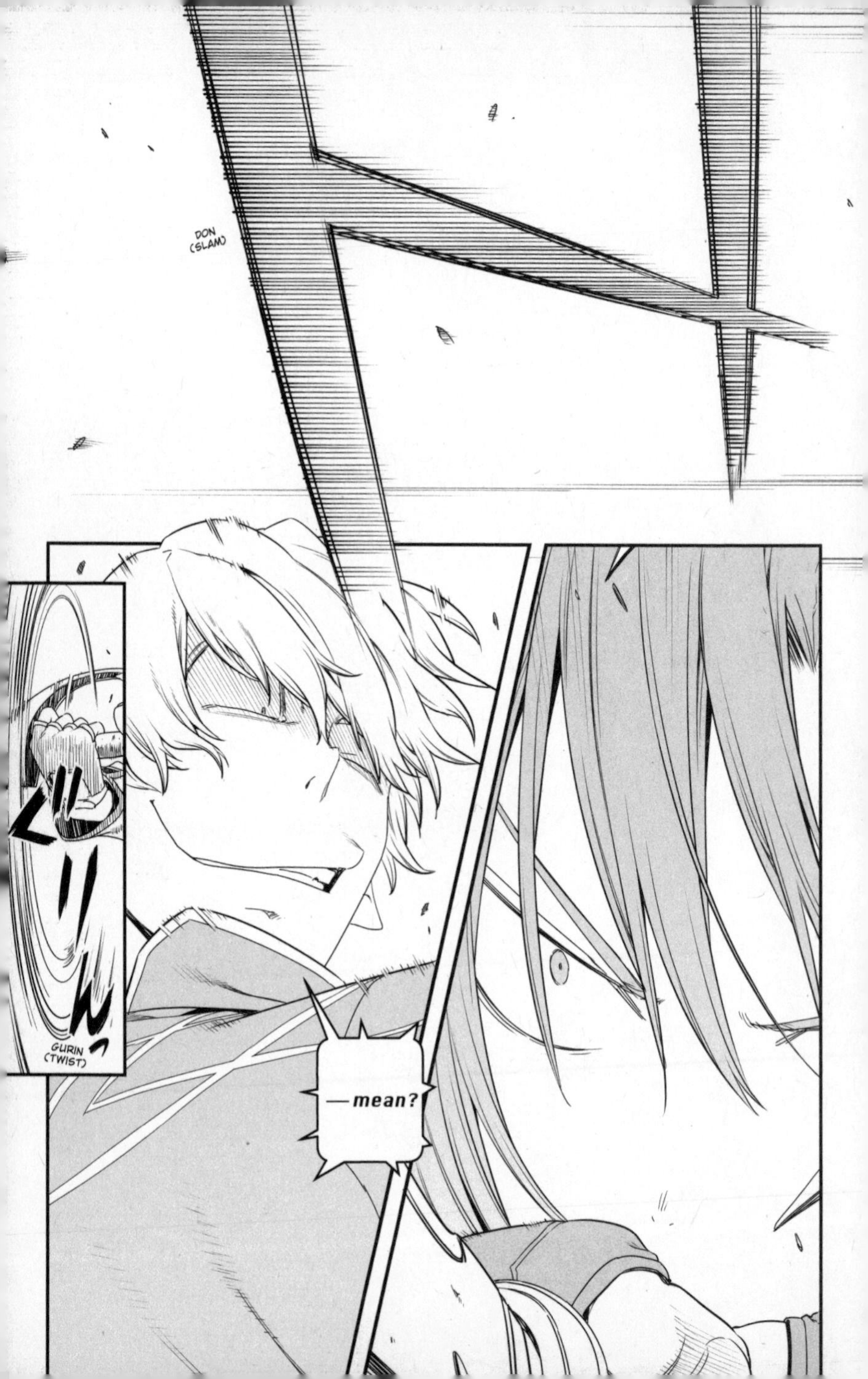
DON (SLAM)
—mean?
GURIN (TWIST)

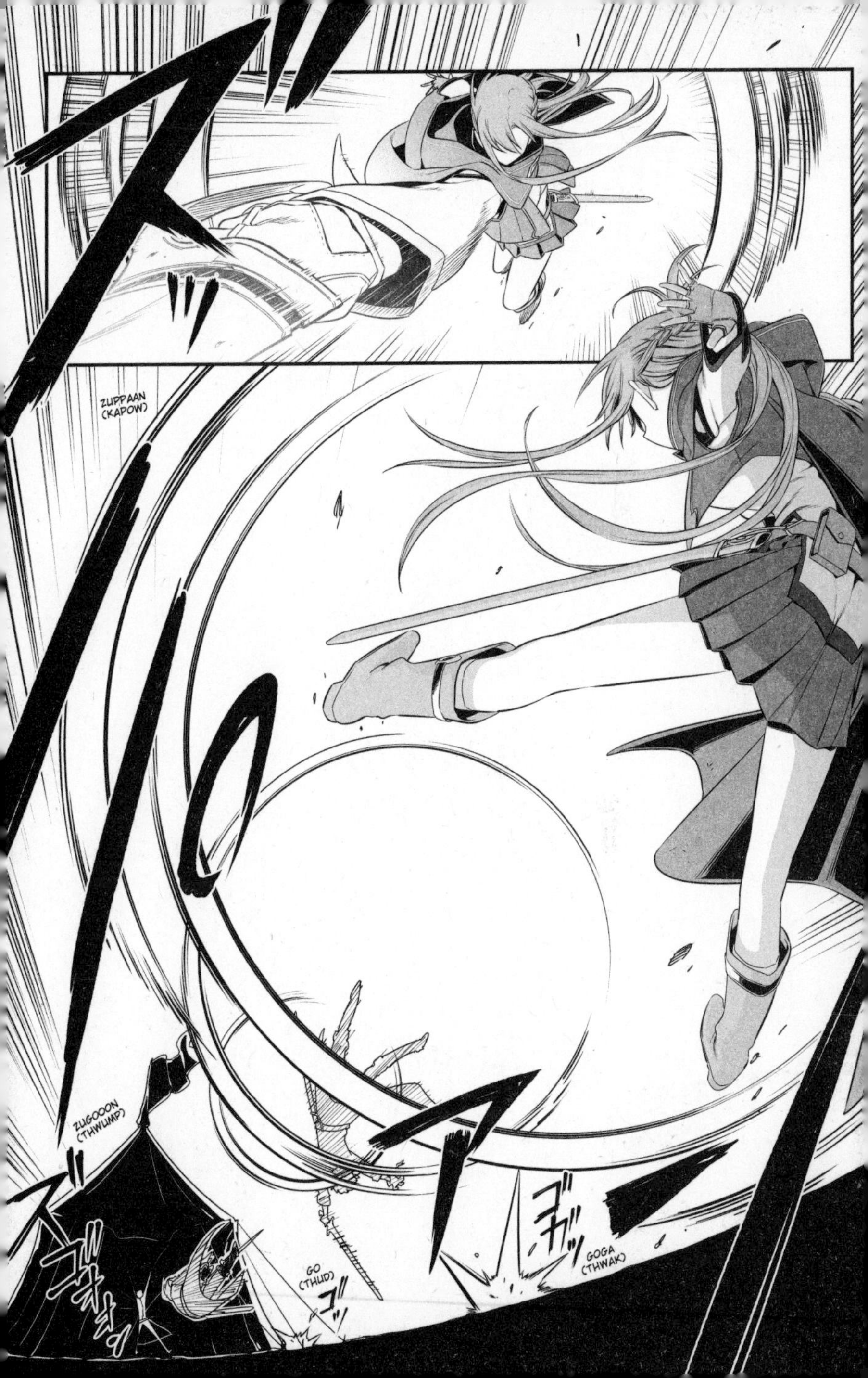
ZUPPAAN
(KAPOW)
GOGA
(THWAK)
GO
(THUD)
ZUGOOON
(THWUMP)

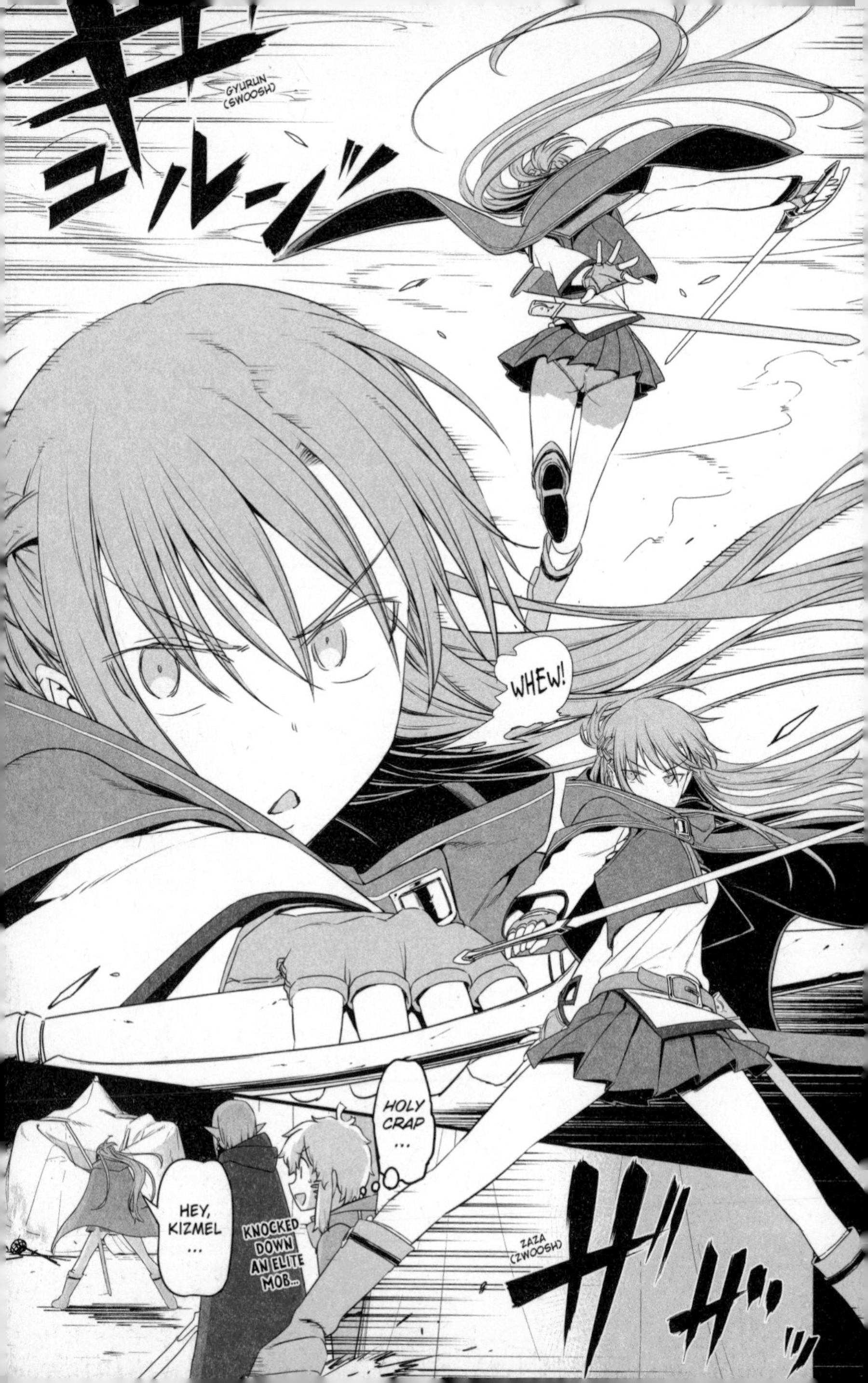

GYURUN (SWOOSH)
WHEW!
HOLY CRAP ...
ZAZA (ZWOOSH)
HEY, KIZMEL ...
KNOCKED DOWN AN ELITE MOB...

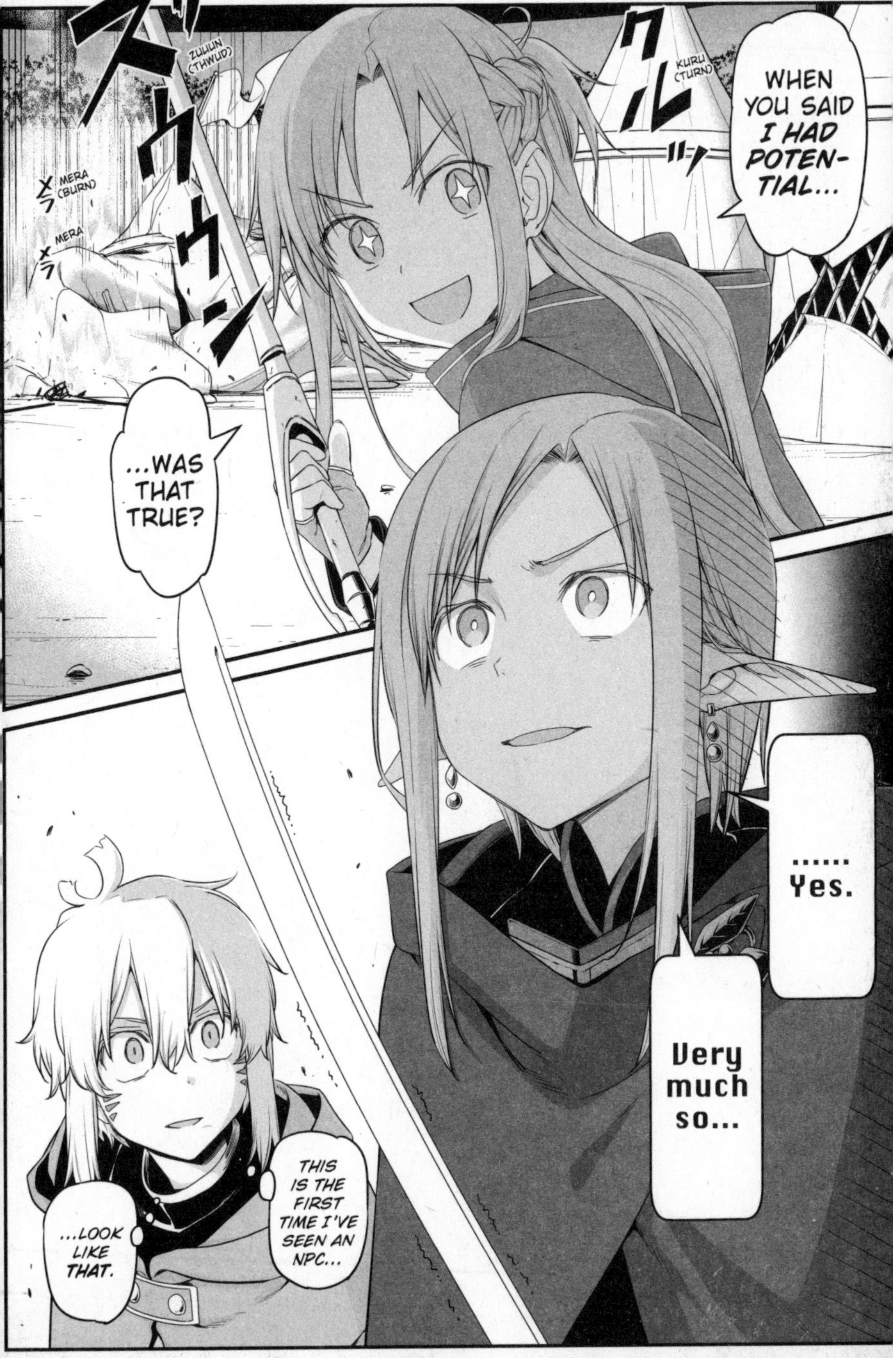
KURU (TURN)
WHEN YOU SAID I HAD POTENTIAL...
ZUUUN (THWUD)
MERA (BURN)
MERA
...WAS THAT TRUE?
...... Yes.
Very much so...
THIS IS THE FIRST TIME I'VE SEEN AN NPC...
...LOOK LIKE THAT.

#038: Challenge

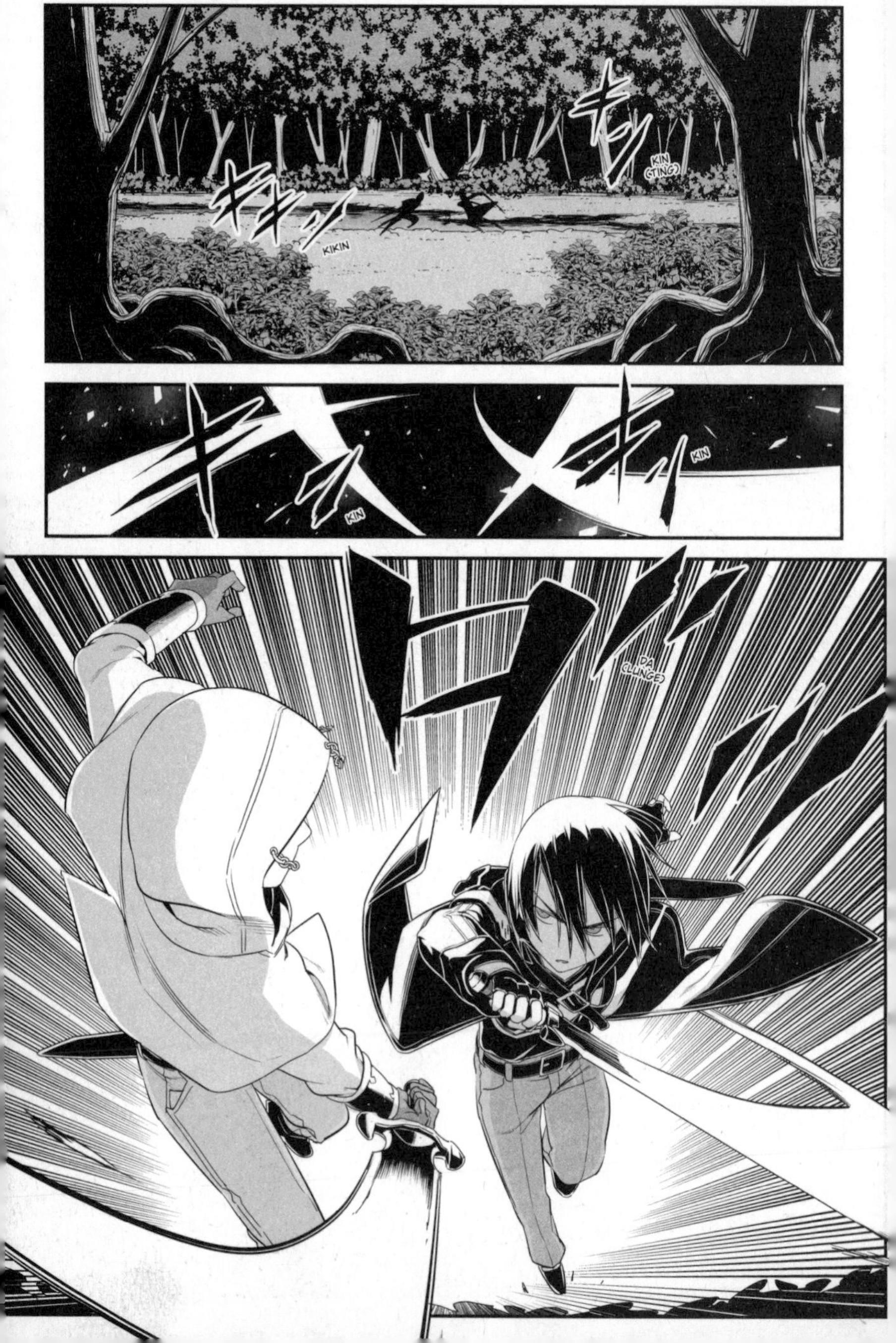
KIN (TING)
KIKIN
KIN
KIN
DA (LUNGE)

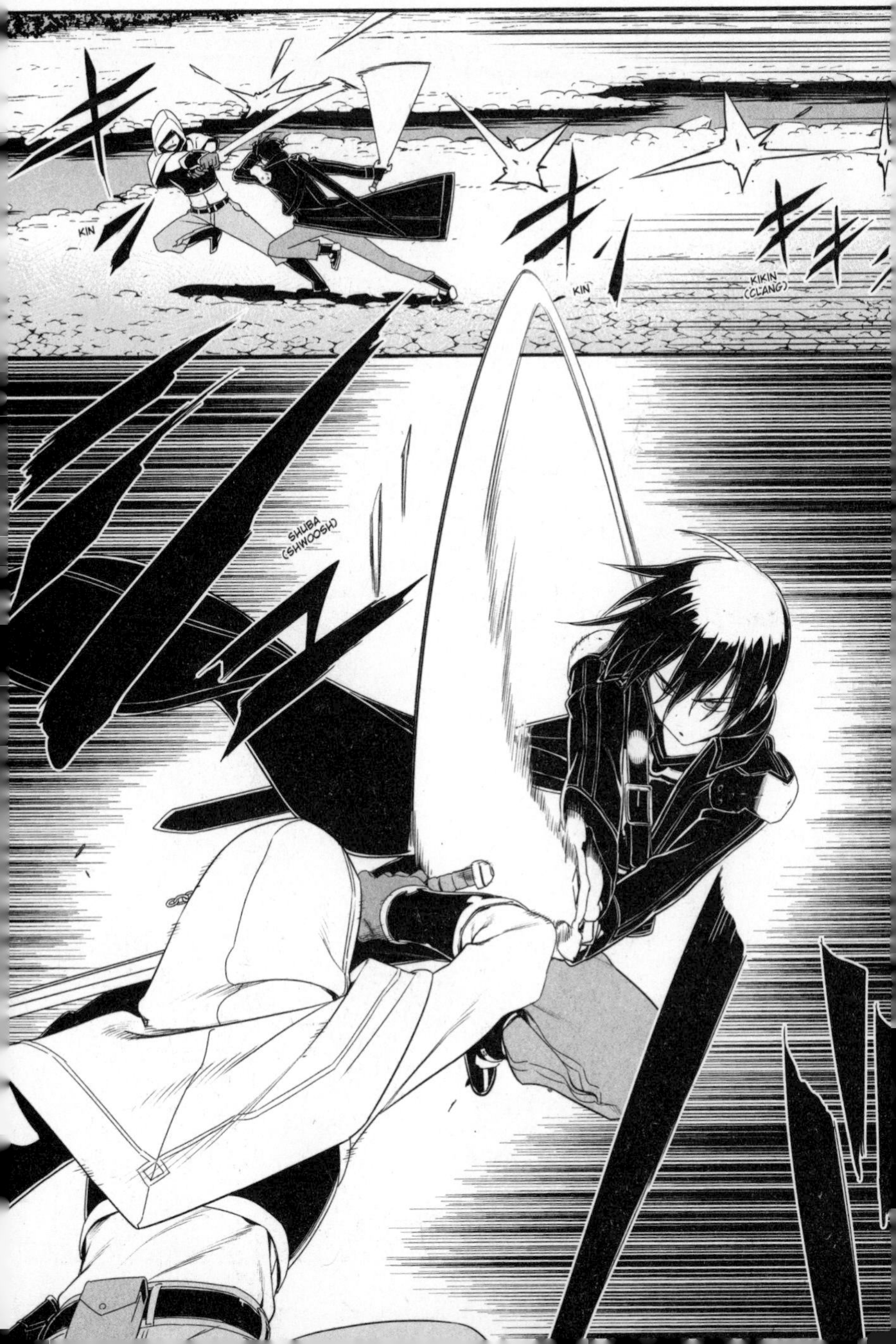
KIKIN (CLANG)
KIN
KIN
SHUBA (SHWOOSH)

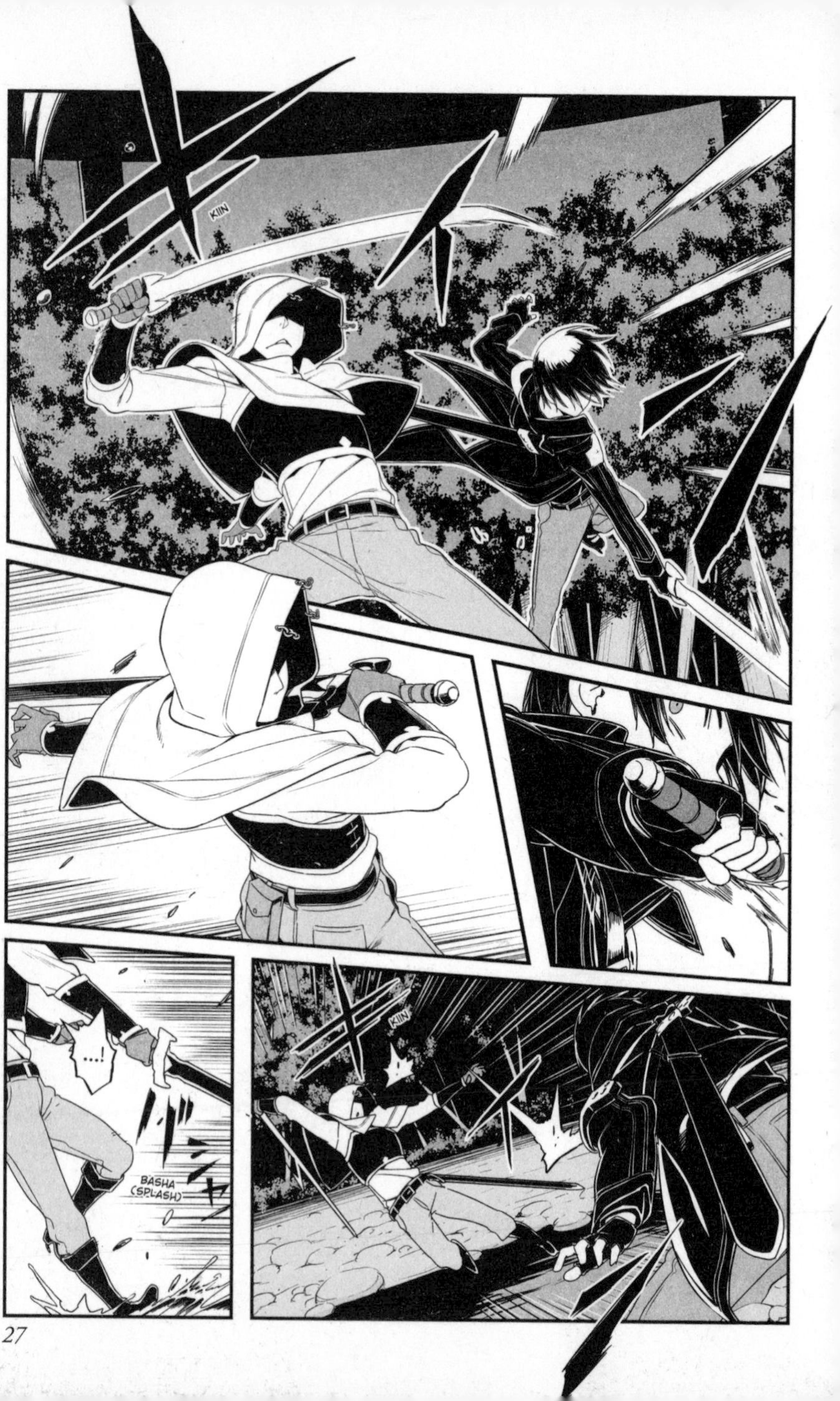
KIIN
KIIN
...!
BASHA
(SPLASH)

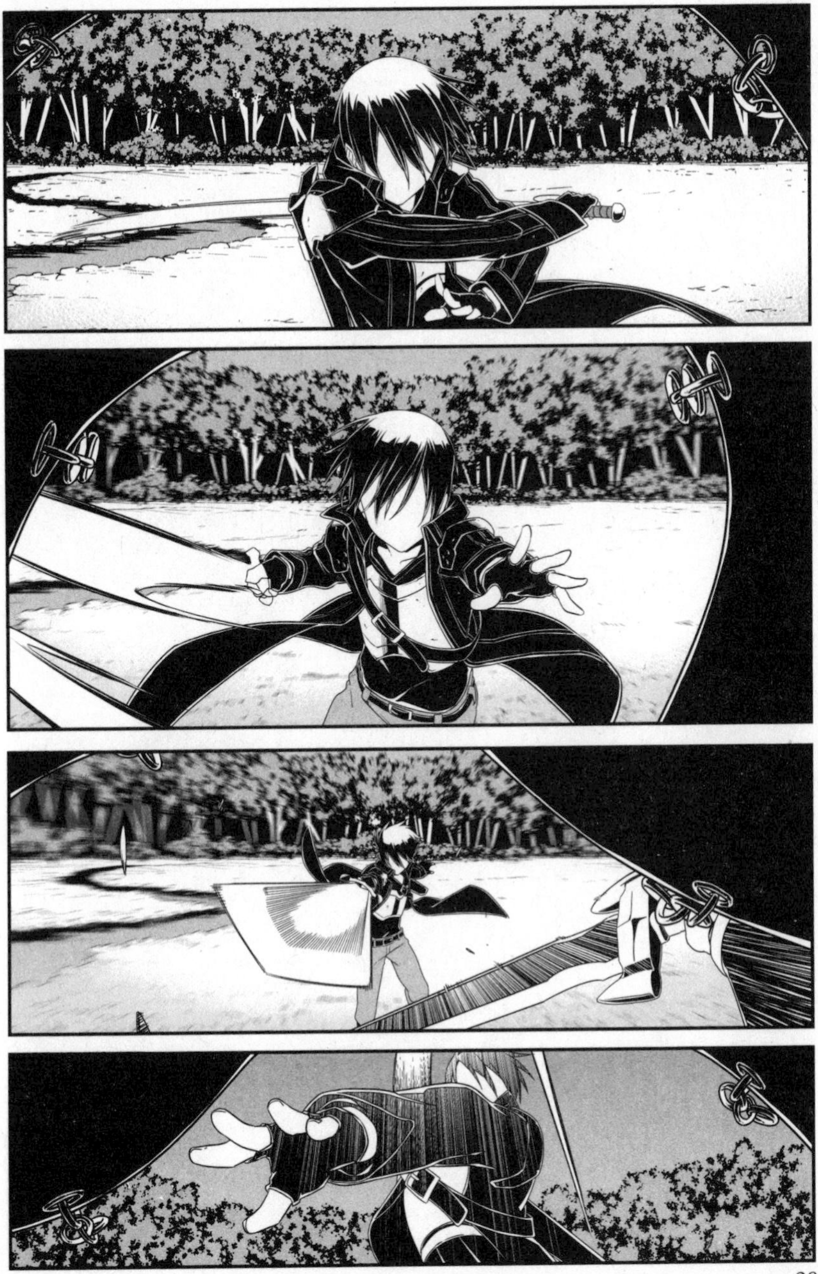

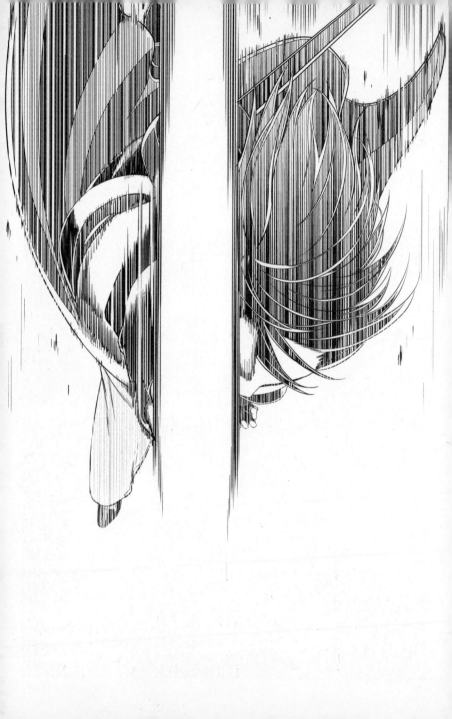

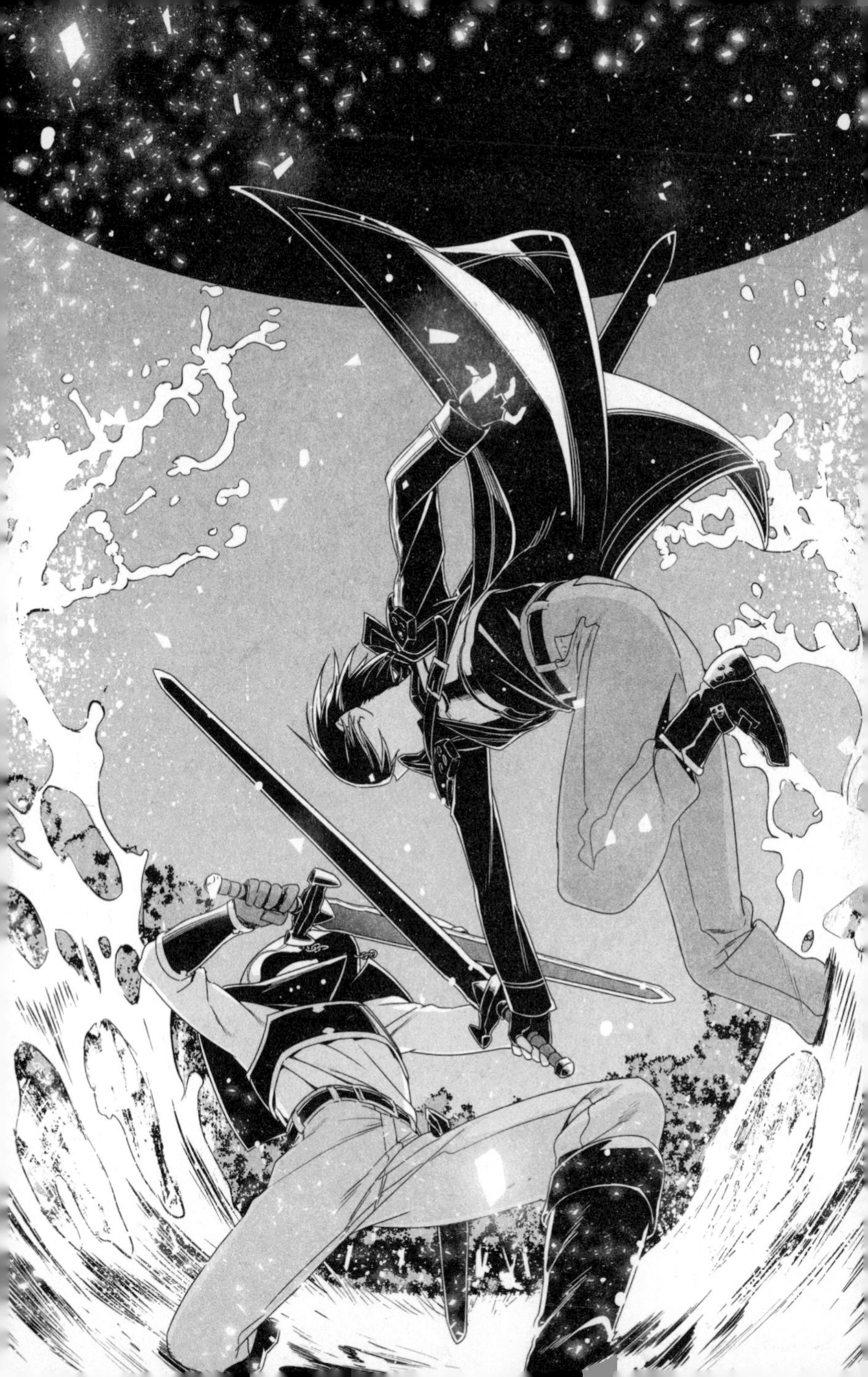

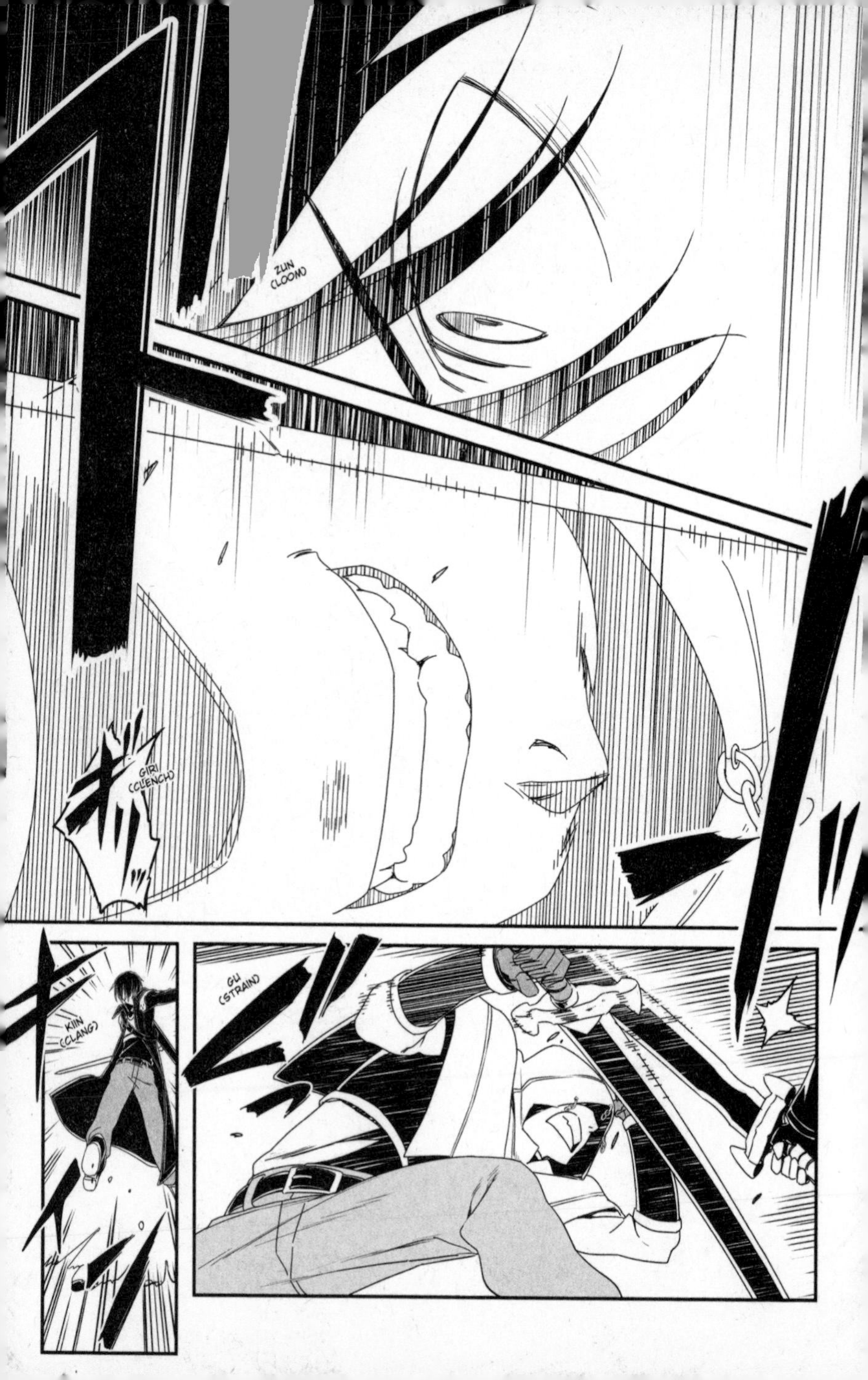
ZUN (LOOM)
GIRI (CLENCH)
GU (STRAIN)
KIIN (CLANG)

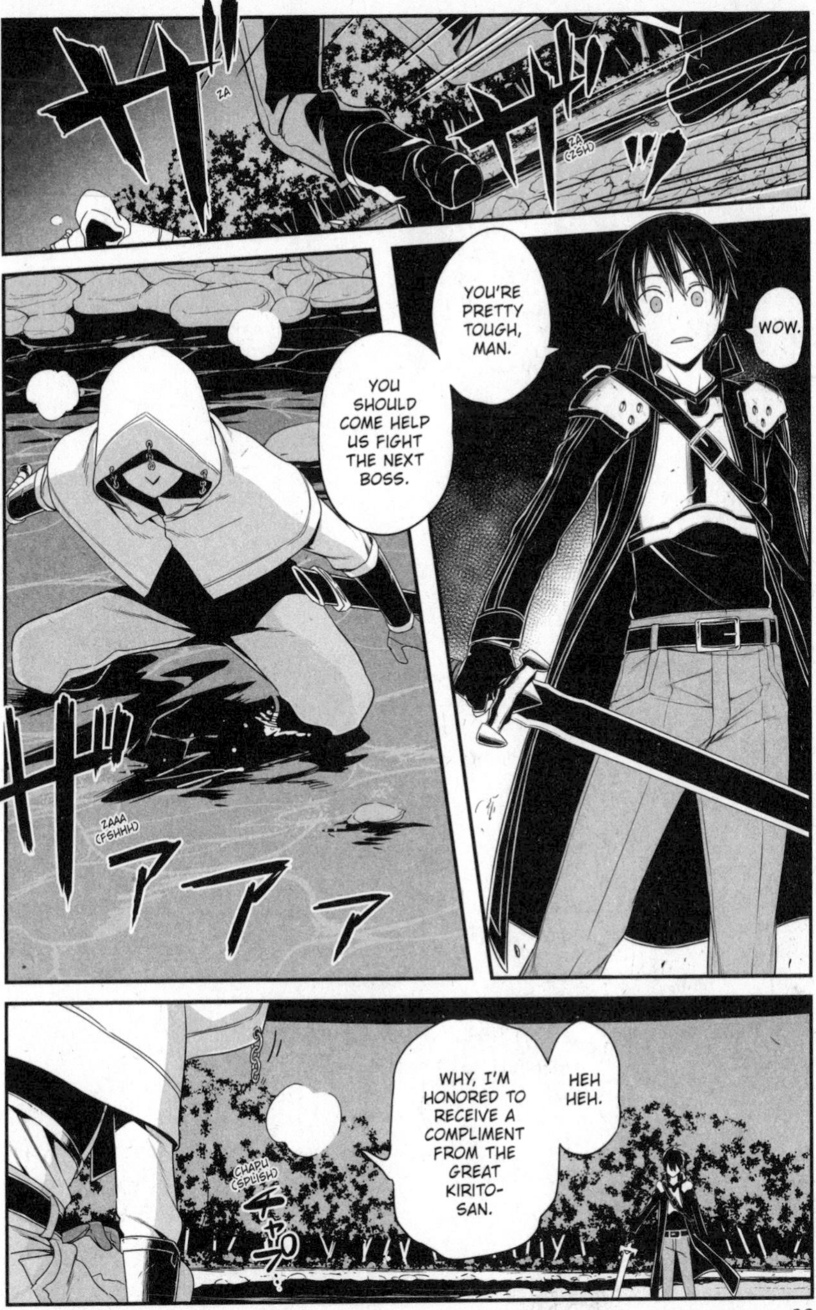
ZA (ZSH)
ZA
WOW.
YOU'RE PRETTY TOUGH, MAN.
YOU SHOULD COME HELP US FIGHT THE NEXT BOSS.
ZAAA (FSHHH)
HEH HEH.
WHY, I'M HONORED TO RECEIVE A COMPLIMENT FROM THE GREAT KIRITO-SAN.
CHAPU (SPLISH)

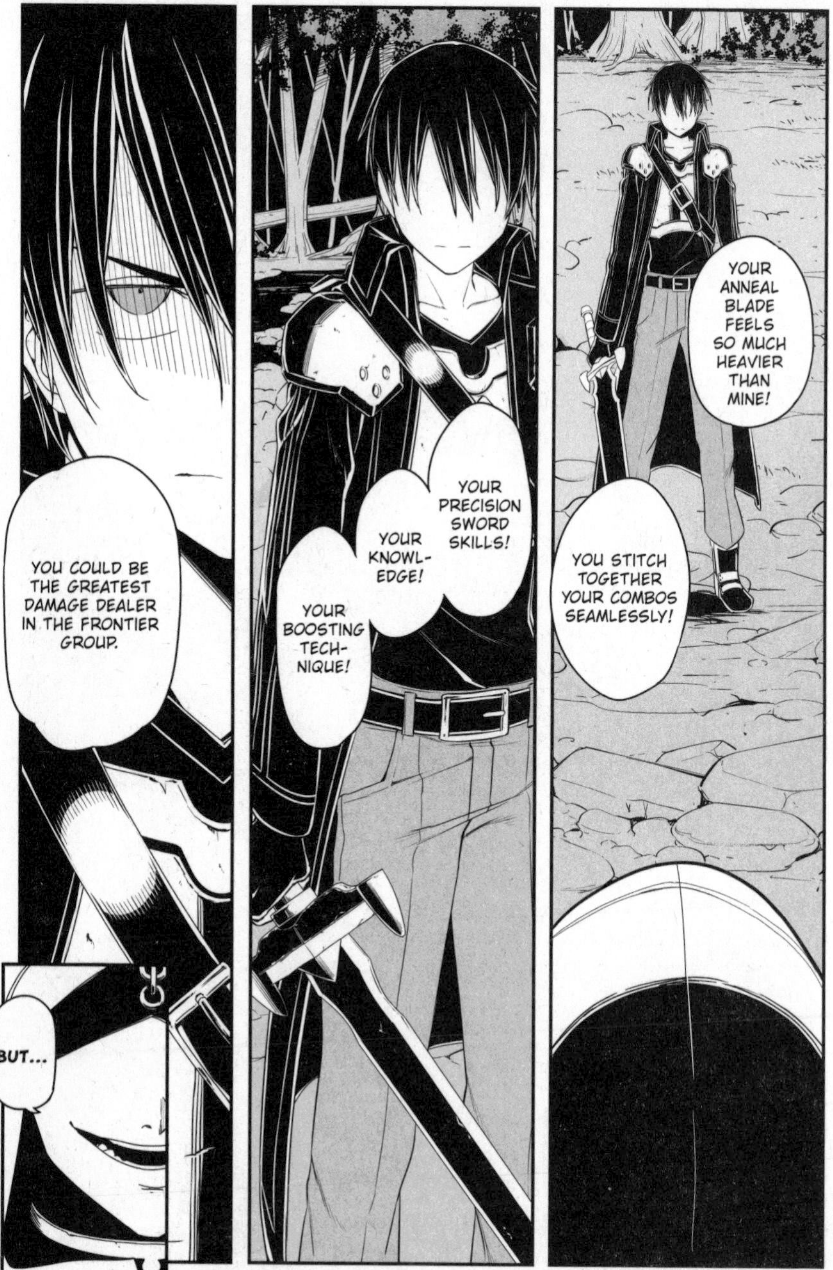
YOUR ANNEAL BLADE FEELS SO MUCH HEAVIER THAN MINE!
YOU STITCH TOGETHER YOUR COMBOS SEAMLESSLY!
YOUR PRECISION SWORD SKILLS!
YOUR KNOWL-EDGE!
YOUR BOOSTING TECH-NIQUE!
YOU COULD BE THE GREATEST DAMAGE DEALER IN THE FRONTIER GROUP.
BUT...

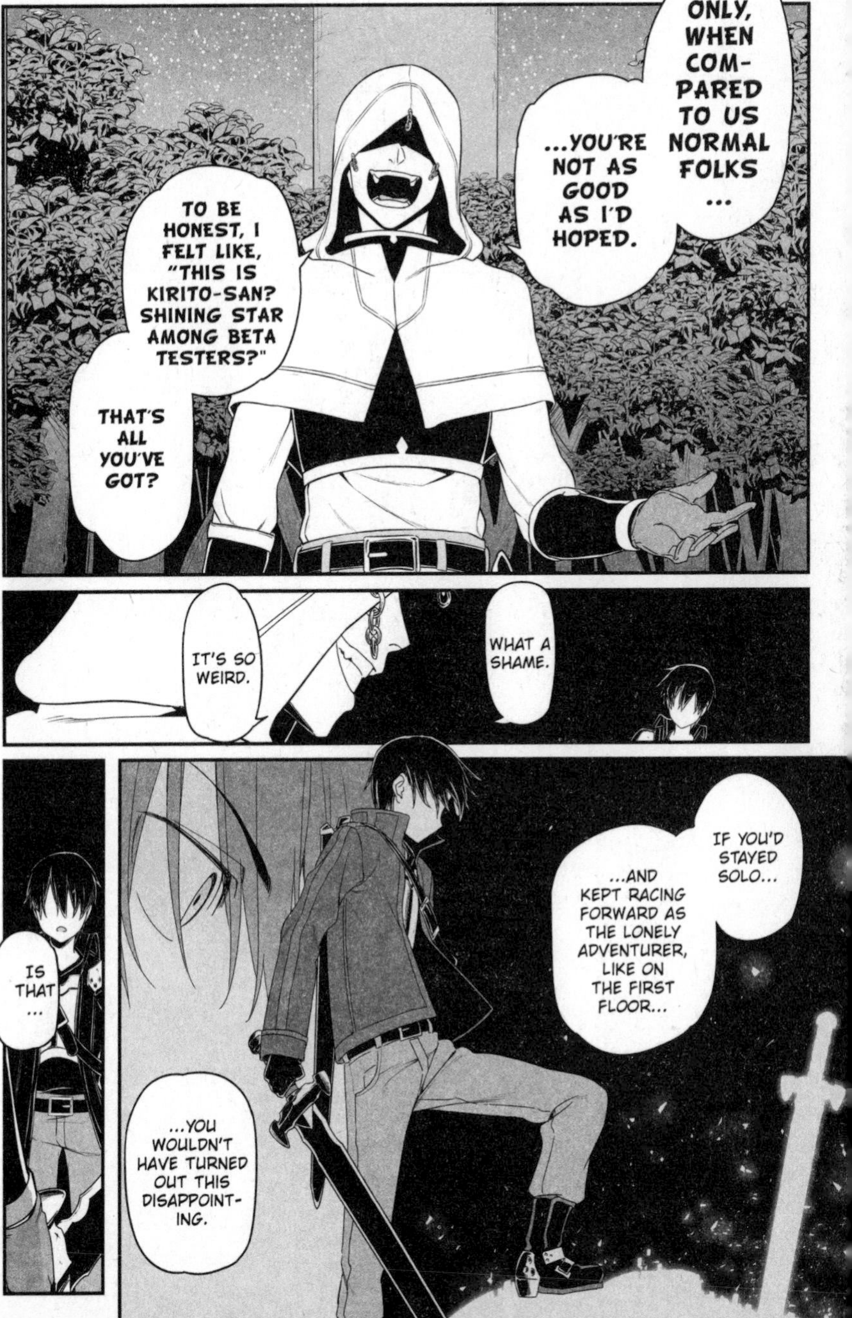
ONLY, WHEN COM-PARED TO US NORMAL FOLKS...
...YOU'RE NOT AS GOOD AS I'D HOPED.
TO BE HONEST, I FELT LIKE, "THIS IS KIRITO-SAN? SHINING STAR AMONG BETA TESTERS?"
THAT'S ALL YOU'VE GOT?
WHAT A SHAME.
IT'S SO WEIRD.
IF YOU'D STAYED SOLO...
...AND KEPT RACING FORWARD AS THE LONELY ADVENTURER, LIKE ON THE FIRST FLOOR...
...YOU WOULDN'T HAVE TURNED OUT THIS DISAPPOINT-ING.
IS THAT...

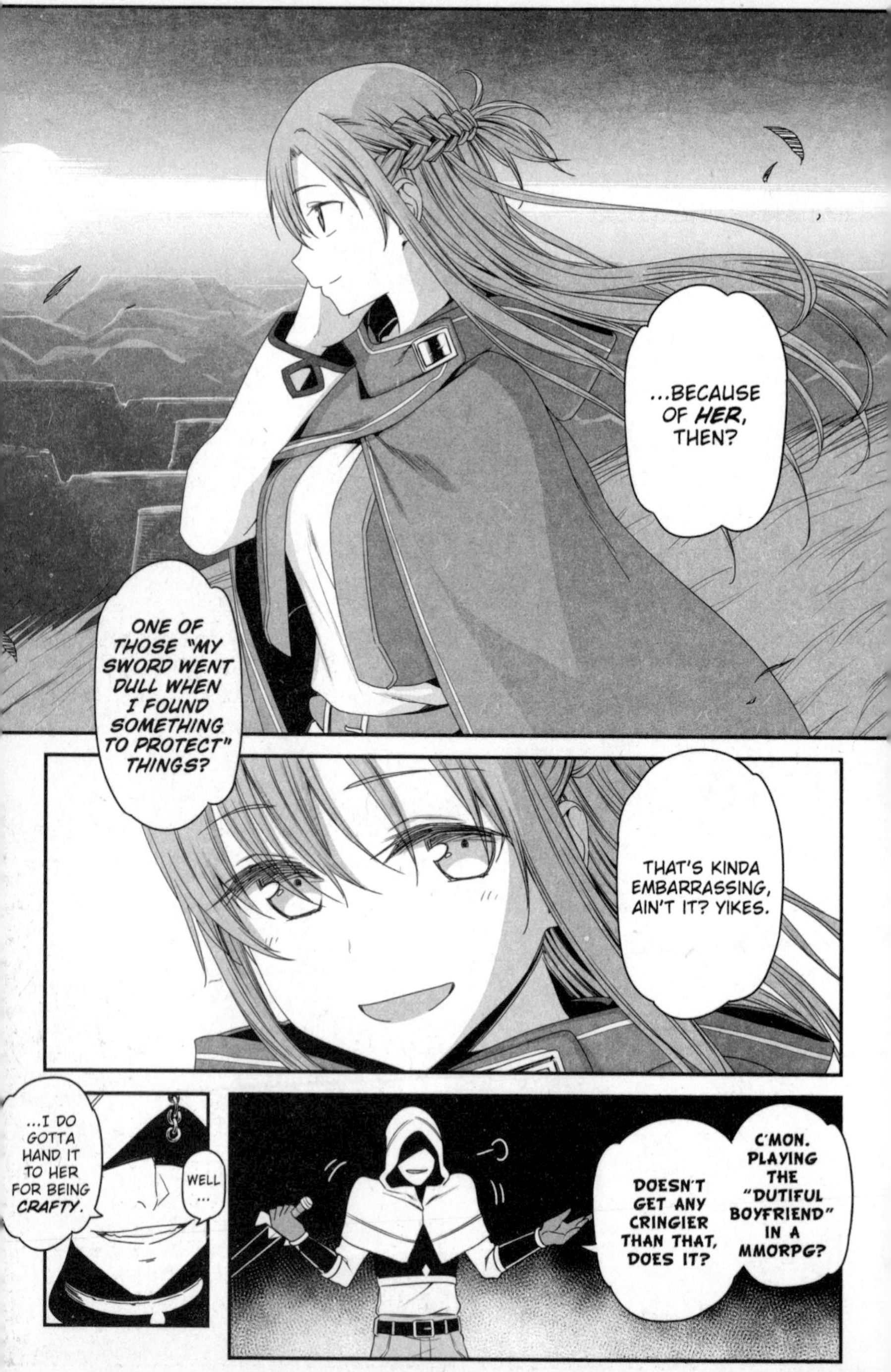
...BECAUSE OF HER, THEN?
ONE OF THOSE "MY SWORD WENT DULL WHEN I FOUND SOMETHING TO PROTECT" THINGS?
THAT'S KINDA EMBARRASSING, AIN'T IT? YIKES.
C'MON. PLAYING THE "DUTIFUL BOYFRIEND" IN A MMORPG?
DOESN'T GET ANY CRINGIER THAN THAT, DOES IT?
WELL ...
...I DO GOTTA HAND IT TO HER FOR BEING CRAFTY.

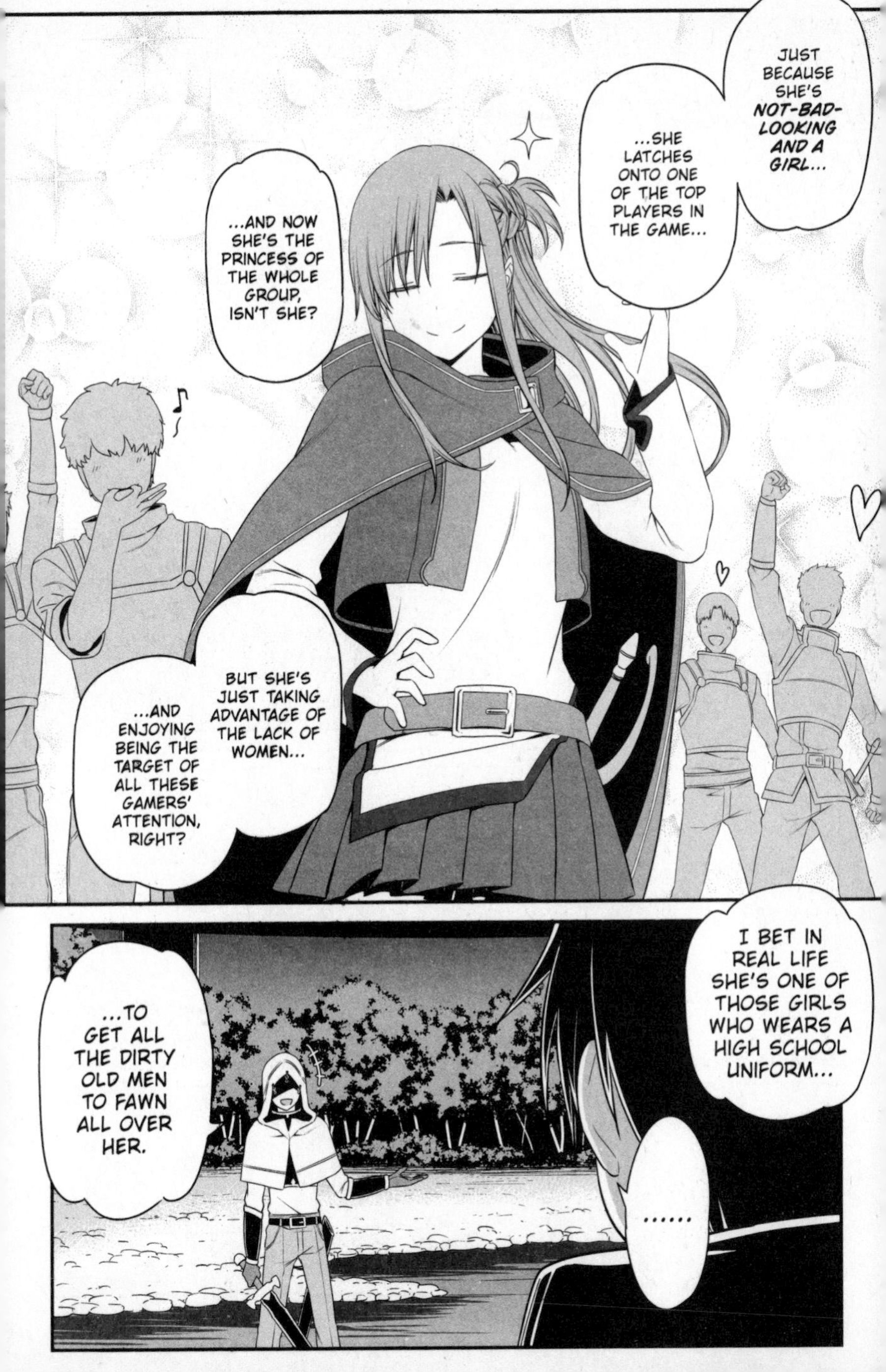
JUST BECAUSE SHE'S NOT-BAD-LOOKING AND A GIRL...
...SHE LATCHES ONTO ONE OF THE TOP PLAYERS IN THE GAME...
...AND NOW SHE'S THE PRINCESS OF THE WHOLE GROUP, ISN'T SHE?
BUT SHE'S JUST TAKING ADVANTAGE OF THE LACK OF WOMEN...
...AND ENJOYING BEING THE TARGET OF ALL THESE GAMERS' ATTENTION, RIGHT?
I BET IN REAL LIFE SHE'S ONE OF THOSE GIRLS WHO WEARS A HIGH SCHOOL UNIFORM...
...TO GET ALL THE DIRTY OLD MEN TO FAWN ALL OVER HER.
......

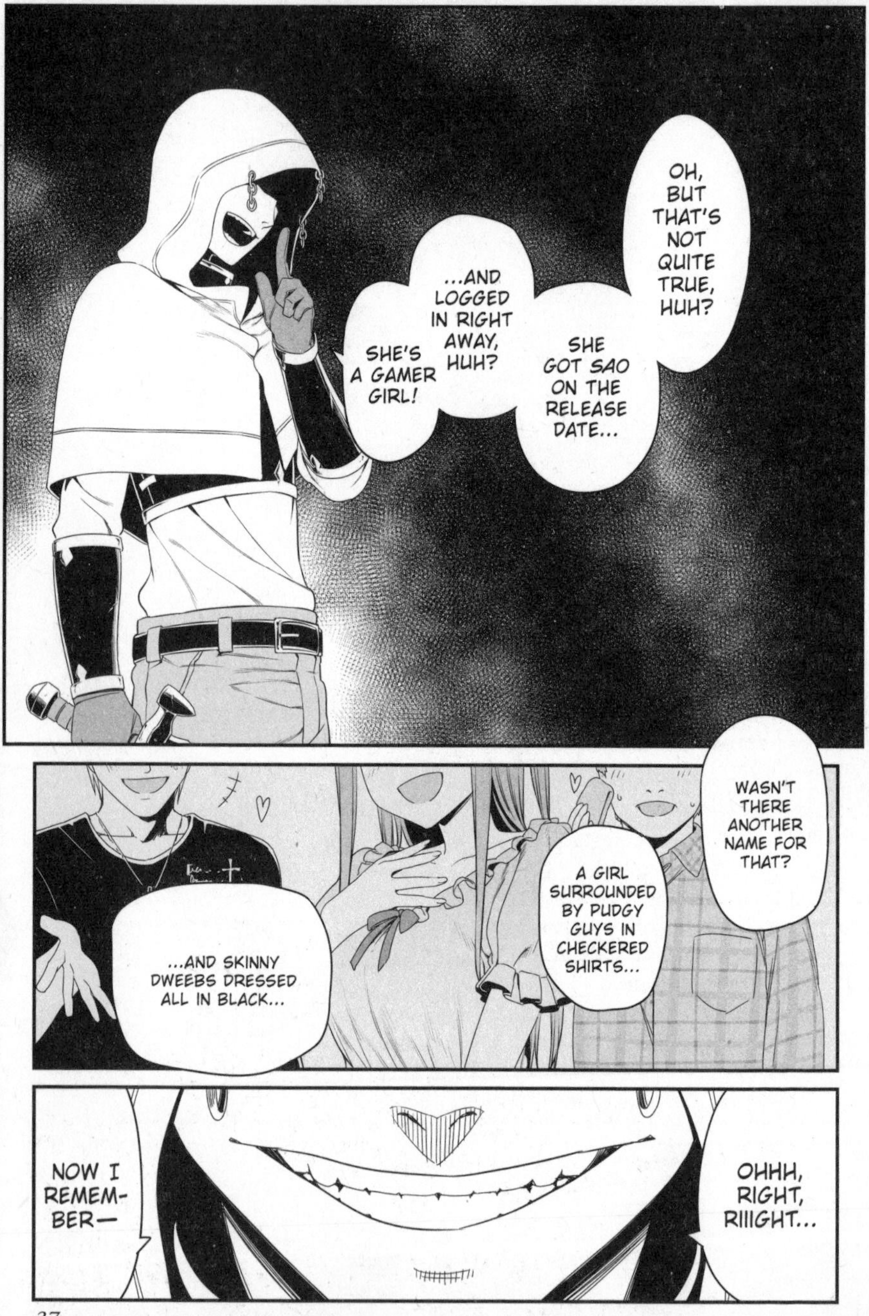
OH, BUT THAT'S NOT QUITE TRUE, HUH?
SHE GOT SAO ON THE RELEASE DATE...
...AND LOGGED IN RIGHT AWAY, HUH?
SHE'S A GAMER GIRL!
WASN'T THERE ANOTHER NAME FOR THAT?
A GIRL SURROUNDED BY PUDGY GUYS IN CHECKERED SHIRTS...
...AND SKINNY DWEEBS DRESSED ALL IN BLACK...
OHHH, RIGHT, RIIIGHT...
NOW I REMEM-BER—

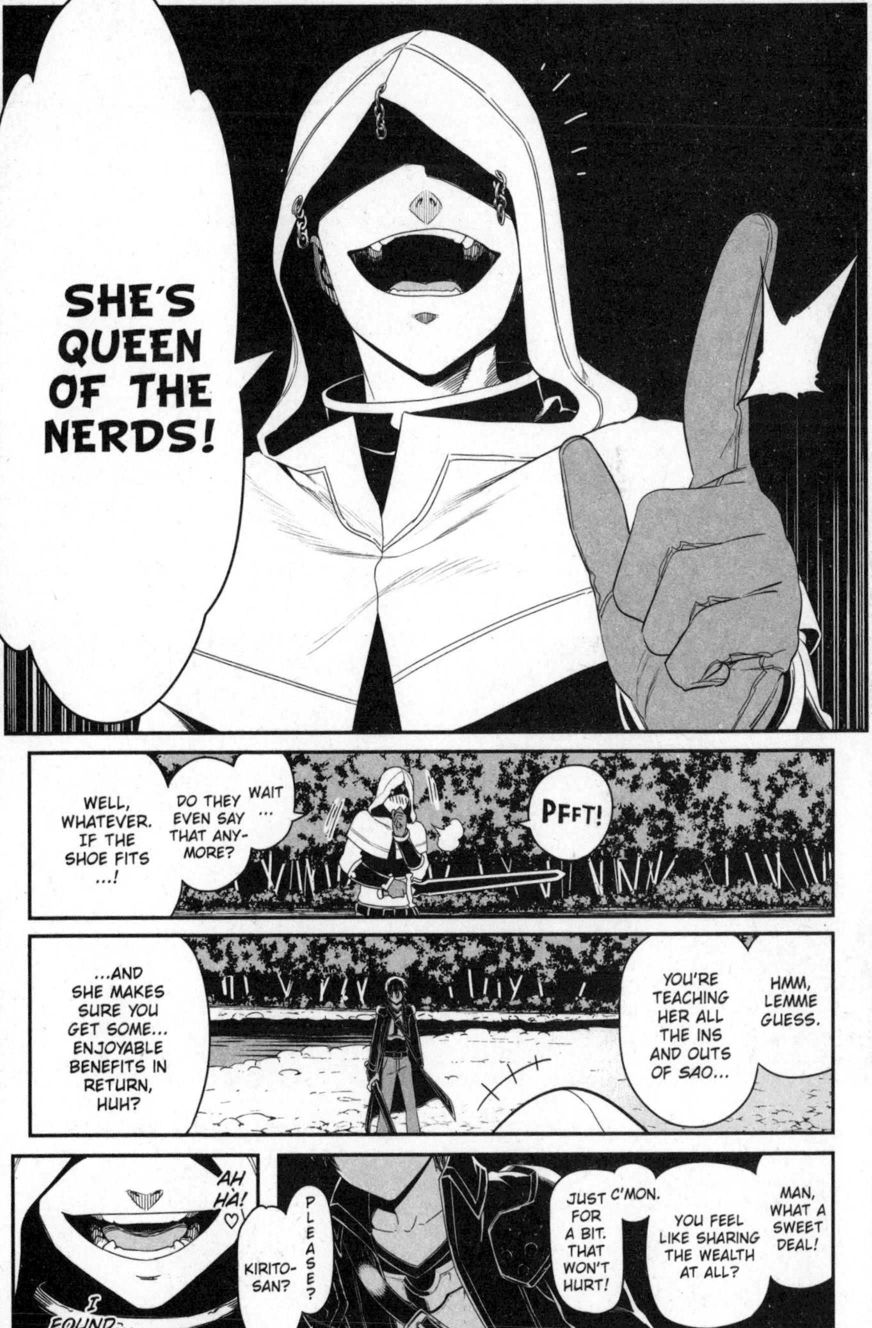
SHE'S QUEEN OF THE NERDS!
PFFT!
WAIT ...
DO THEY EVEN SAY THAT ANYMORE?
WELL, WHATEVER. IF THE SHOE FITS ...!
HMM, LEMME GUESS.
YOU'RE TEACHING HER ALL THE INS AND OUTS OF SAO...
...AND SHE MAKES SURE YOU GET SOME... ENJOYABLE BENEFITS IN RETURN, HUH?
MAN, WHAT A SWEET DEAL!
YOU FEEL LIKE SHARING THE WEALTH AT ALL?
C'MON.
JUST FOR A BIT. THAT WON'T HURT!
PLEASE?
KIRITO-SAN?
AH HA! ♡
I FOUND...

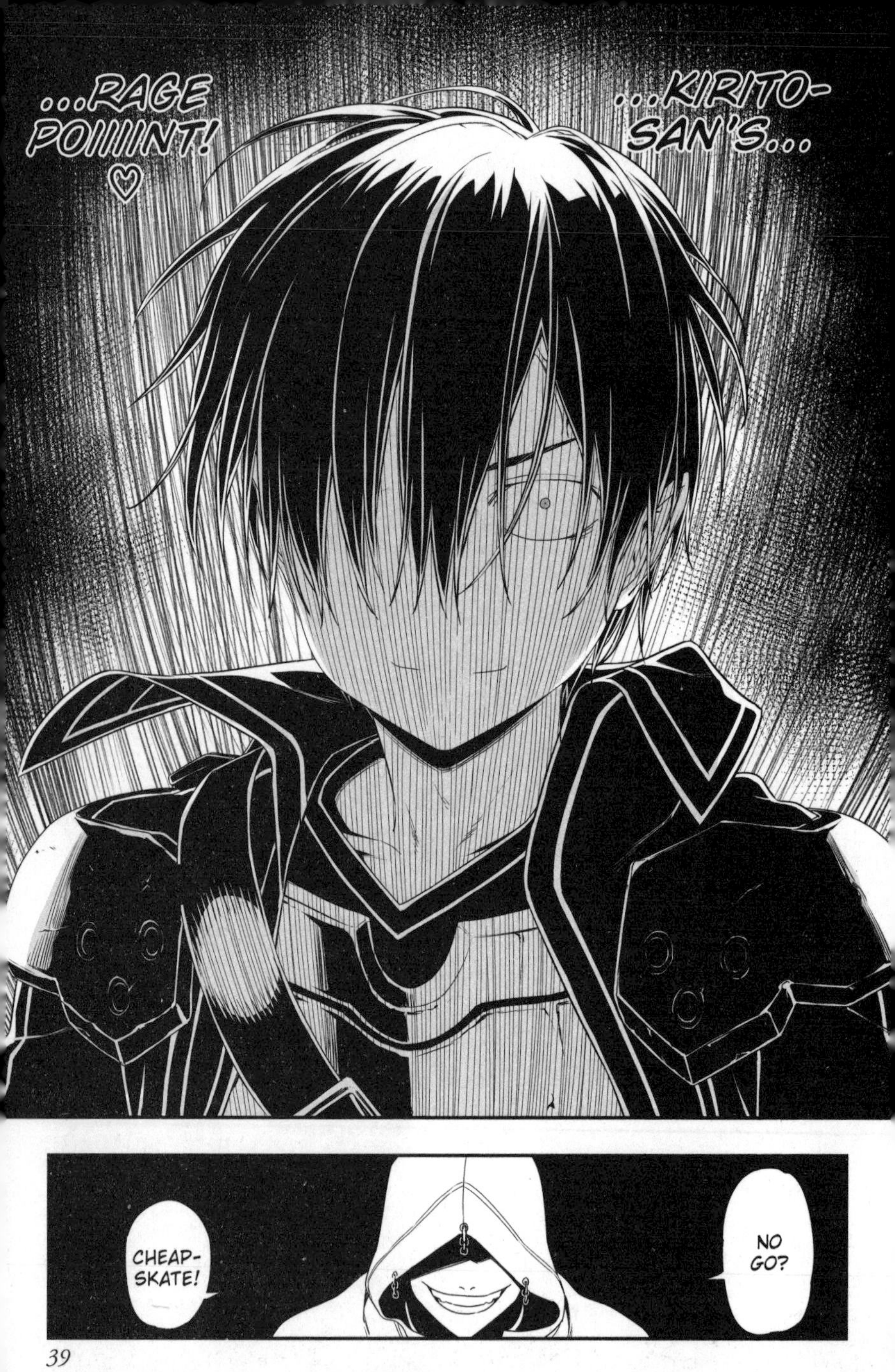
...KIRITO-SAN'S...
...RAGE POIIIIINT! ♡
NO GO?
CHEAP-SKATE!

#039: Divide and Conquer

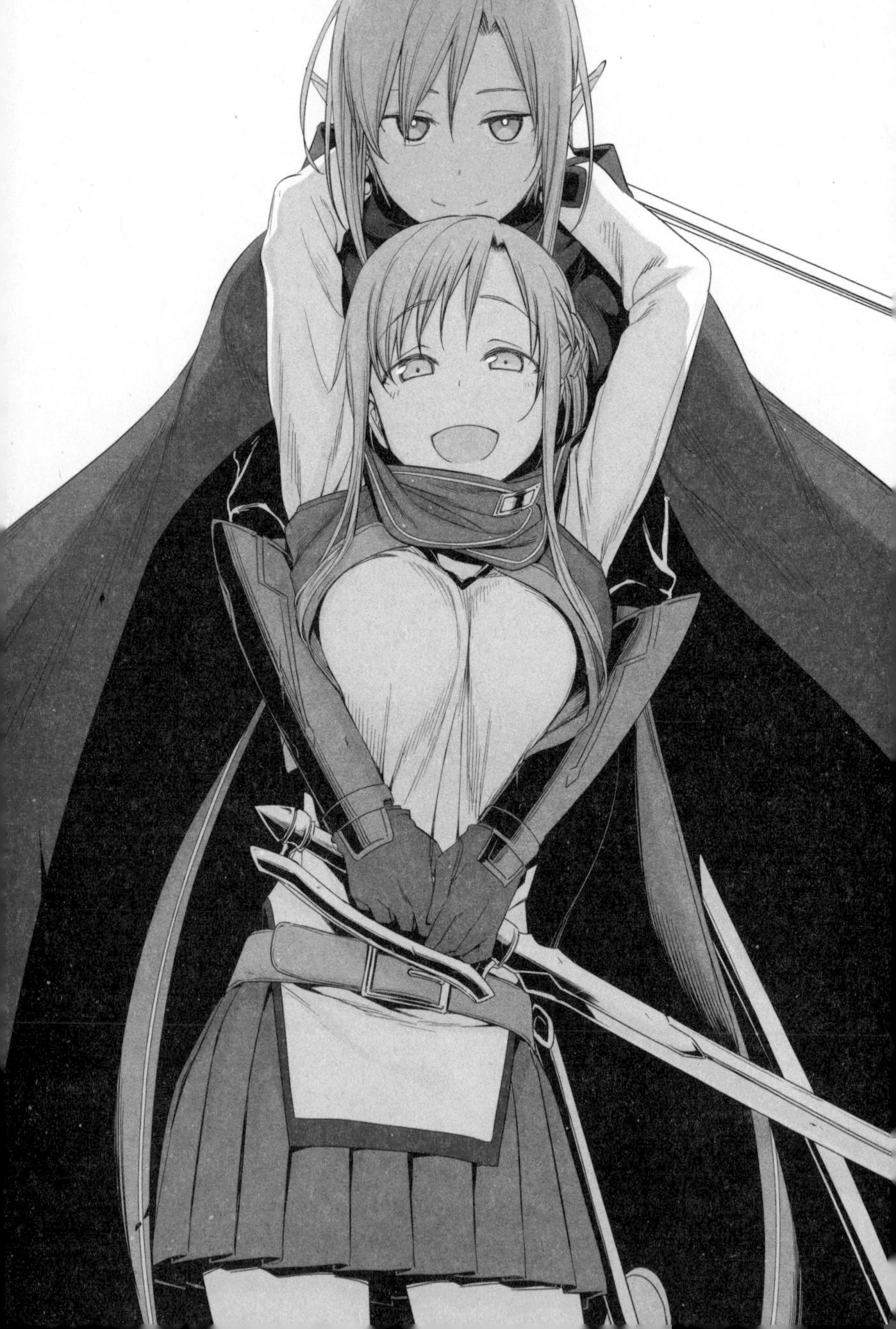

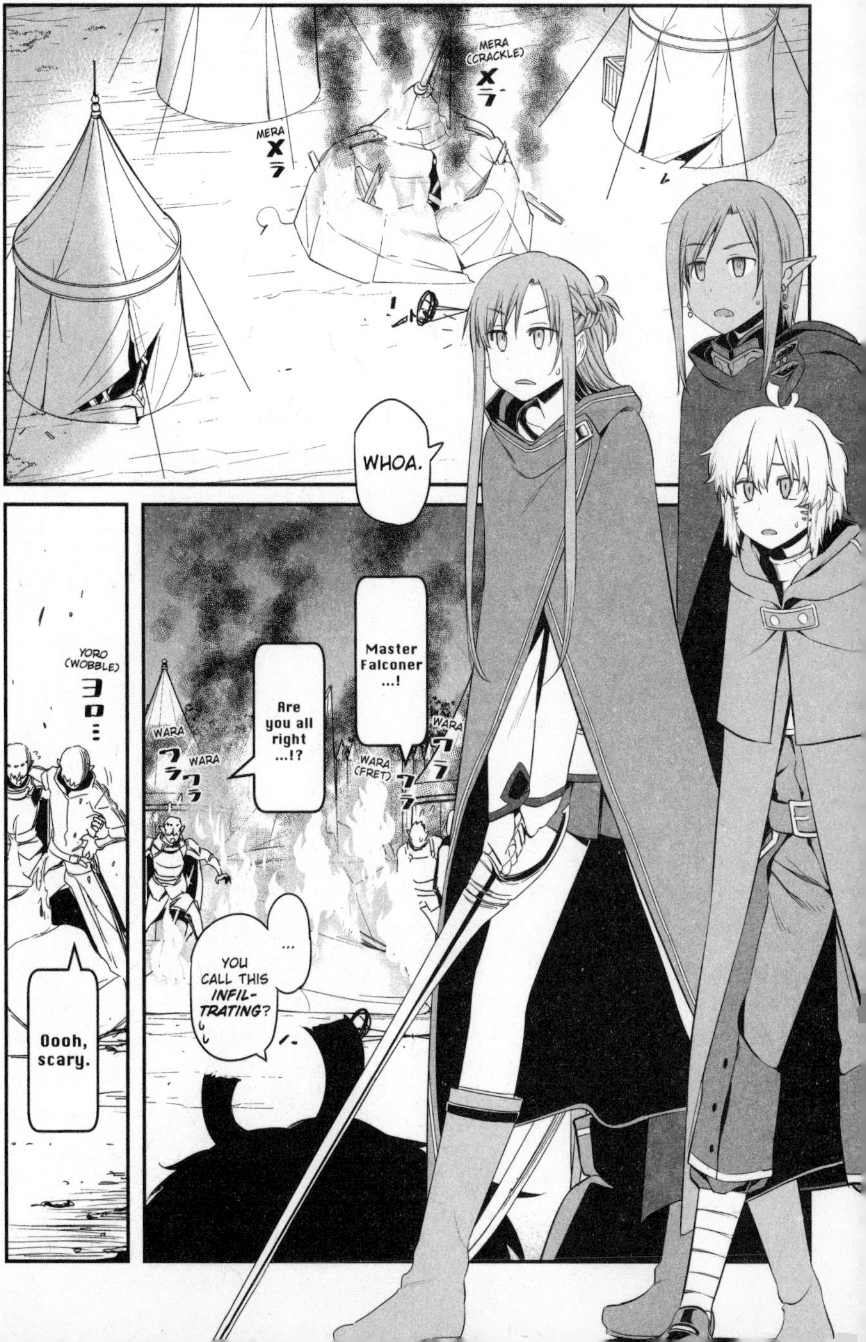
MERA (CRACKLE)
MERA
WHOA.
Master Falconer ...!
WARA
WARA (FRET)
Are you all right ...!?
WARA
WARA
... YOU CALL THIS *INFIL-TRATING*?
YORO (WOBBLE)
Oooh, scary.

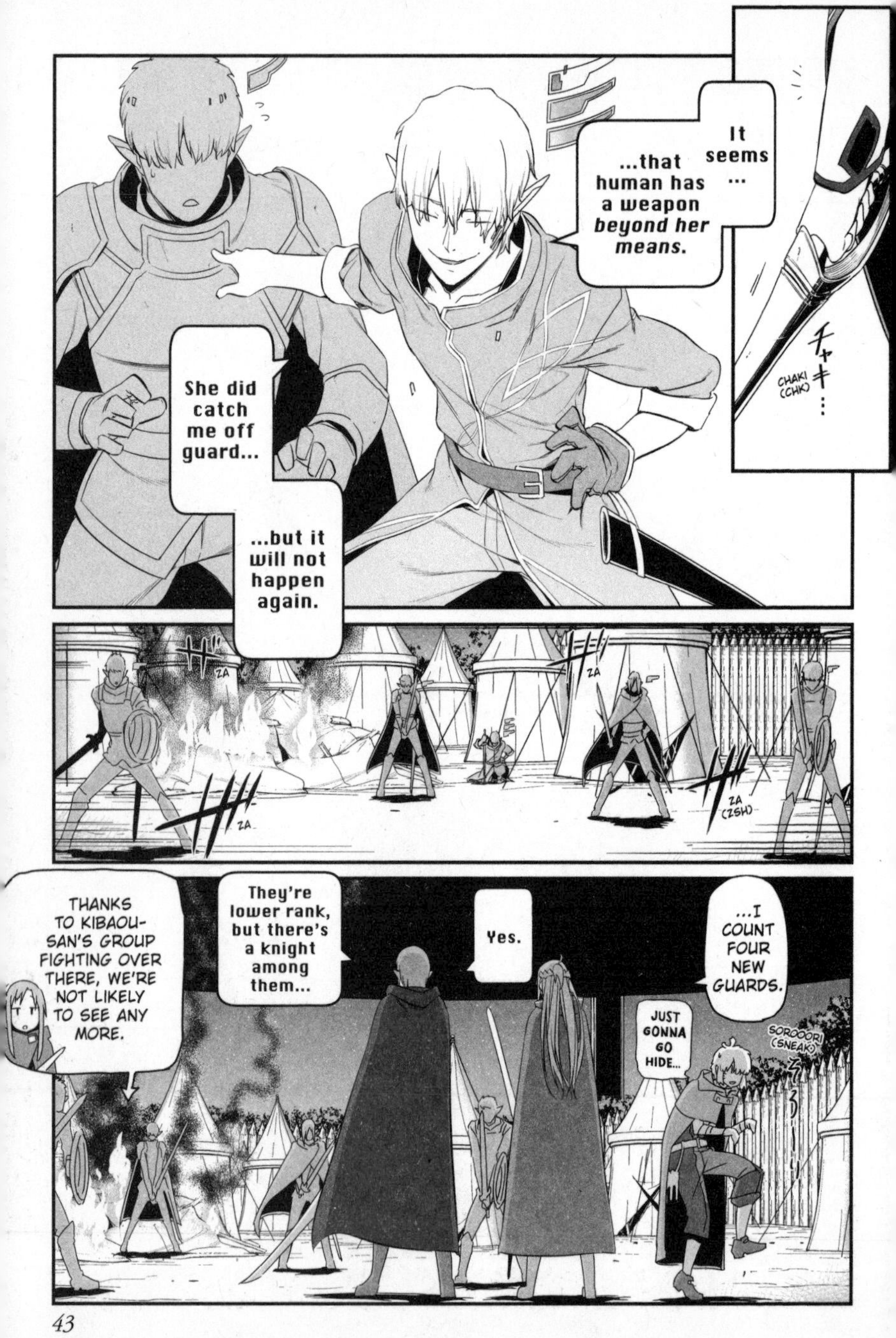
CHAKI (CHK)
It seems...
...that human has a weapon beyond her means.
She did catch me off guard...
...but it will not happen again.
ZA
ZA
ZA (ZSH)
ZA
...I COUNT FOUR NEW GUARDS.
SOROOORI (SNEAK)
JUST GONNA GO HIDE...
Yes.
They're lower rank, but there's a knight among them...
THANKS TO KIBAOU-SAN'S GROUP FIGHTING OVER THERE, WE'RE NOT LIKELY TO SEE ANY MORE.

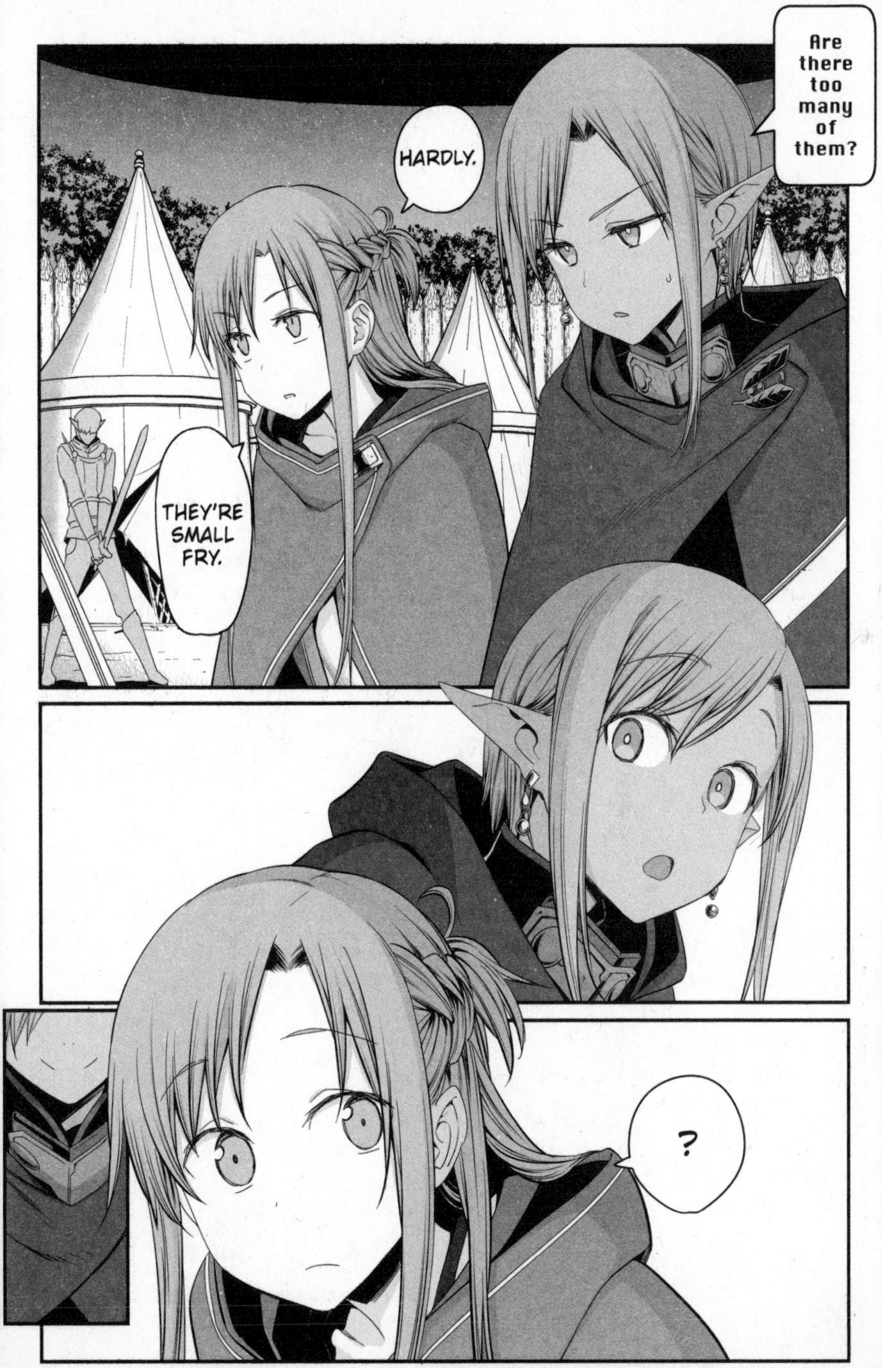
Are there too many of them?
HARDLY.
THEY'RE SMALL FRY.
?

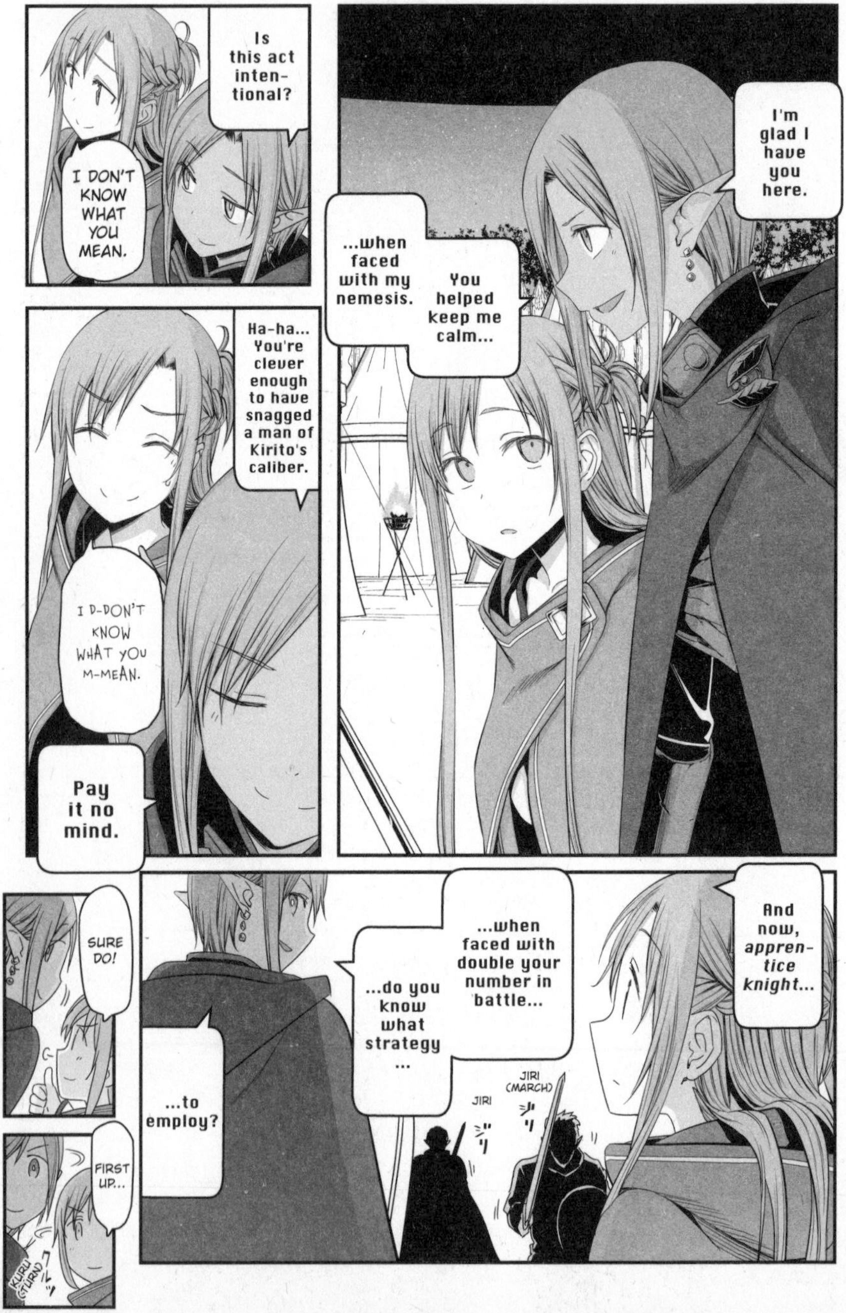
I'm glad I have you here.
You helped keep me calm...
...when faced with my nemesis.
Is this act inten-tional?
I DON'T KNOW WHAT YOU MEAN.
Ha-ha... You're clever enough to have snagged a man of Kirito's caliber.
I D-DON'T KNOW WHAT YOU M-MEAN.
Pay it no mind.
And now, *appren-tice knight*...
...when faced with double your number in battle...
...do you know what strategy...
...to employ?
JIRI (MARCH)
JIRI
SURE DO!
FIRST UP...
KURU (TURN)

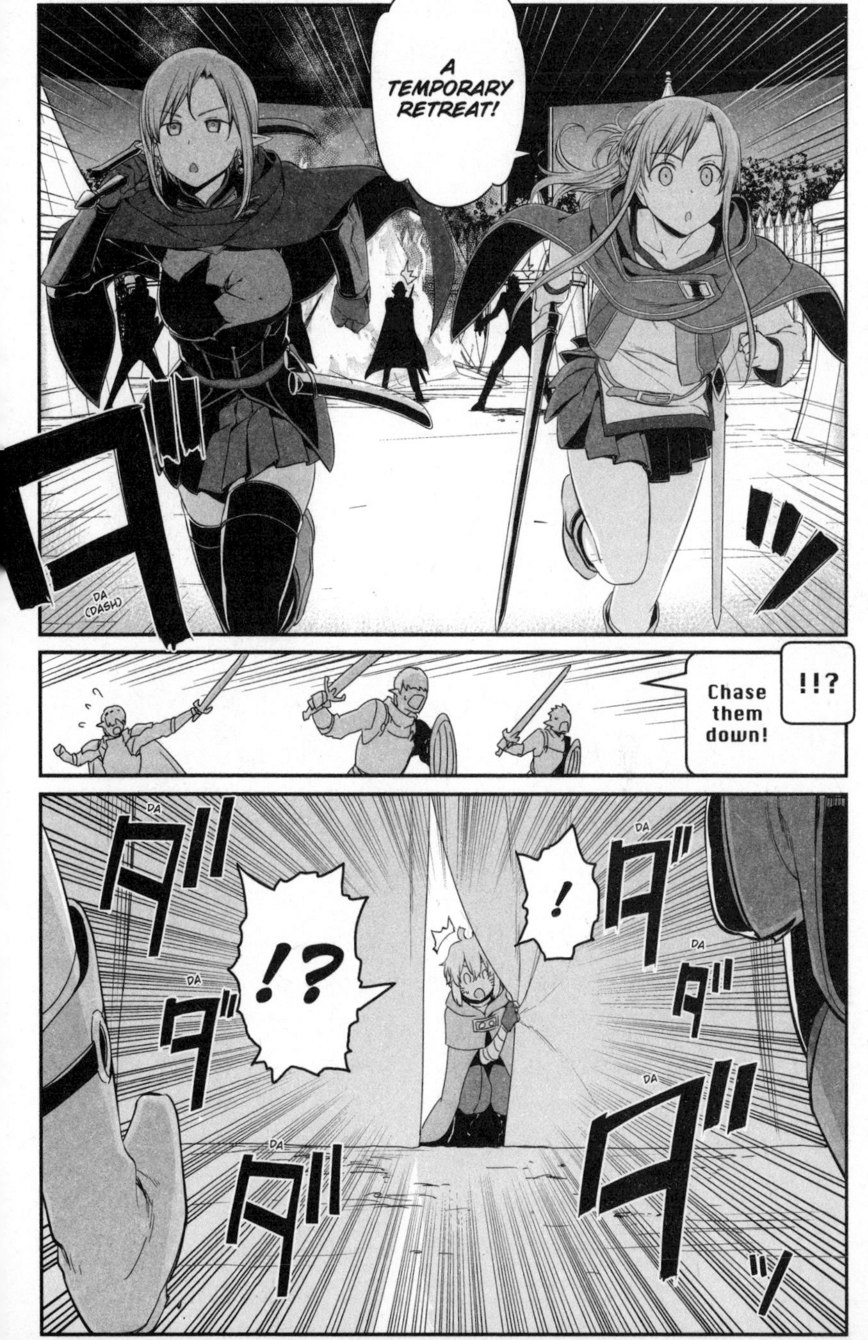
A TEMPORARY RETREAT!
DA (DASH)
!!?
Chase them down!
DA
!
DA
DA
!?
DA
DA

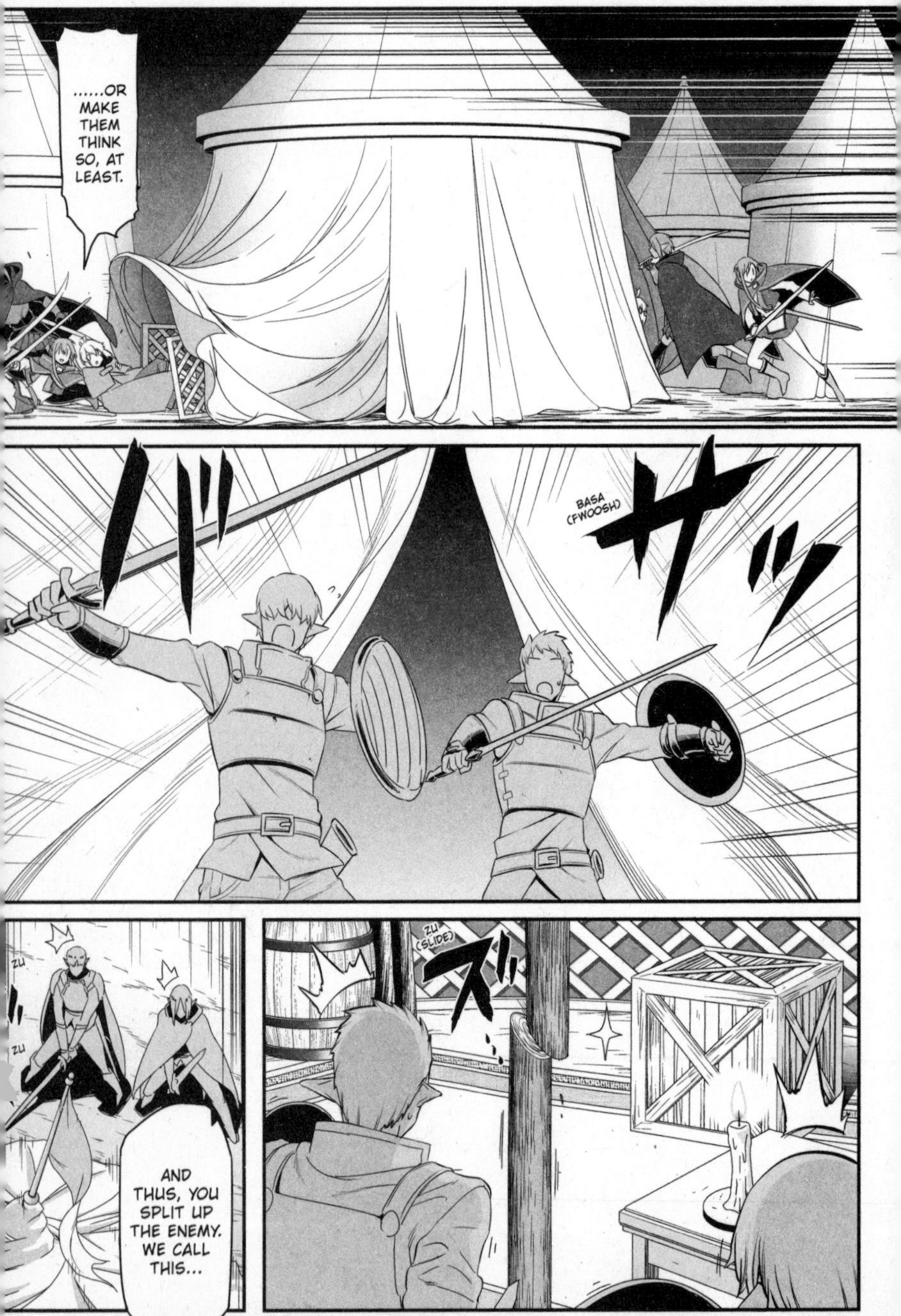
......OR MAKE THEM THINK SO, AT LEAST.
BASA (FWOOSH)
ZU (SLIDE)
ZU
ZU
AND THUS, YOU SPLIT UP THE ENEMY. WE CALL THIS...

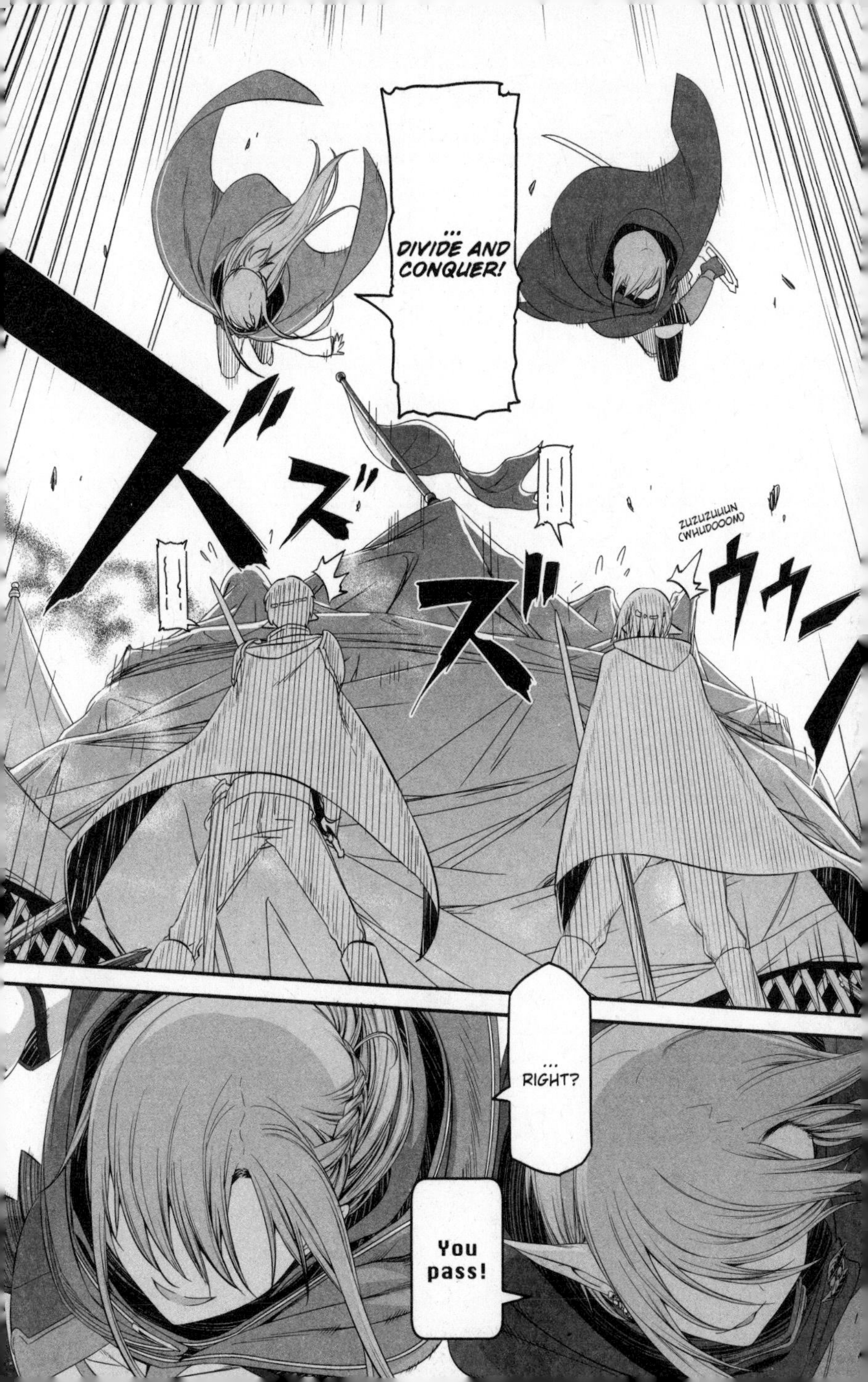
...DIVIDE AND CONQUER!
!!
!!
ZUZUZUUUN (WHUDOOOM)
ズズズズウウーン
...RIGHT?
You pass!

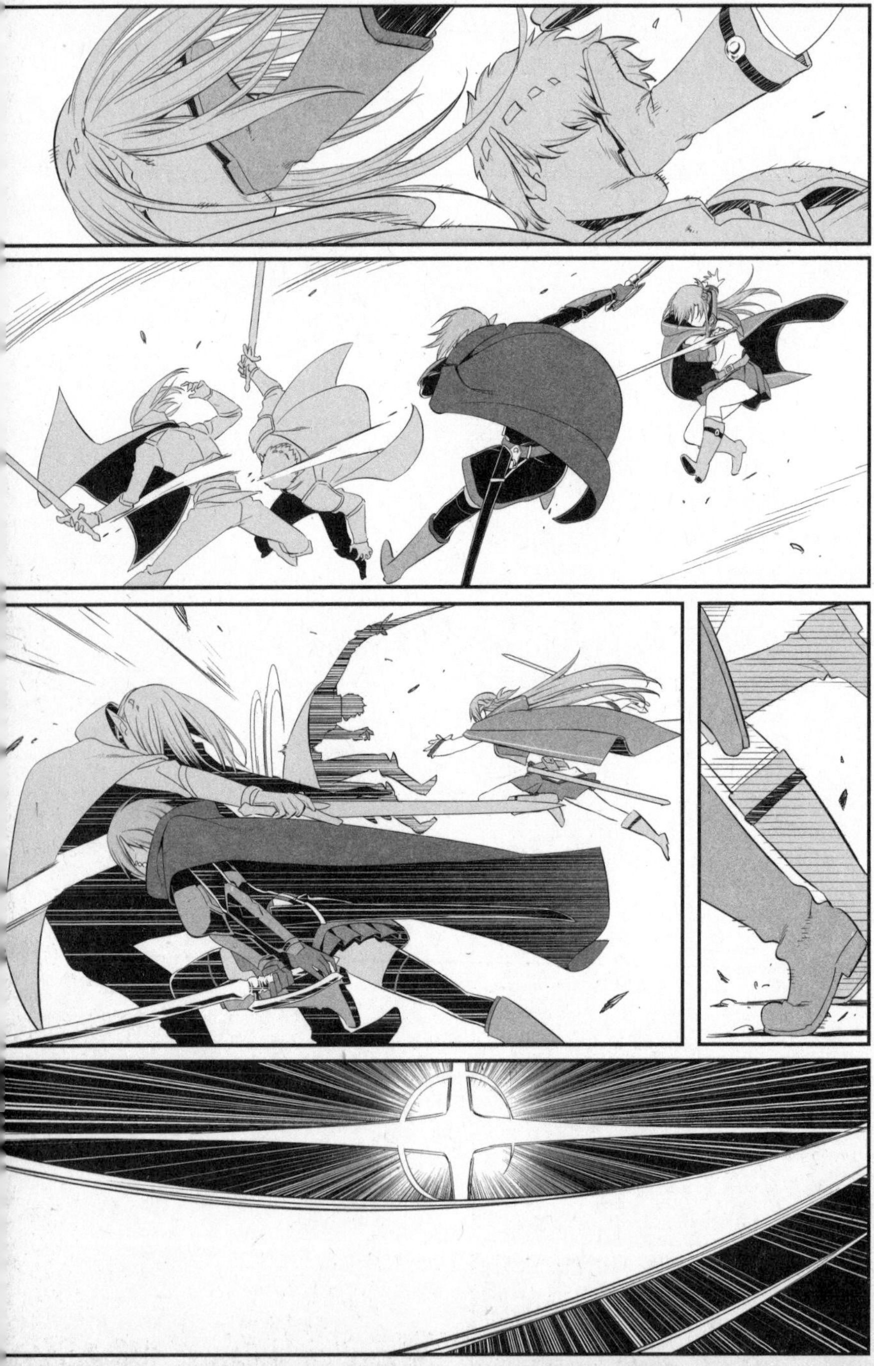

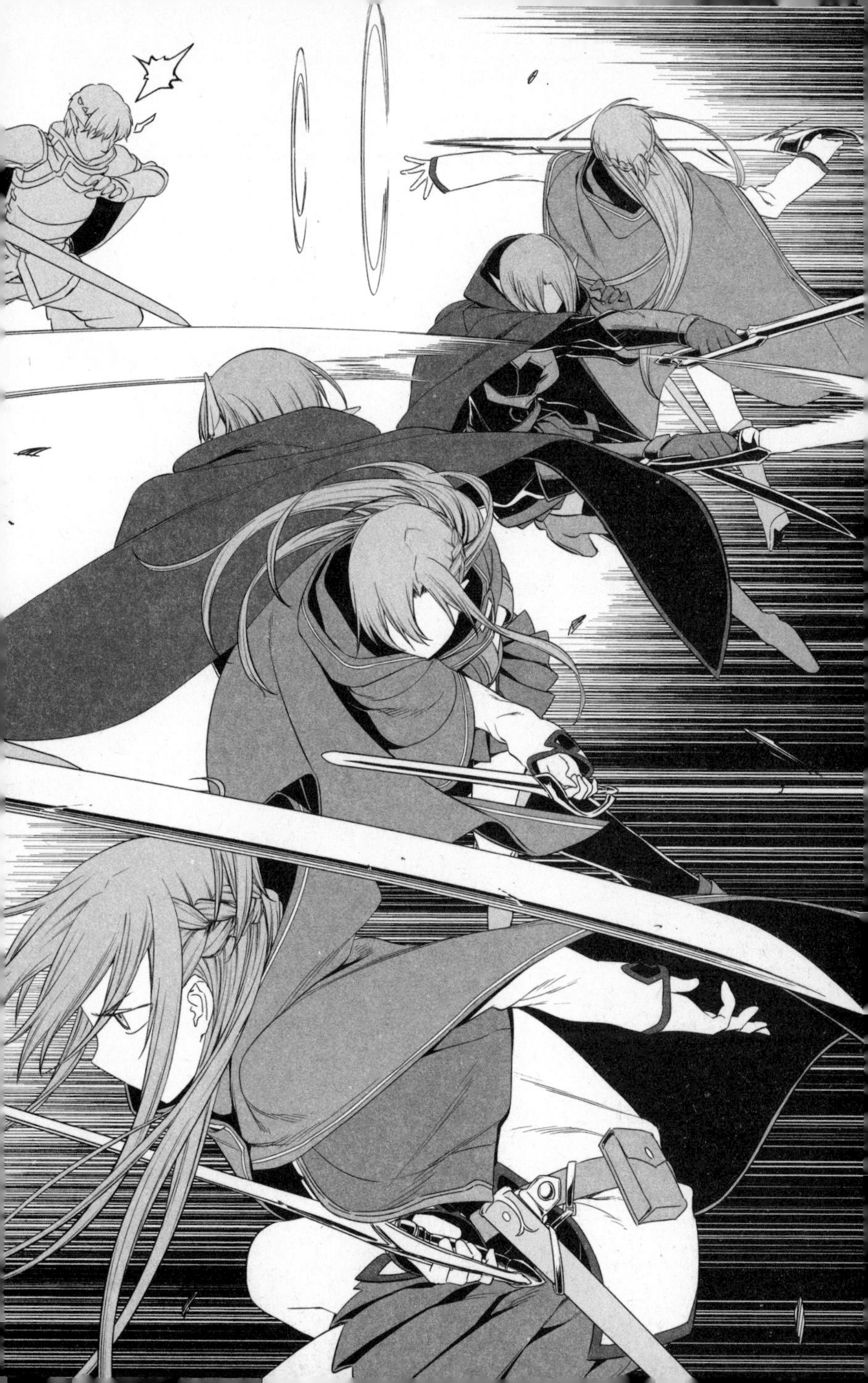

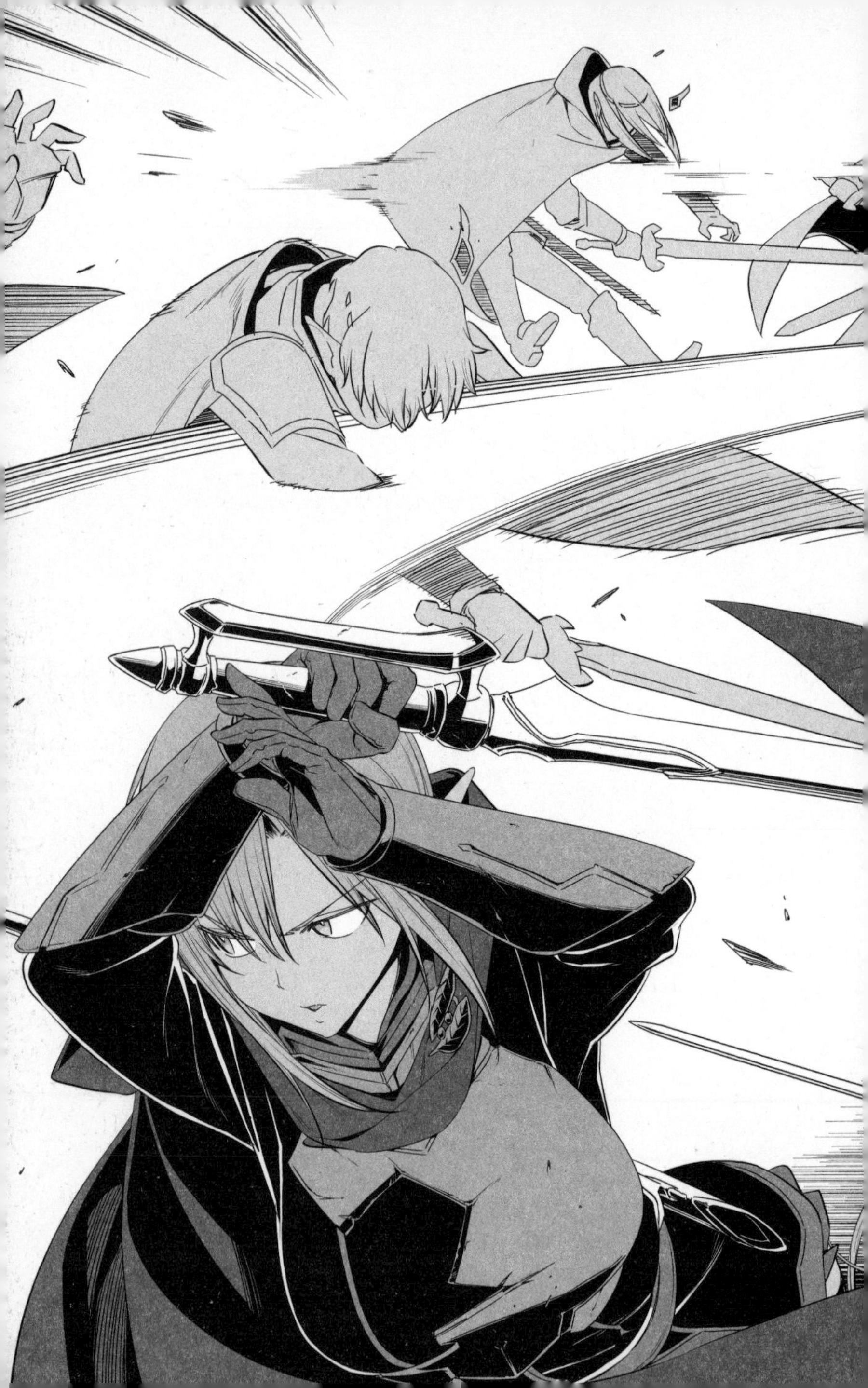

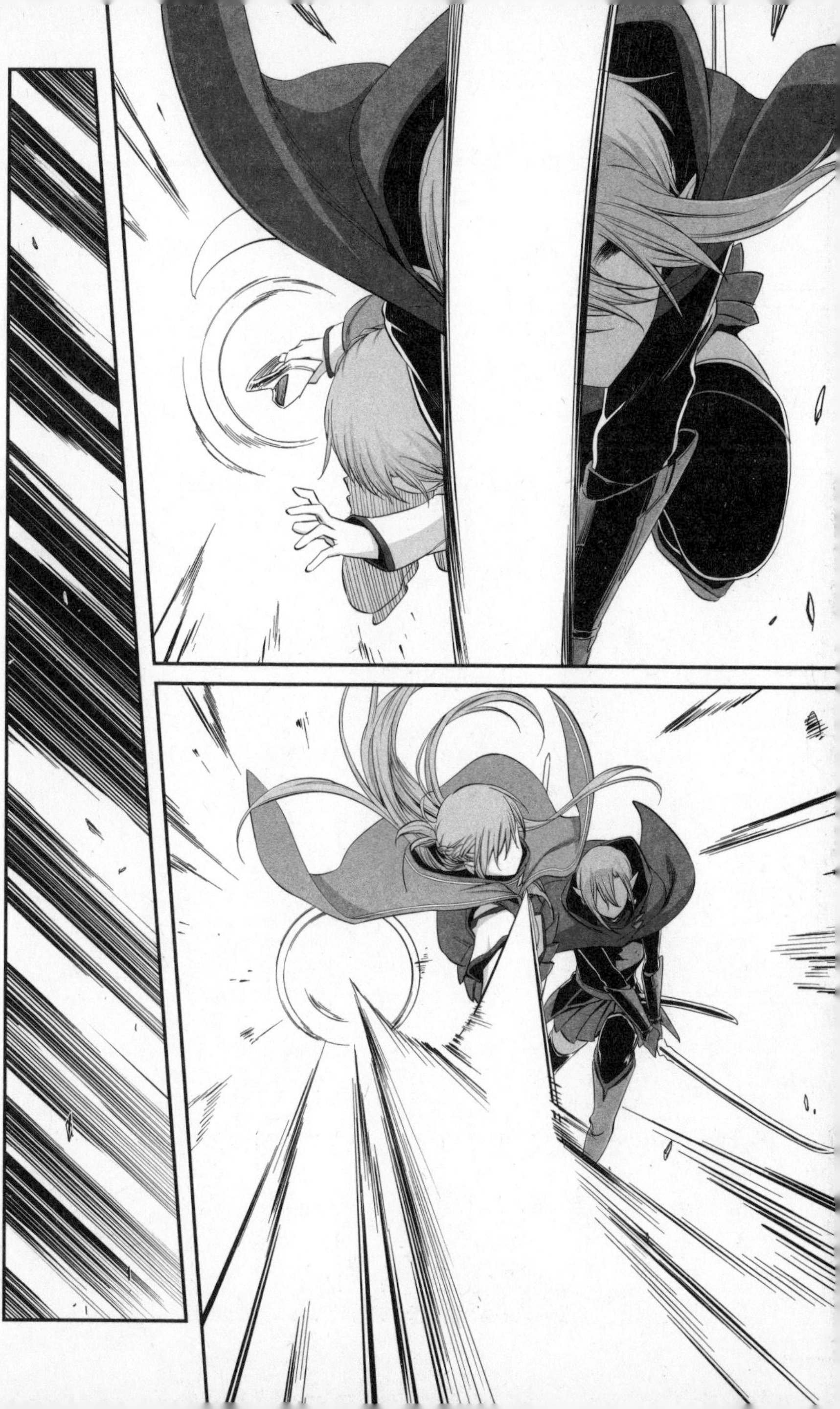

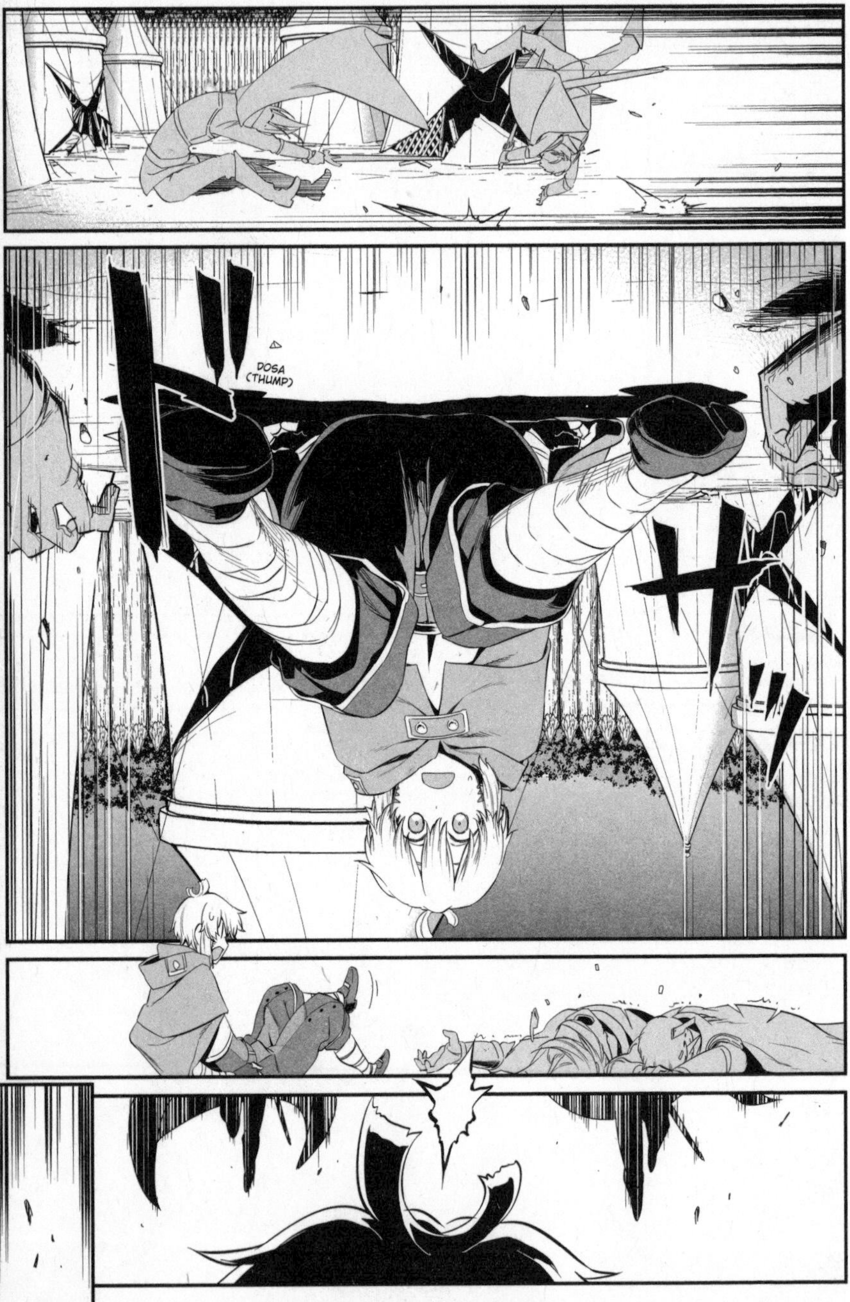
DOSA
(THUMP)

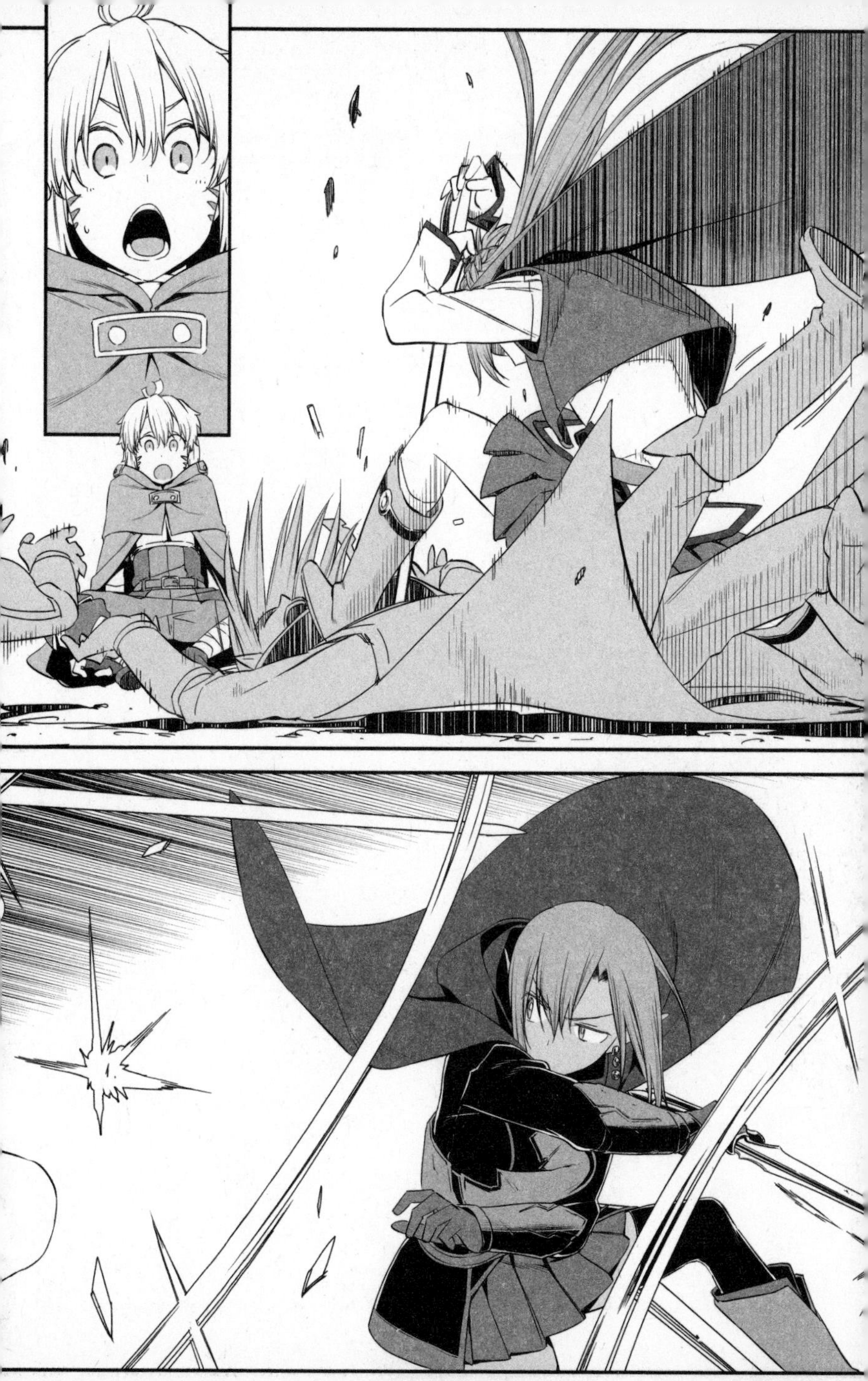

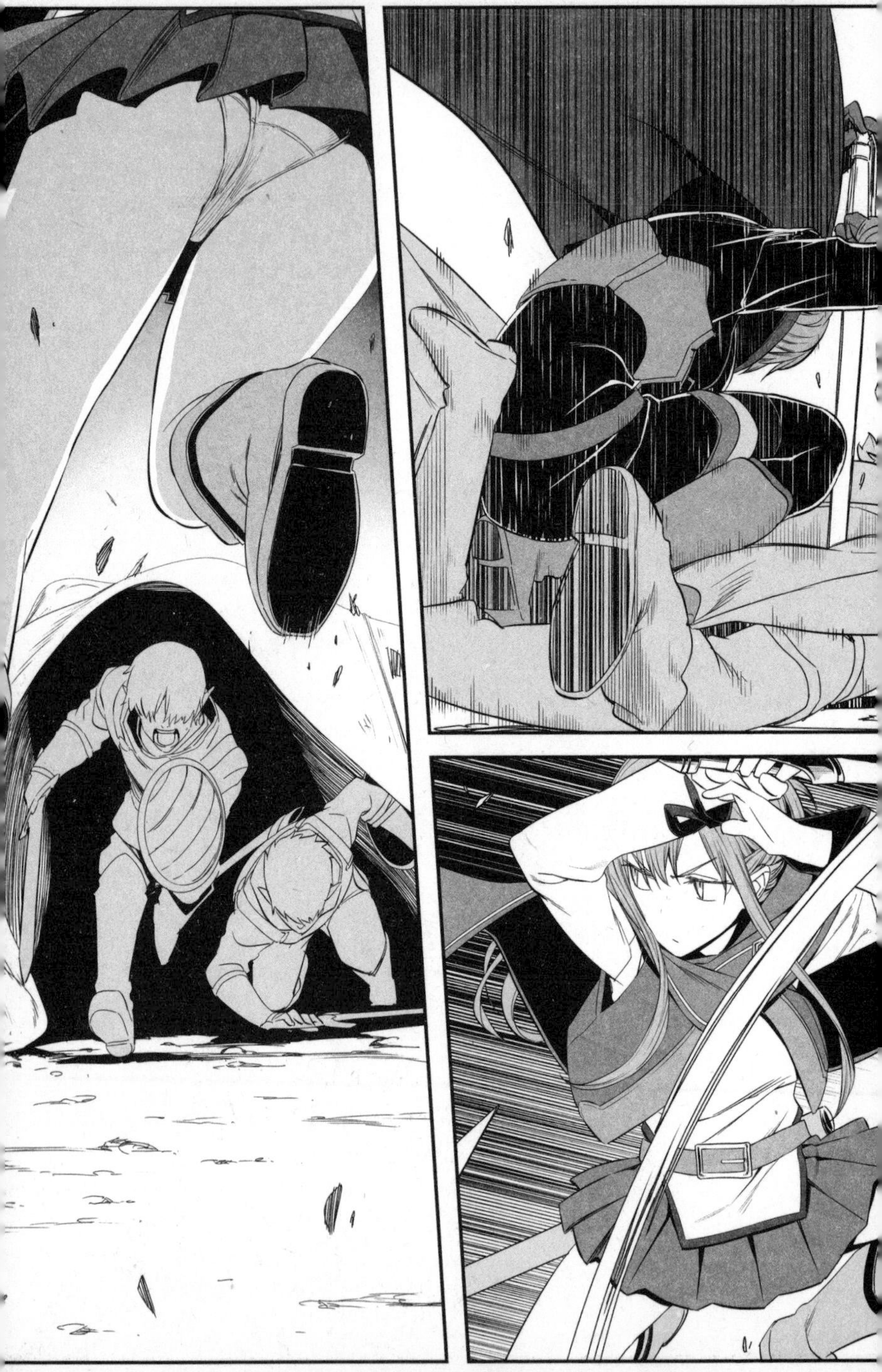

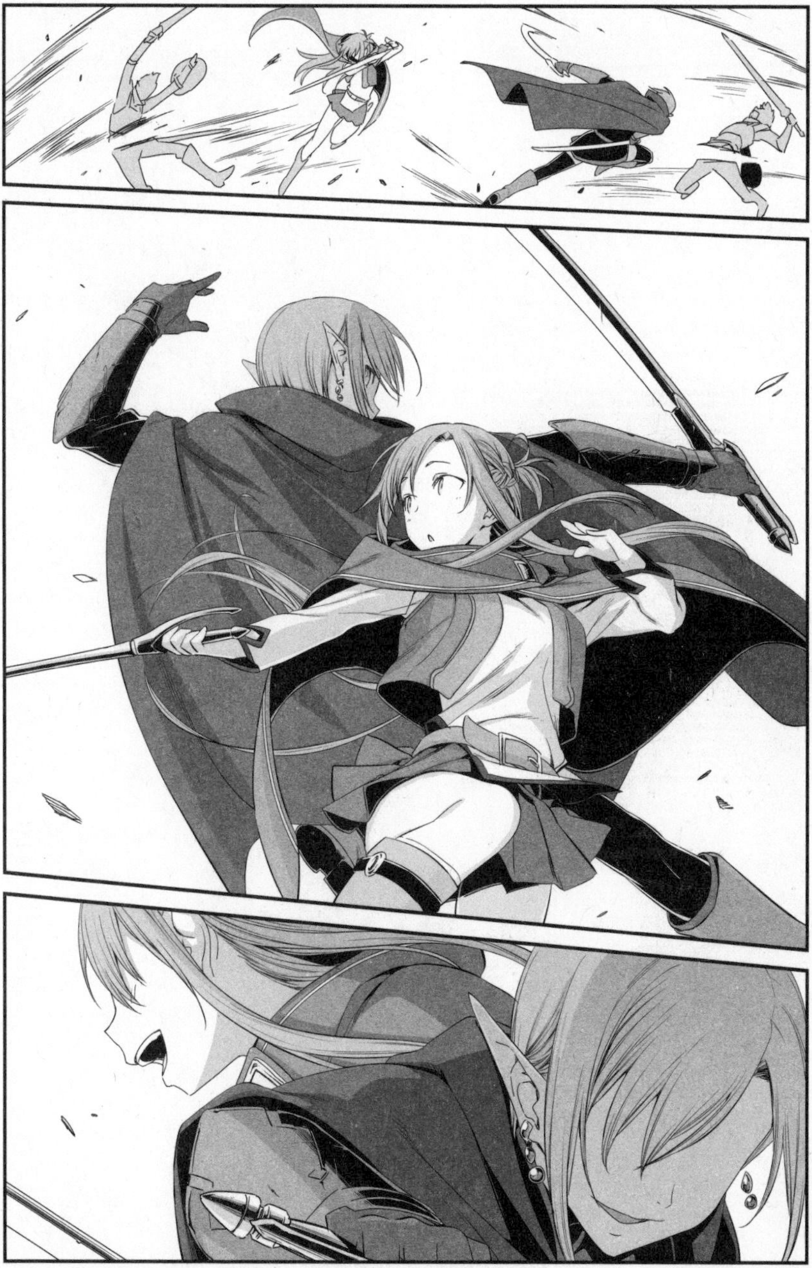

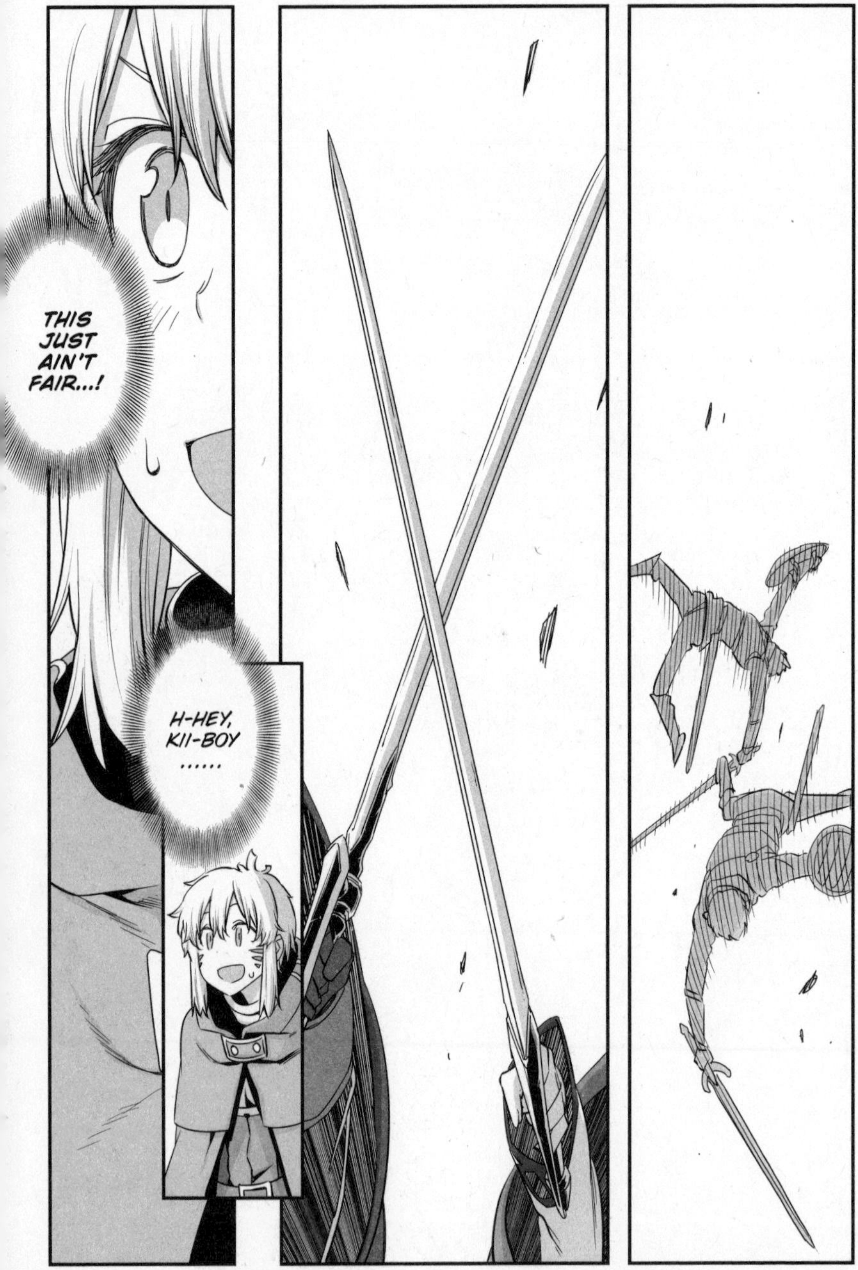
THIS JUST AIN'T FAIR...!
H-HEY, KII-BOY ......

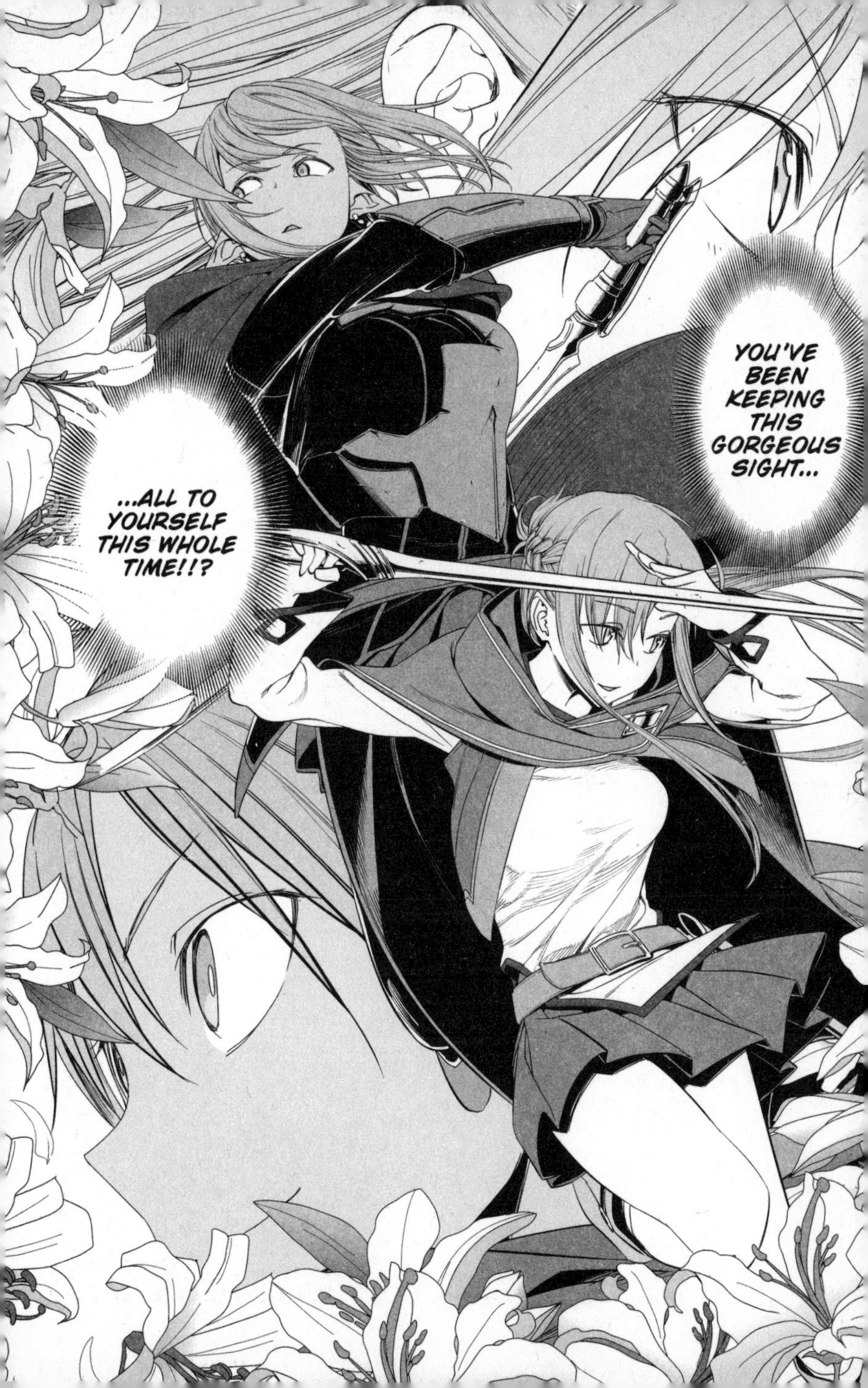
YOU'VE BEEN KEEPING THIS GORGEOUS SIGHT...
...ALL TO YOURSELF THIS WHOLE TIME!!?

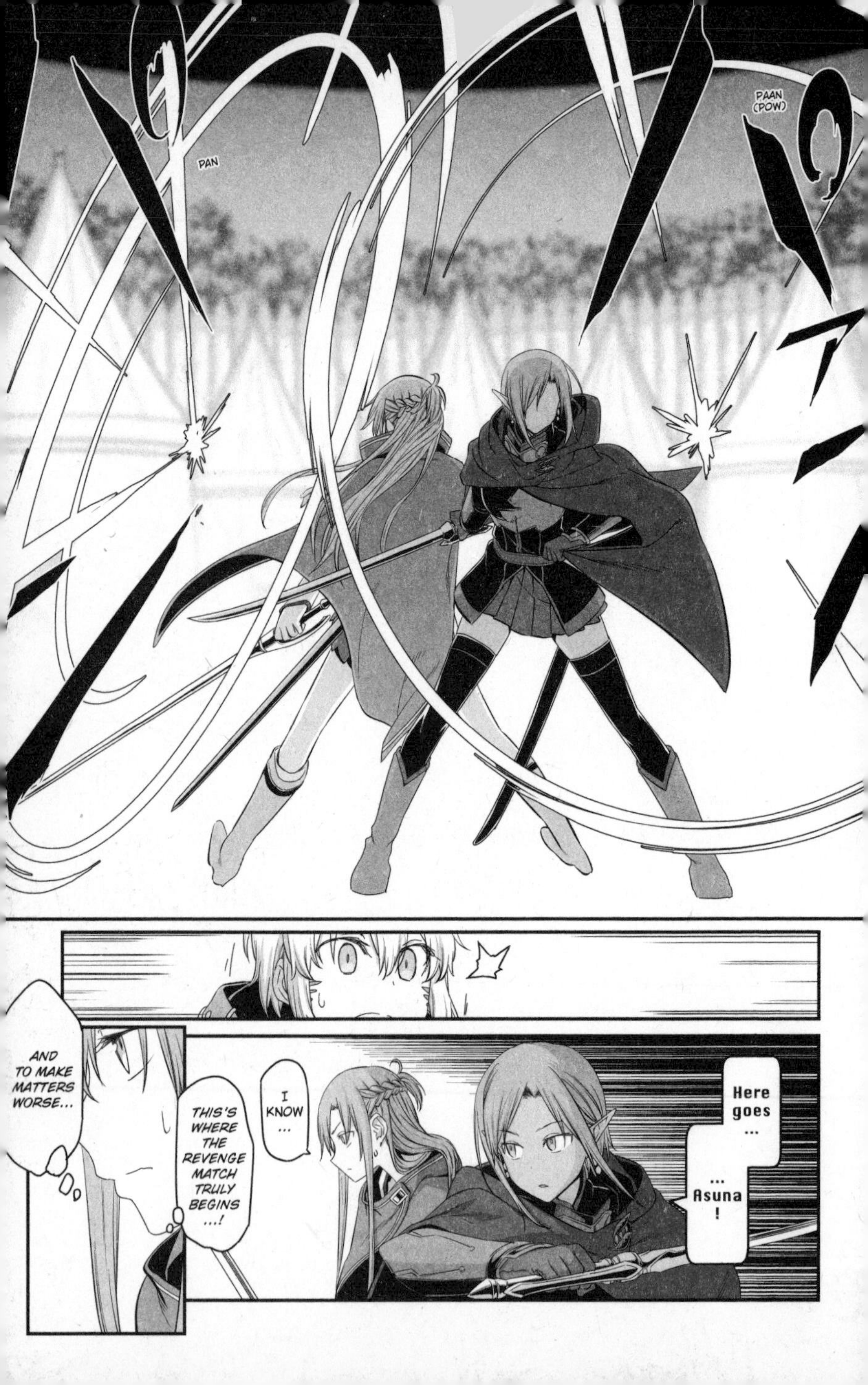
PAAN (POW)
PAN
Here goes ...
... Asuna !
I KNOW ...
THIS'S WHERE THE REVENGE MATCH TRULY BEGINS ...!
AND TO MAKE MATTERS WORSE...

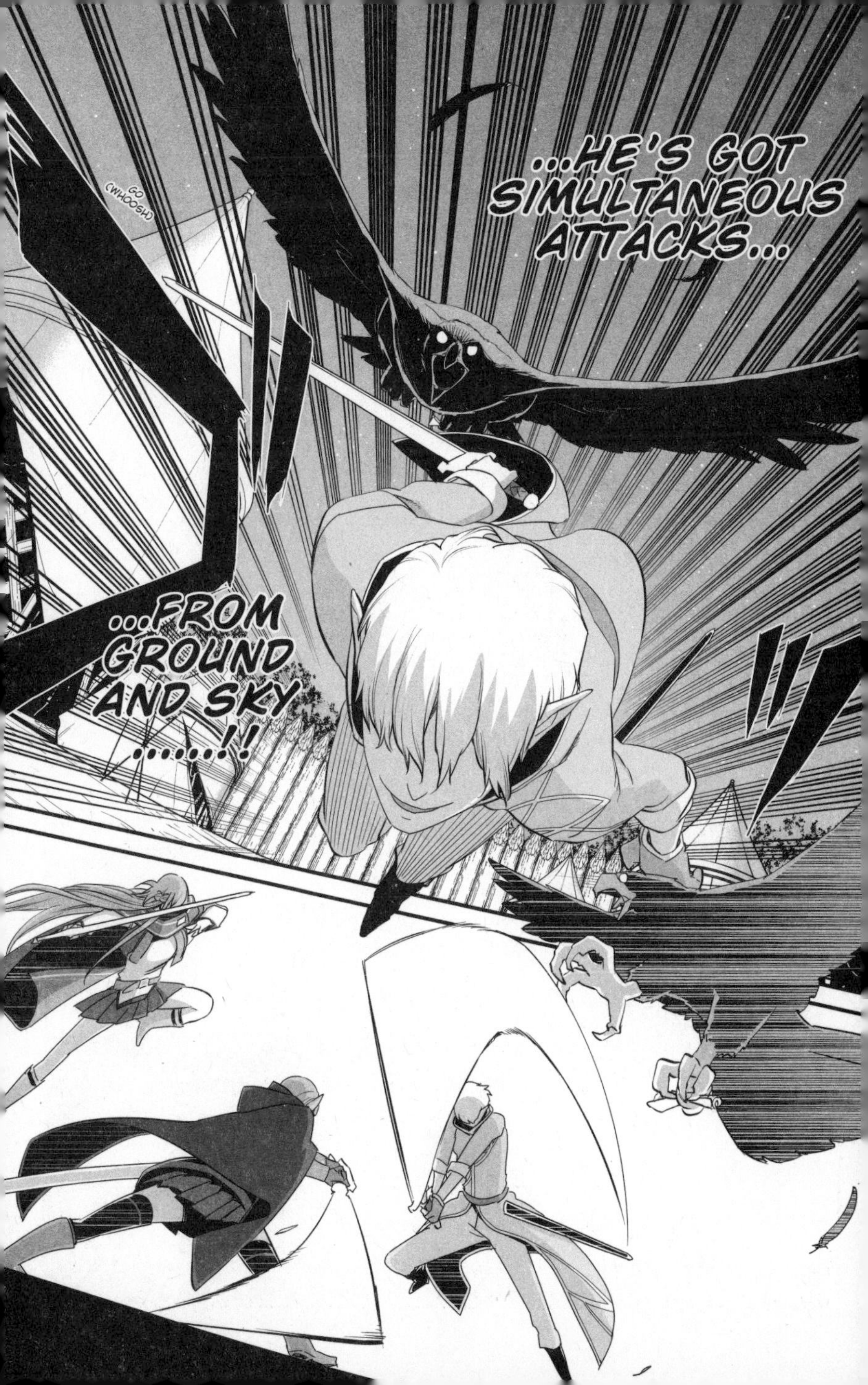
...HE'S GOT SIMULTANEOUS ATTACKS...
GO (WHOOSH)
...FROM GROUND AND SKY ......!!

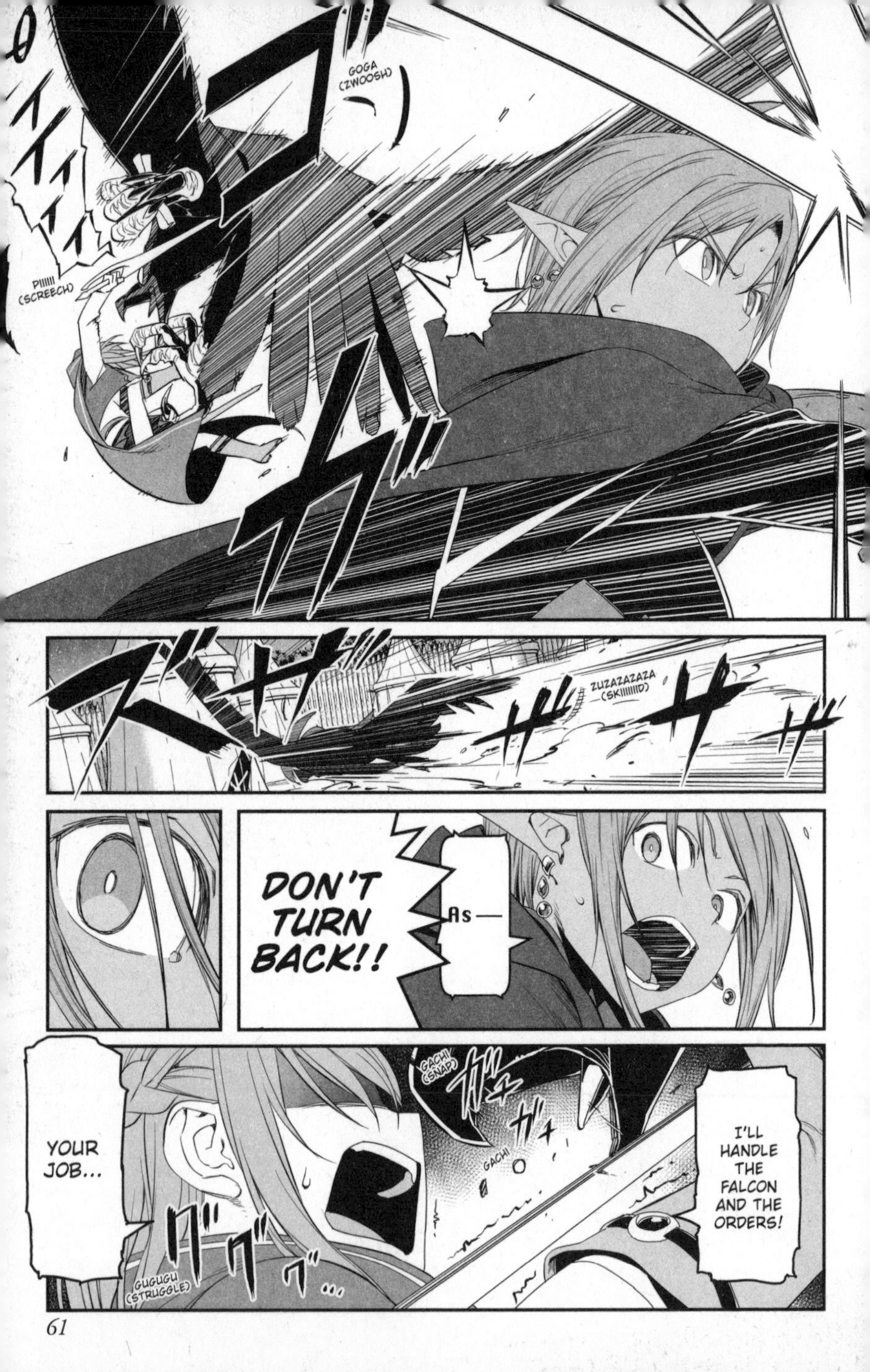
GOGA (ZWOOSH)
PIIIIII (SCREECH)
ZUZAZAZAZA (SKIIIIIIID)
As—
DON'T TURN BACK!!
I'LL HANDLE THE FALCON AND THE ORDERS!
GACHI (SNAP)
GACHI
YOUR JOB...
GUGUGU (STRUGGLE)

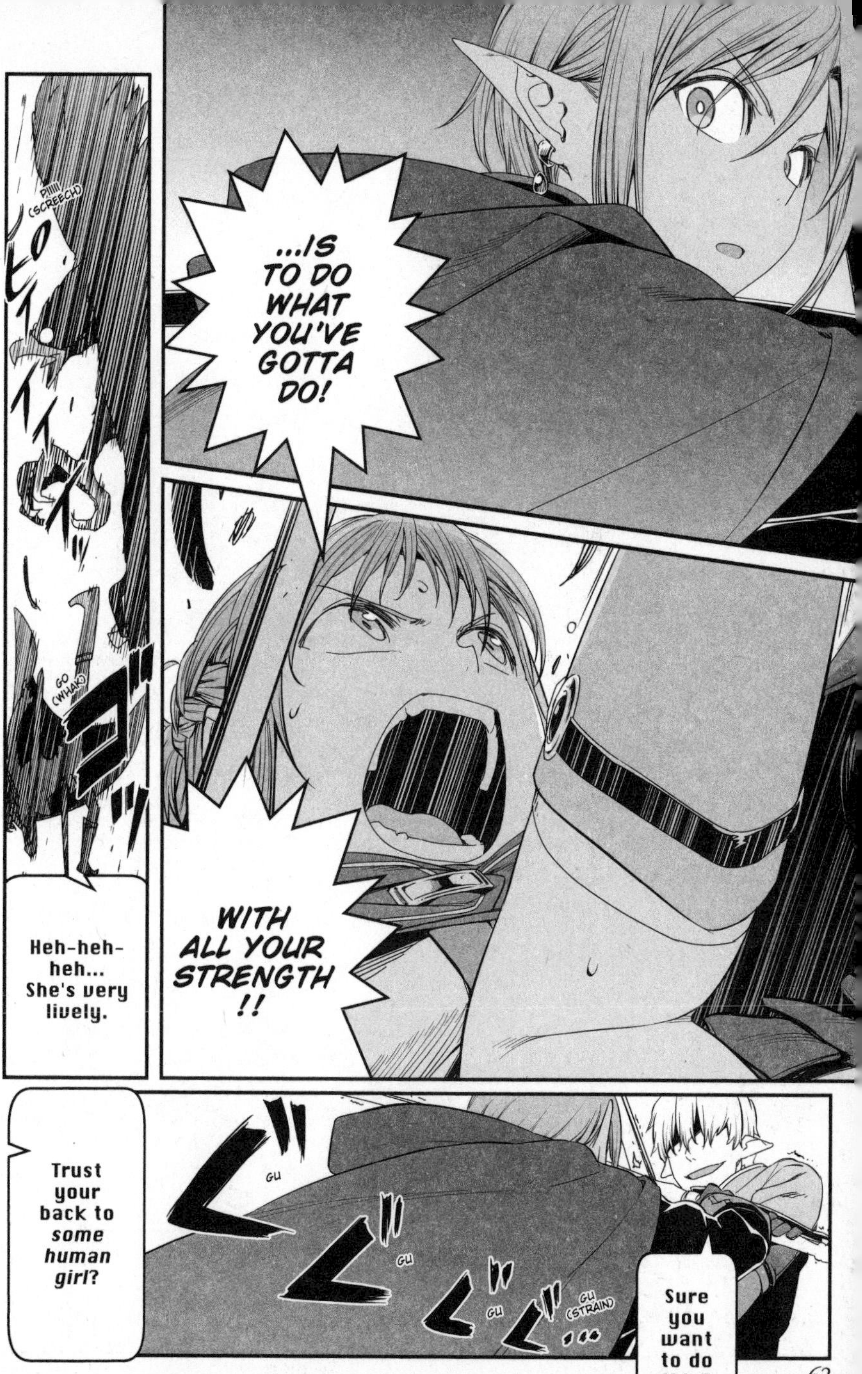
...IS TO DO WHAT YOU'VE GOTTA DO!
WITH ALL YOUR STRENGTH!!
PIIII (SCREECH)
GO (WHAK)
Heh-heh-heh... She's very lively.
Sure you want to do this?
GU (STRAIN)
GU
GU
GU
Trust your back to some human girl?

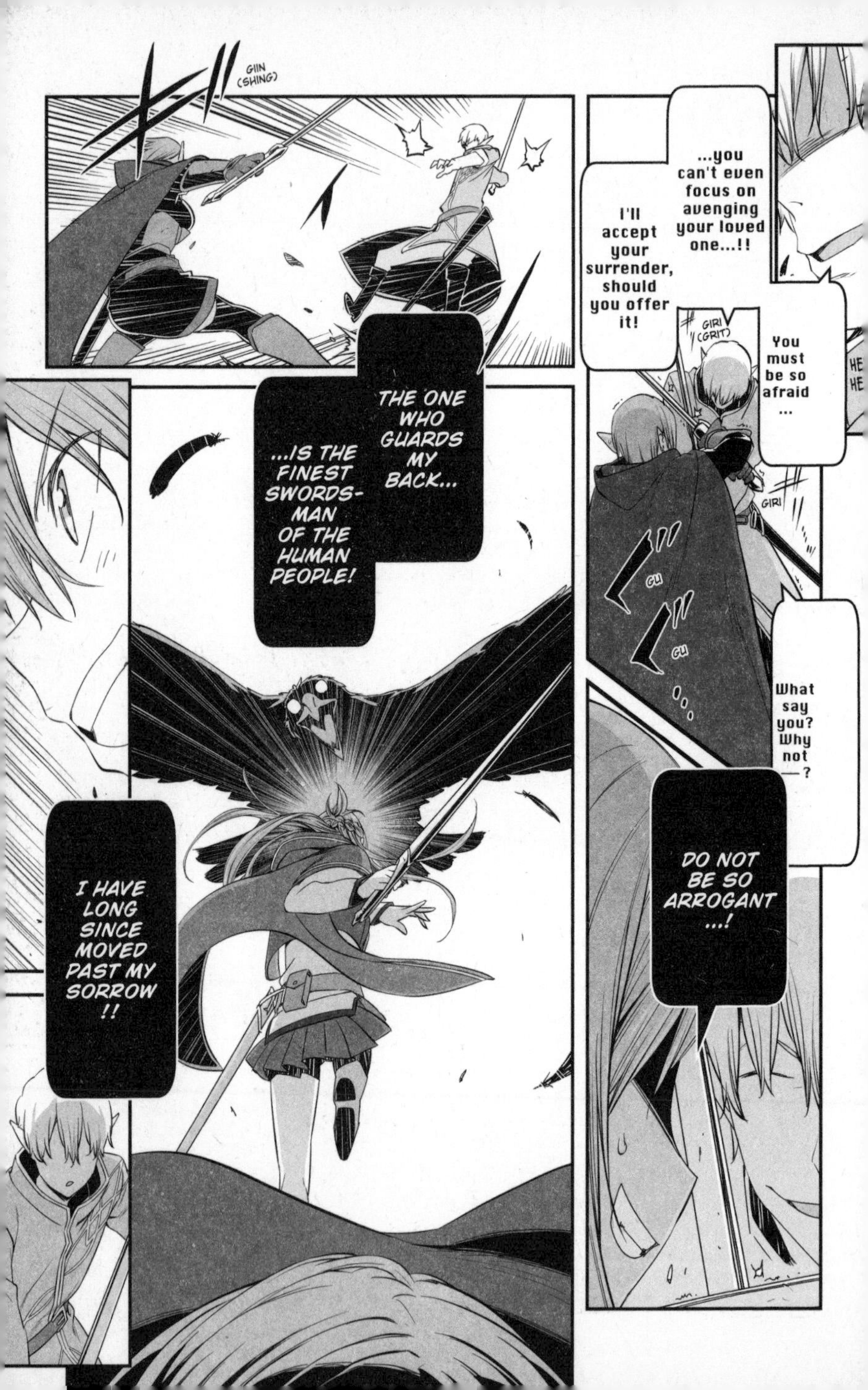
You must be so afraid...
HE HE
...you can't even focus on avenging your loved one...!!
I'll accept your surrender, should you offer it!
GIRI (GRIT)
GIRI
GU
GU
What say you? Why not—?
DO NOT BE SO ARROGANT...!
GIIN (SHING)
THE ONE WHO GUARDS MY BACK...
...IS THE FINEST SWORDS-MAN OF THE HUMAN PEOPLE!
I HAVE LONG SINCE MOVED PAST MY SORROW!!

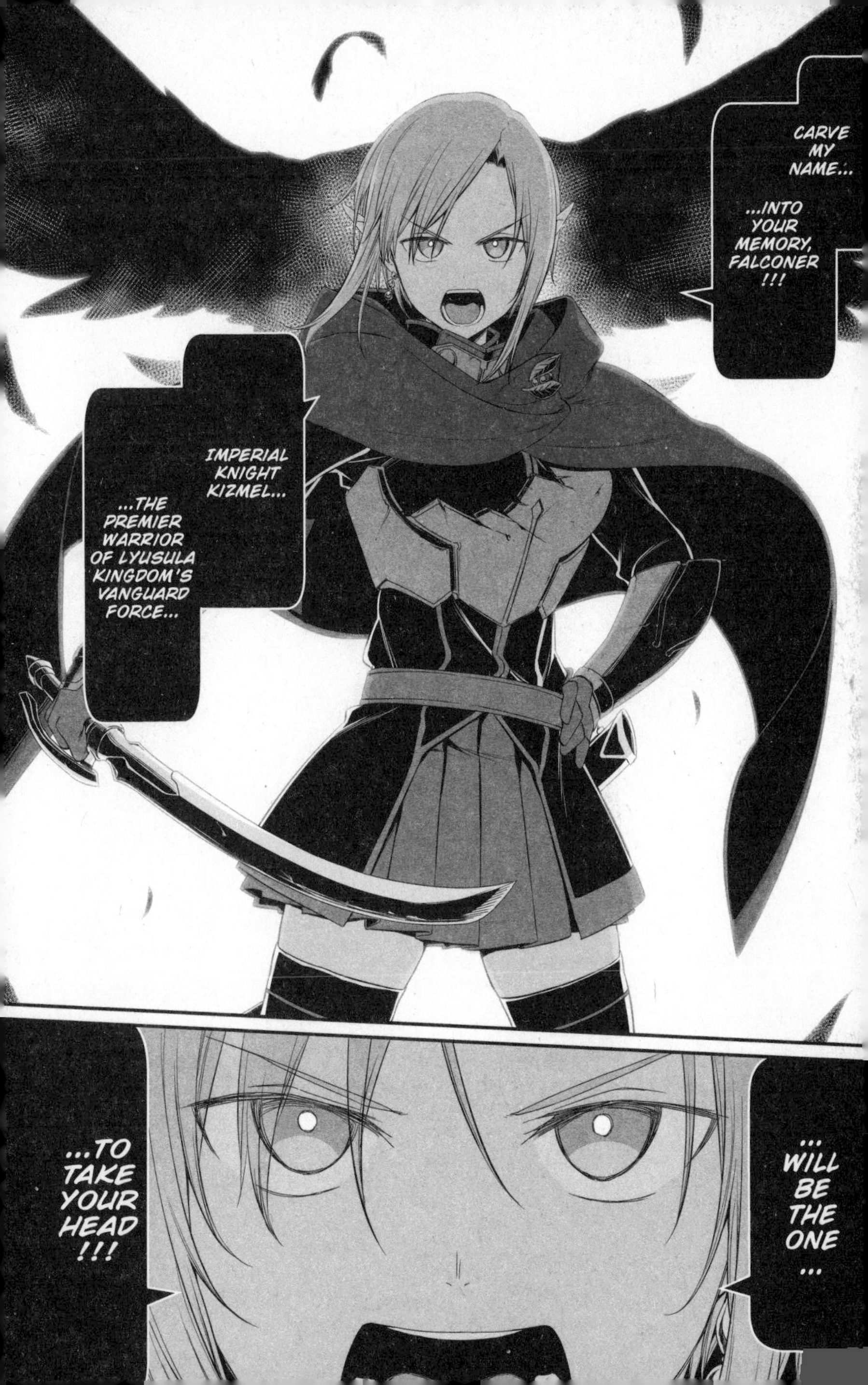
CARVE MY NAME...
...INTO YOUR MEMORY, FALCONER !!!
IMPERIAL KNIGHT KIZMEL...
...THE PREMIER WARRIOR OF LYUSULA KINGDOM'S VANGUARD FORCE...
... WILL BE THE ONE ...
...TO TAKE YOUR HEAD !!!

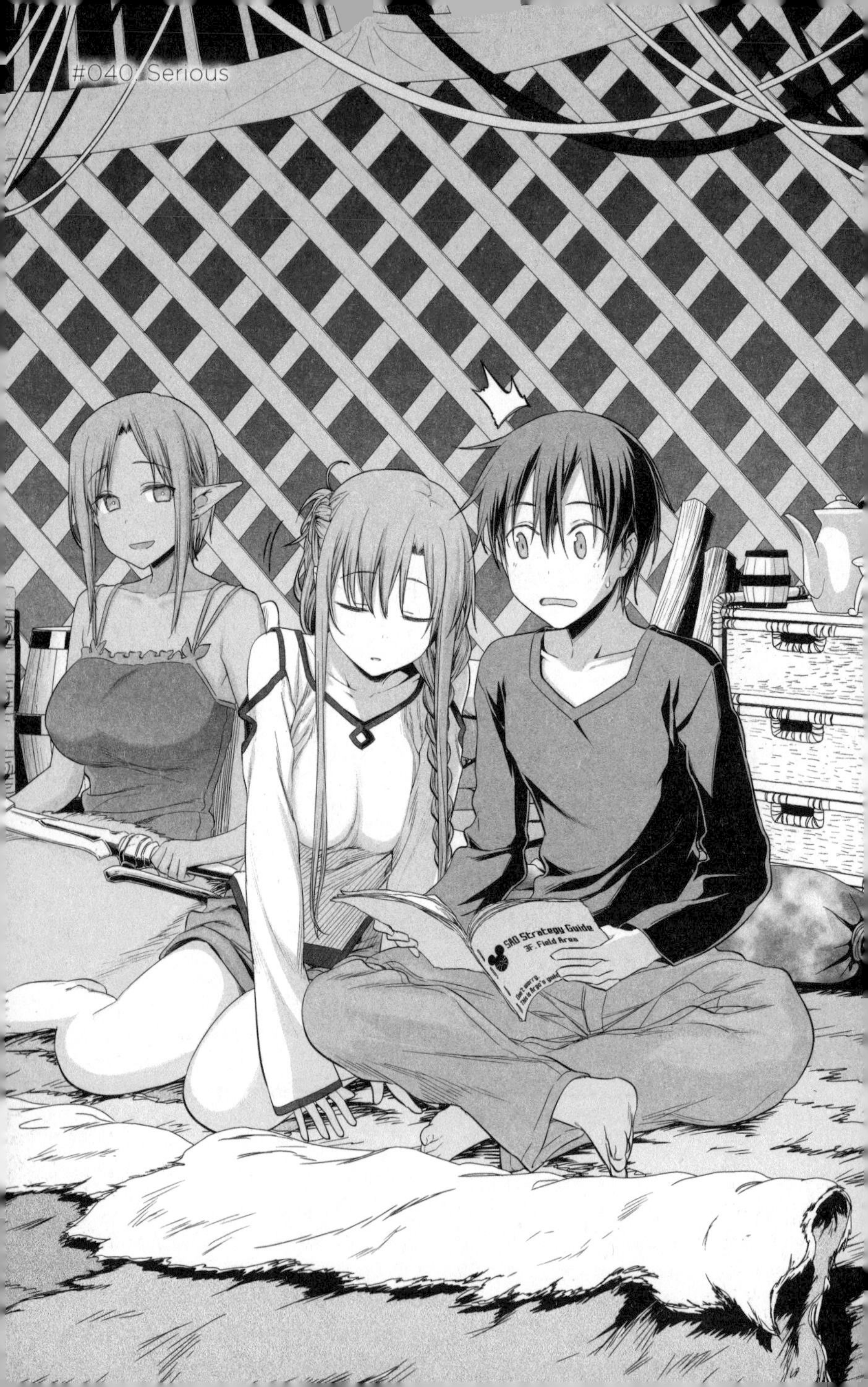
#040: Serious
SAO Strategy Guide
3F. Field Area
Don't worry.
This is Argo's guid

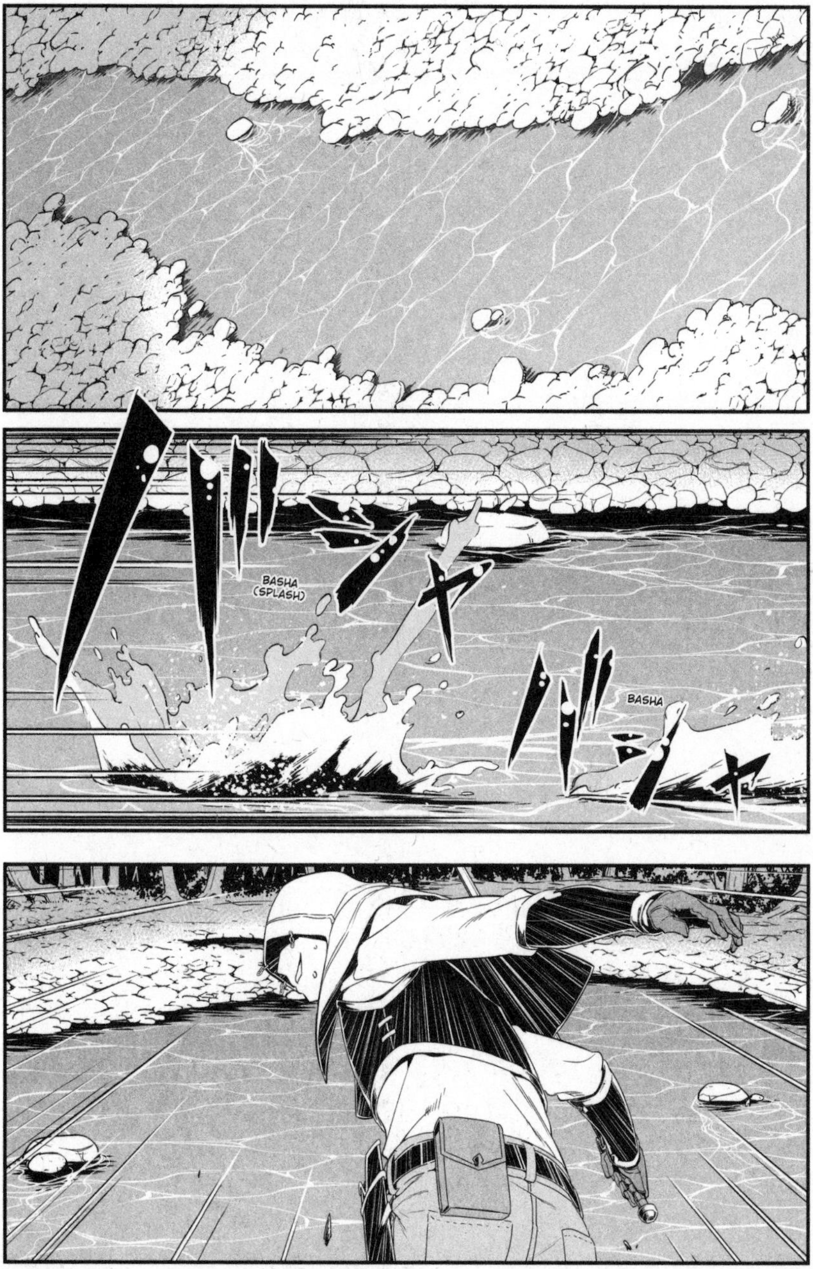
BASHA
(SPLASH)
BASHA

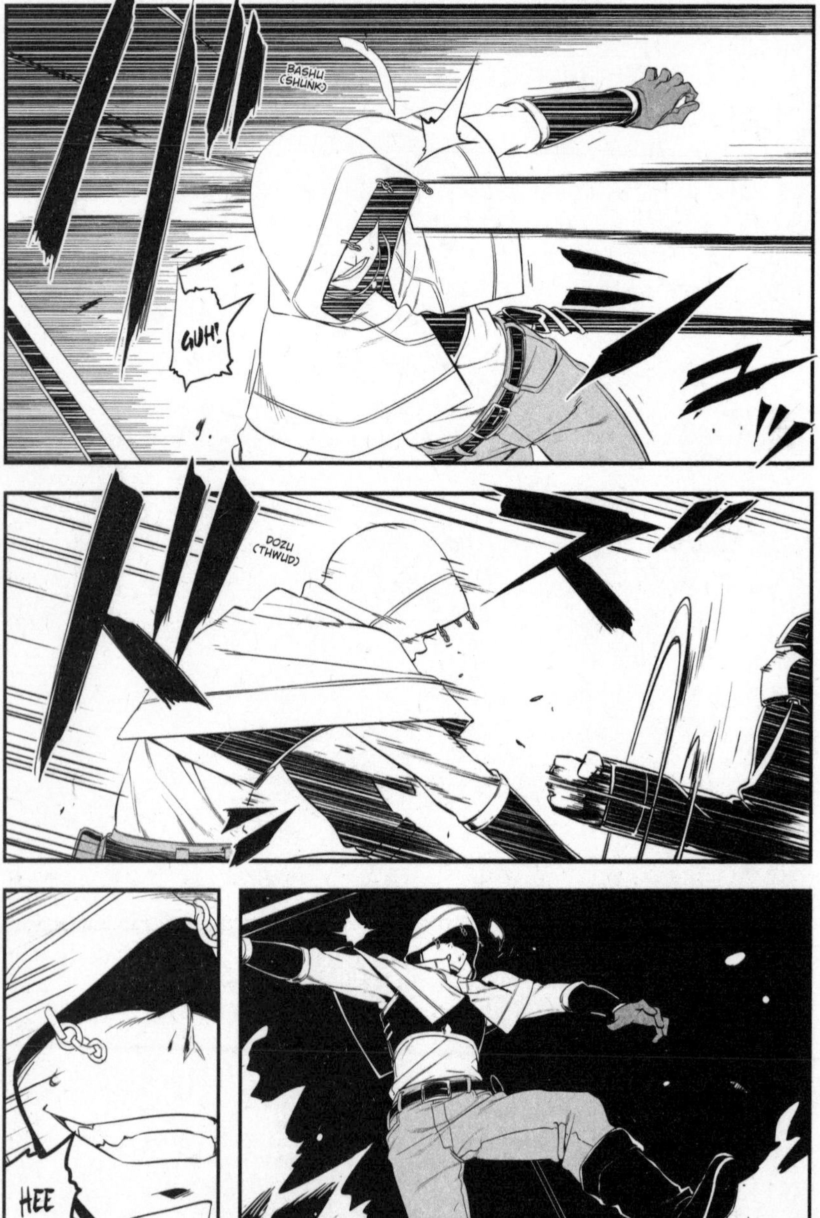
BASHU (SHUNK)
GUH!
DOZU (THWUD)
HEE HEE!

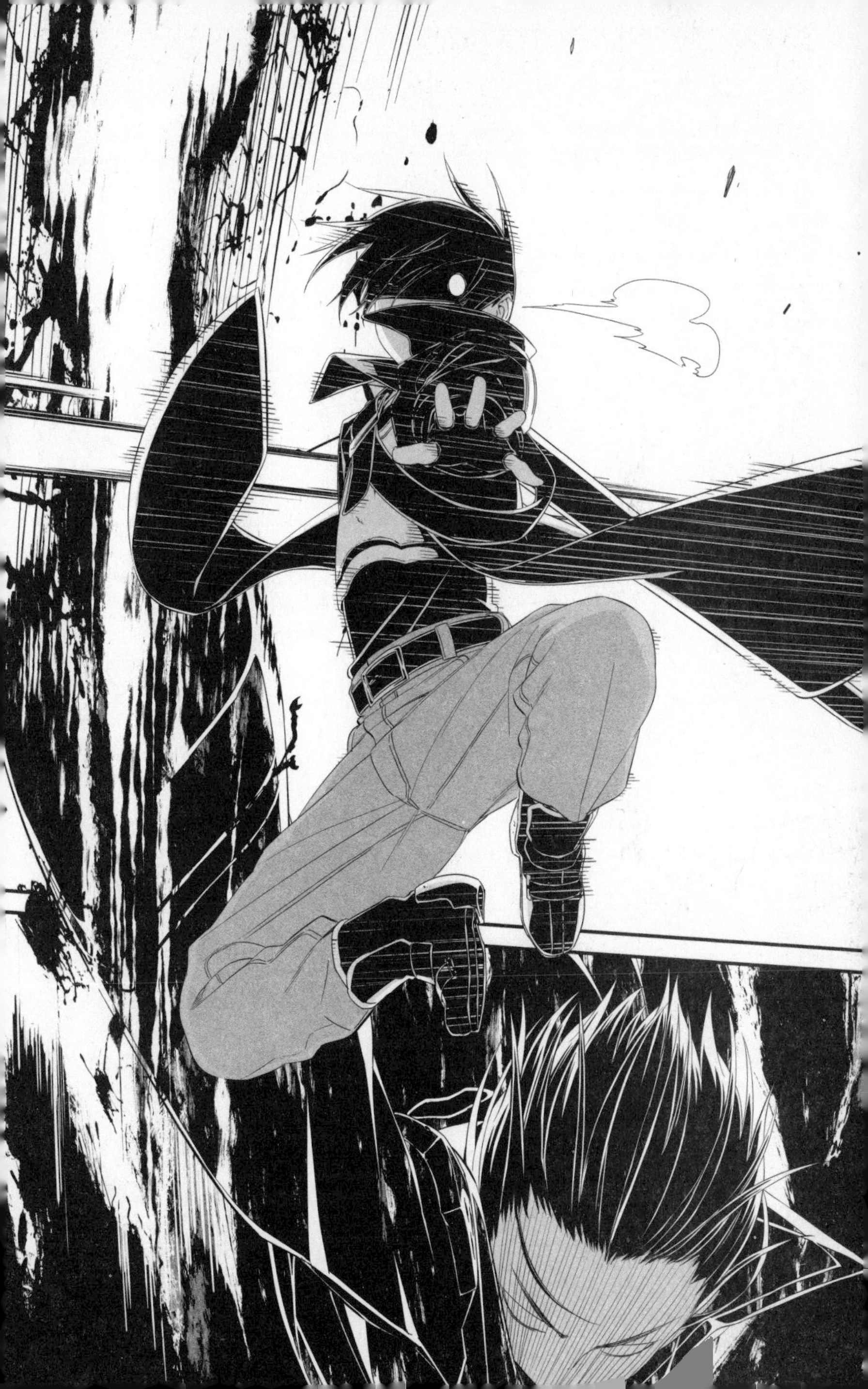

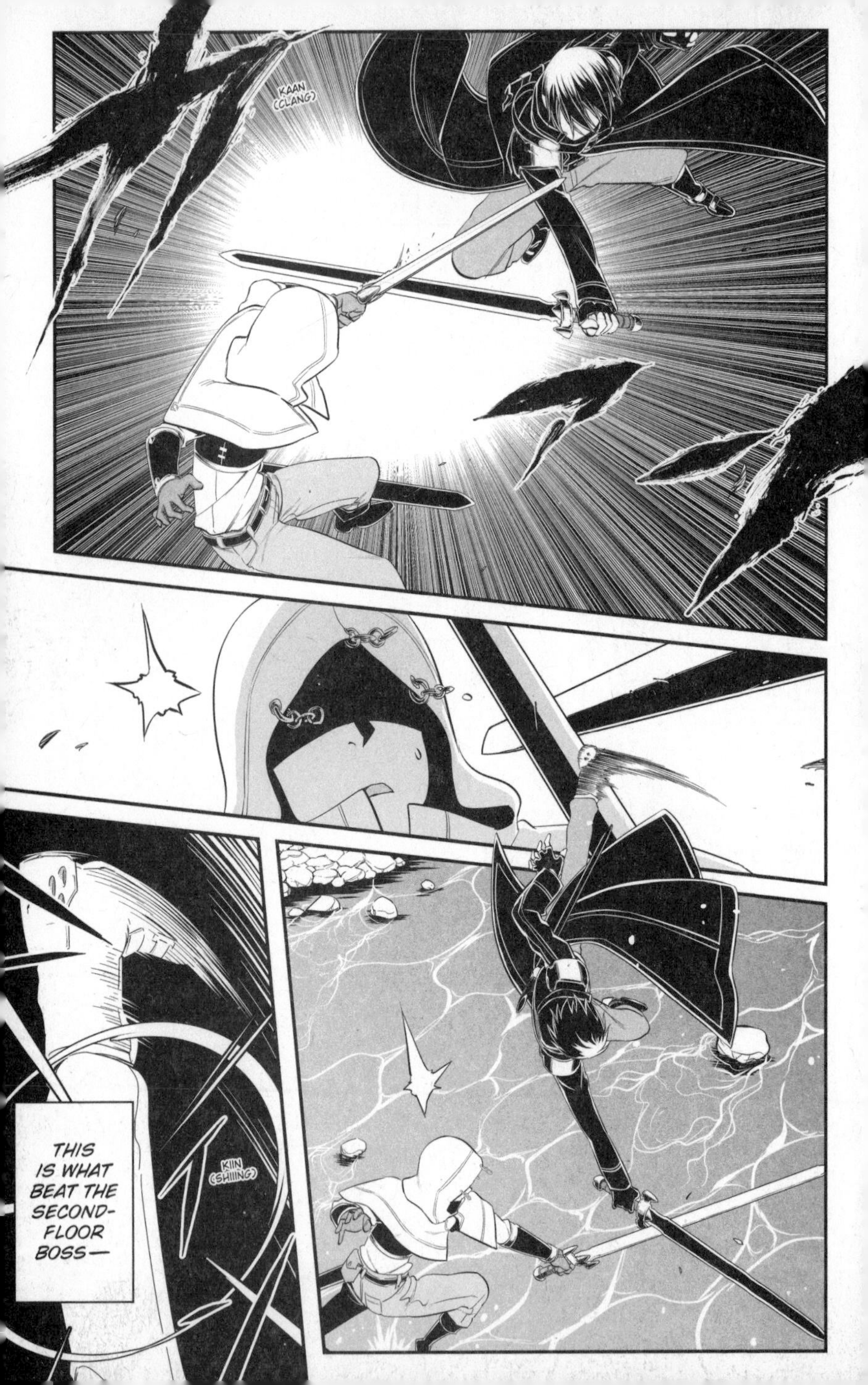
KAAN
(CLANG)
KIIN
(SHIING)
THIS IS WHAT BEAT THE SECOND-FLOOR BOSS—

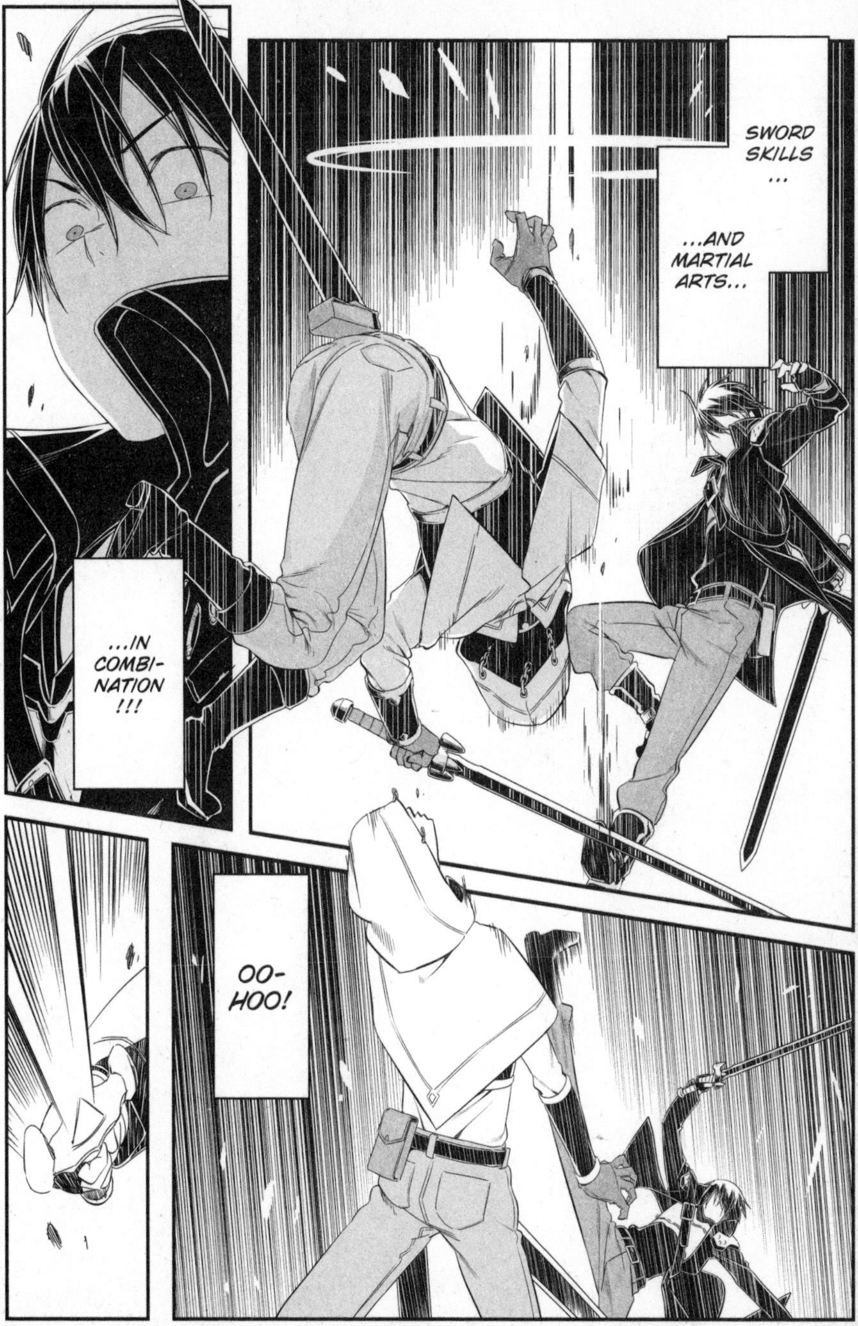

SWORD SKILLS ...
...AND MARTIAL ARTS...
...IN COMBI-NATION !!!
OO-HOO!

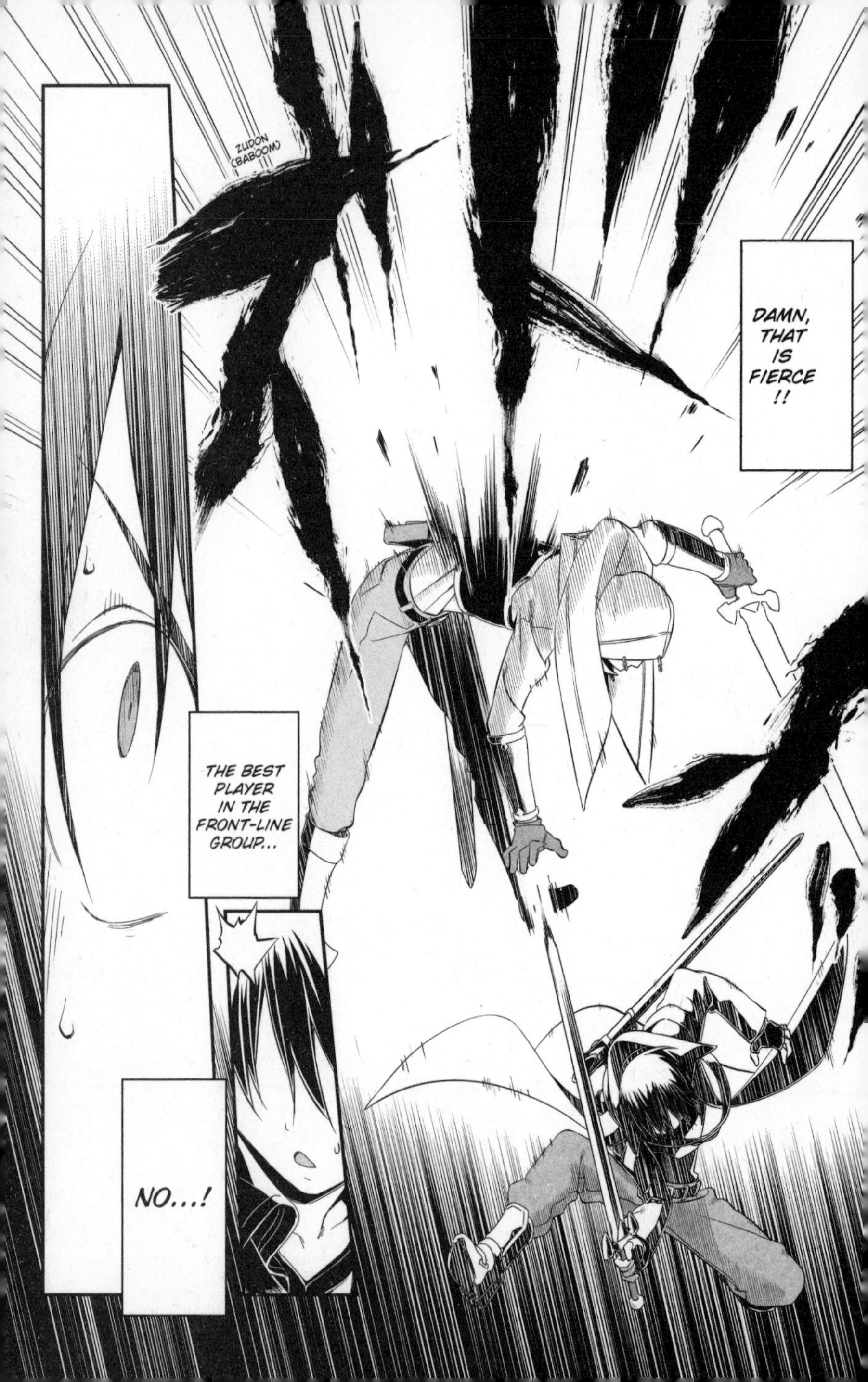

DAMN, THAT IS FIERCE!!
ZUDON (BABOOM)
THE BEST PLAYER IN THE FRONT-LINE GROUP...
NO...!

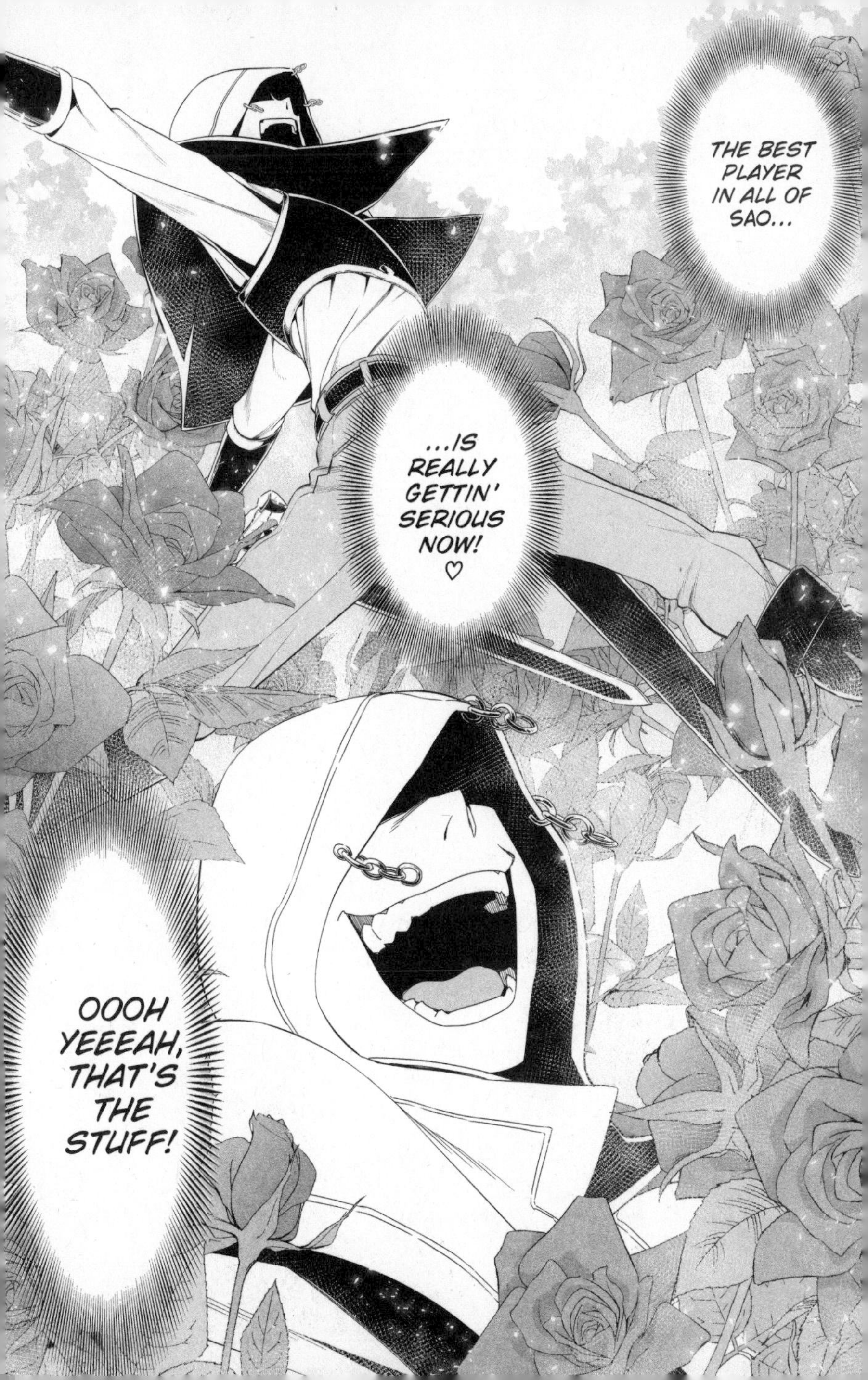
THE BEST PLAYER IN ALL OF SAO...
...IS REALLY GETTIN' SERIOUS NOW! ♡
OOOH YEEEAH, THAT'S THE STUFF!

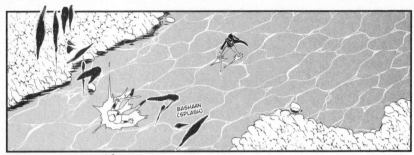

BASHAAN
(SPLASH)

HEH HEH HEH!

HEH.

ZAAAAA
(FSHHH)

AND...

I GIVE, I GIVE! WHEN YOU GET INTO IT, YOU'RE EVEN BETTER THAN I IMAGINED, KIRITO-SAN!!

WELL, WELL!

HUFF

HUFF

AH HA HA HA HA!

HUFF

HUFF

...YOU'RE MORE *LOVE-STRUCK* THAN I EXPECTED!

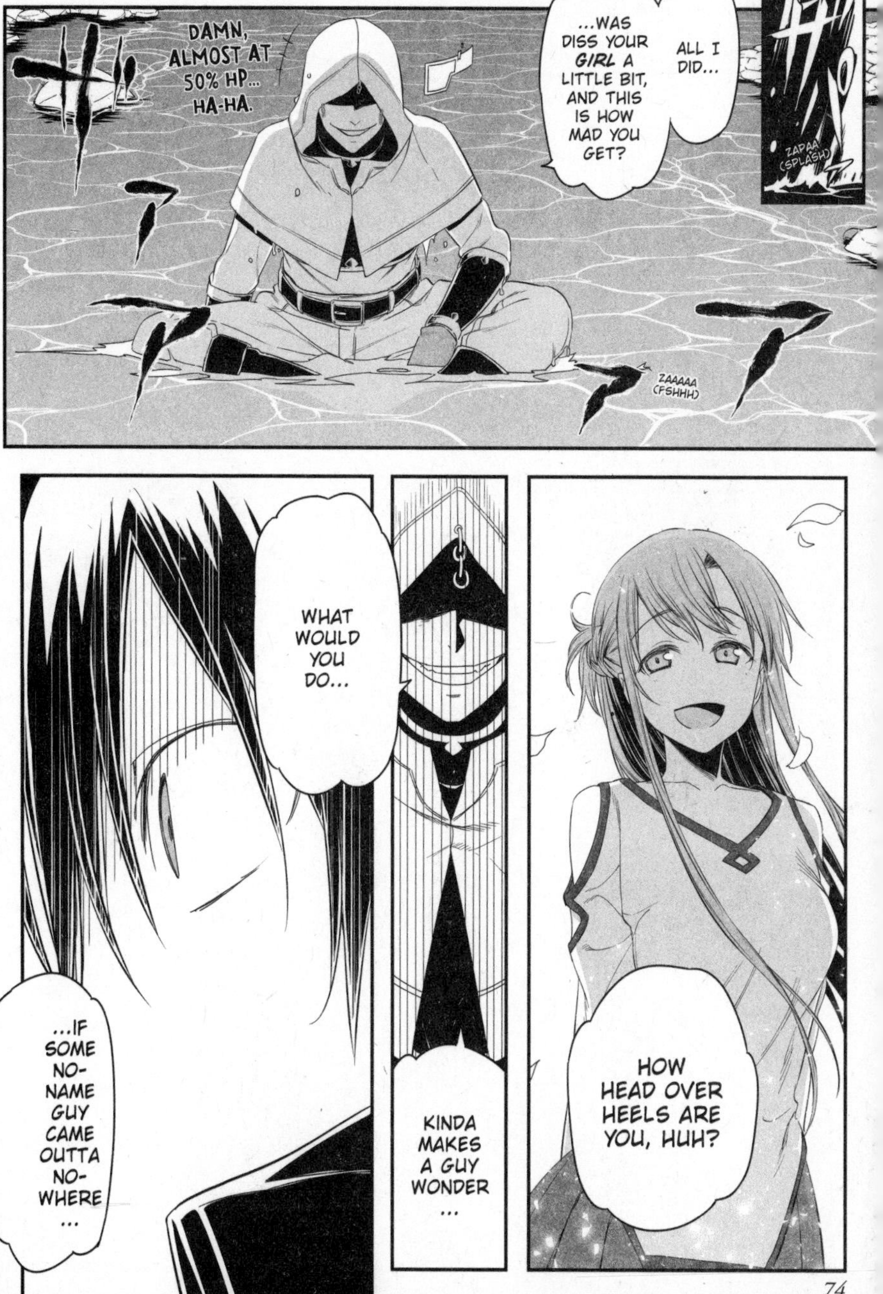
ZAPAA (SPLASH)
ALL I DID...
...WAS DISS YOUR GIRL A LITTLE BIT, AND THIS IS HOW MAD YOU GET?
DAMN, ALMOST AT 50% HP... HA-HA.
ZAAAAA (FSHHH)
HOW HEAD OVER HEELS ARE YOU, HUH?
KINDA MAKES A GUY WONDER...
WHAT WOULD YOU DO...
...IF SOME NO-NAME GUY CAME OUTTA NO-WHERE...

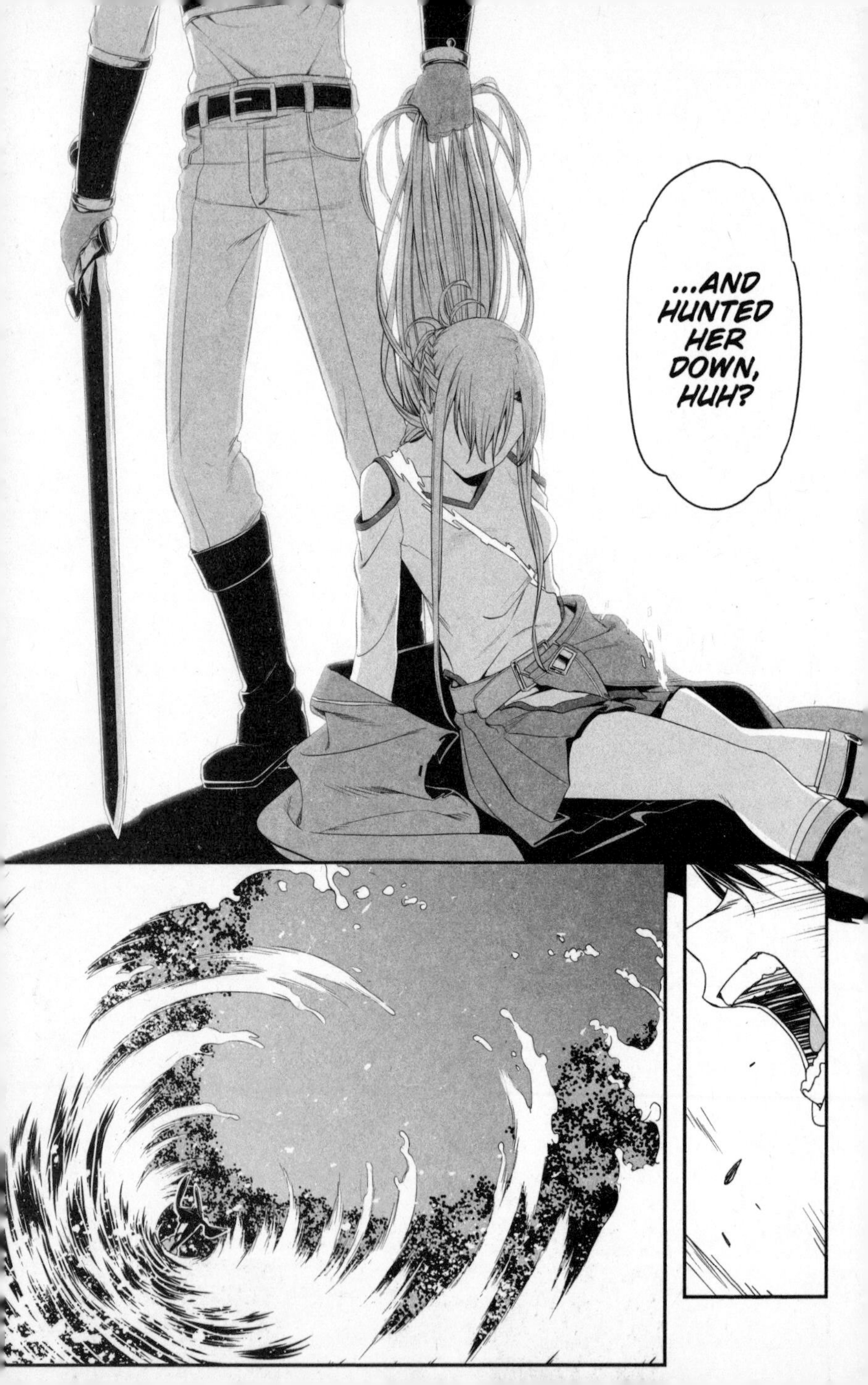
...AND HUNTED HER DOWN, HUH?

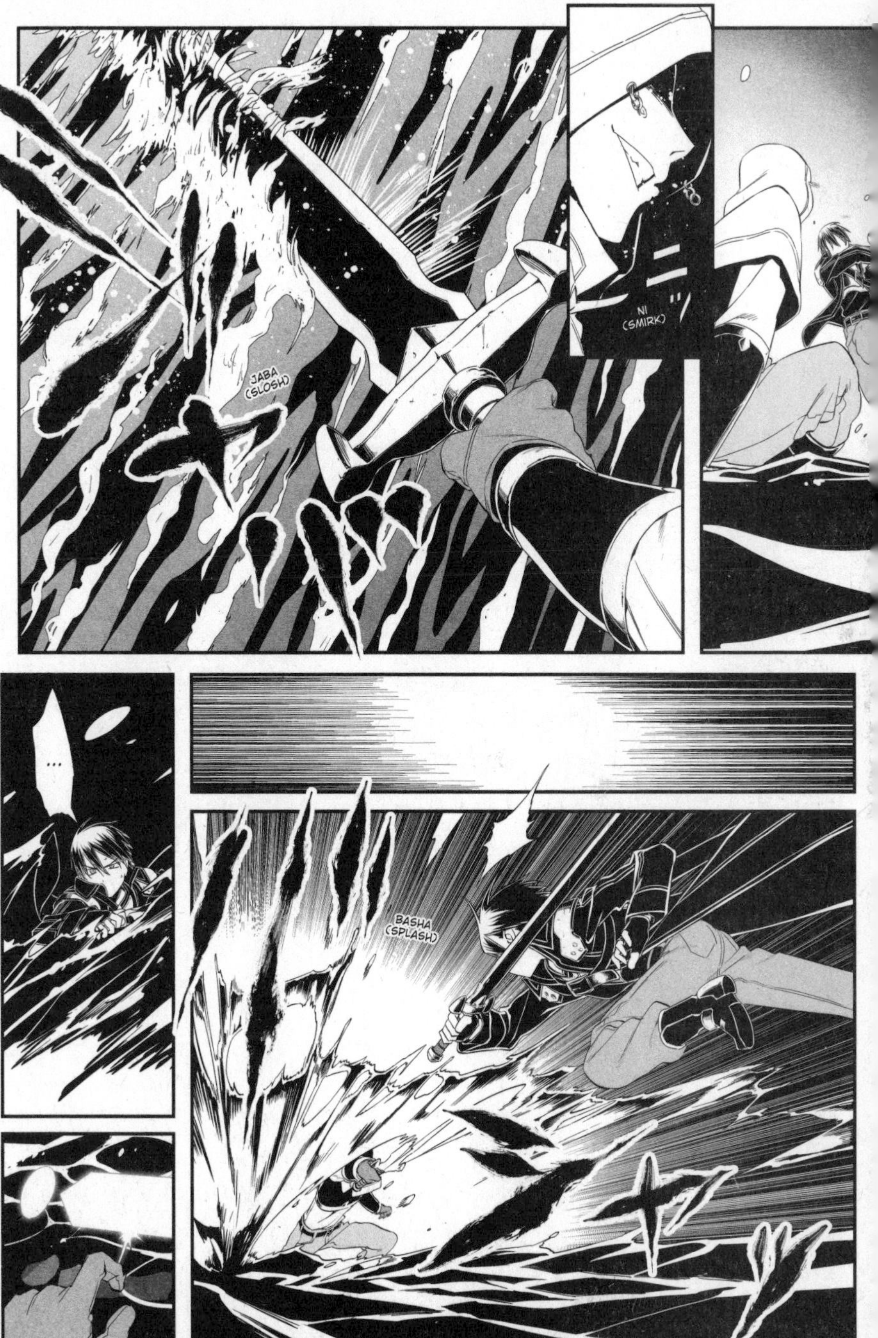
NI
(SMIRK)
JABA
(SLOSH)
BASHA
(SPLASH)
...

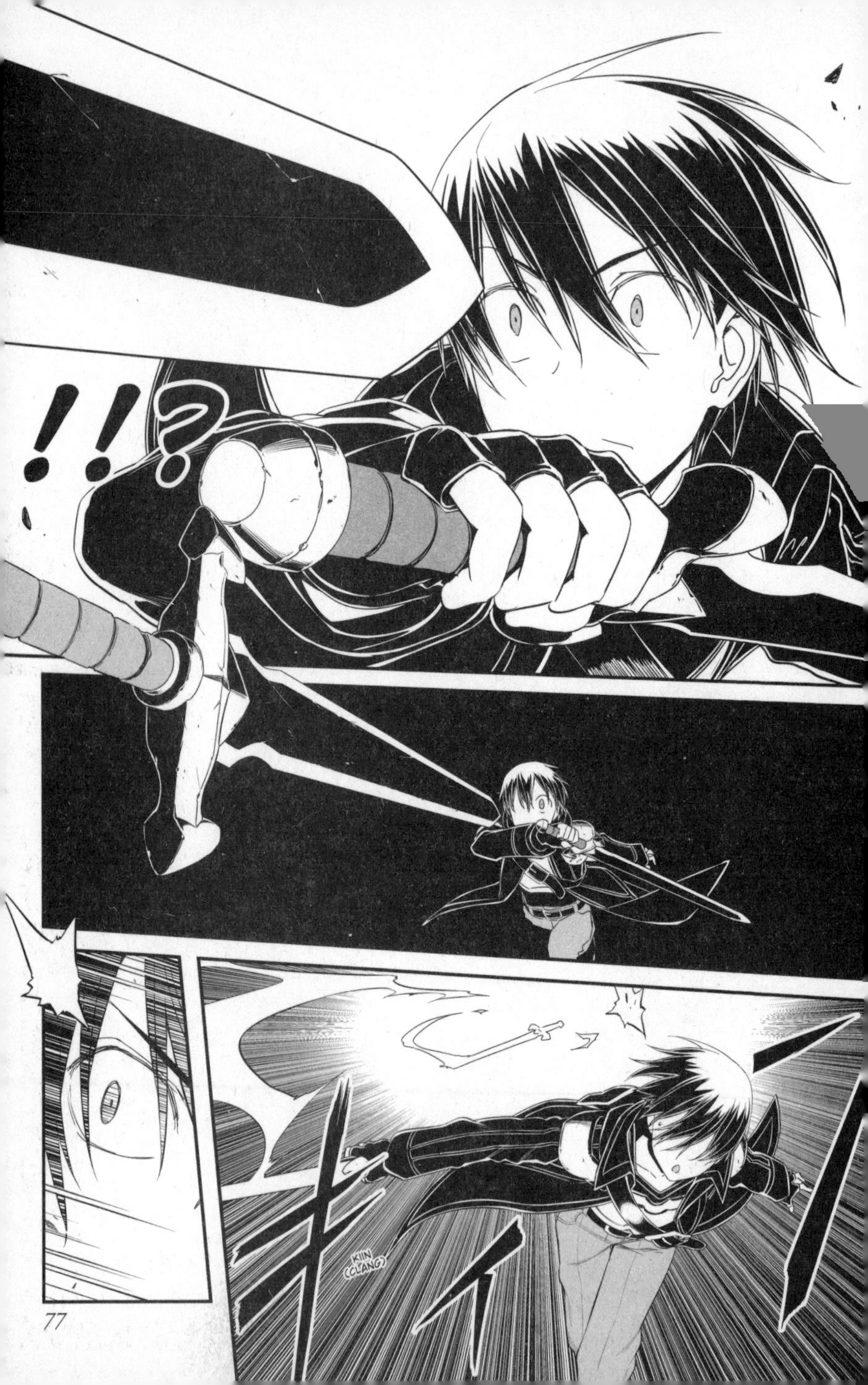
!!?
KIIN (CLANG)

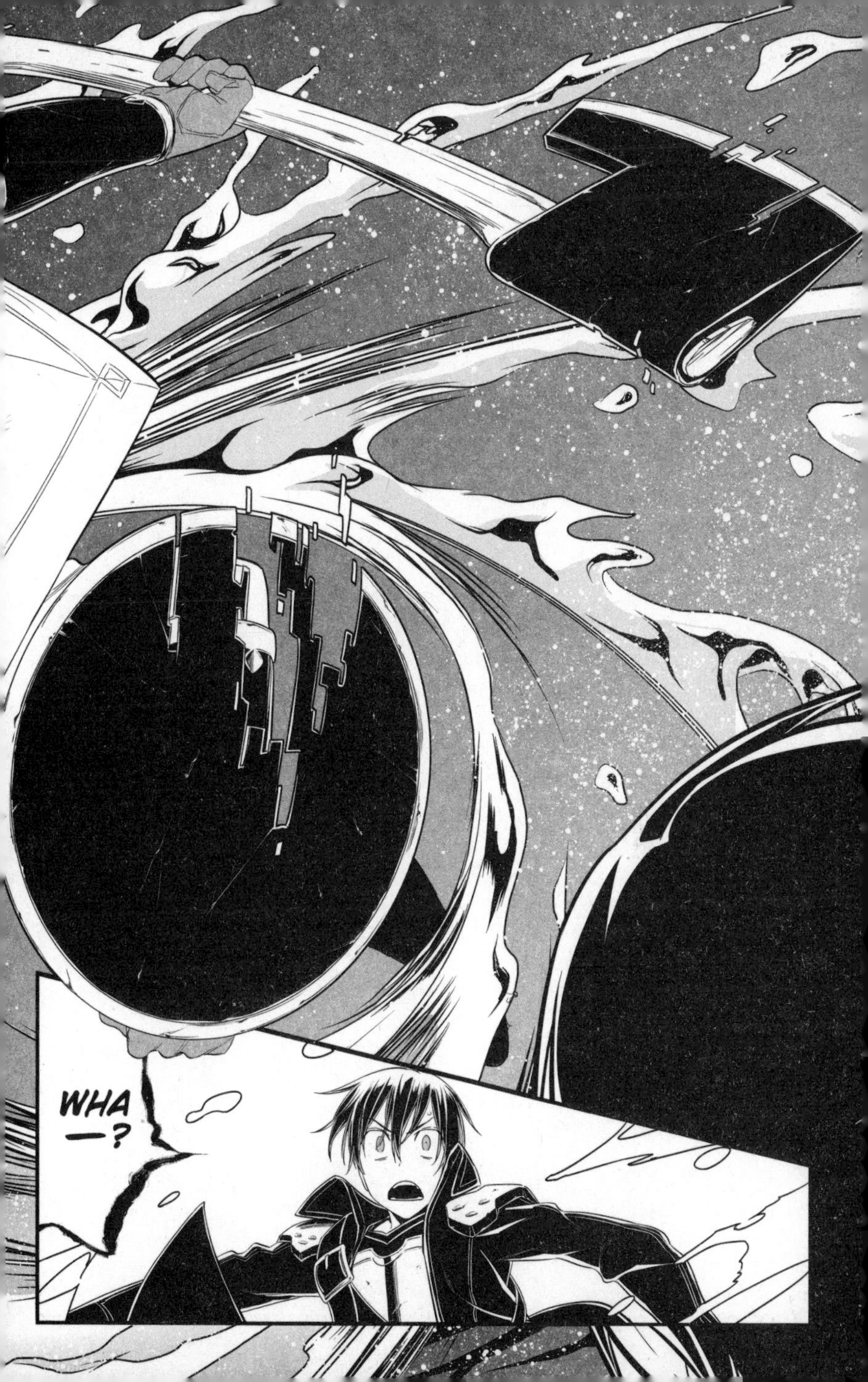
WHA—?

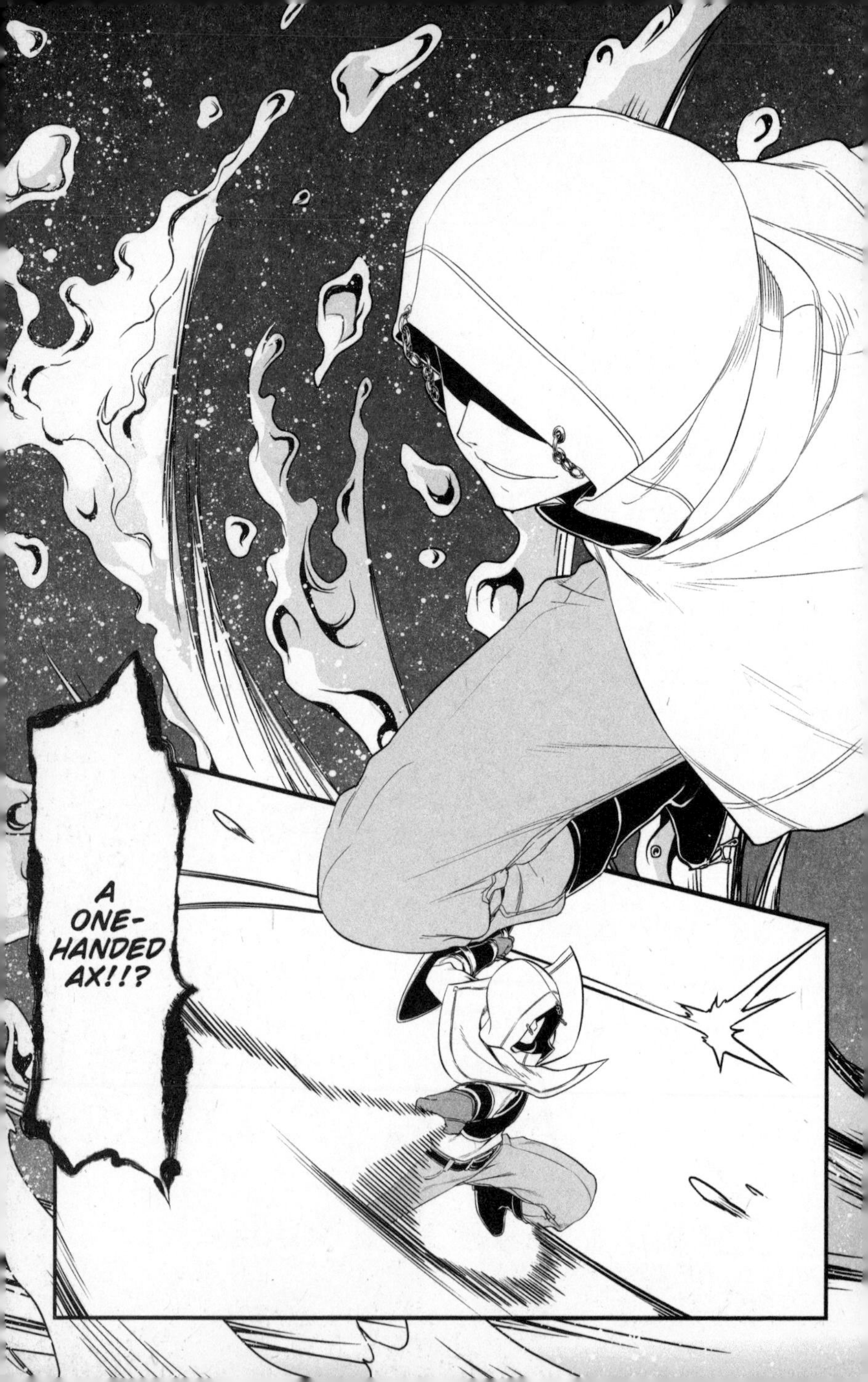
A ONE-HANDED AX!!?

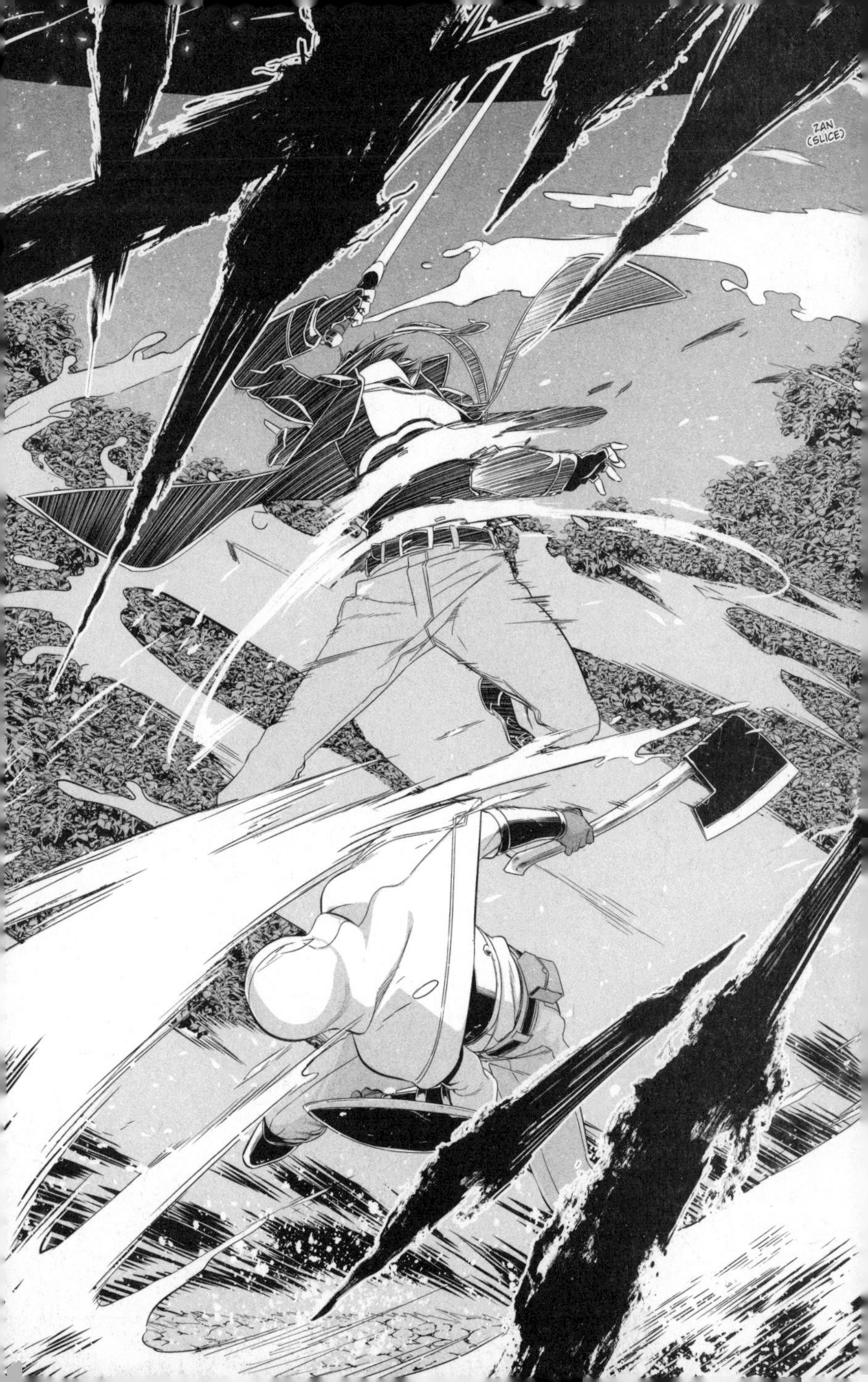
ZAN
(SLICE)

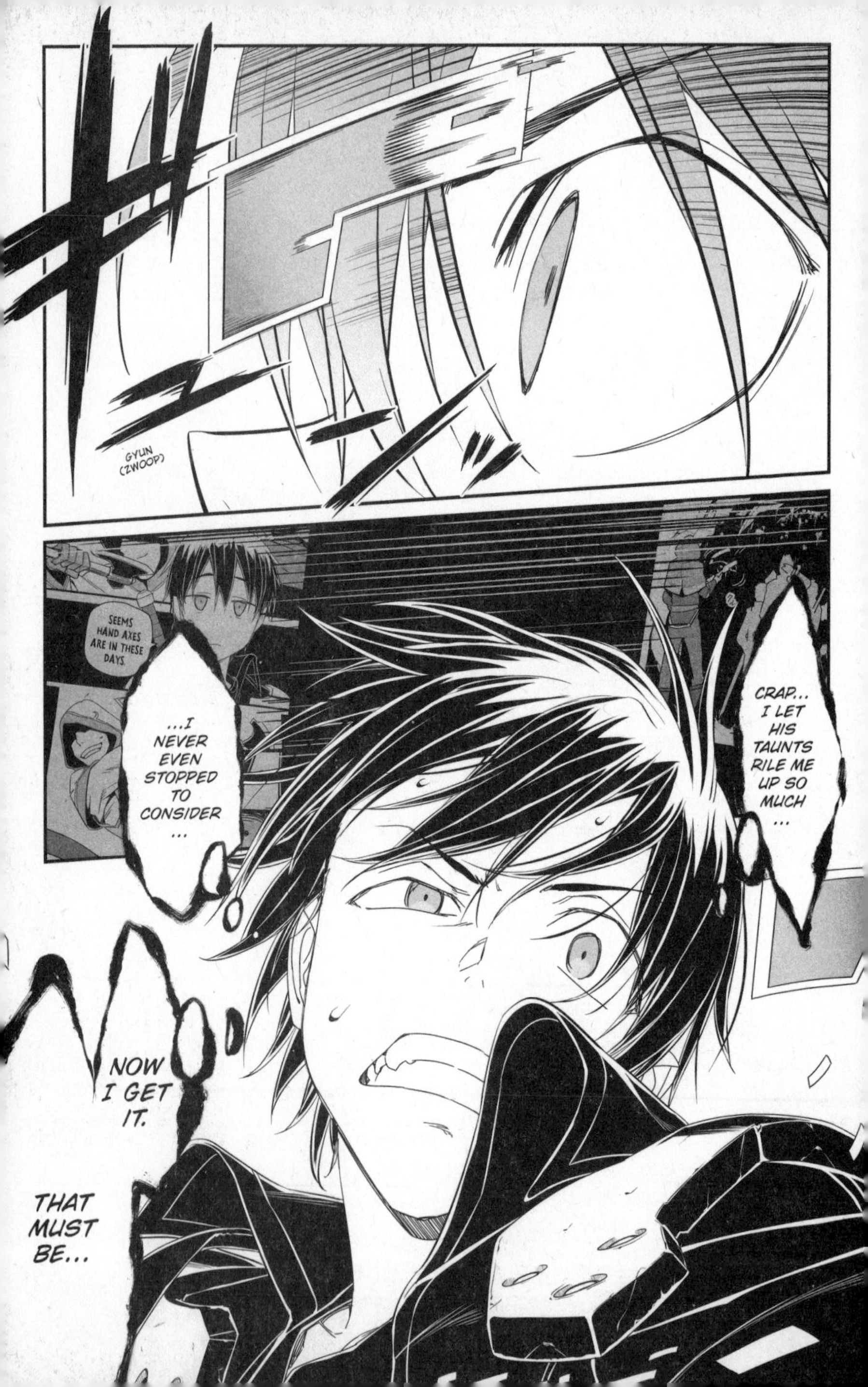
GYUN (ZWOOP)
CRAP... I LET HIS TAUNTS RILE ME UP SO MUCH...
SEEMS HAND AXES ARE IN THESE DAYS.
...I NEVER EVEN STOPPED TO CONSIDER...
NOW I GET IT.
THAT MUST BE...

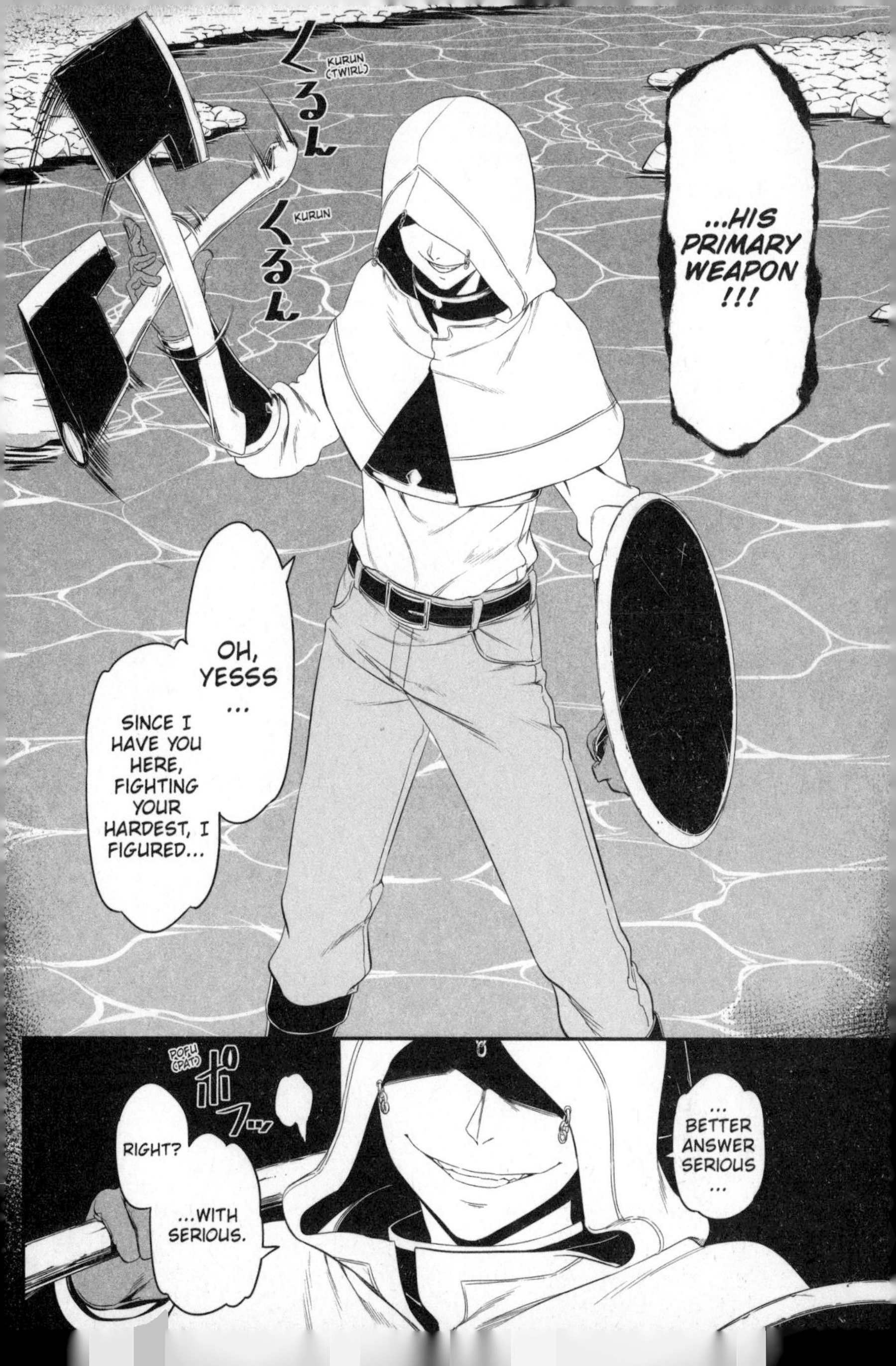
...HIS PRIMARY WEAPON!!!
くるん
KURUN (TWIRL)
くるん
KURUN
OH, YESSS...
SINCE I HAVE YOU HERE, FIGHTING YOUR HARDEST, I FIGURED...
...BETTER ANSWER SERIOUS...
ポフッ
POFU (PAT)
RIGHT?
...WITH SERIOUS.

#041: Humankind

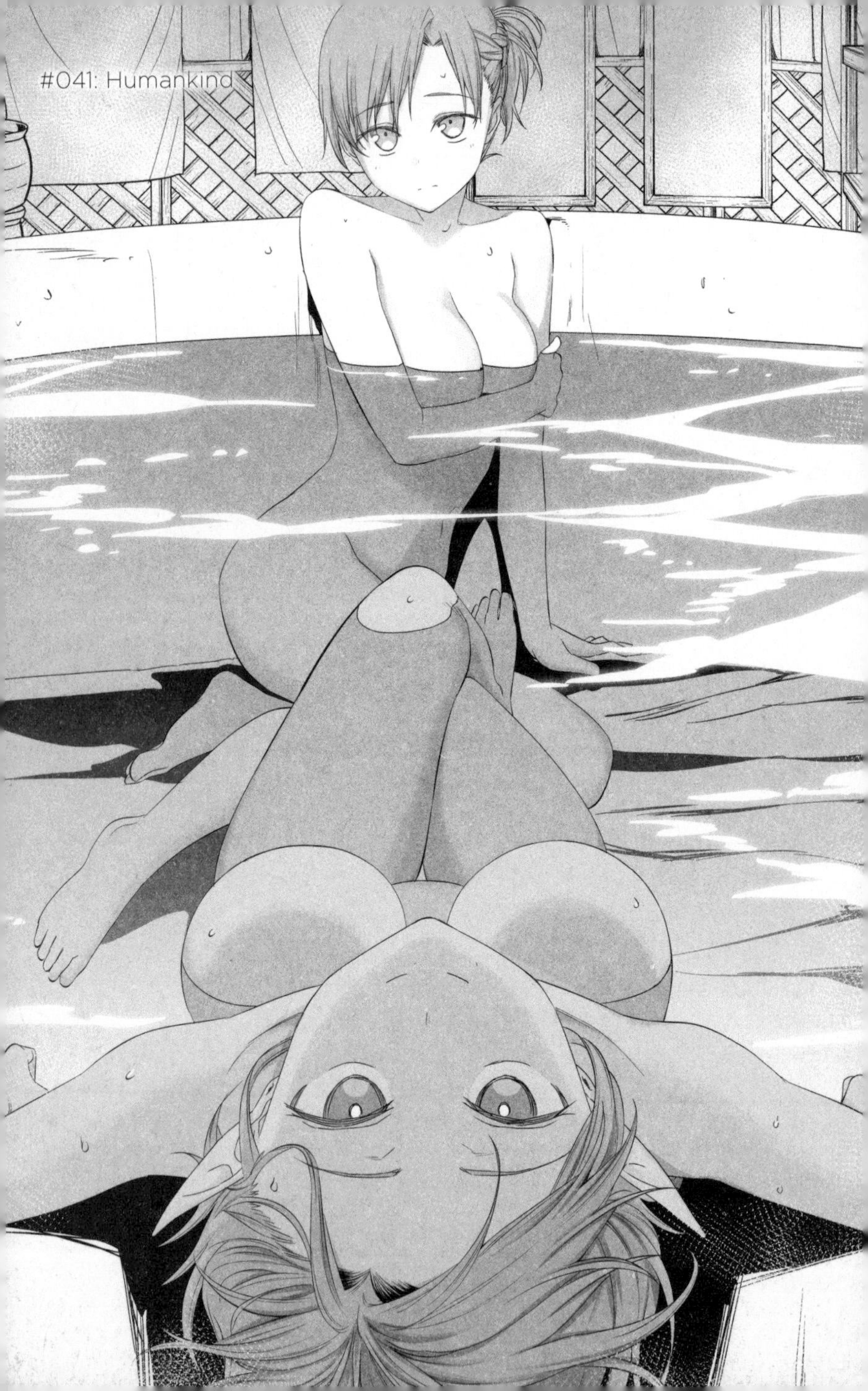

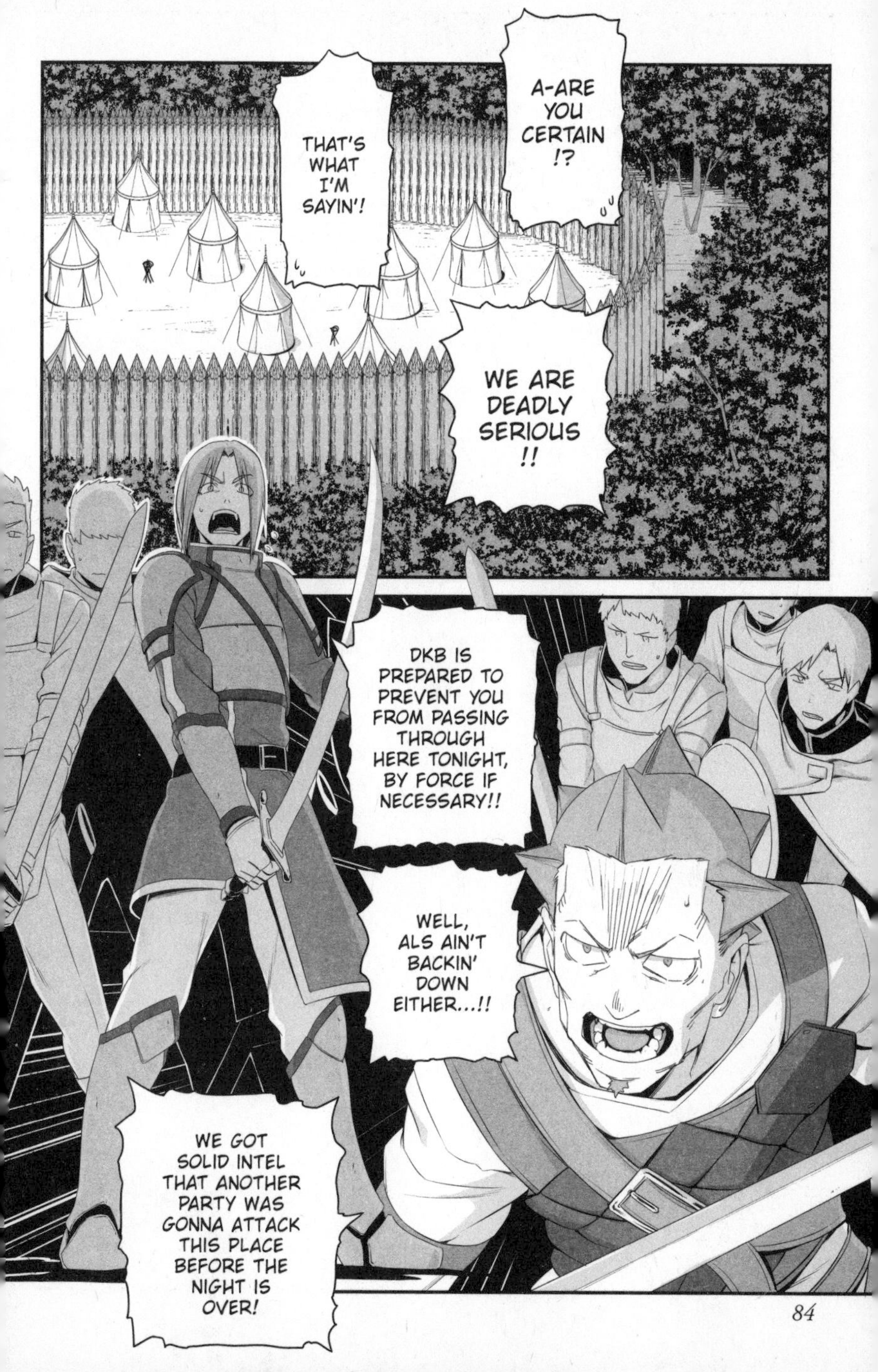
A-ARE YOU CERTAIN!?
THAT'S WHAT I'M SAYIN'!
WE ARE DEADLY SERIOUS!!
DKB IS PREPARED TO PREVENT YOU FROM PASSING THROUGH HERE TONIGHT, BY FORCE IF NECESSARY!!
WELL, ALS AIN'T BACKIN' DOWN EITHER...!!
WE GOT SOLID INTEL THAT ANOTHER PARTY WAS GONNA ATTACK THIS PLACE BEFORE THE NIGHT IS OVER!

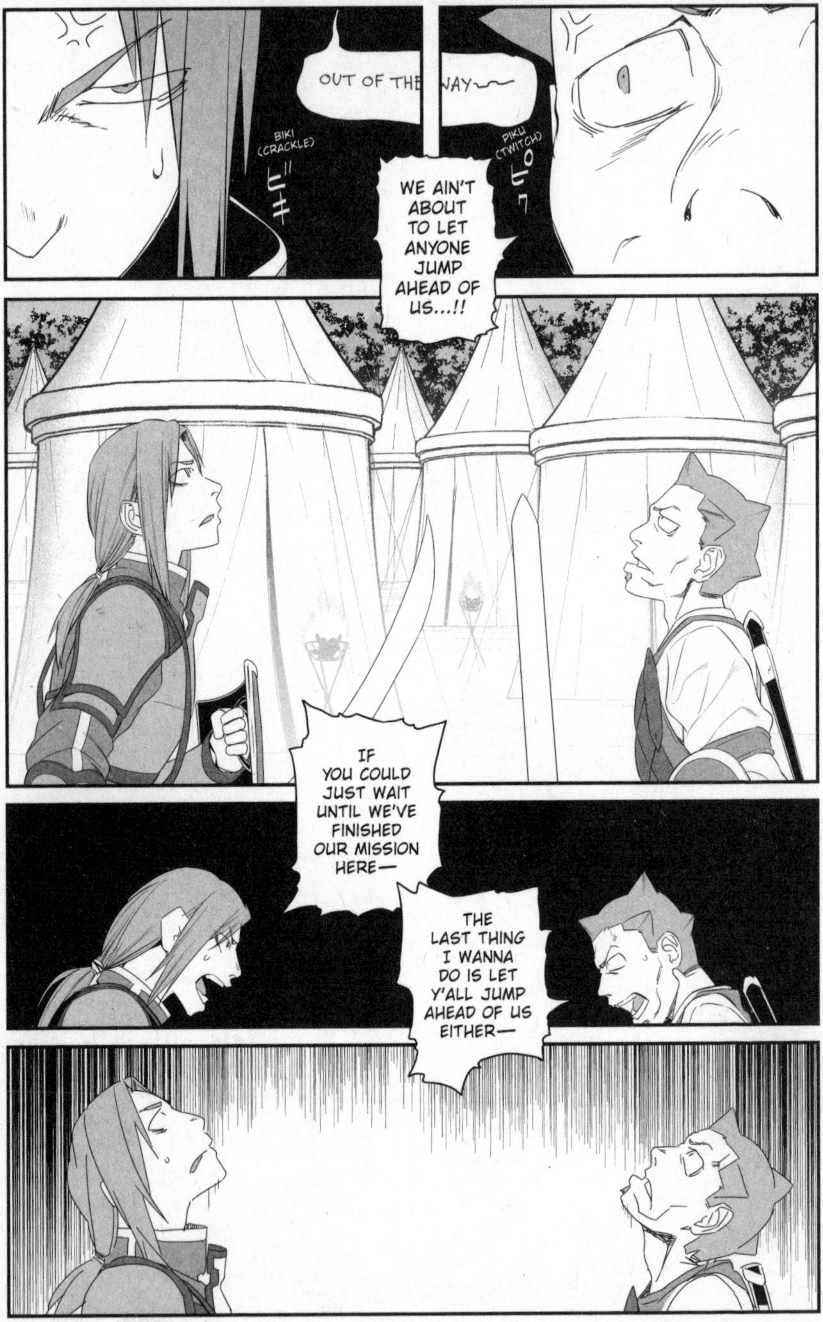
PIKU (TWITCH)
ピク
OUT OF THE WAY~~
BIKI (CRACKLE)
ビキ
WE AIN'T ABOUT TO LET ANYONE JUMP AHEAD OF US...!!
IF YOU COULD JUST WAIT UNTIL WE'VE FINISHED OUR MISSION HERE—
THE LAST THING I WANNA DO IS LET Y'ALL JUMP AHEAD OF US EITHER—

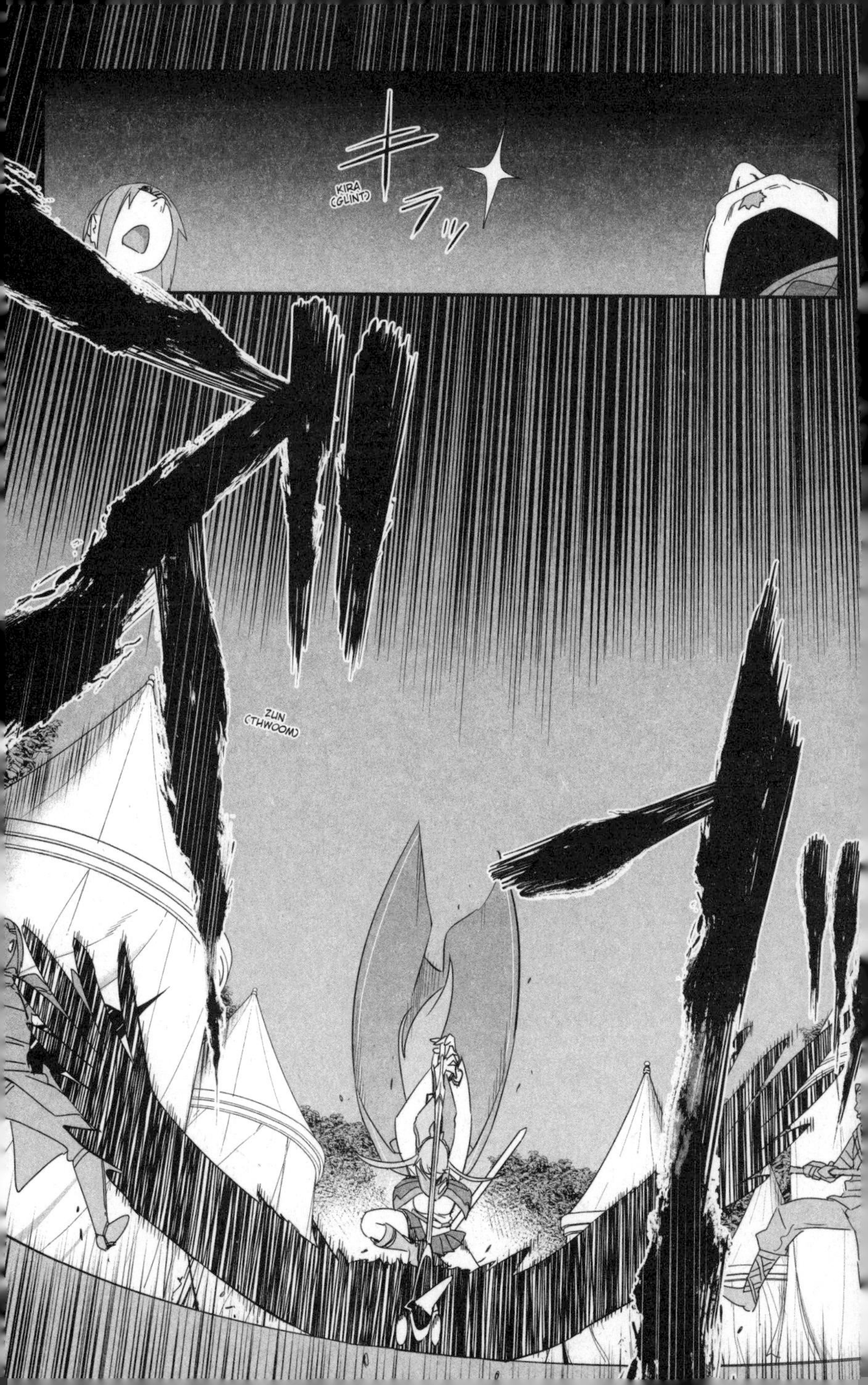

キラッ
KIRA (GLINT)
ZUN (THWOOM)

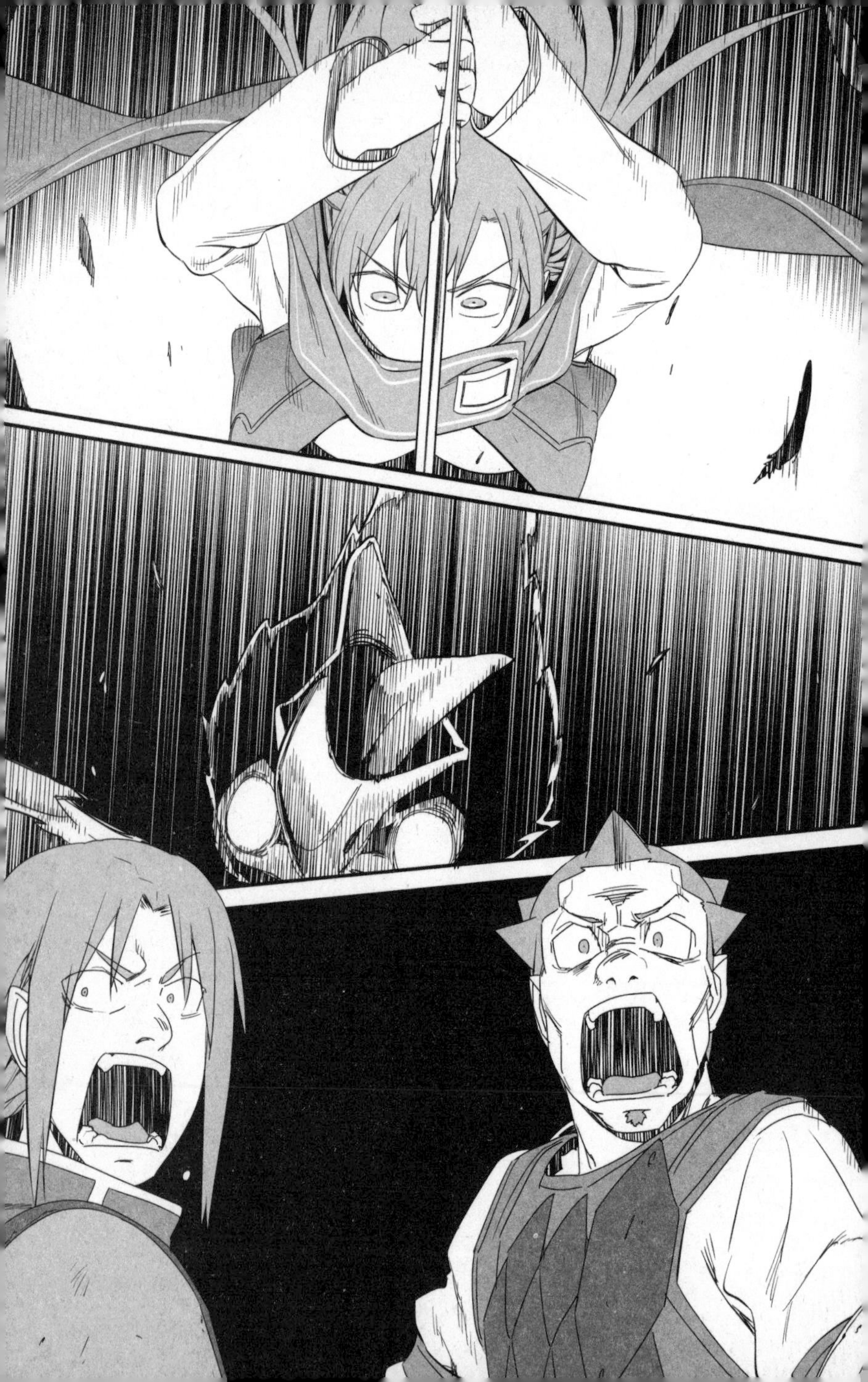

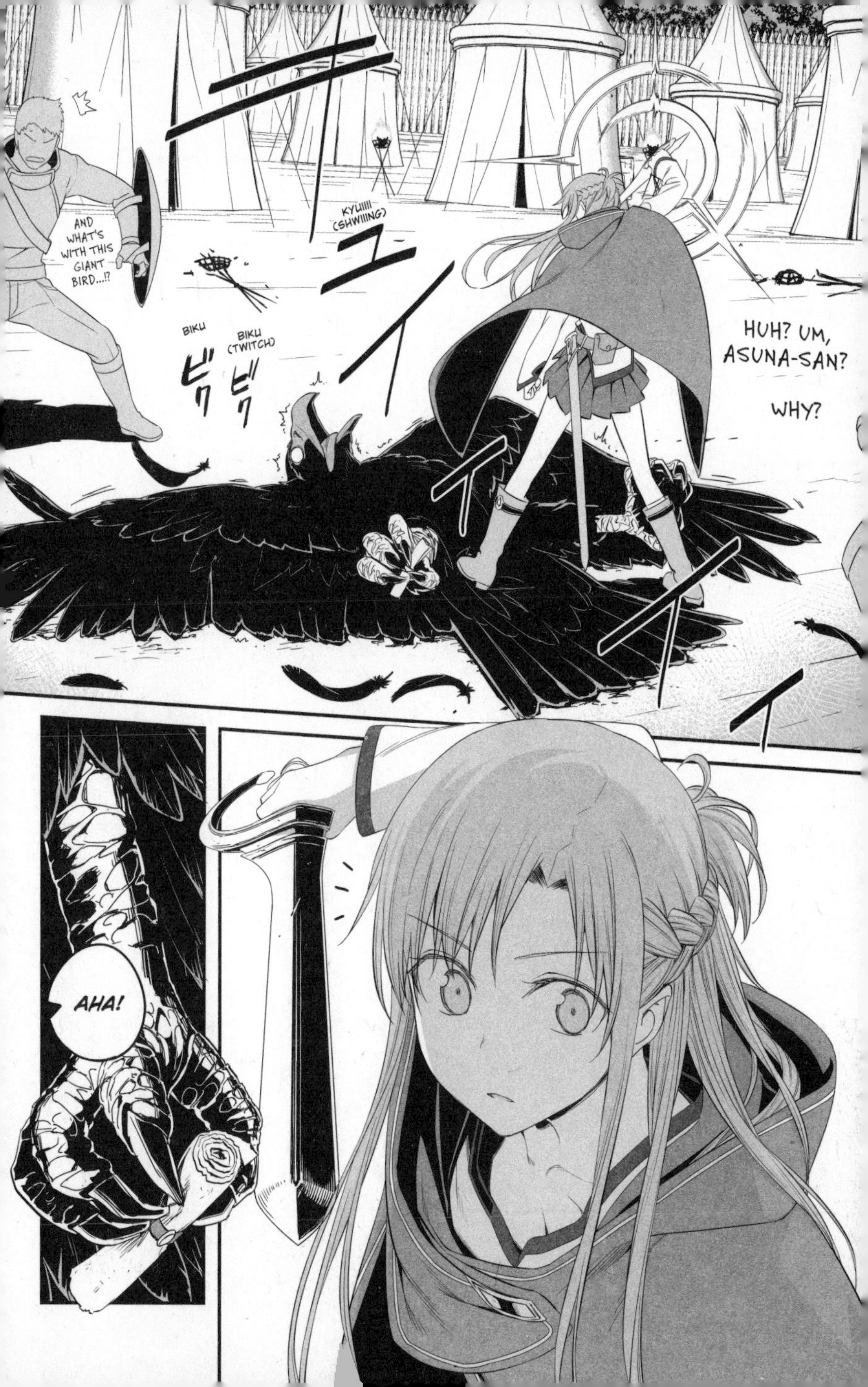
HUH? UM, ASUNA-SAN?
WHY?
KYUIIII (SHWIIING)
BIKU
BIKU (TWITCH)
AND WHAT'S WITH THIS GIANT BIRD...!?
AHA!

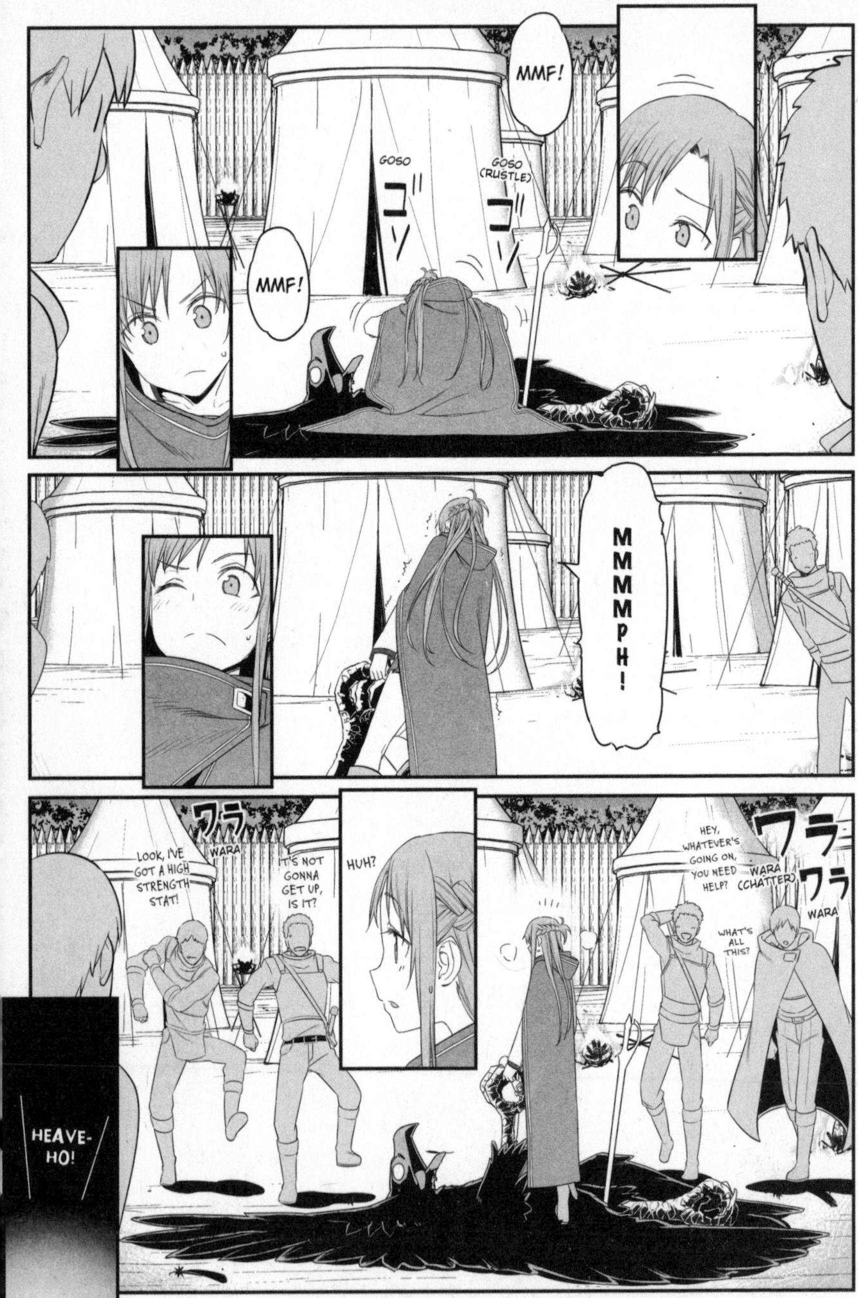

MMF!
ゴソ
GOSO (RUSTLE)
ゴソ
GOSO
MMF!
MMMMPH!
HEY, WHATEVER'S GOING ON, YOU NEED HELP?
ワラ
WARA (CHATTER)
ワラ
WARA
WHAT'S ALL THIS?
HUH?
IT'S NOT GONNA GET UP, IS IT?
ワラ
WARA
LOOK, I'VE GOT A HIGH STRENGTH STAT!
HEAVE-HO!

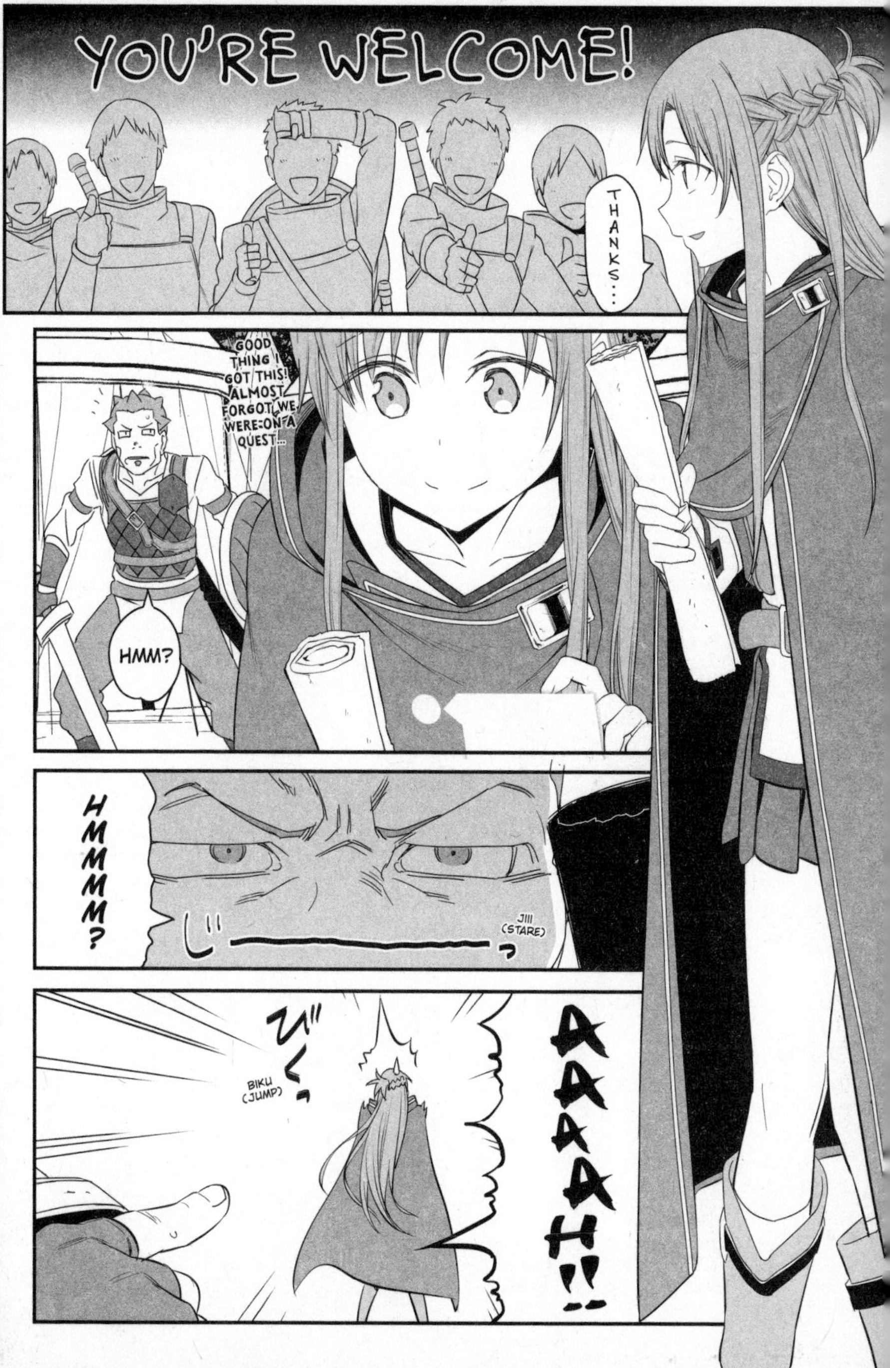
THANKS...
YOU'RE WELCOME!
GOOD THING I GOT THIS! ALMOST FORGOT WE WERE ON A QUEST...
HMM?
JIII (STARE)
HMMMMM?
AAAAH!!
BIKU (JUMP)

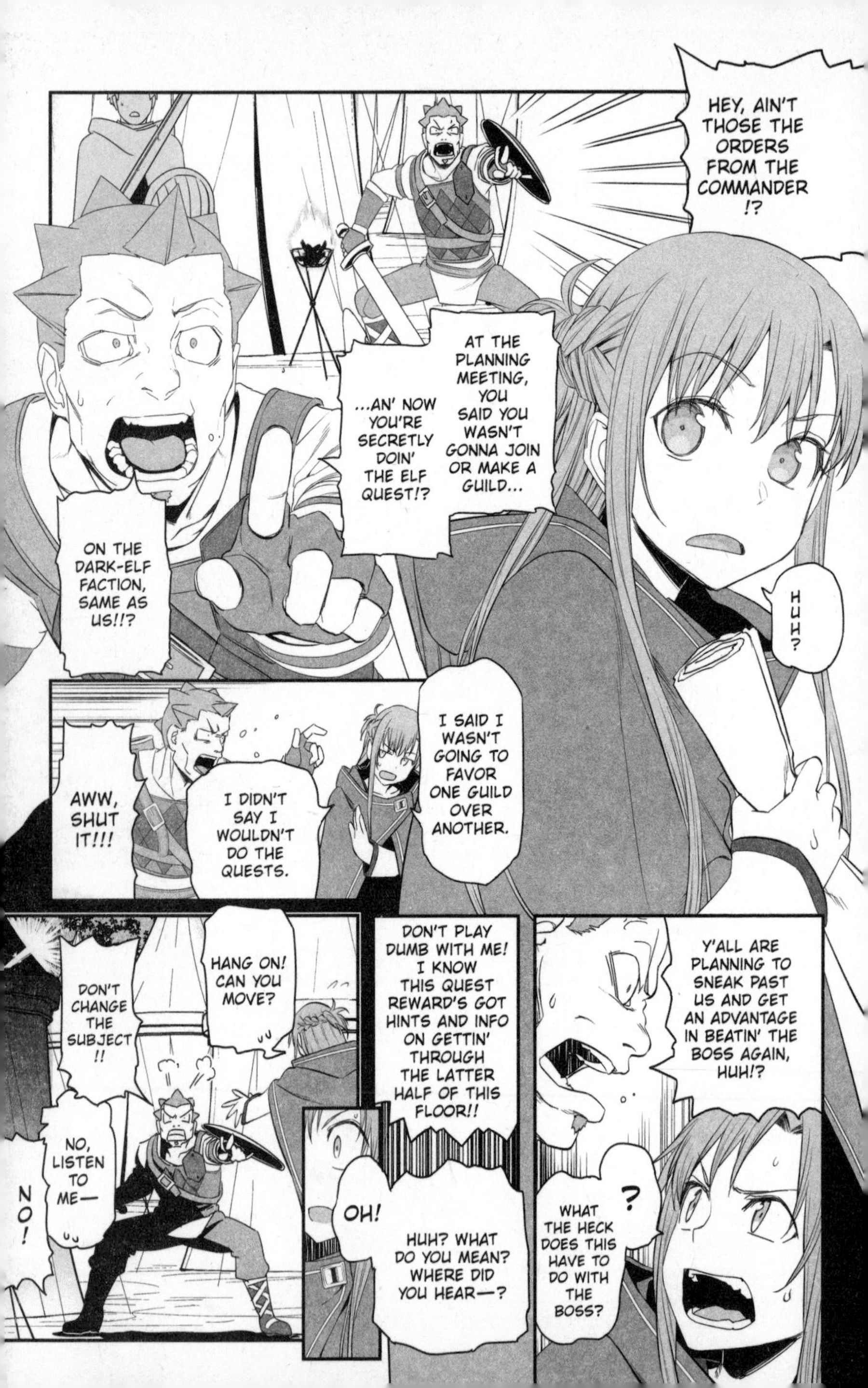
HEY, AIN'T THOSE THE ORDERS FROM THE COMMANDER !?
AT THE PLANNING MEETING, YOU SAID YOU WASN'T GONNA JOIN OR MAKE A GUILD...
...AN' NOW YOU'RE SECRETLY DOIN' THE ELF QUEST!?
ON THE DARK-ELF FACTION, SAME AS US!!?
HUH?
I SAID I WASN'T GOING TO FAVOR ONE GUILD OVER ANOTHER.
I DIDN'T SAY I WOULDN'T DO THE QUESTS.
AWW, SHUT IT!!!
Y'ALL ARE PLANNING TO SNEAK PAST US AND GET AN ADVANTAGE IN BEATIN' THE BOSS AGAIN, HUH!?
?
WHAT THE HECK DOES THIS HAVE TO DO WITH THE BOSS?
DON'T PLAY DUMB WITH ME! I KNOW THIS QUEST REWARD'S GOT HINTS AND INFO ON GETTIN' THROUGH THE LATTER HALF OF THIS FLOOR!!
OH!
HUH? WHAT DO YOU MEAN? WHERE DID YOU HEAR—?
HANG ON! CAN YOU MOVE?
DON'T CHANGE THE SUBJECT!!
NO, LISTEN TO ME—
NO!

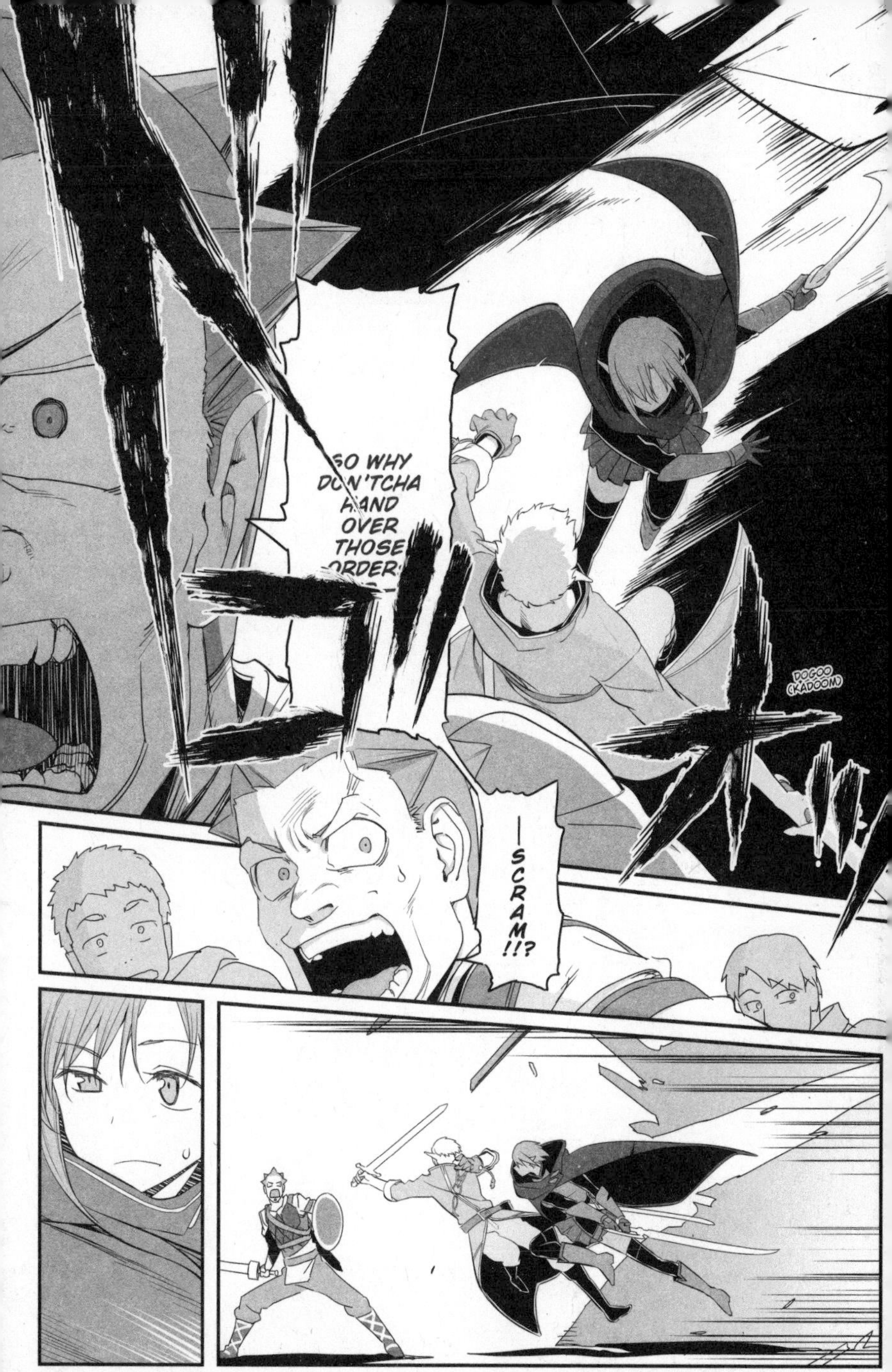
SO WHY DON'TCHA HAND OVER THOSE ORDERS
DOGOO (KADOOM)
—SCRAM!!?

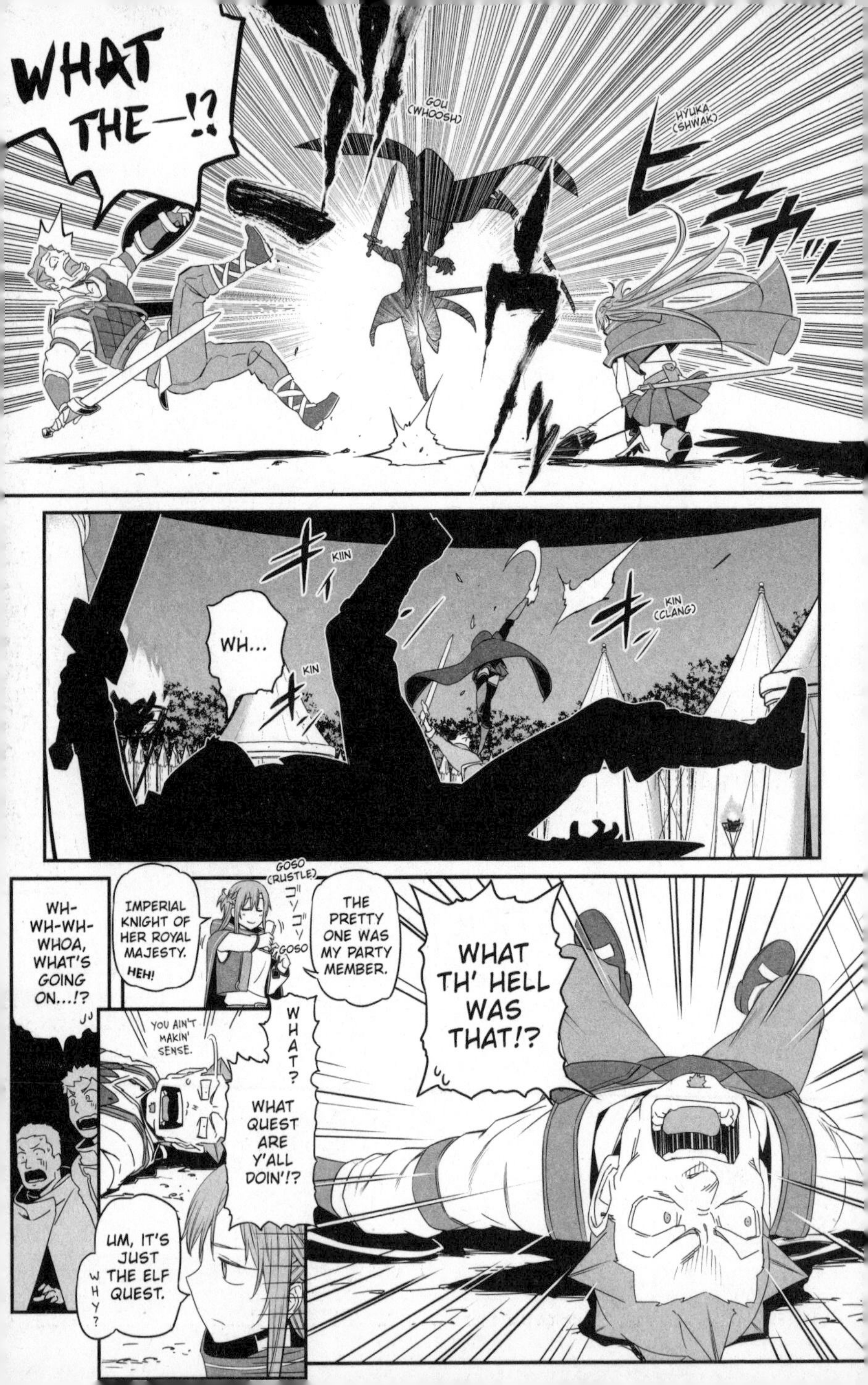
HYUKA (SHWAK)
GOU (WHOOSH)
WHAT THE—!?
KIN (CLANG)
KIIN
KIN
WH...
WHAT TH' HELL WAS THAT!?
THE PRETTY ONE WAS MY PARTY MEMBER.
GOSO (RUSTLE)
GOSO
IMPERIAL KNIGHT OF HER ROYAL MAJESTY.
HEH!
WH-WH-WH-WHOA, WHAT'S GOING ON...!?
WHAT?
WHAT QUEST ARE Y'ALL DOIN'!?
YOU AIN'T MAKIN' SENSE.
UM, IT'S JUST THE ELF QUEST.
WHY?

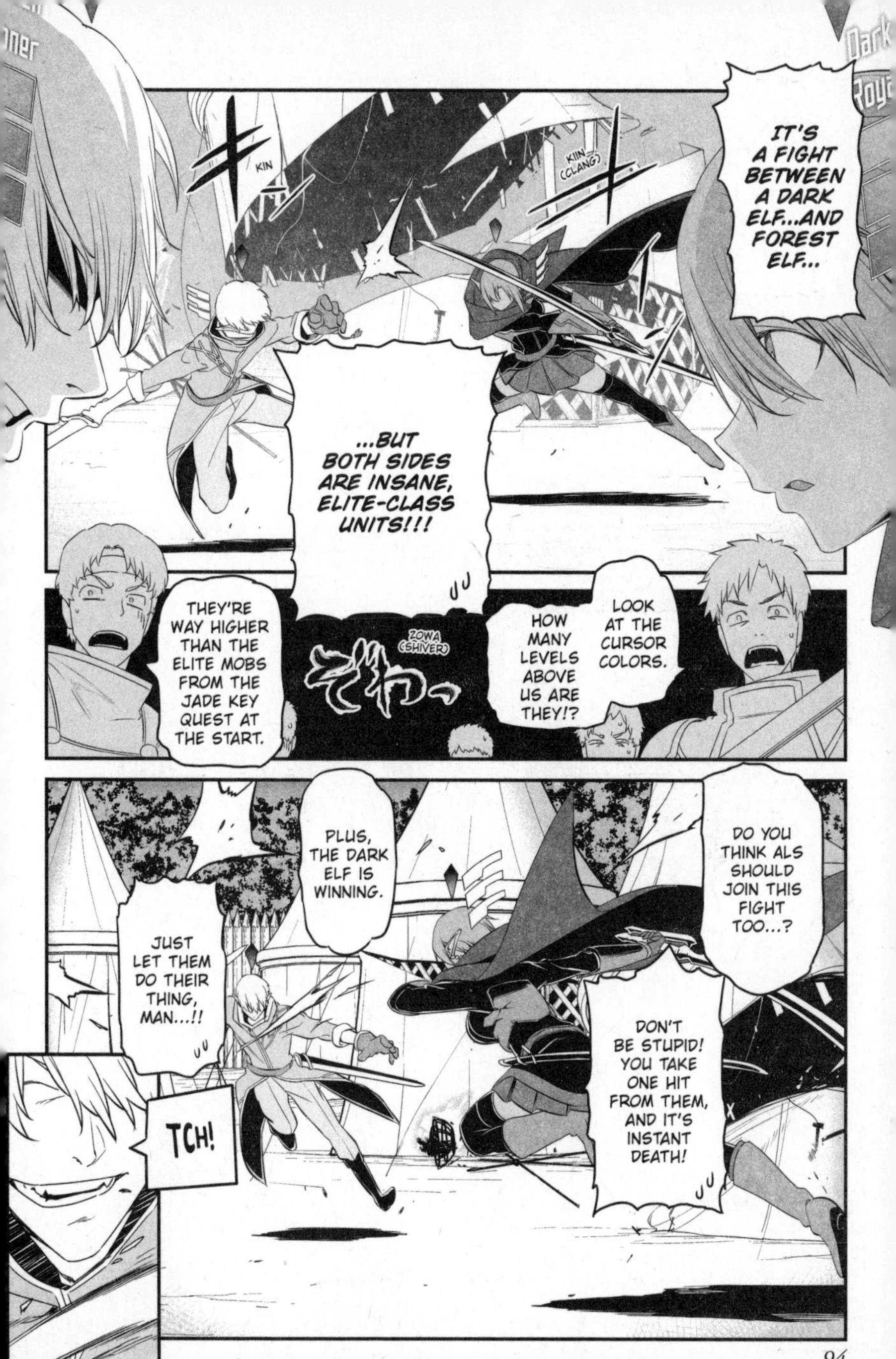
IT'S A FIGHT BETWEEN A DARK ELF...AND FOREST ELF...
KIIN (CLANG)
KIN
...BUT BOTH SIDES ARE INSANE, ELITE-CLASS UNITS!!!
LOOK AT THE CURSOR COLORS.
HOW MANY LEVELS ABOVE US ARE THEY!?
ZOWA (SHIVER)
THEY'RE WAY HIGHER THAN THE ELITE MOBS FROM THE JADE KEY QUEST AT THE START.
DO YOU THINK ALS SHOULD JOIN THIS FIGHT TOO...?
PLUS, THE DARK ELF IS WINNING.
DON'T BE STUPID! YOU TAKE ONE HIT FROM THEM, AND IT'S INSTANT DEATH!
JUST LET THEM DO THEIR THING, MAN...!!
TCH!

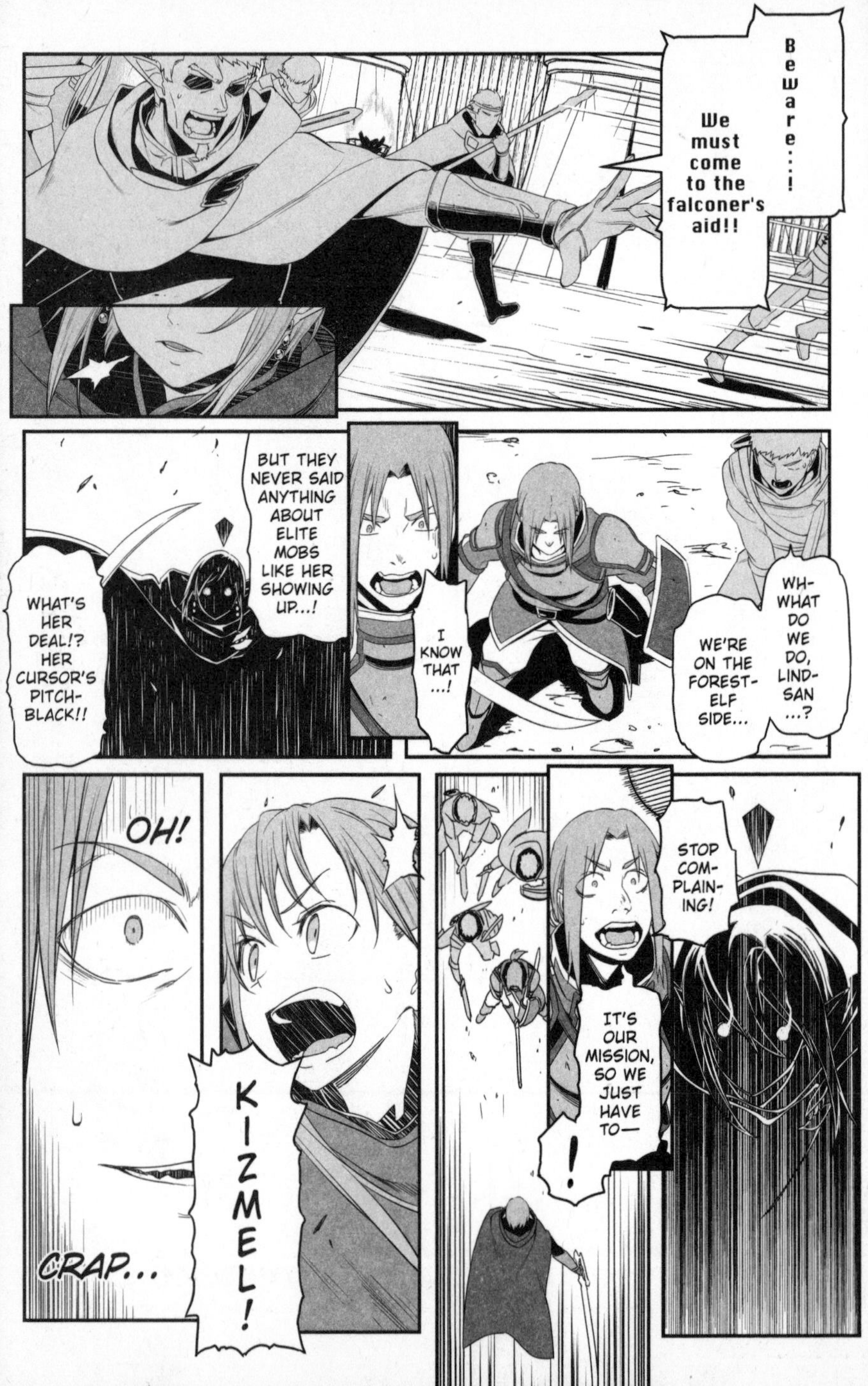
Beware...!
We must come to the falconer's aid!!
WH-WHAT DO WE DO, LIND-SAN...?
WE'RE ON THE FOREST-ELF SIDE...
I KNOW THAT...!
BUT THEY NEVER SAID ANYTHING ABOUT ELITE MOBS LIKE HER SHOWING UP...!
WHAT'S HER DEAL!? HER CURSOR'S PITCH-BLACK!!
STOP COMPLAINING!
IT'S OUR MISSION, SO WE JUST HAVE TO—
!
KIZMEL!
OH!
CRAP...

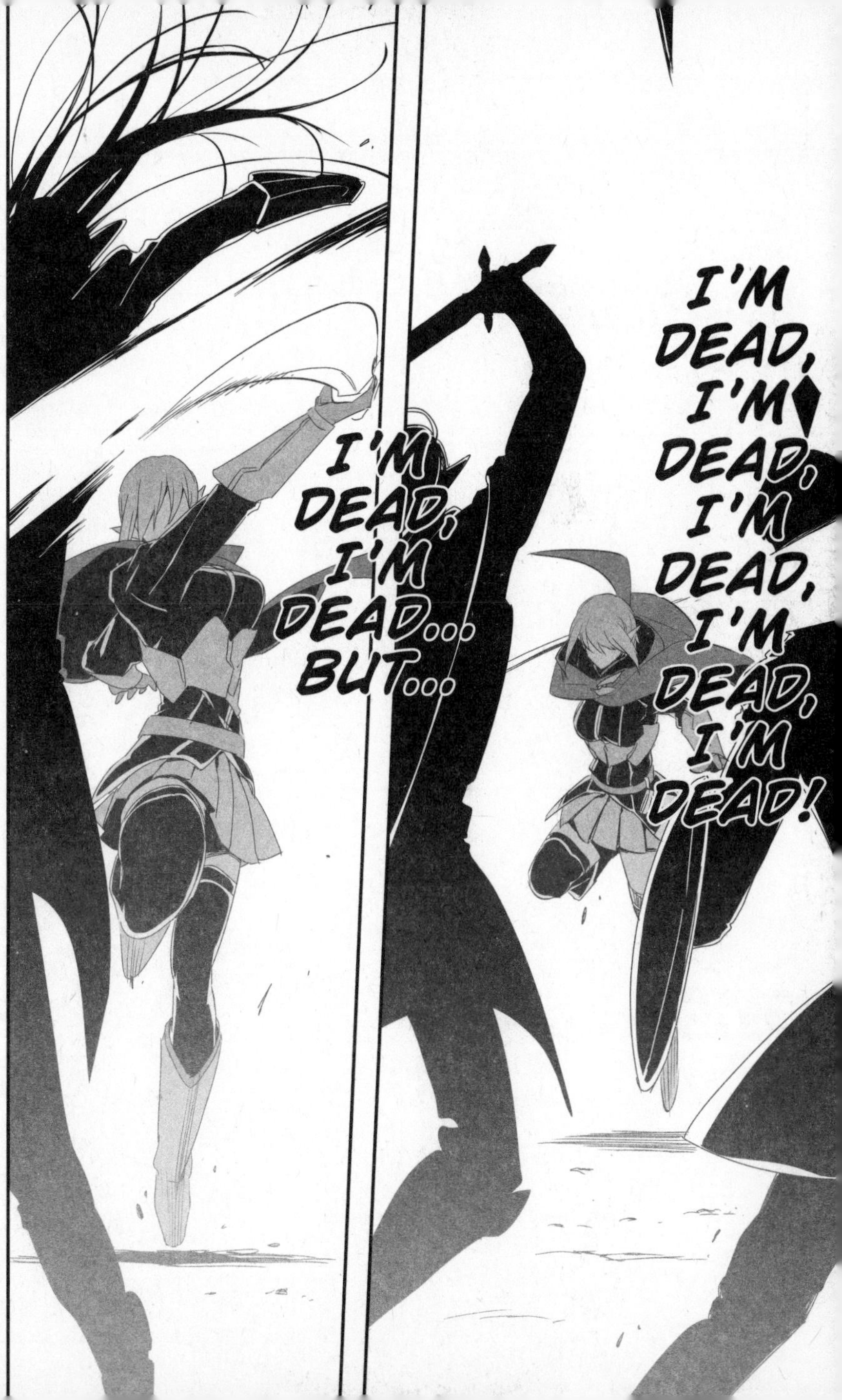
I'M DEAD, I'M DEAD, I'M DEAD, I'M DEAD, I'M DEAD!
I'M DEAD, I'M DEAD... BUT...

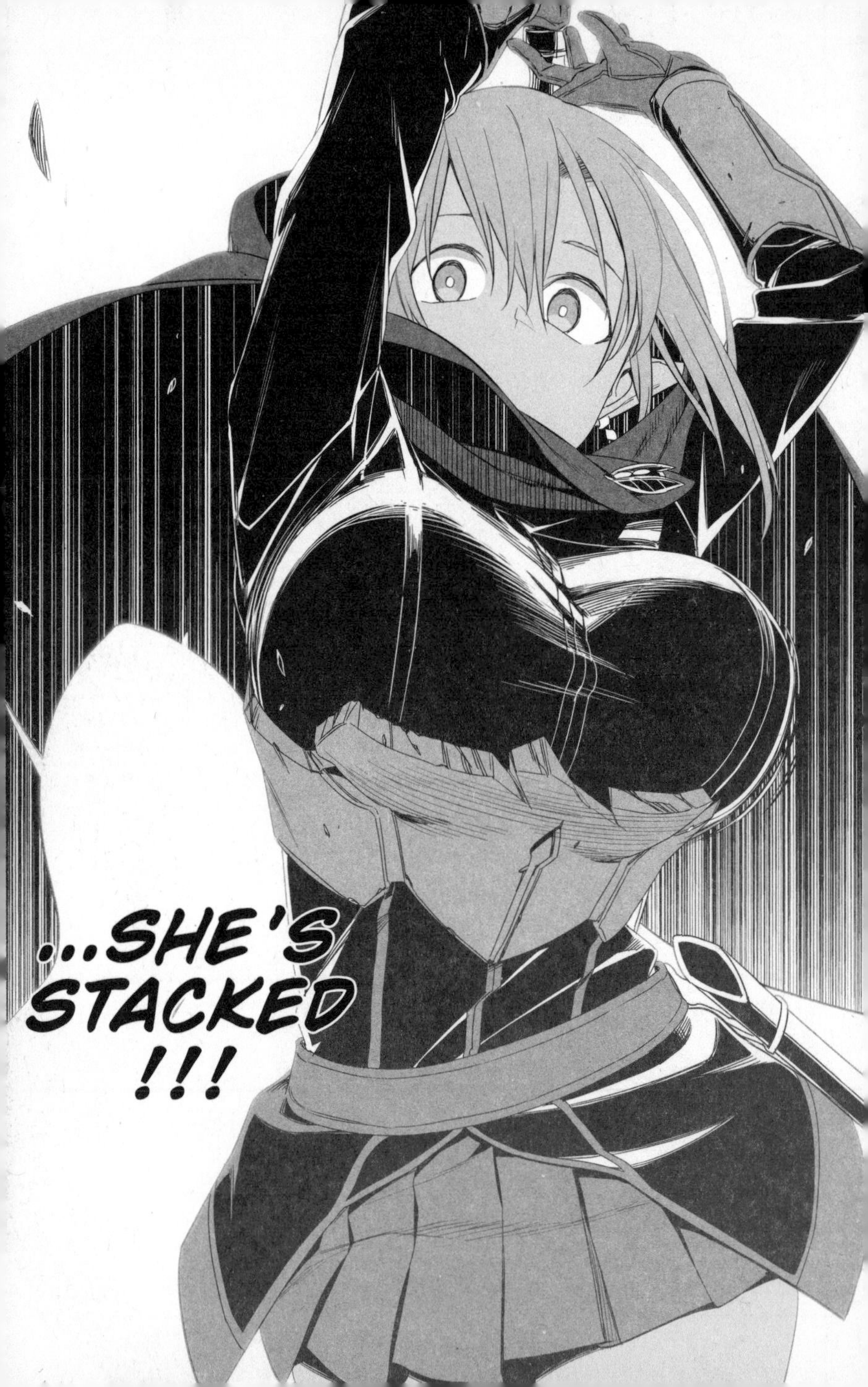
...SHE'S STACKED!!!

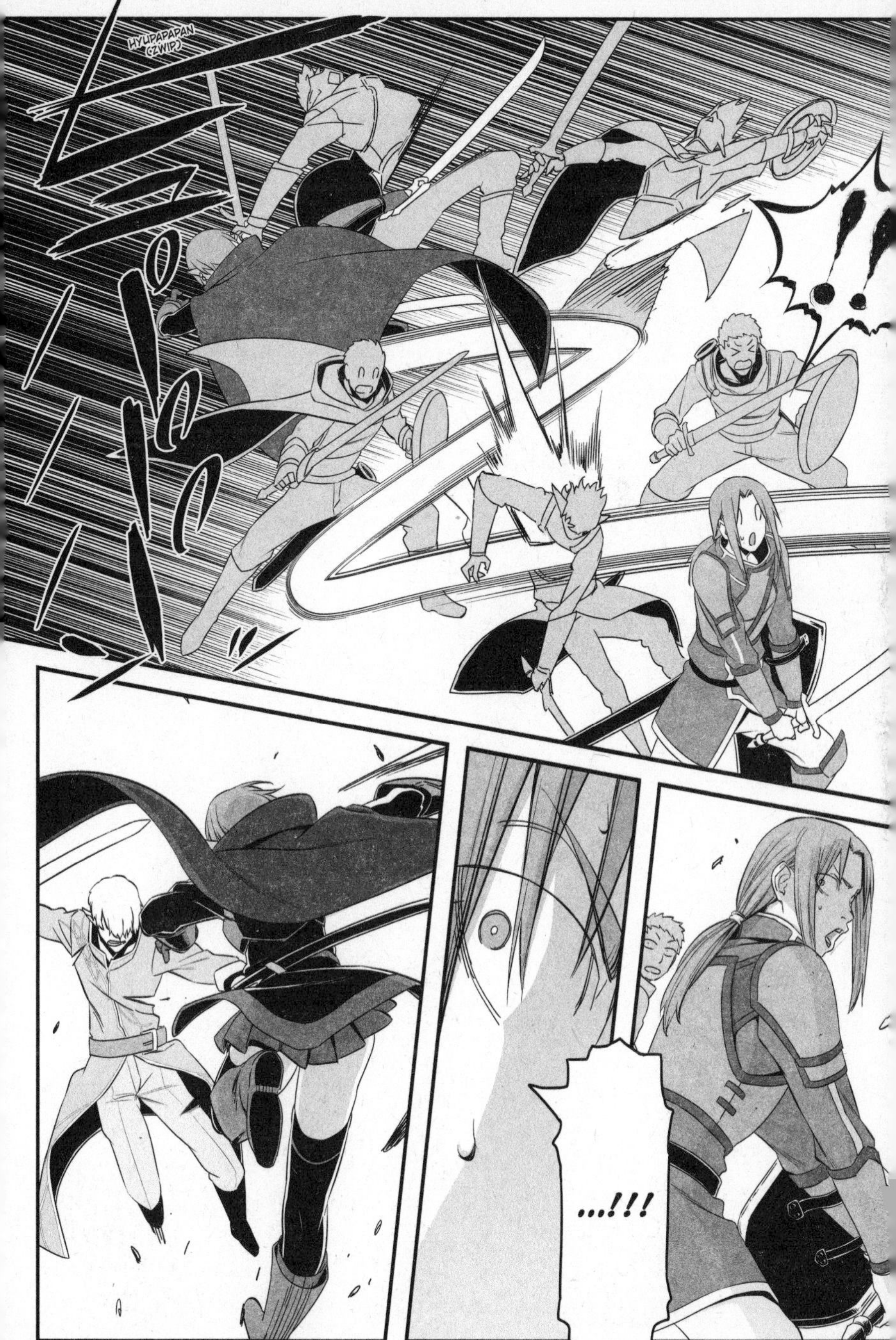
HYUPAPAPAN (ZWIP)
!!
...!!!

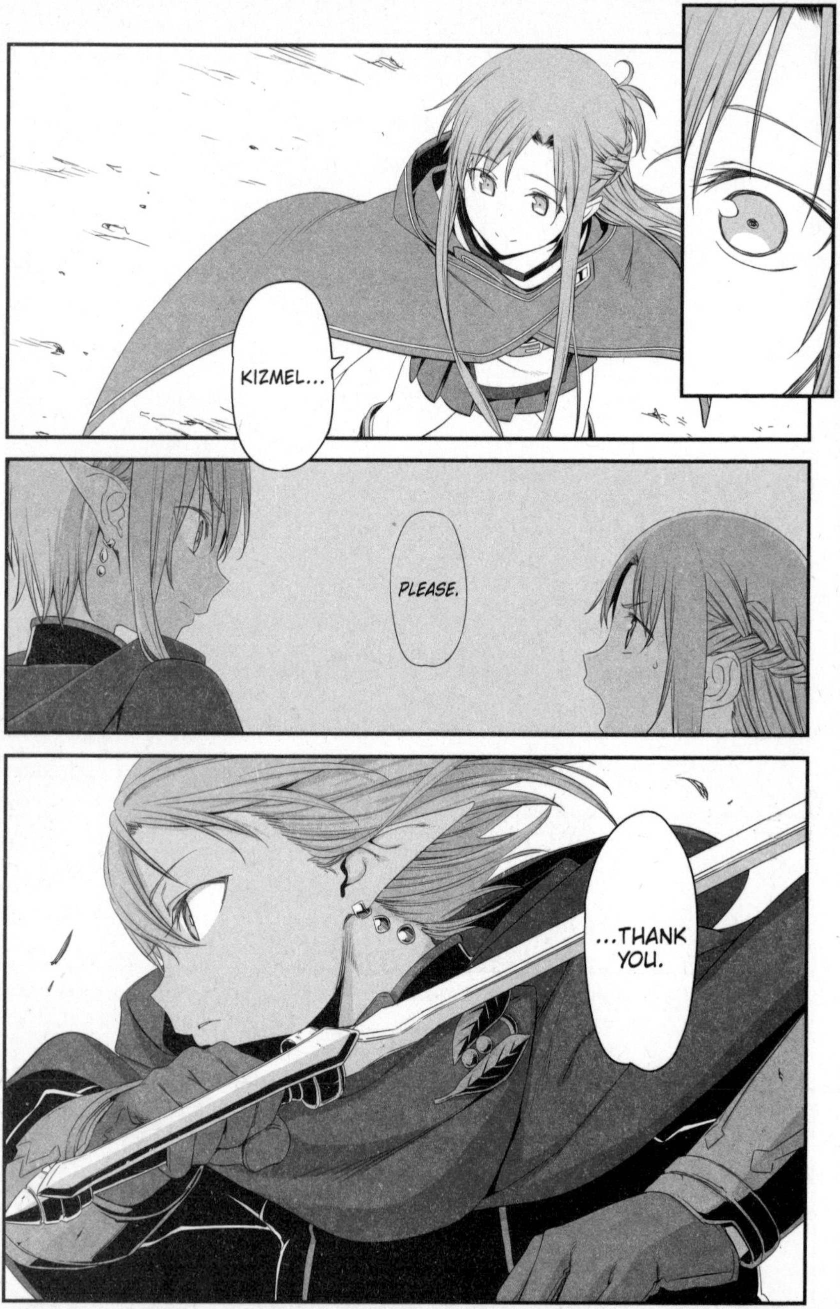
KIZMEL...
PLEASE.
...THANK YOU.

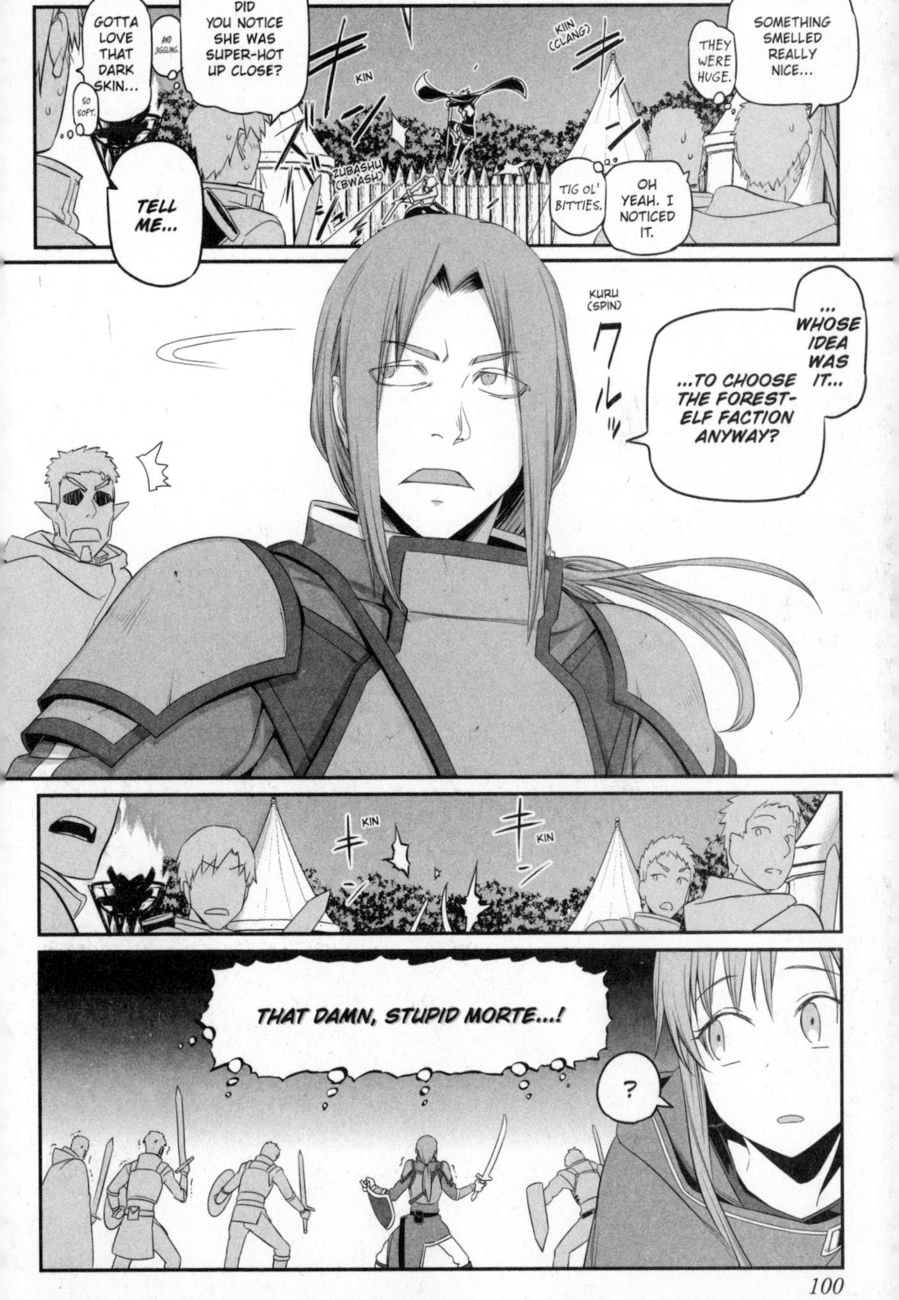
SOMETHING SMELLED REALLY NICE...
THEY WERE HUGE.
OH YEAH. I NOTICED IT.
TIG OL' BITTIES.
KIIN (CLANG)
KIN
ZUBASHU (CBWASH)
DID YOU NOTICE SHE WAS SUPER-HOT UP CLOSE?
AND JIGGLING.
GOTTA LOVE THAT DARK SKIN...
SO SOFT.
TELL ME...
...WHOSE IDEA WAS IT...
...TO CHOOSE THE FOREST-ELF FACTION ANYWAY?
KURU (SPIN)
KIN
KIN
?
THAT DAMN, STUPID MORTE...!

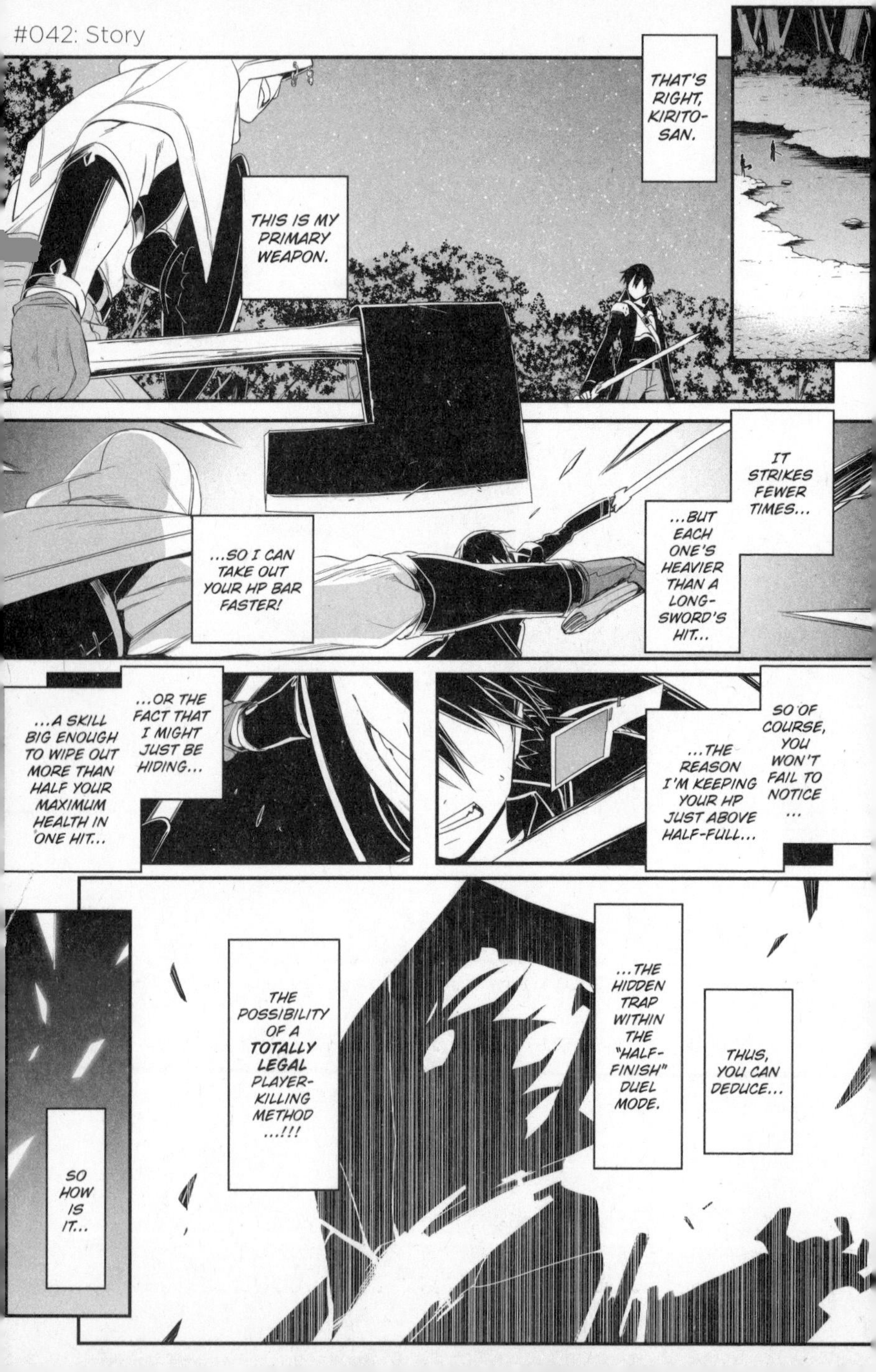
THAT'S RIGHT, KIRITO-SAN.
THIS IS MY PRIMARY WEAPON.
IT STRIKES FEWER TIMES...
...BUT EACH ONE'S HEAVIER THAN A LONG-SWORD'S HIT...
...SO I CAN TAKE OUT YOUR HP BAR FASTER!
SO OF COURSE, YOU WON'T FAIL TO NOTICE...
...THE REASON I'M KEEPING YOUR HP JUST ABOVE HALF-FULL...
...OR THE FACT THAT I MIGHT JUST BE HIDING...
...A SKILL BIG ENOUGH TO WIPE OUT MORE THAN HALF YOUR MAXIMUM HEALTH IN ONE HIT...
THUS, YOU CAN DEDUCE...
...THE HIDDEN TRAP WITHIN THE "HALF-FINISH" DUEL MODE.
THE POSSIBILITY OF A **TOTALLY LEGAL** PLAYER-KILLING METHOD ...!!!
SO HOW IS IT...

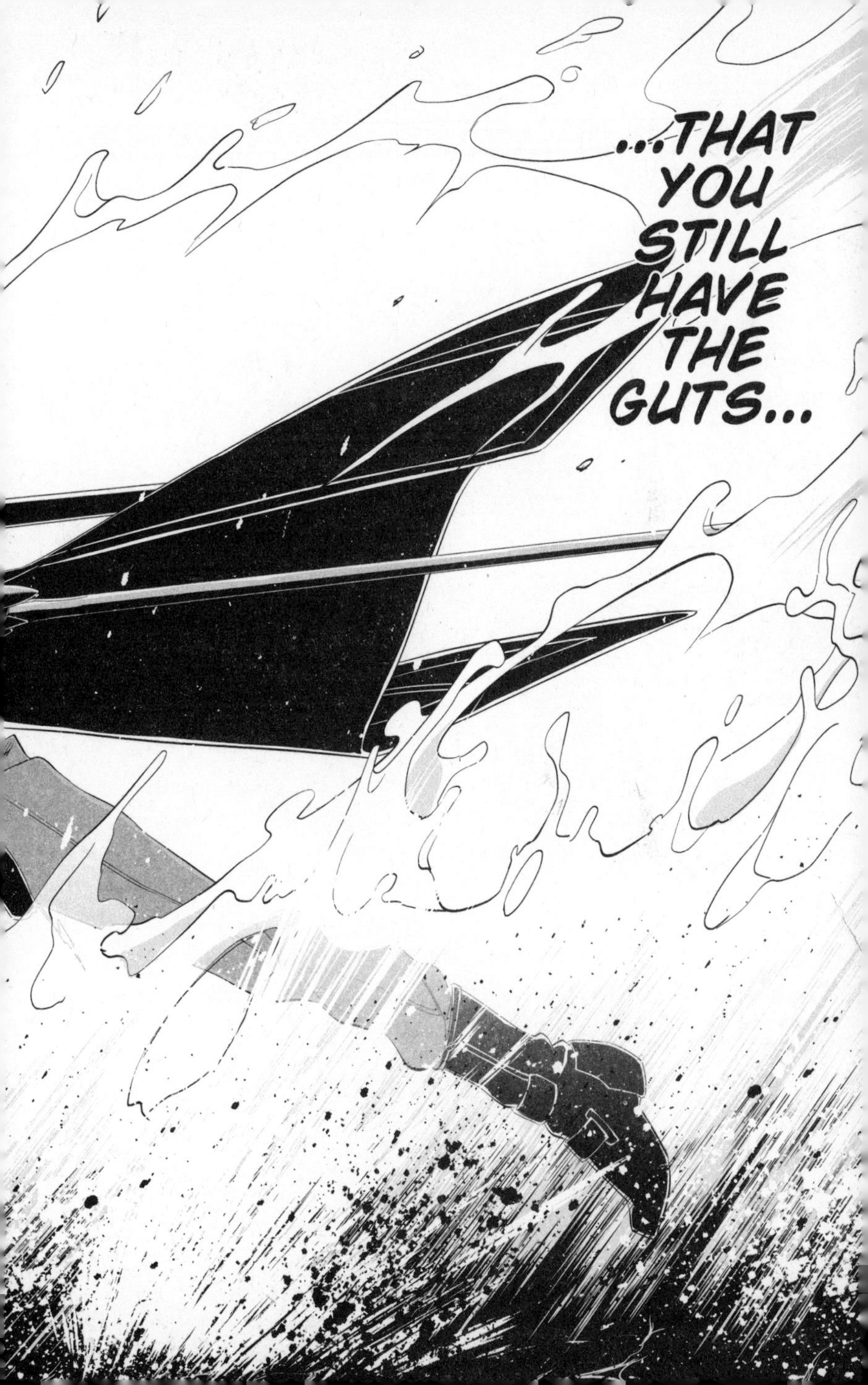
...THAT YOU STILL HAVE THE GUTS...

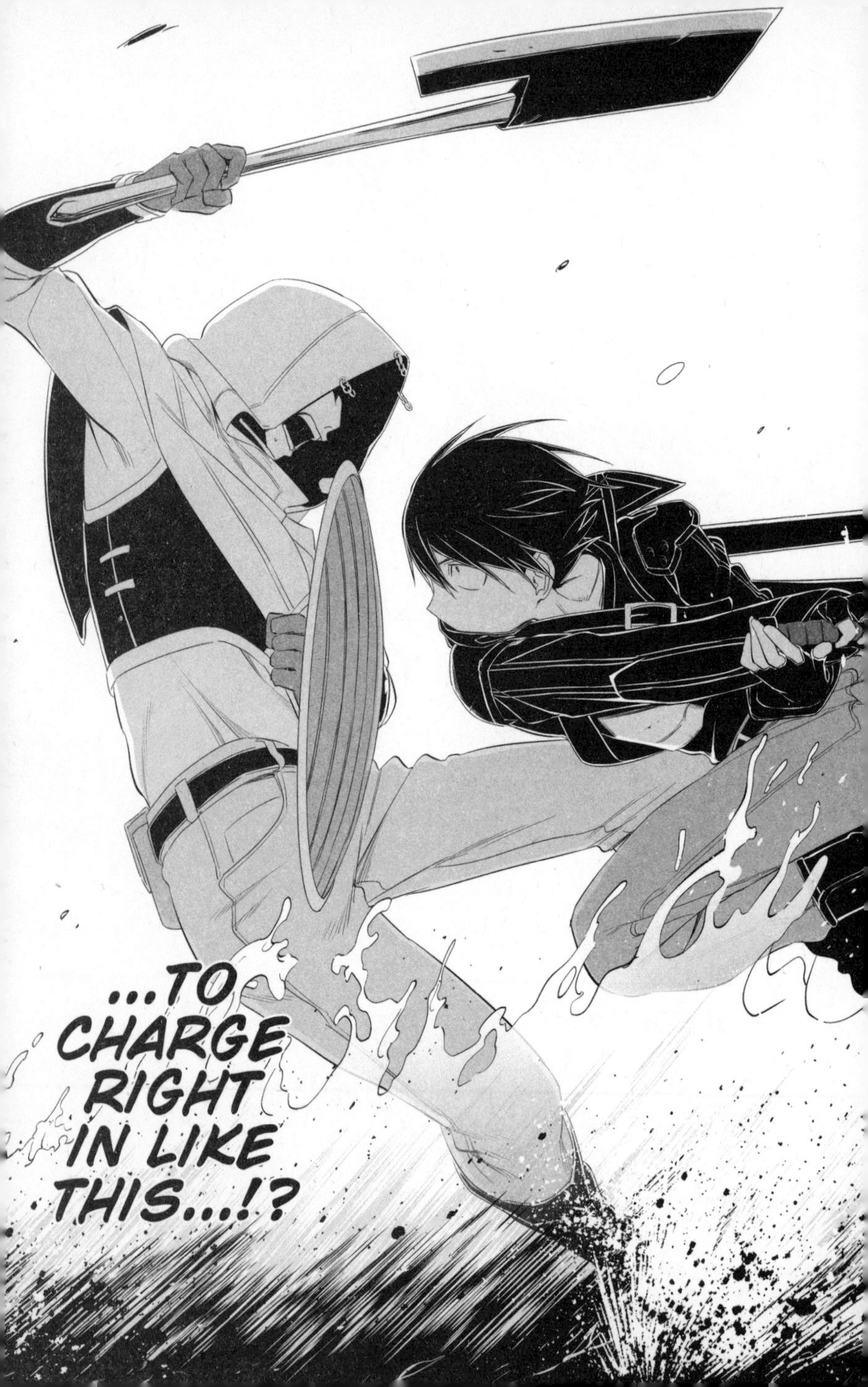
...TO CHARGE RIGHT IN LIKE THIS...!?

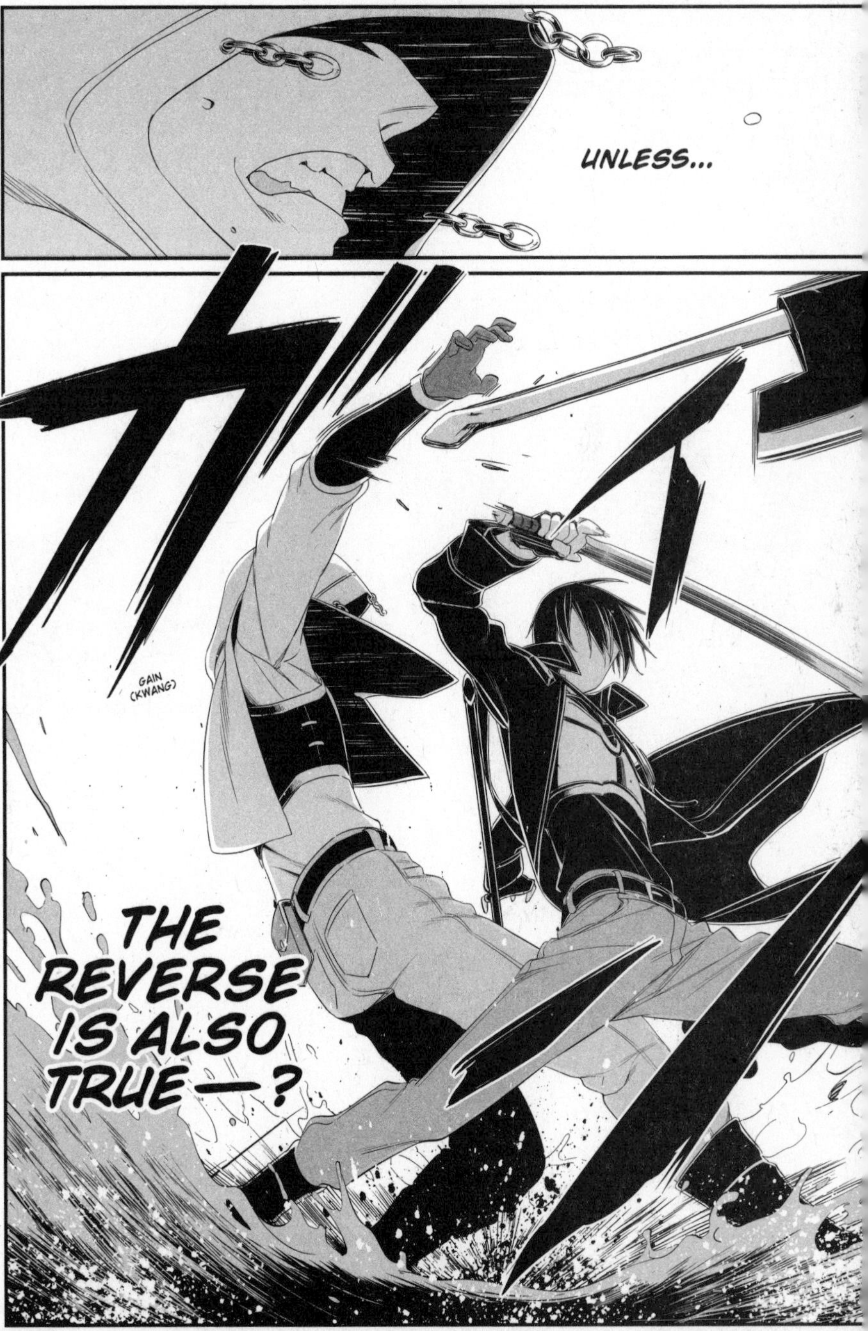
UNLESS...
GAIN
(KWANG)
THE REVERSE IS ALSO TRUE—?

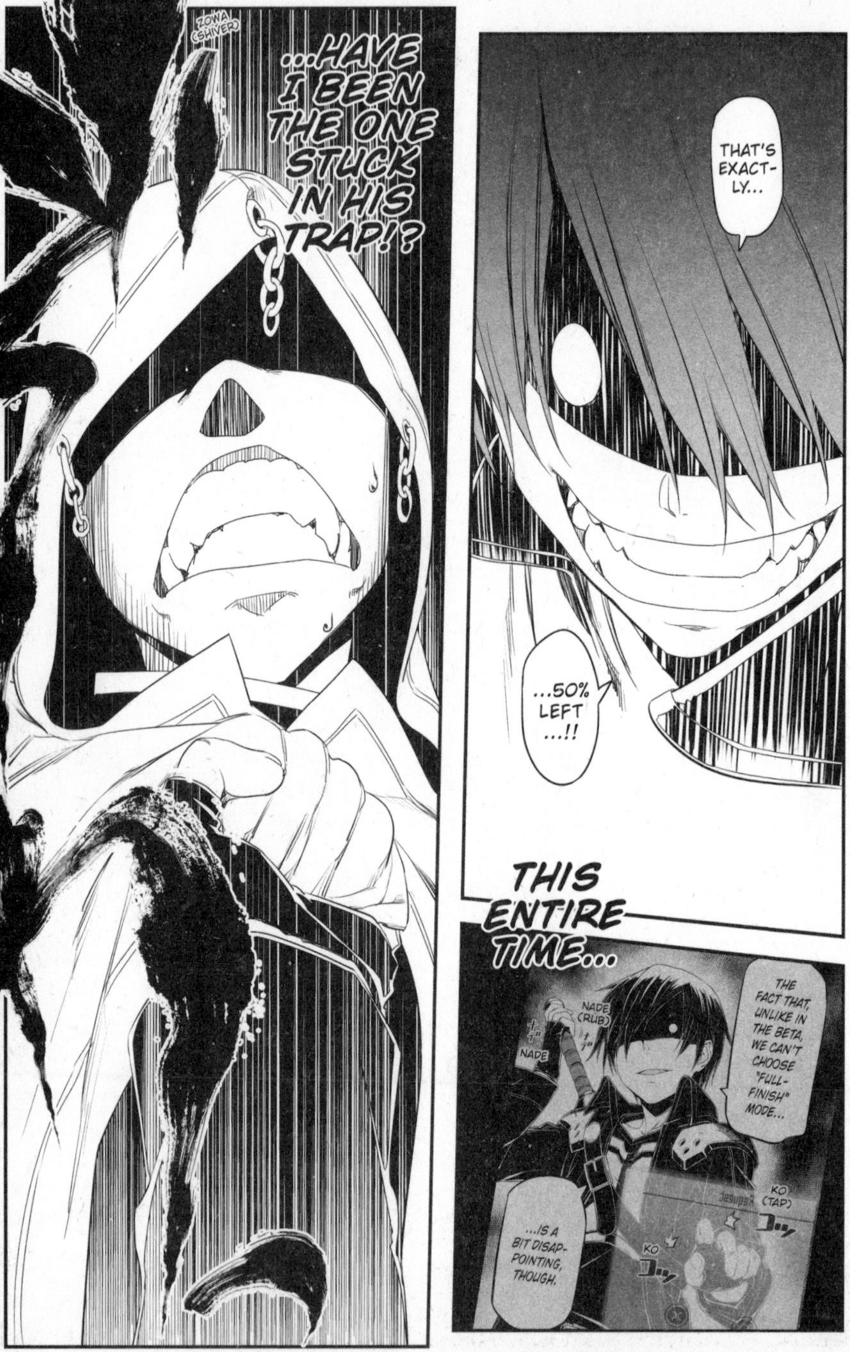
THAT'S EXACT-LY...
...50% LEFT ...!!
THIS ENTIRE TIME...
THE FACT THAT, UNLIKE IN THE BETA, WE CAN'T CHOOSE "FULL-FINISH" MODE...
NADE (RUB)
NADE
KO (TAP)
KO
...IS A BIT DISAPPOINTING, THOUGH.
ZOWA (SHIVER)
...HAVE I BEEN THE ONE STUCK IN HIS TRAP!?

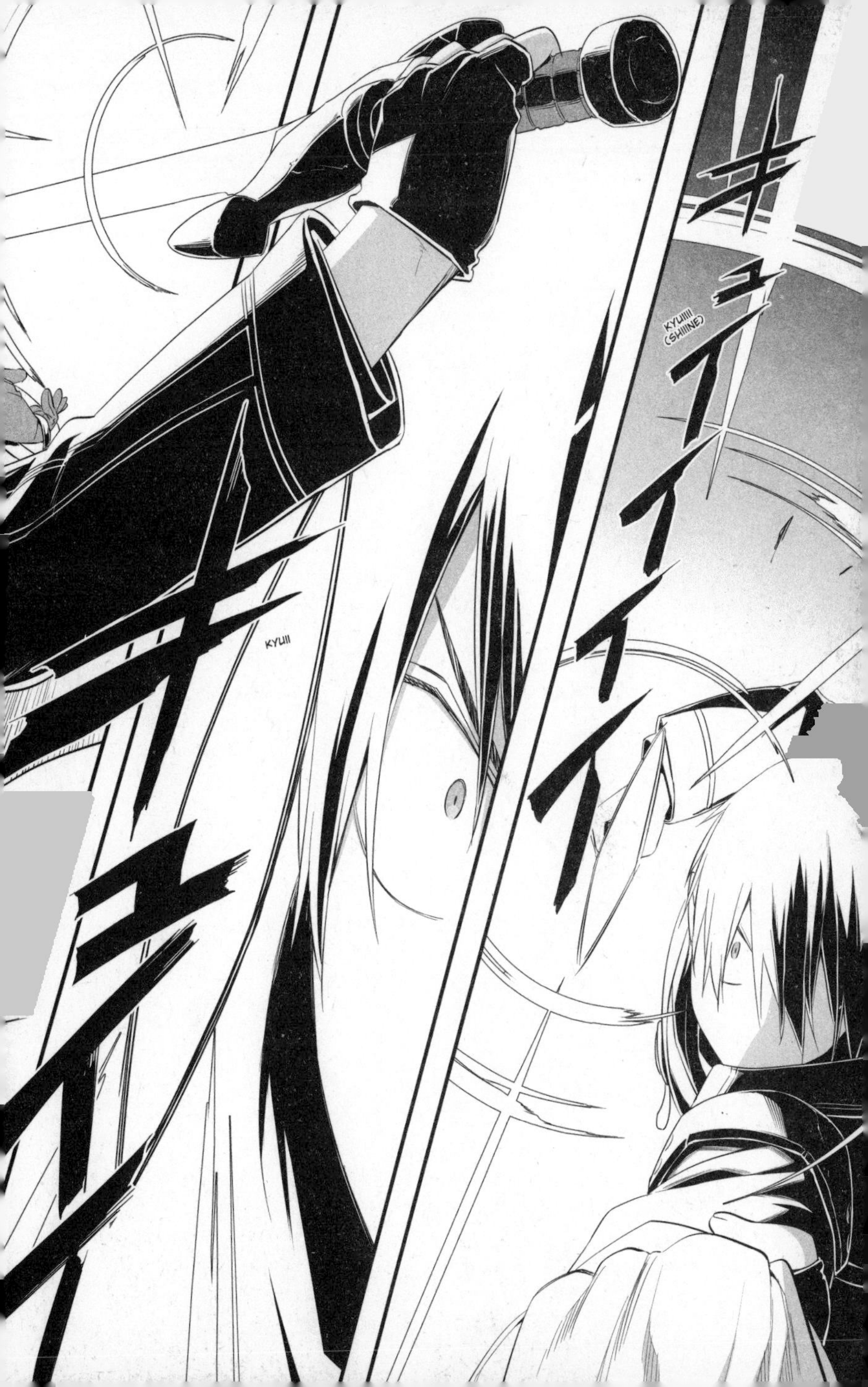
KYUIIIII (SHIIINE)
KYUII

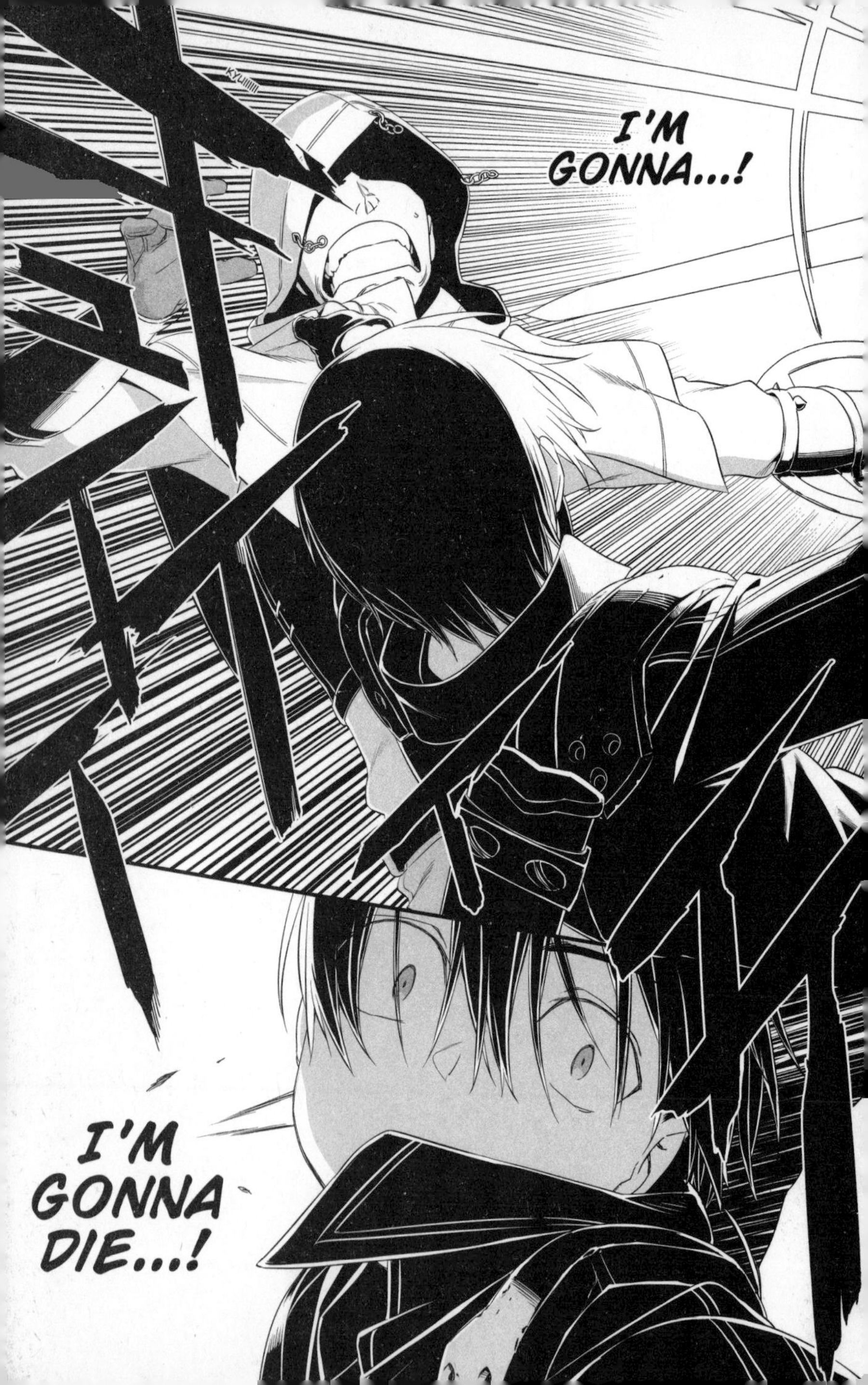
I'M GONNA...!
KYUIIIIIII
I'M GONNA DIE...!

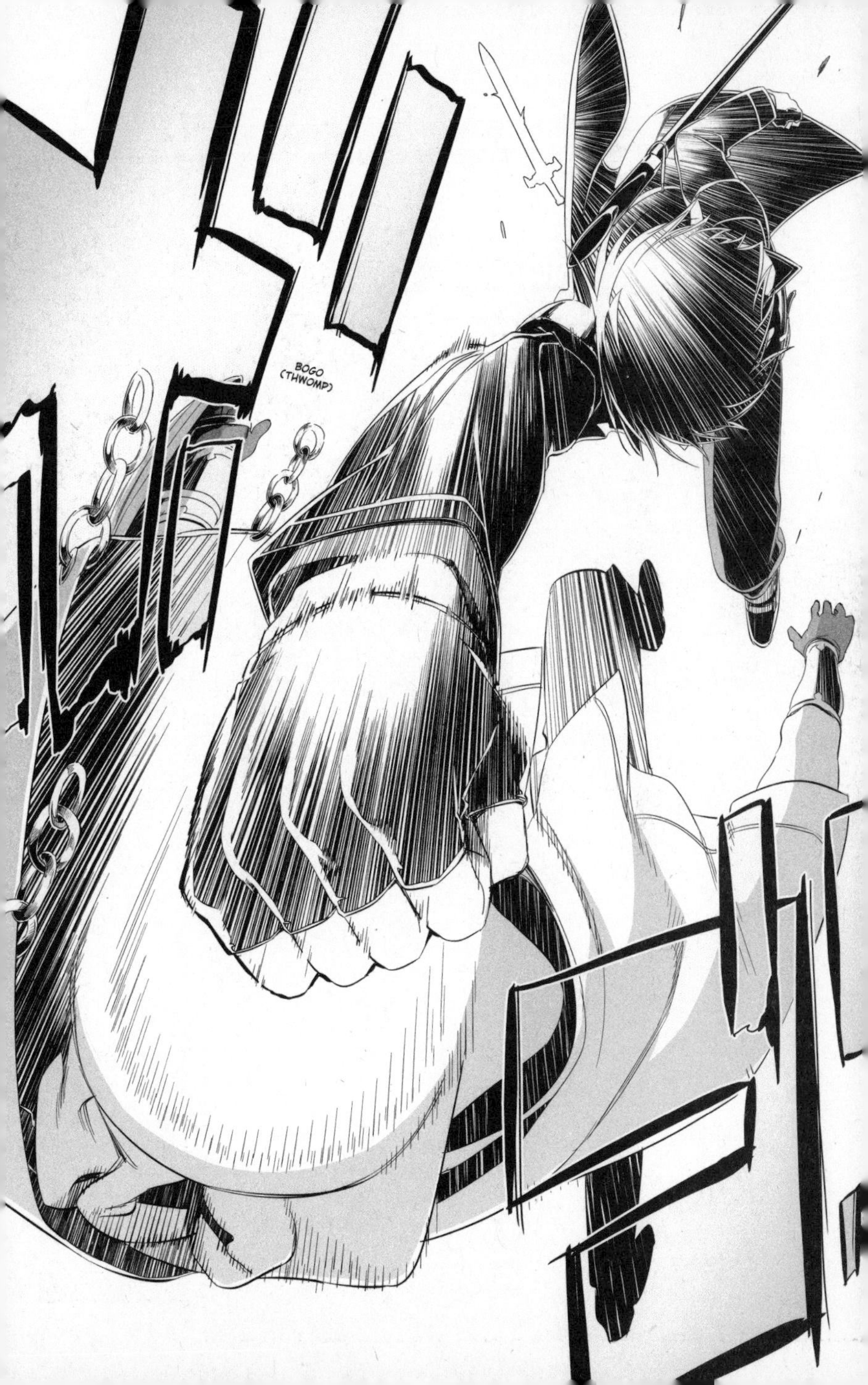
BOGO
(THWOMP)

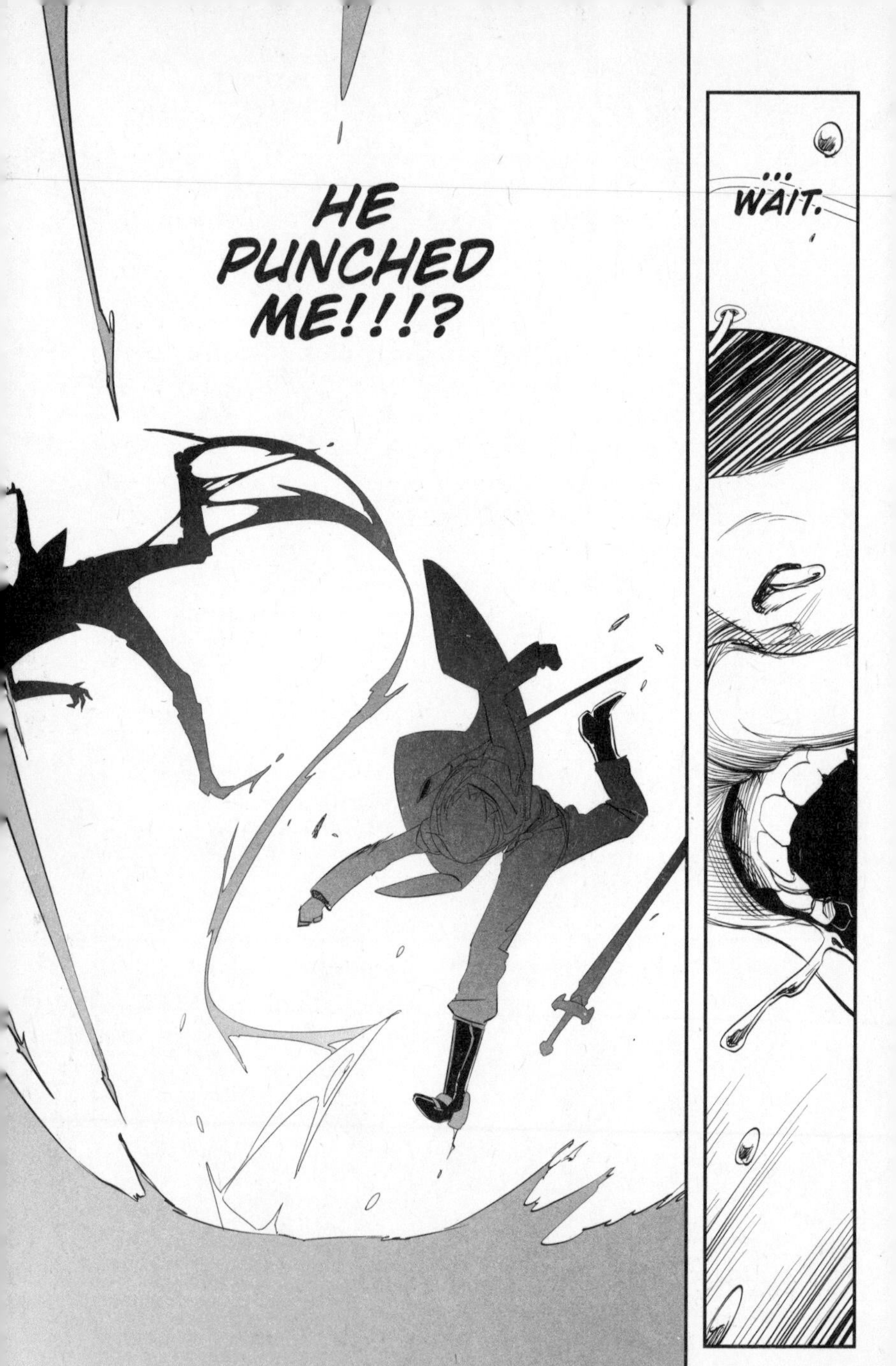
...WAIT.
HE PUNCHED ME!!!?

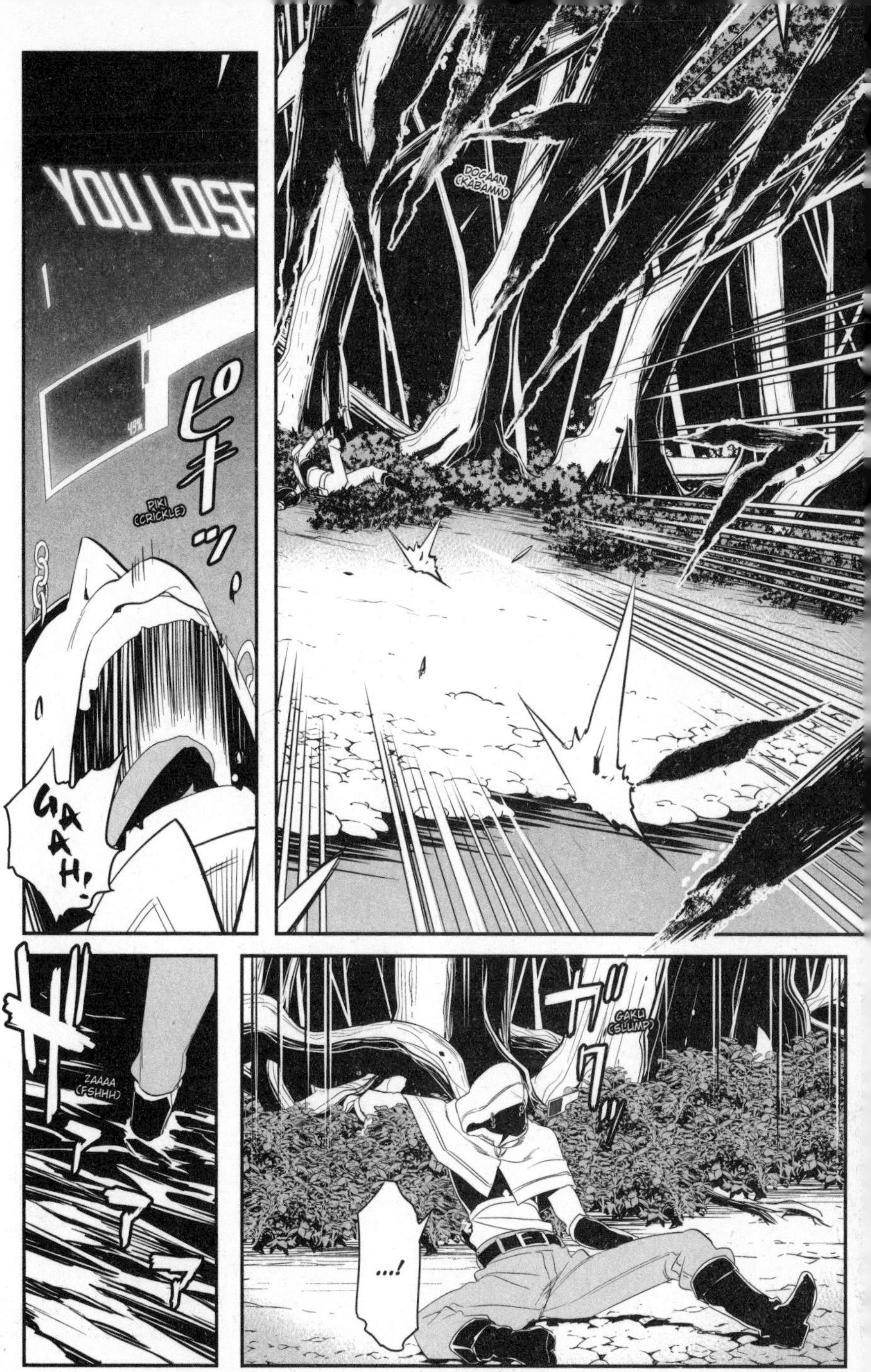
DOGAAN (KABAMM)
YOU LOSE
49%
PIKI (CRICKLE)
UAAH!
GAKU (SLUMP)
...!
ZAAAA (FSHHH)

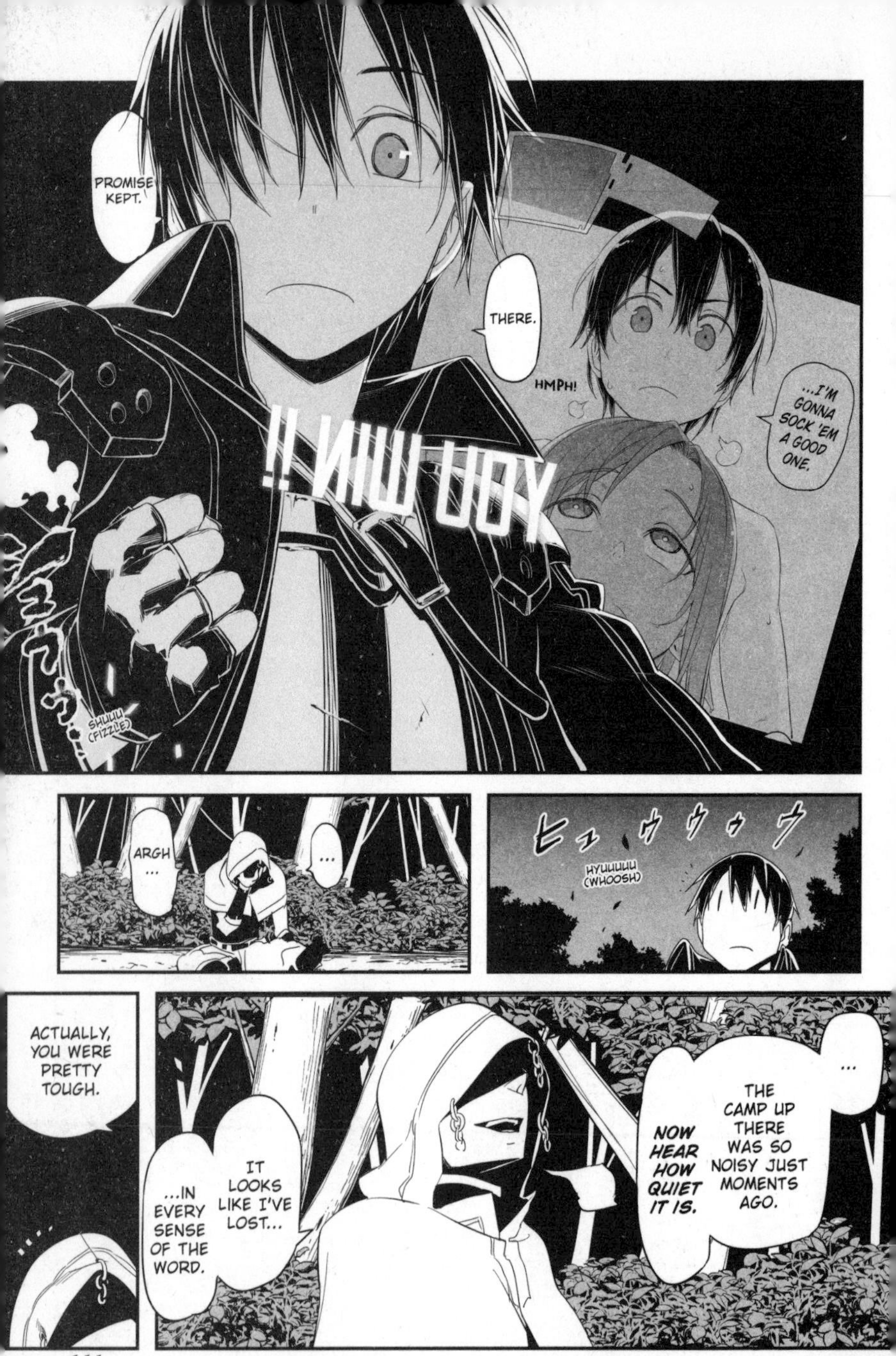
...I'M GONNA SOCK 'EM A GOOD ONE.
HMPH!
THERE.
YOU WIN!!
PROMISE KEPT.
SHUUU (FIZZLE)
HYUUUUU (WHOOSH)
...
ARGH ...
...
THE CAMP UP THERE WAS SO NOISY JUST MOMENTS AGO.
NOW HEAR HOW QUIET IT IS.
IT LOOKS LIKE I'VE LOST...
...IN EVERY SENSE OF THE WORD.
ACTUALLY, YOU WERE PRETTY TOUGH.
....

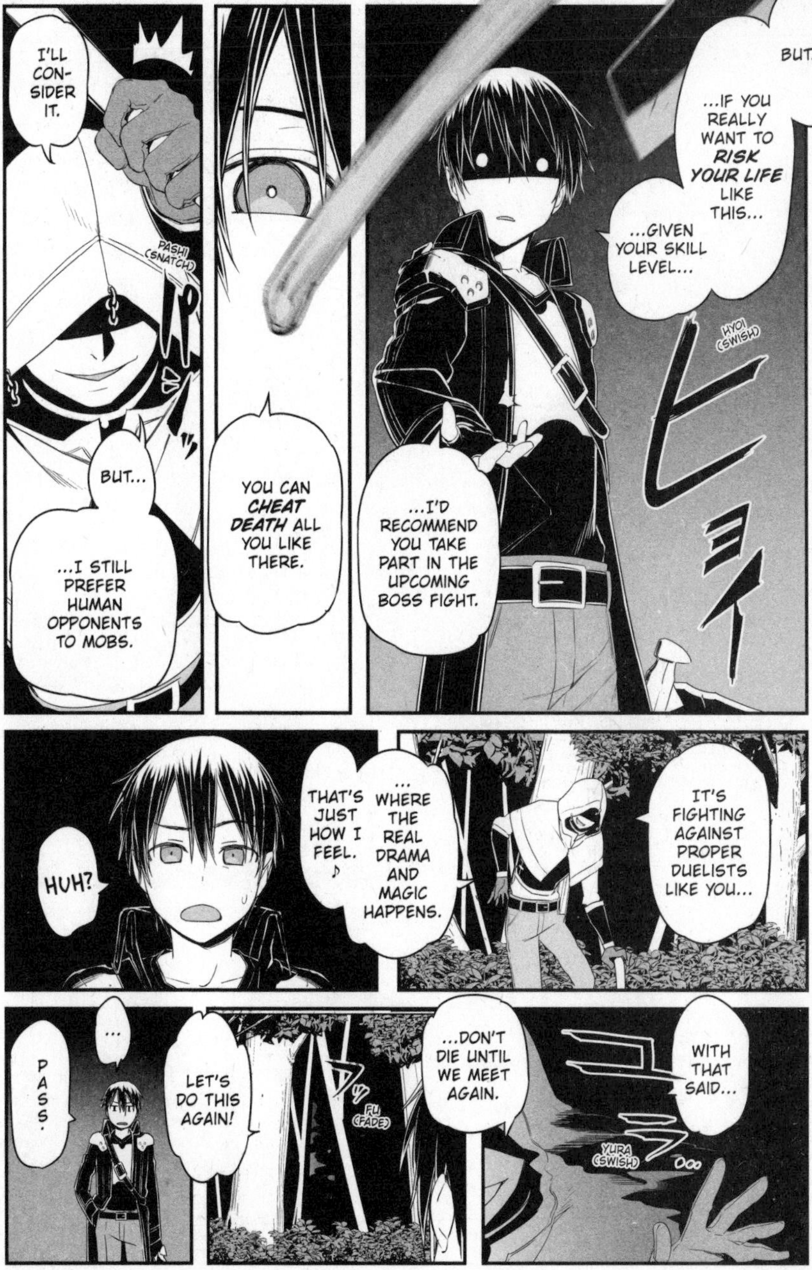
BUT...
...IF YOU REALLY WANT TO RISK YOUR LIFE LIKE THIS...
...GIVEN YOUR SKILL LEVEL...
HYOI (SWISH)
...I'D RECOMMEND YOU TAKE PART IN THE UPCOMING BOSS FIGHT.
YOU CAN CHEAT DEATH ALL YOU LIKE THERE.
I'LL CONSIDER IT.
PASHI (SNATCH)
BUT...
...I STILL PREFER HUMAN OPPONENTS TO MOBS.
IT'S FIGHTING AGAINST PROPER DUELISTS LIKE YOU...
...WHERE THE REAL DRAMA AND MAGIC HAPPENS.
THAT'S JUST HOW I FEEL. ♪
HUH?
WITH THAT SAID...
...DON'T DIE UNTIL WE MEET AGAIN.
YURA (SWISH)
FU (FADE)
LET'S DO THIS AGAIN!
...
PASS.

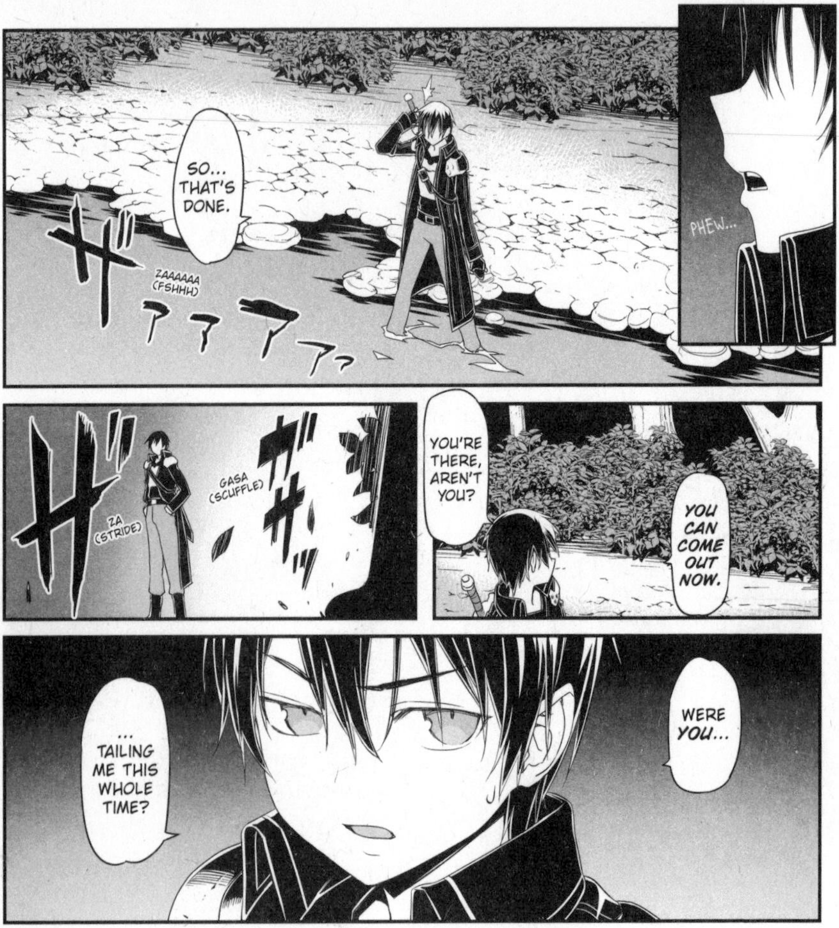
PHEW...
SO... THAT'S DONE.
ZAAAAAA (FSHHH)
YOU'RE THERE, AREN'T YOU?
YOU CAN COME OUT NOW.
GASA (SCUFFLE)
ZA (STRIDE)
WERE YOU...
... TAILING ME THIS WHOLE TIME?
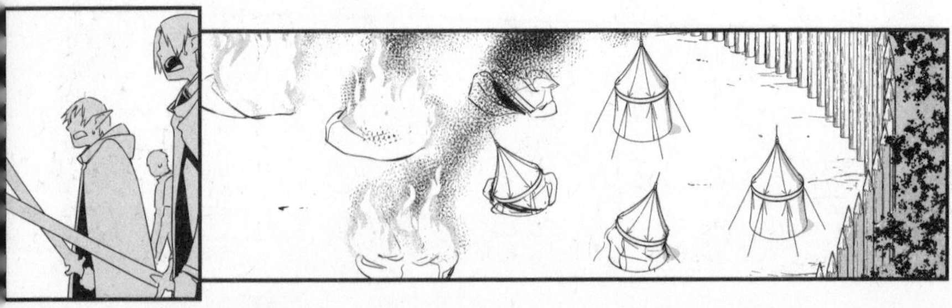

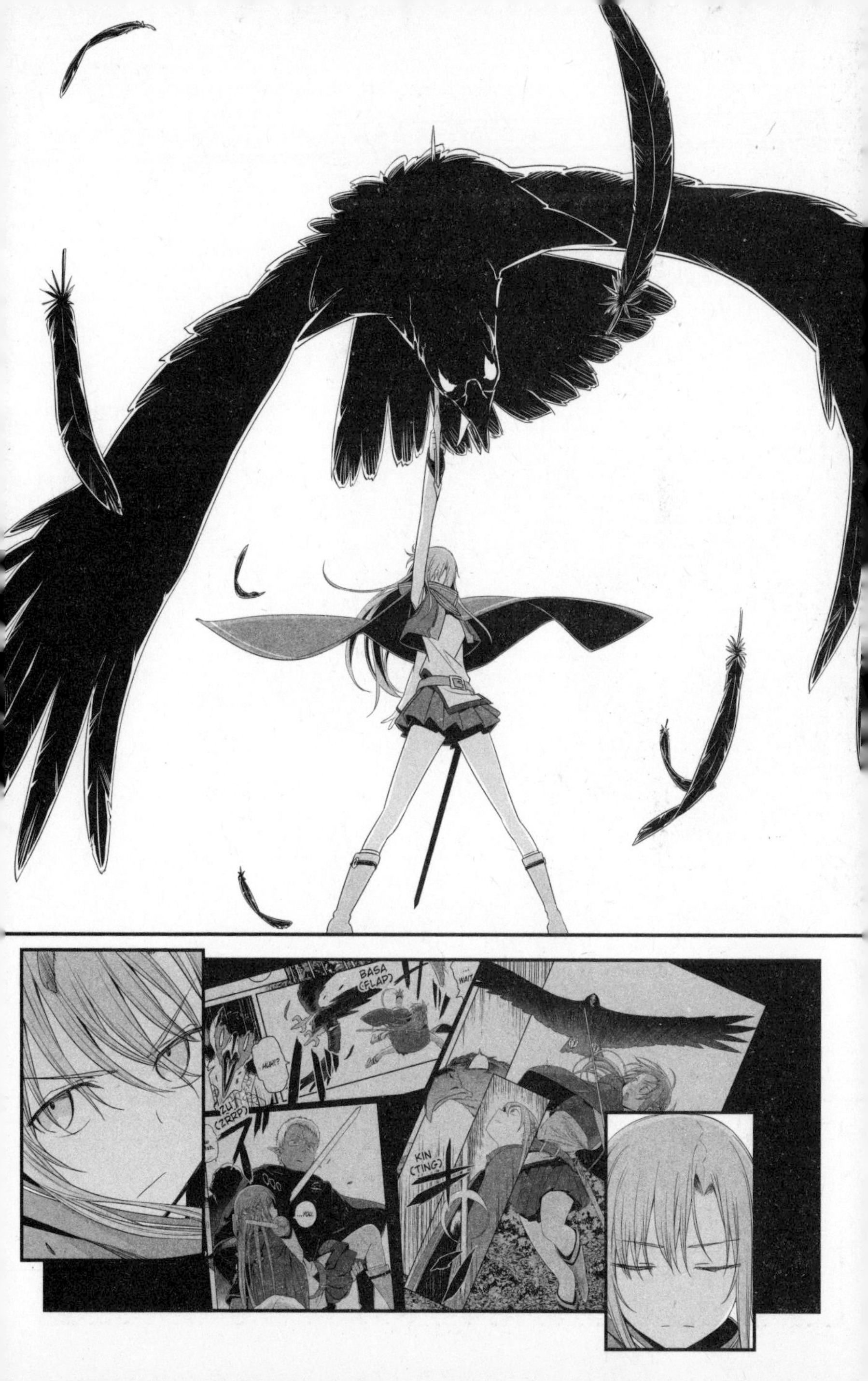
KIN (TING)
...WAIT
BASA (FLAP)
HUH!?
ZU!! (ZRRP)
...YOU!

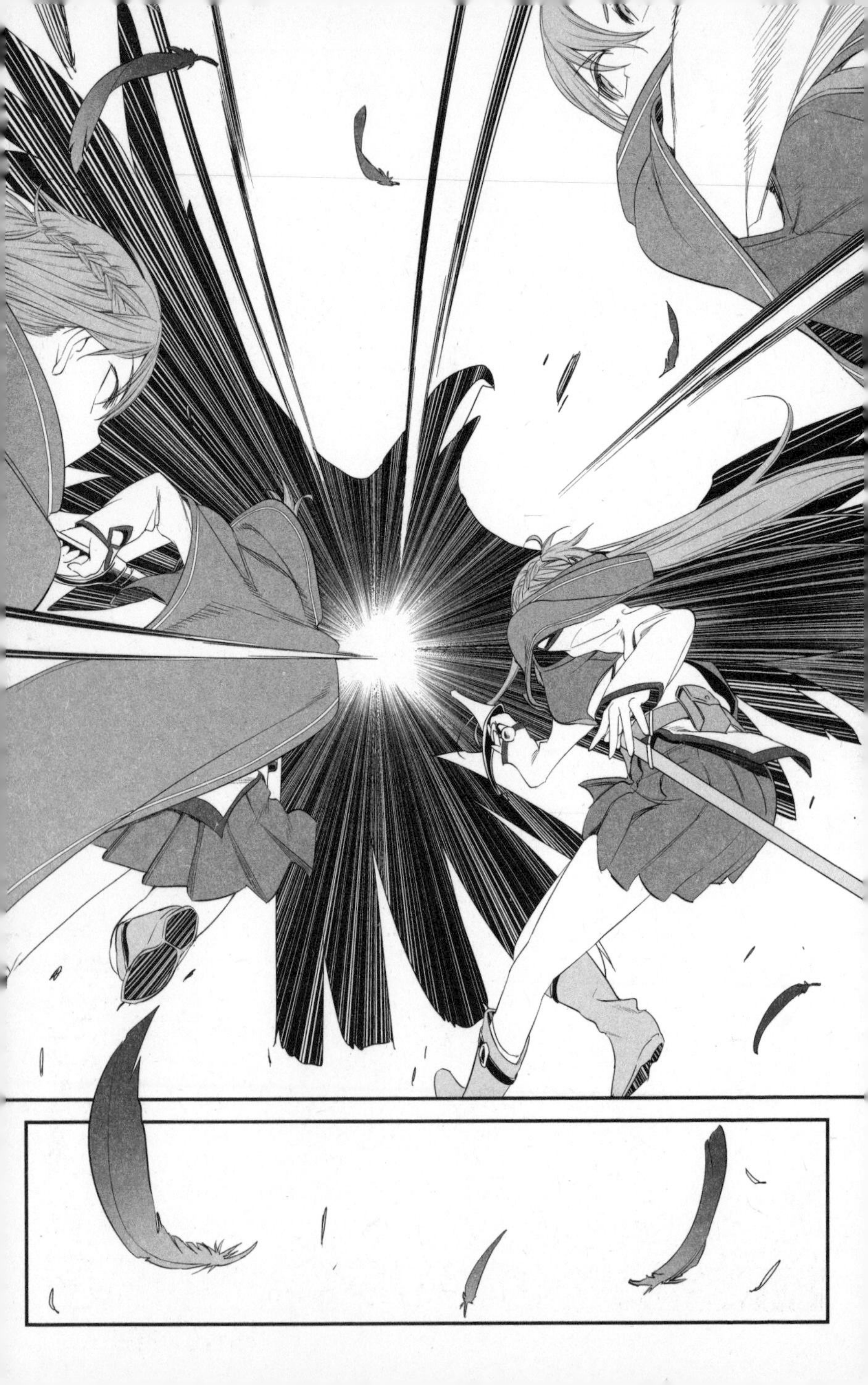

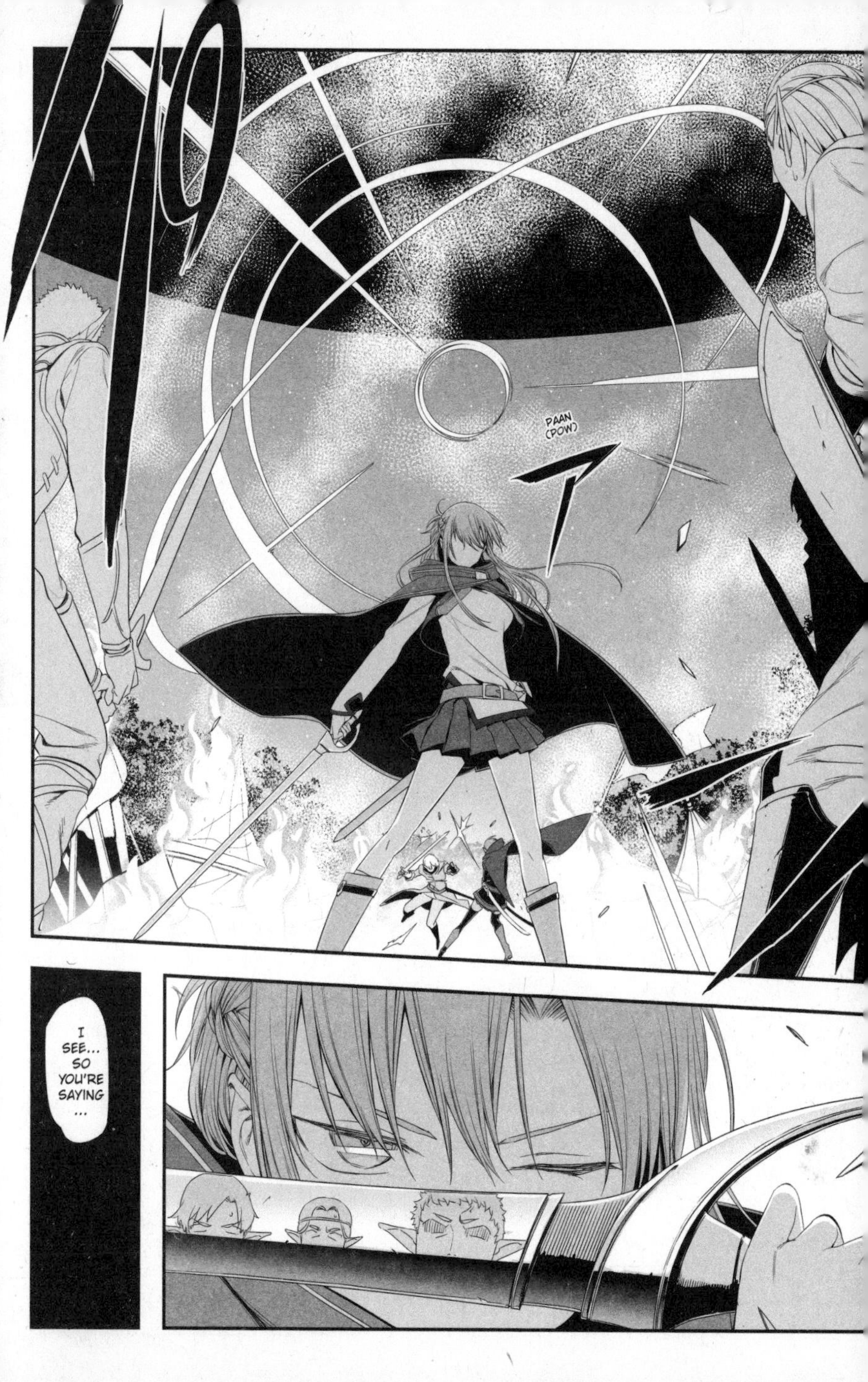
PAAN (POW)
I SEE... SO YOU'RE SAYING...

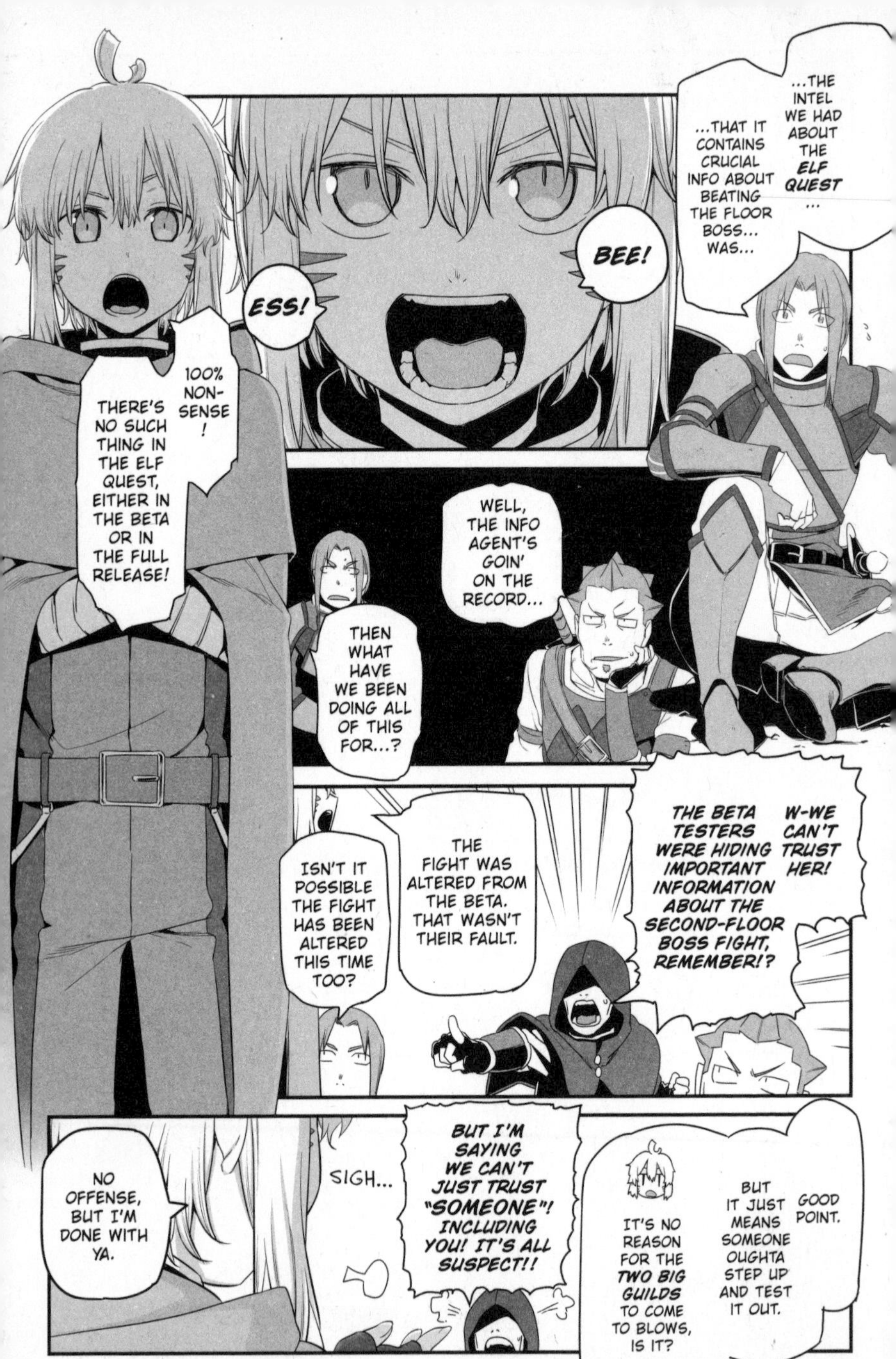

...THE INTEL WE HAD ABOUT THE ELF QUEST...
...THAT IT CONTAINS CRUCIAL INFO ABOUT BEATING THE FLOOR BOSS... WAS...
BEE!
ESS!
100% NONSENSE!
THERE'S NO SUCH THING IN THE ELF QUEST, EITHER IN THE BETA OR IN THE FULL RELEASE!
WELL, THE INFO AGENT'S GOIN' ON THE RECORD...
THEN WHAT HAVE WE BEEN DOING ALL OF THIS FOR...?
W-WE CAN'T TRUST HER!
THE BETA TESTERS WERE HIDING IMPORTANT INFORMATION ABOUT THE SECOND-FLOOR BOSS FIGHT, REMEMBER!?
THE FIGHT WAS ALTERED FROM THE BETA. THAT WASN'T THEIR FAULT.
ISN'T IT POSSIBLE THE FIGHT HAS BEEN ALTERED THIS TIME TOO?
GOOD POINT.
BUT IT JUST MEANS SOMEONE OUGHTA STEP UP AND TEST IT OUT.
IT'S NO REASON FOR THE TWO BIG GUILDS TO COME TO BLOWS, IS IT?
BUT I'M SAYING WE CAN'T JUST TRUST "SOMEONE"! INCLUDING YOU! IT'S ALL SUSPECT!!
SIGH...
NO OFFENSE, BUT I'M DONE WITH YA.

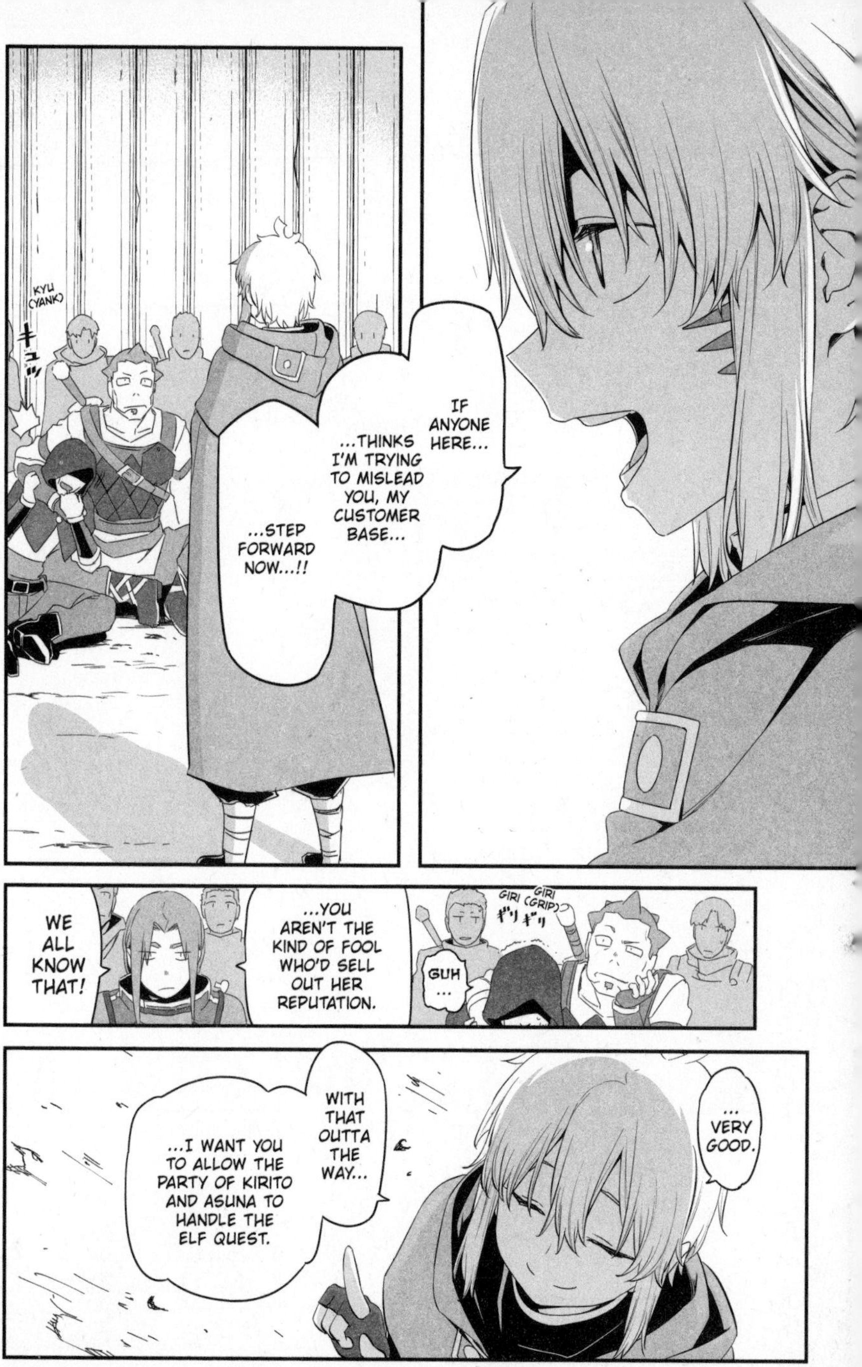
IF ANYONE HERE...
...THINKS I'M TRYING TO MISLEAD YOU, MY CUSTOMER BASE...
...STEP FORWARD NOW...!!
KYU (YANK)
キュッ
GIRI GIRI (GRIP)
ギリギリ
GUH ...
...YOU AREN'T THE KIND OF FOOL WHO'D SELL OUT HER REPUTATION.
WE ALL KNOW THAT!
... VERY GOOD.
WITH THAT OUTTA THE WAY...
...I WANT YOU TO ALLOW THE PARTY OF KIRITO AND ASUNA TO HANDLE THE ELF QUEST.

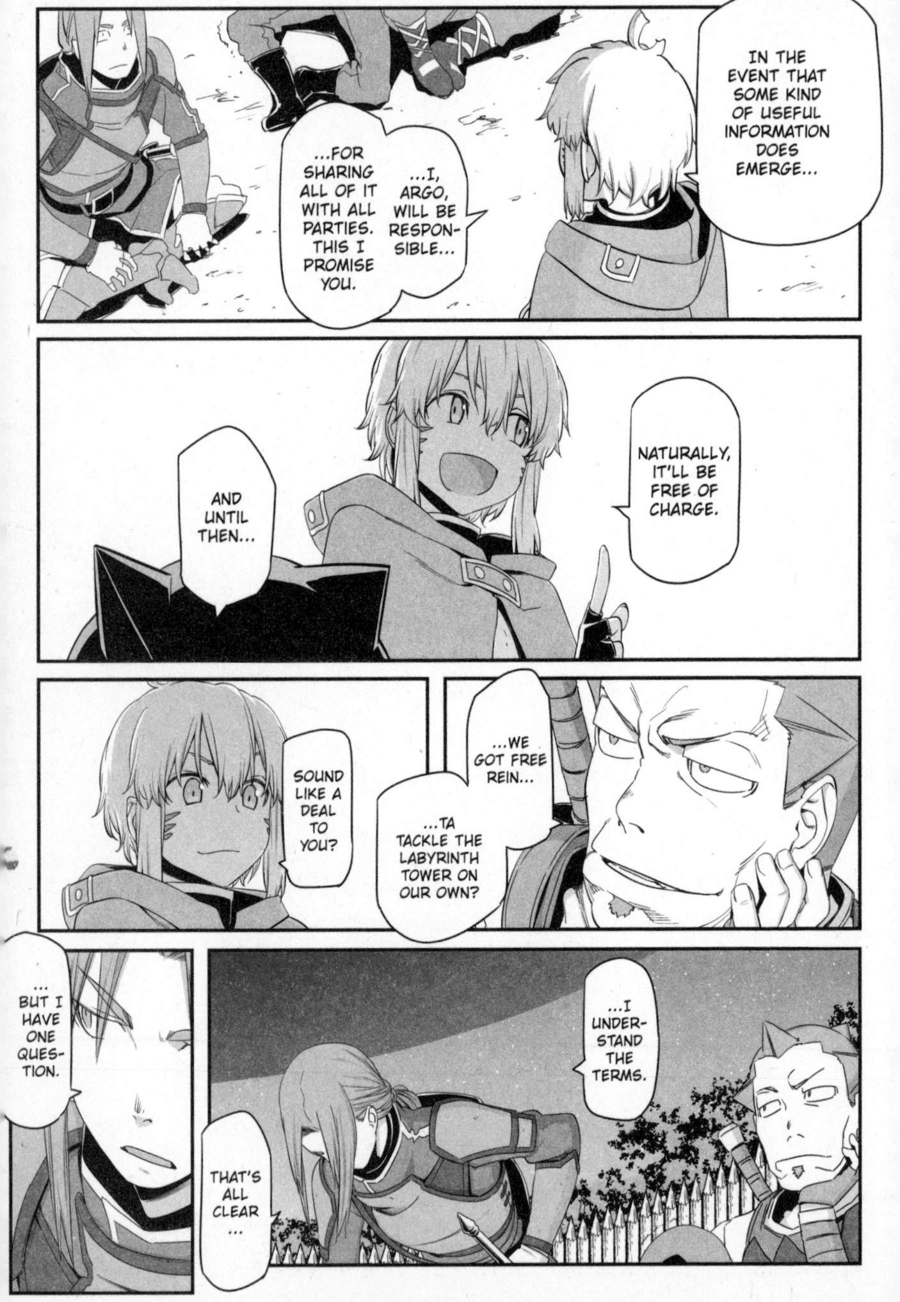
IN THE EVENT THAT SOME KIND OF USEFUL INFORMATION DOES EMERGE...
...I, ARGO, WILL BE RESPONSIBLE...
...FOR SHARING ALL OF IT WITH ALL PARTIES. THIS I PROMISE YOU.
NATURALLY, IT'LL BE FREE OF CHARGE.
AND UNTIL THEN...
...WE GOT FREE REIN...
...TA TACKLE THE LABYRINTH TOWER ON OUR OWN?
SOUND LIKE A DEAL TO YOU?
...I UNDERSTAND THE TERMS.
THAT'S ALL CLEAR...
...BUT I HAVE ONE QUESTION.

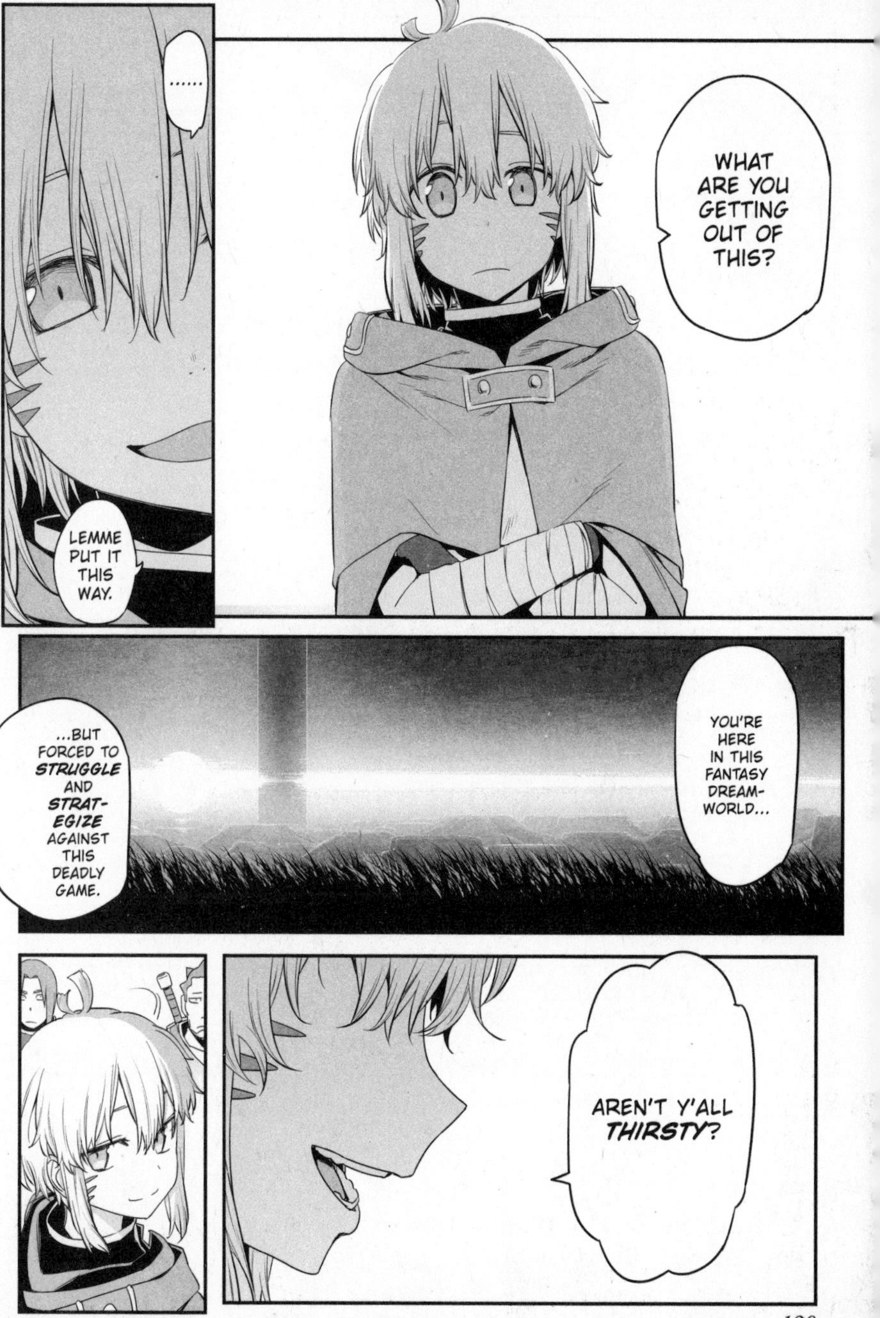
WHAT ARE YOU GETTING OUT OF THIS?
......
LEMME PUT IT THIS WAY.
YOU'RE HERE IN THIS FANTASY DREAM-WORLD...
...BUT FORCED TO *STRUGGLE* AND *STRAT-EGIZE* AGAINST THIS DEADLY GAME.
AREN'T Y'ALL *THIRSTY*?

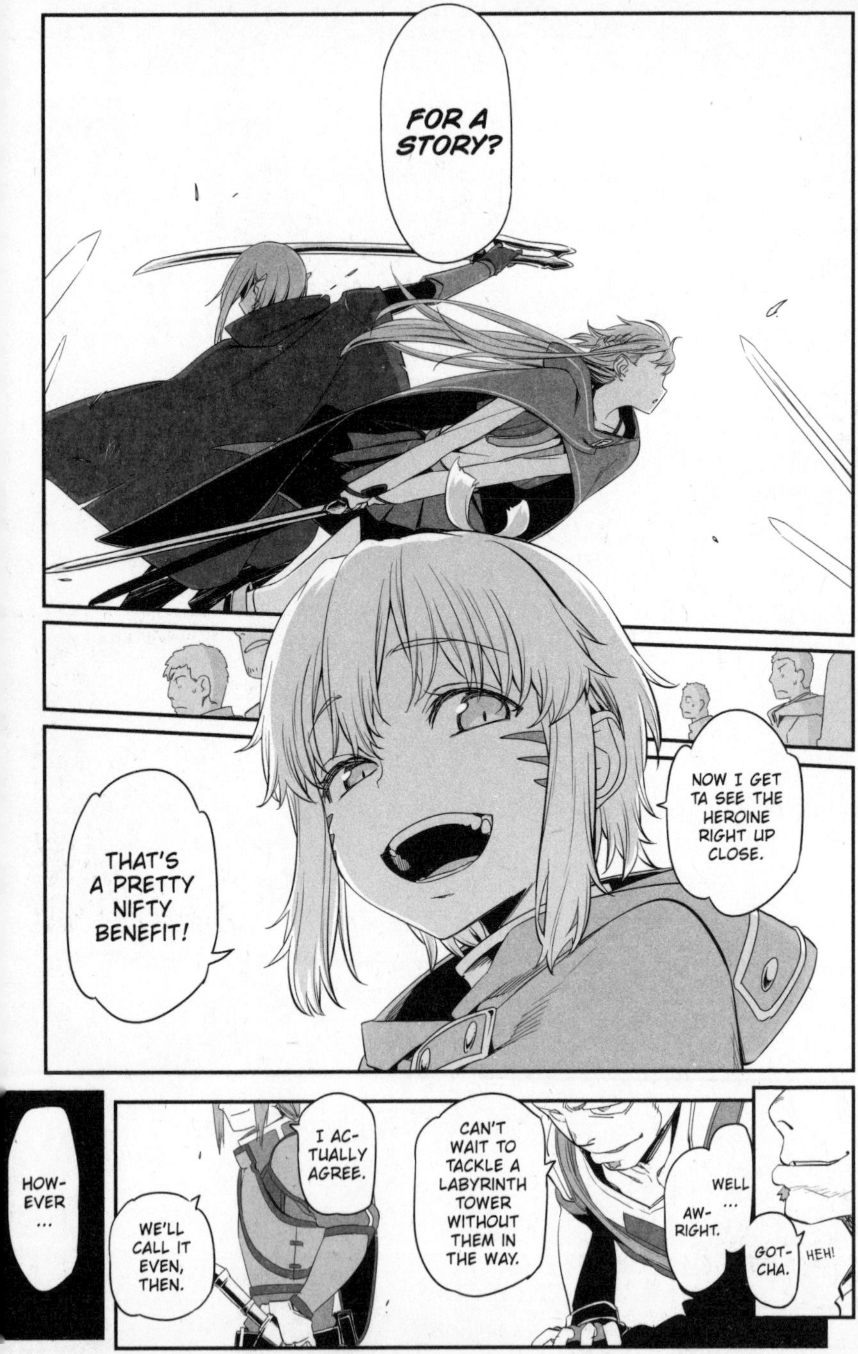
FOR A STORY?
NOW I GET TA SEE THE HEROINE RIGHT UP CLOSE.
THAT'S A PRETTY NIFTY BENEFIT!
HEH!
GOT-CHA.
WELL ... AW-RIGHT.
CAN'T WAIT TO TACKLE A LABYRINTH TOWER WITHOUT THEM IN THE WAY.
I AC-TUALLY AGREE.
WE'LL CALL IT EVEN, THEN.
HOW-EVER ...

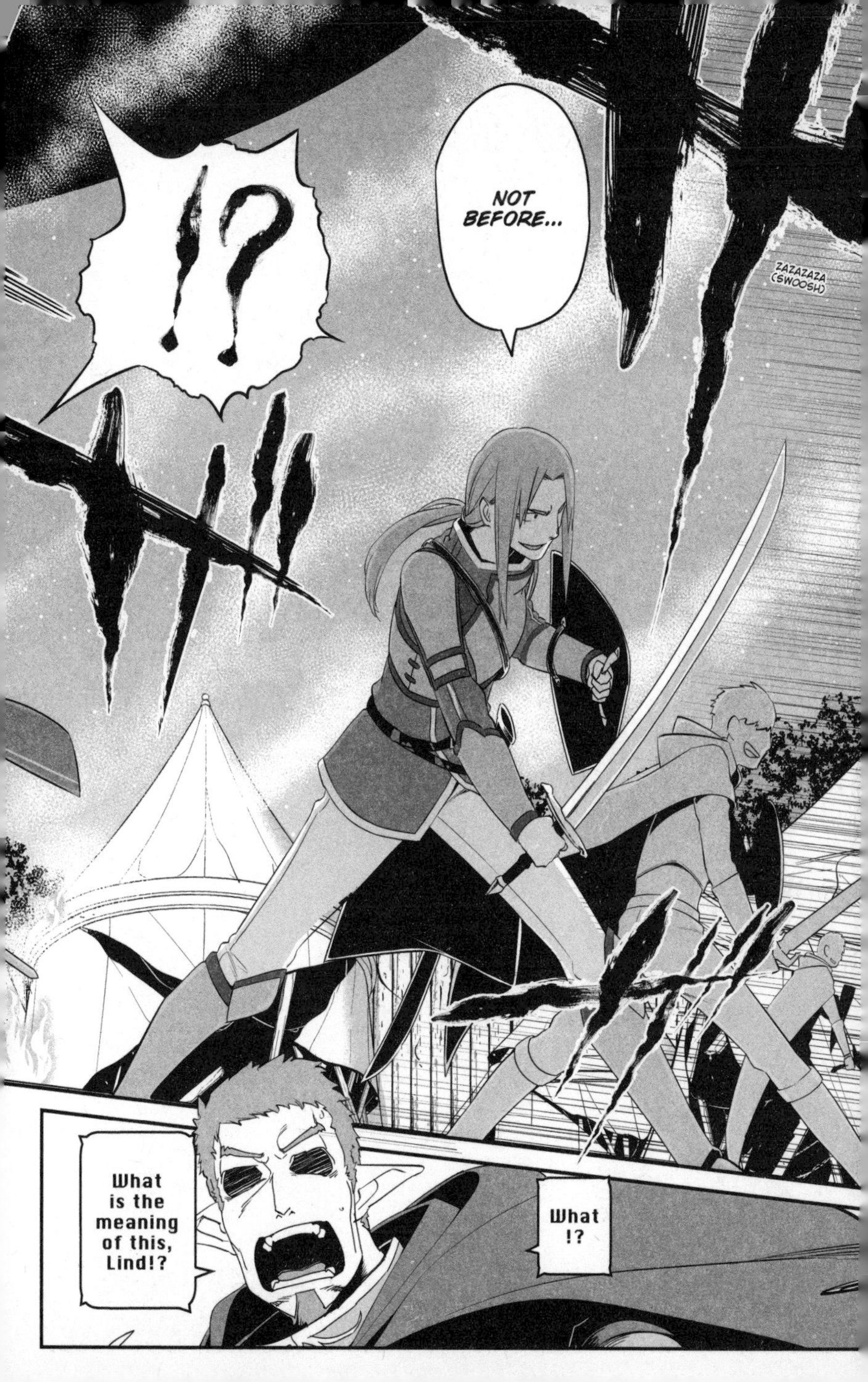
NOT BEFORE...
!?
ZAZAZAZA (SWOOSH)
What !?
What is the meaning of this, Lind!?

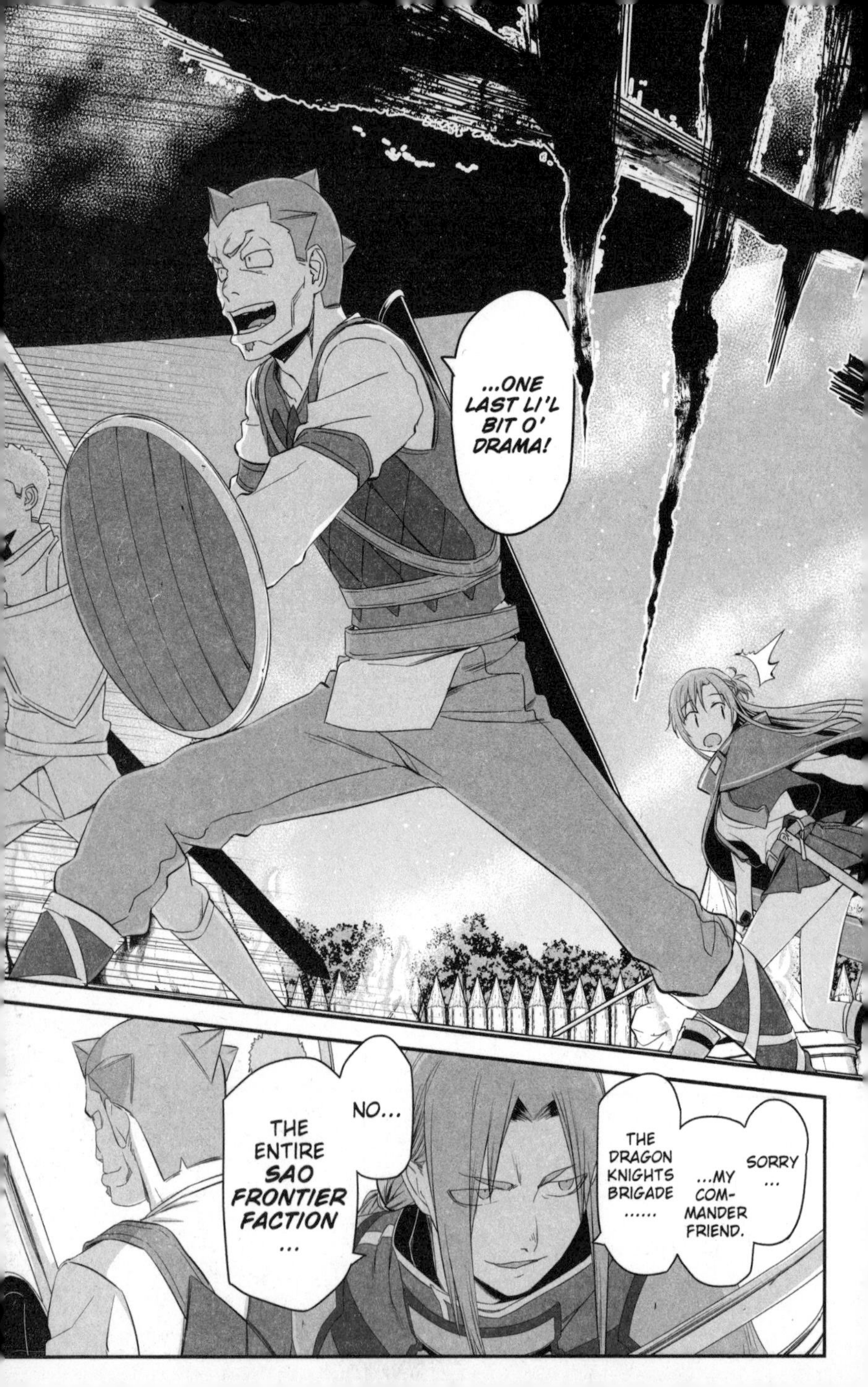
...ONE LAST LI'L BIT O' DRAMA!
SORRY ...
...MY COM-MANDER FRIEND.
THE DRAGON KNIGHTS BRIGADE ......
NO...
THE ENTIRE *SAO FRONTIER FACTION* ...

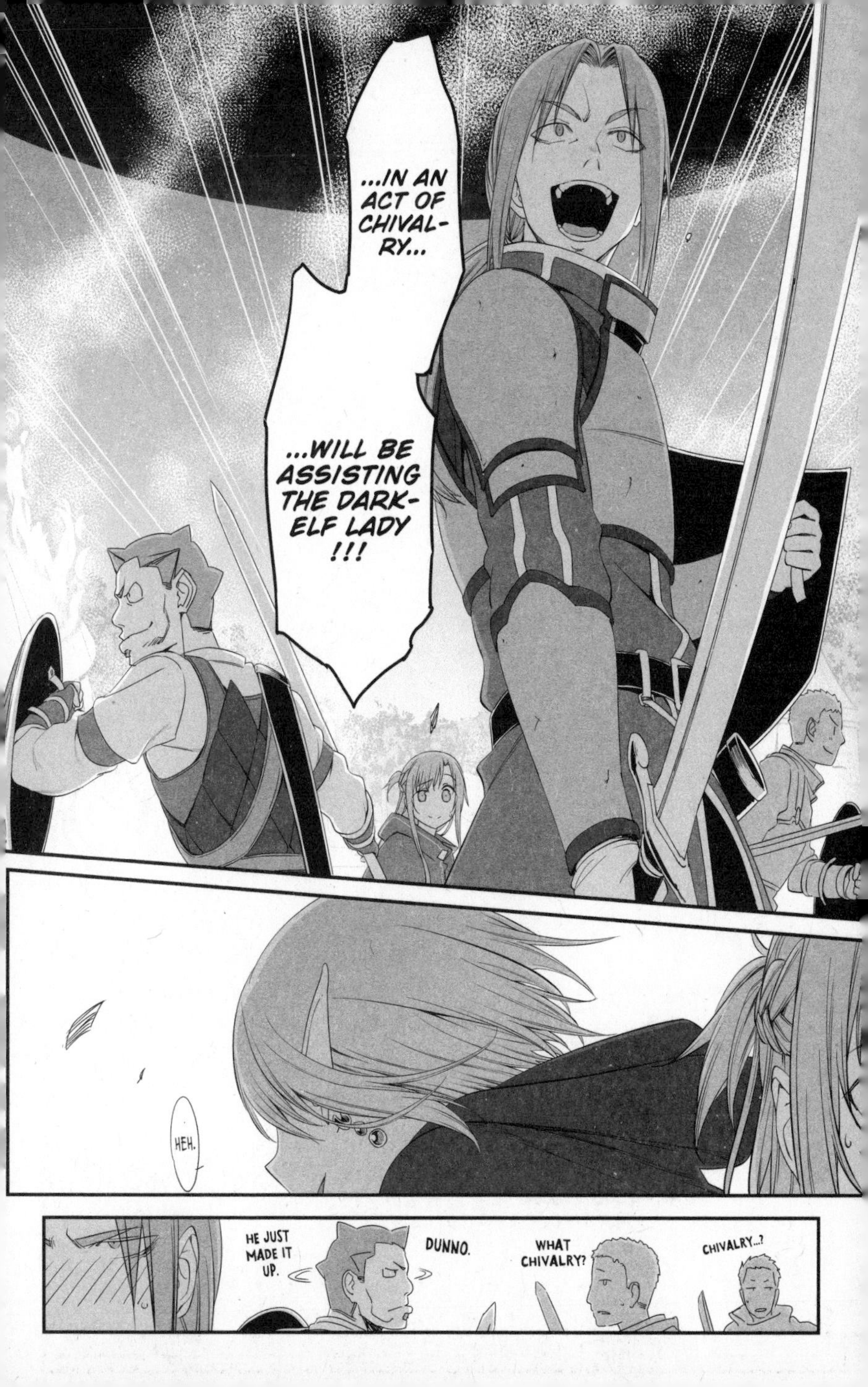
...IN AN ACT OF CHIVAL-RY...
...WILL BE ASSISTING THE DARK-ELF LADY!!!
HEH.
CHIVALRY...?
WHAT CHIVALRY?
DUNNO.
HE JUST MADE IT UP.

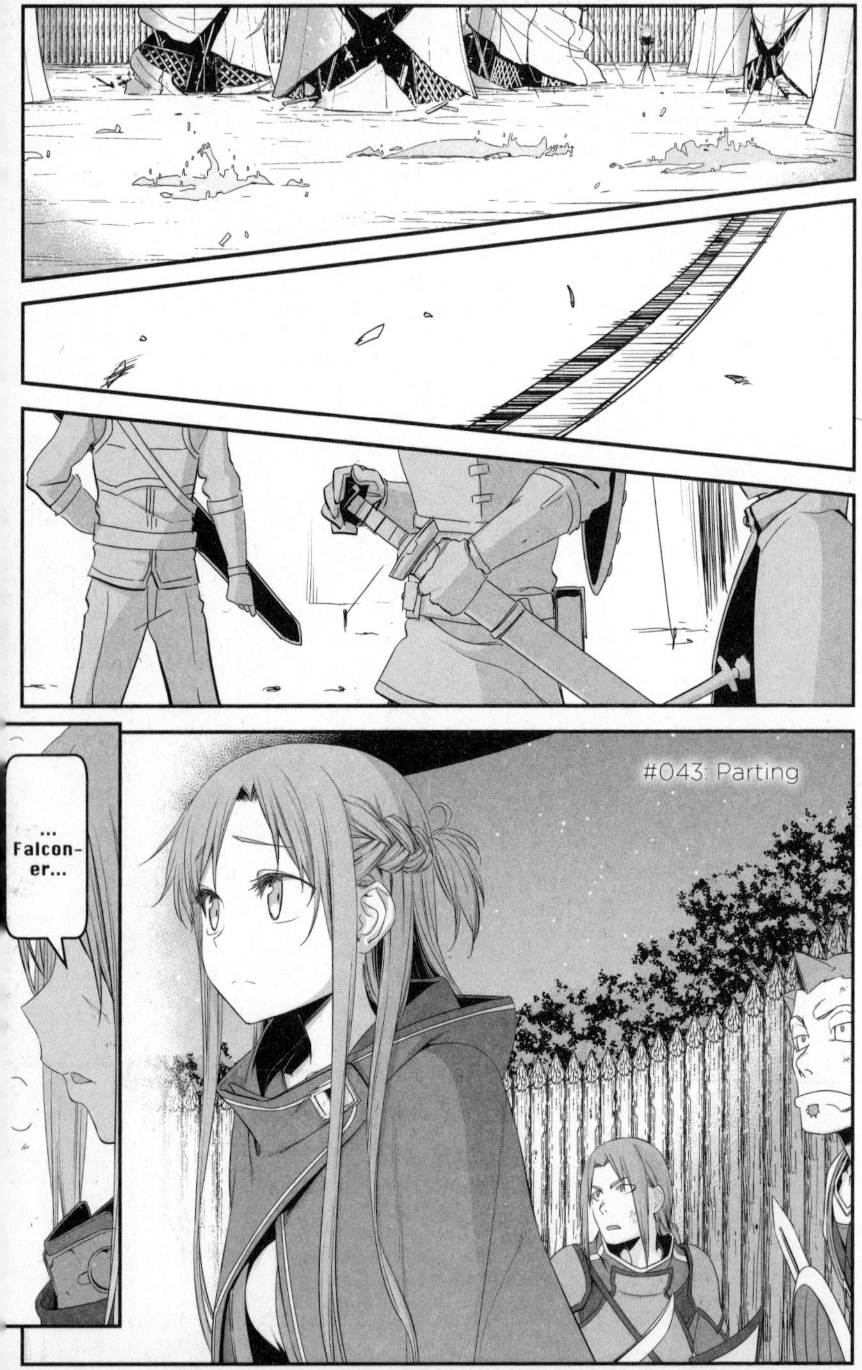
#043: Parting
... Falcon- er...

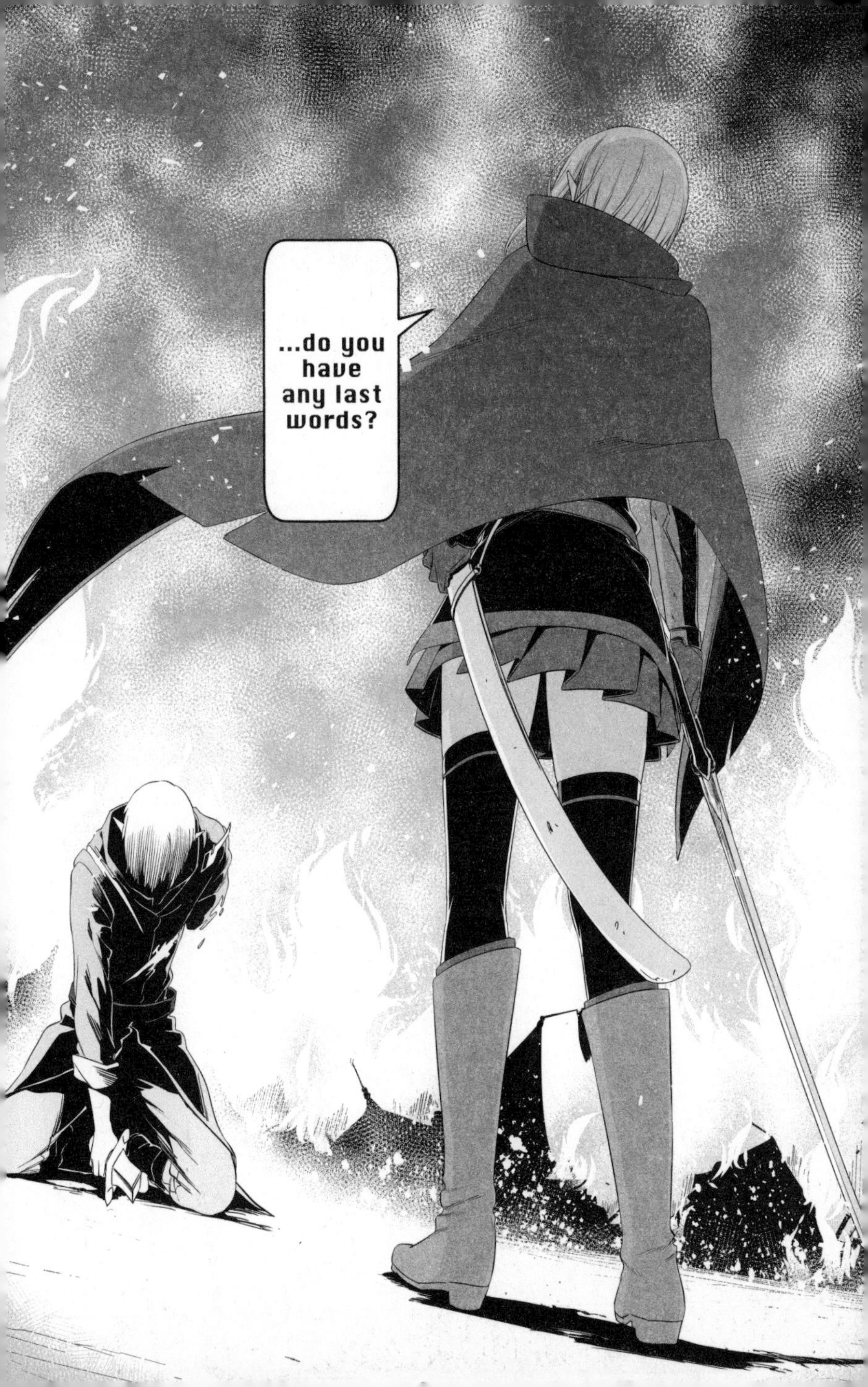
...do you have any last words?

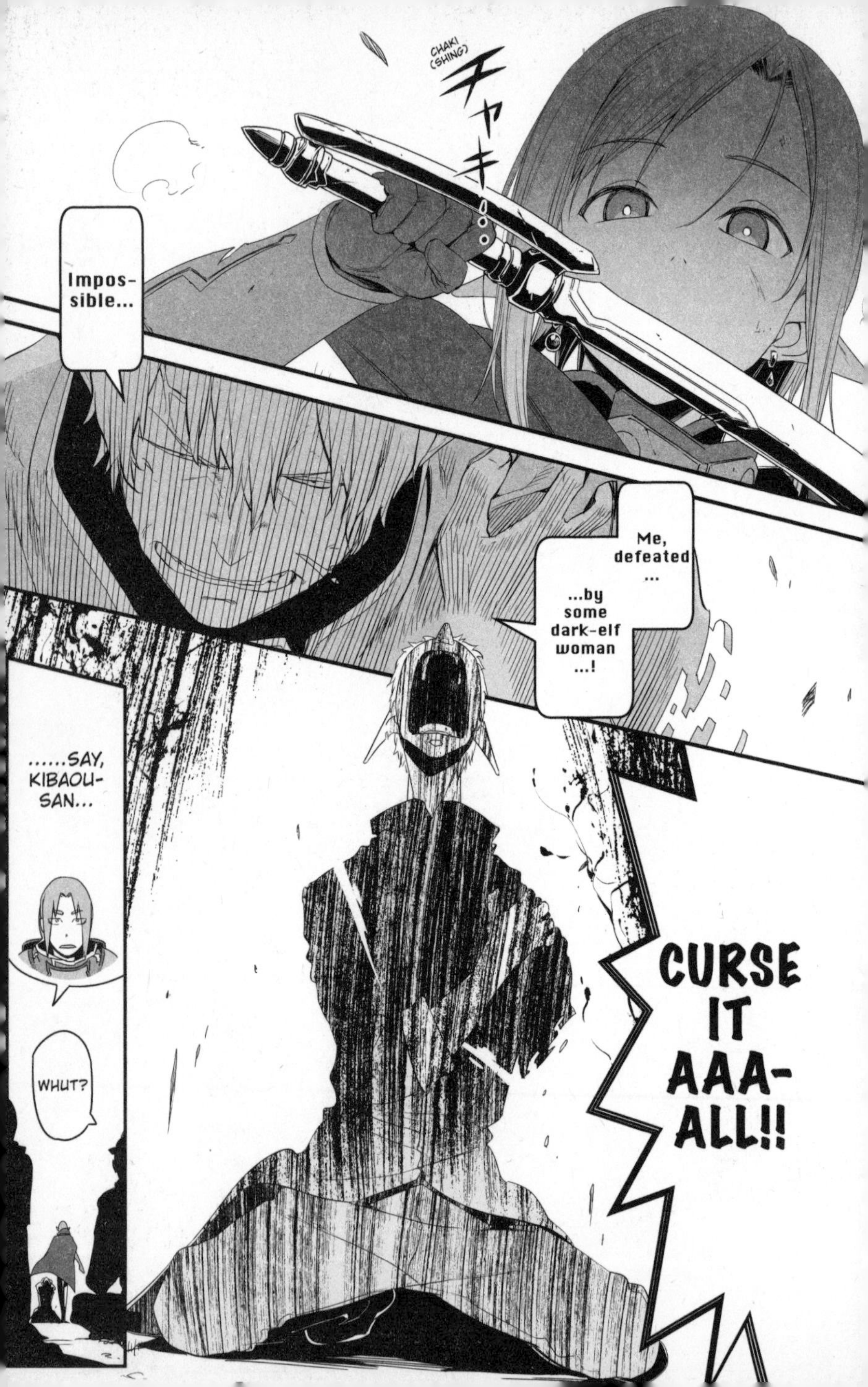
CHAKI (SHING)
チャキ
Impos-sible...
Me, defeated ...
...by some dark-elf woman ...!
CURSE IT AAA-ALL!!
......SAY, KIBAOU-SAN...
WHUT?

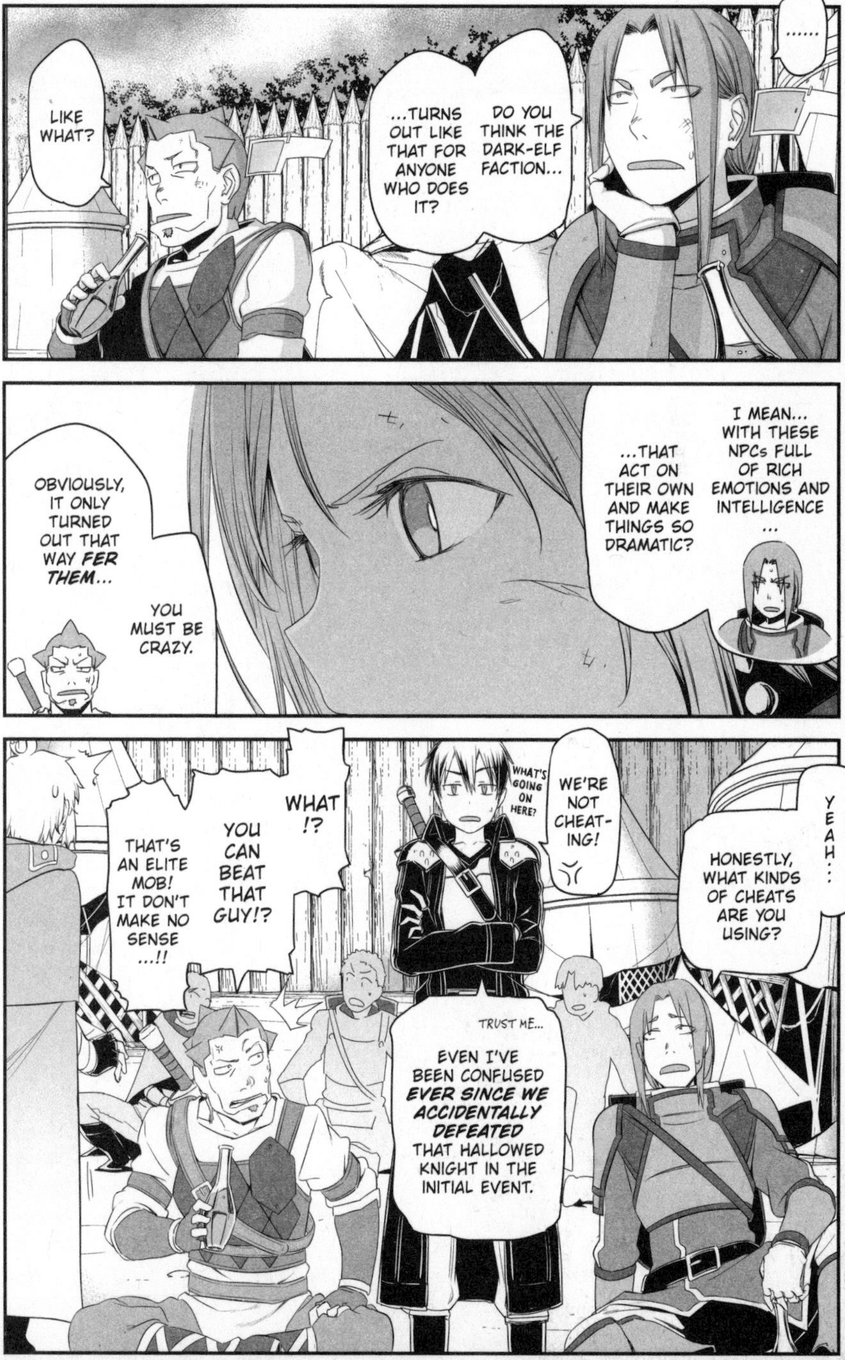
......
DO YOU THINK THE DARK-ELF FACTION...
...TURNS OUT LIKE THAT FOR ANYONE WHO DOES IT?
LIKE WHAT?
I MEAN... WITH THESE NPCs FULL OF RICH EMOTIONS AND INTELLIGENCE ...
...THAT ACT ON THEIR OWN AND MAKE THINGS SO DRAMATIC?
OBVIOUSLY, IT ONLY TURNED OUT THAT WAY ***FER THEM***...
YOU MUST BE CRAZY.
YEAH...
HONESTLY, WHAT KINDS OF CHEATS ARE YOU USING?
WE'RE NOT CHEATING!
WHAT'S GOING ON HERE?
WHAT!?
YOU CAN BEAT THAT GUY!?
THAT'S AN ELITE MOB! IT DON'T MAKE NO SENSE...!!
TRUST ME...
EVEN I'VE BEEN CONFUSED ***EVER SINCE WE ACCIDENTALLY DEFEATED*** THAT HALLOWED KNIGHT IN THE INITIAL EVENT.

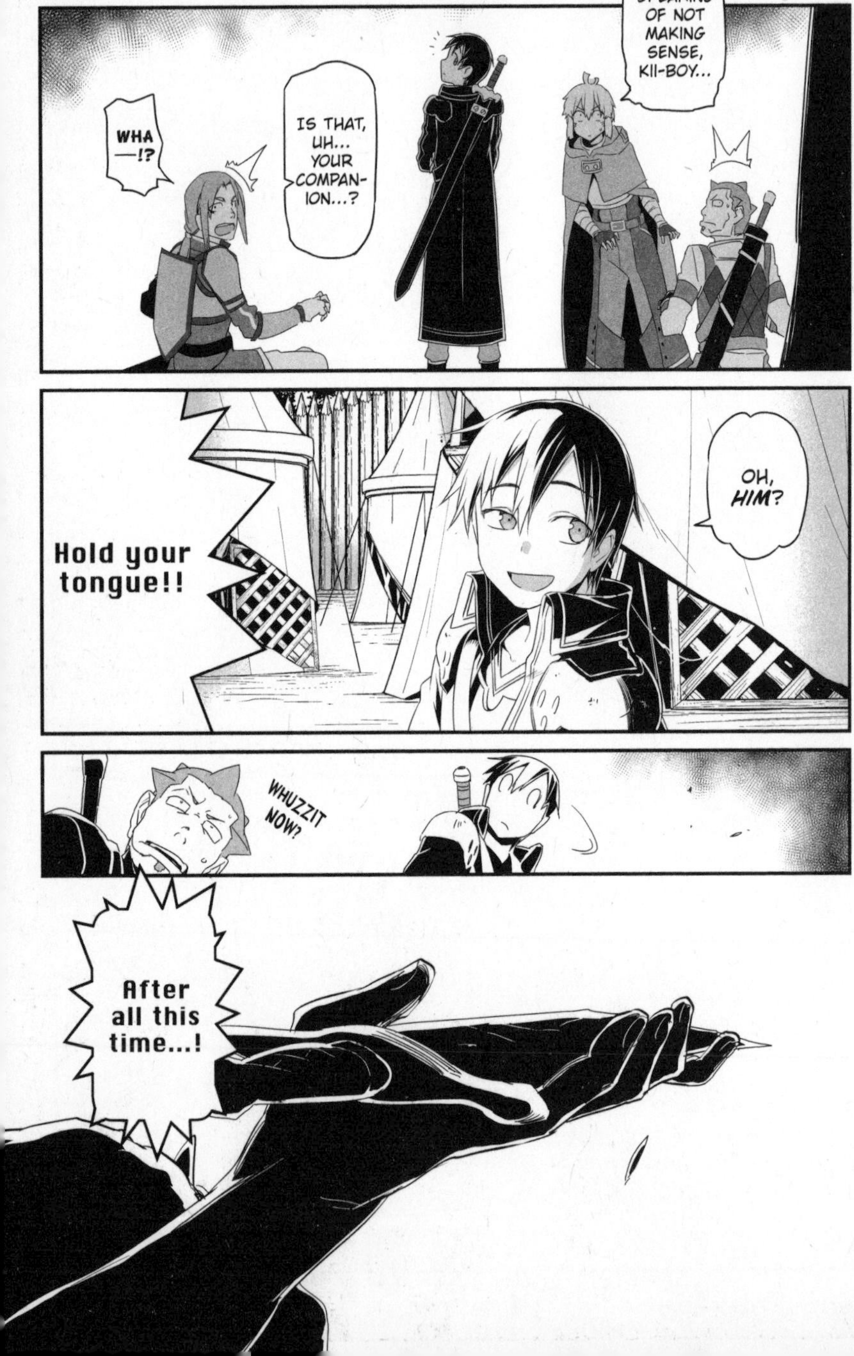
SPEAKING OF NOT MAKING SENSE, KII-BOY...
IS THAT, UH... YOUR COMPANION...?
WHA—!?
OH, HIM?
Hold your tongue!!
WHUZZIT NOW?
After all this time...!

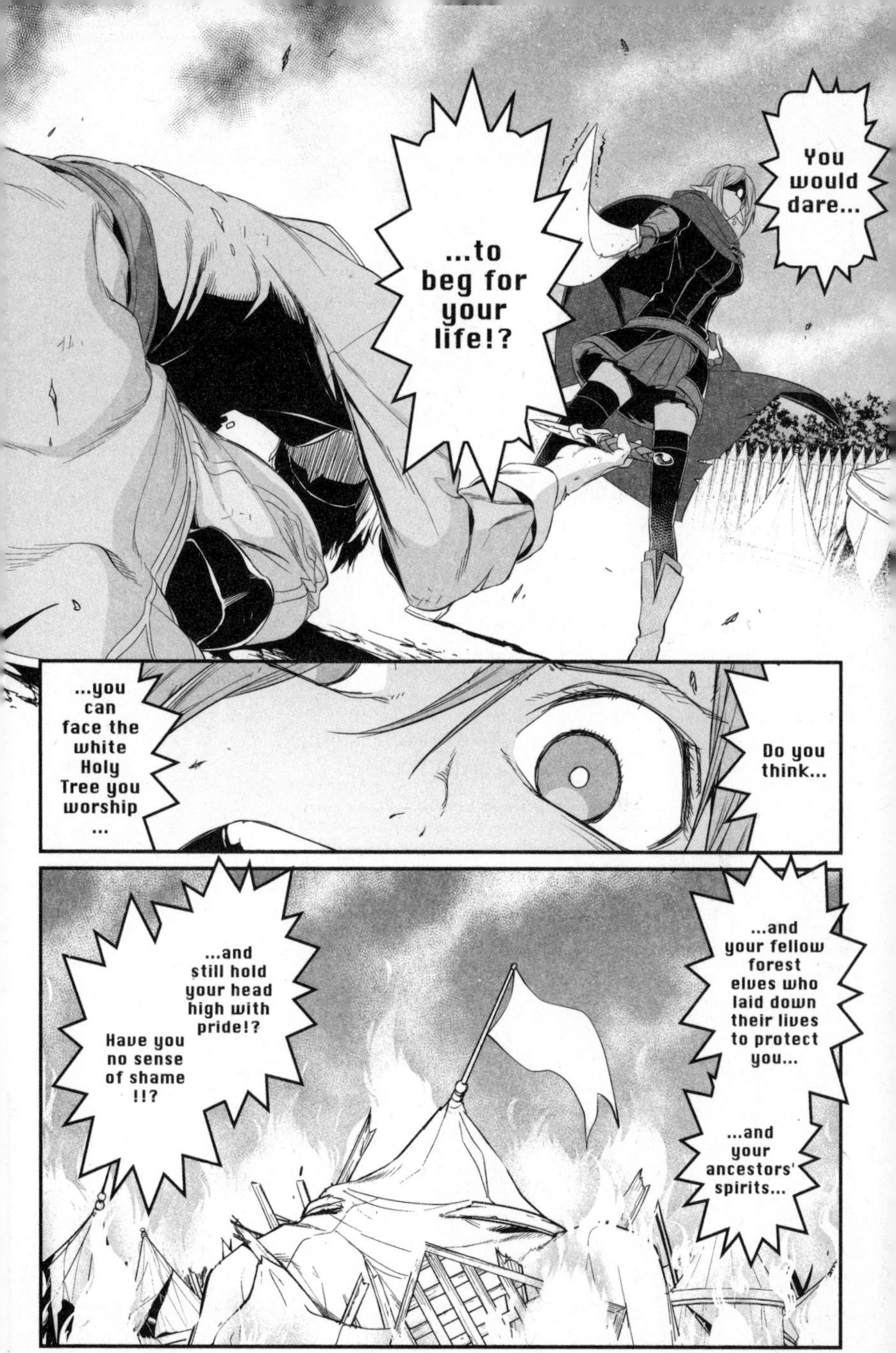
You would dare...
...to beg for your life!?
Do you think...
...you can face the white Holy Tree you worship ...
...and your fellow forest elves who laid down their lives to protect you...
...and your ancestors' spirits...
...and still hold your head high with pride!?
Have you no sense of shame !!?

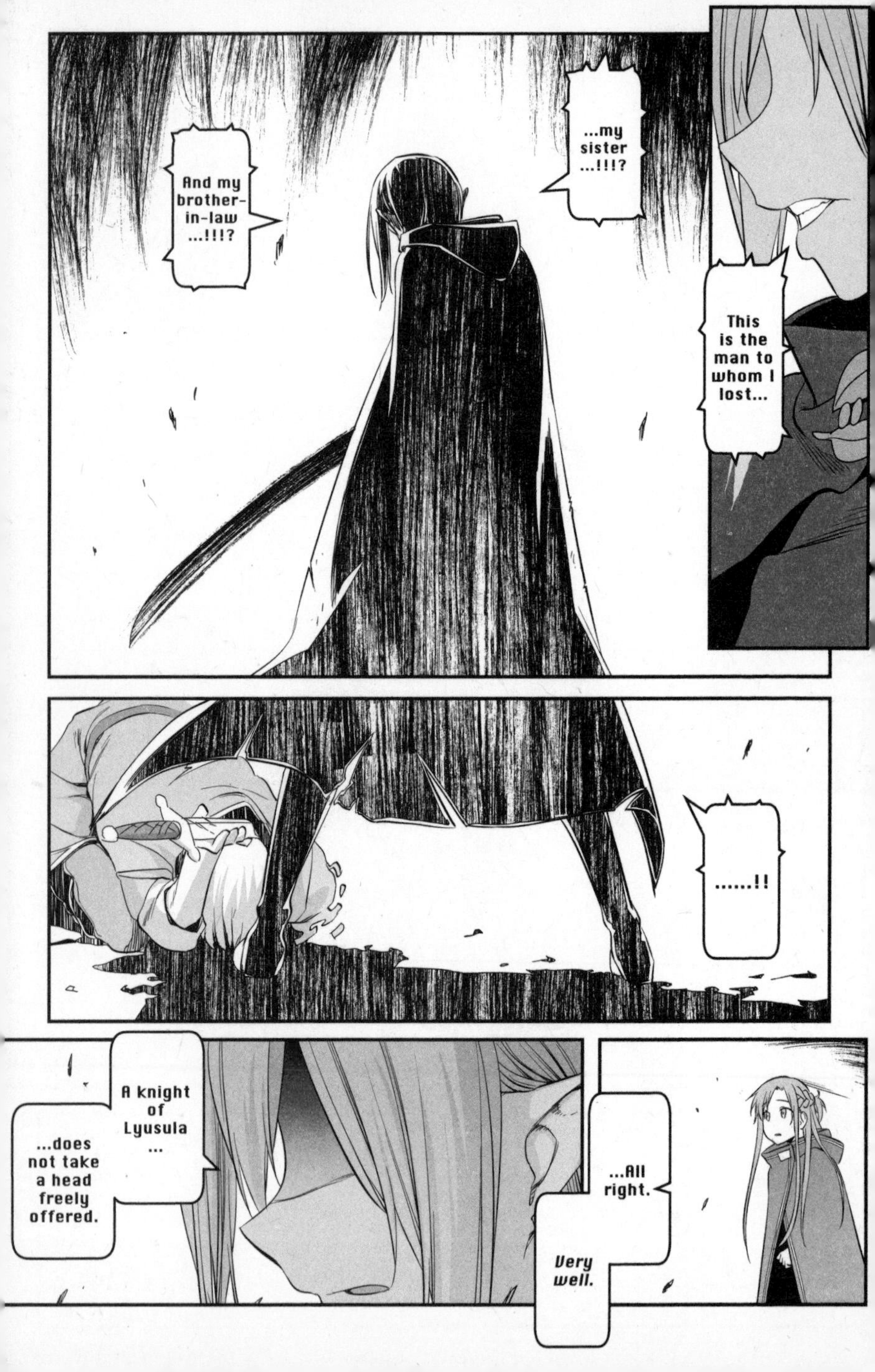
This is the man to whom I lost...
...my sister ...!!!?
And my brother-in-law ...!!!?
......!!
...All right.
Very well.
A knight of Lyusula ...
...does not take a head freely offered.

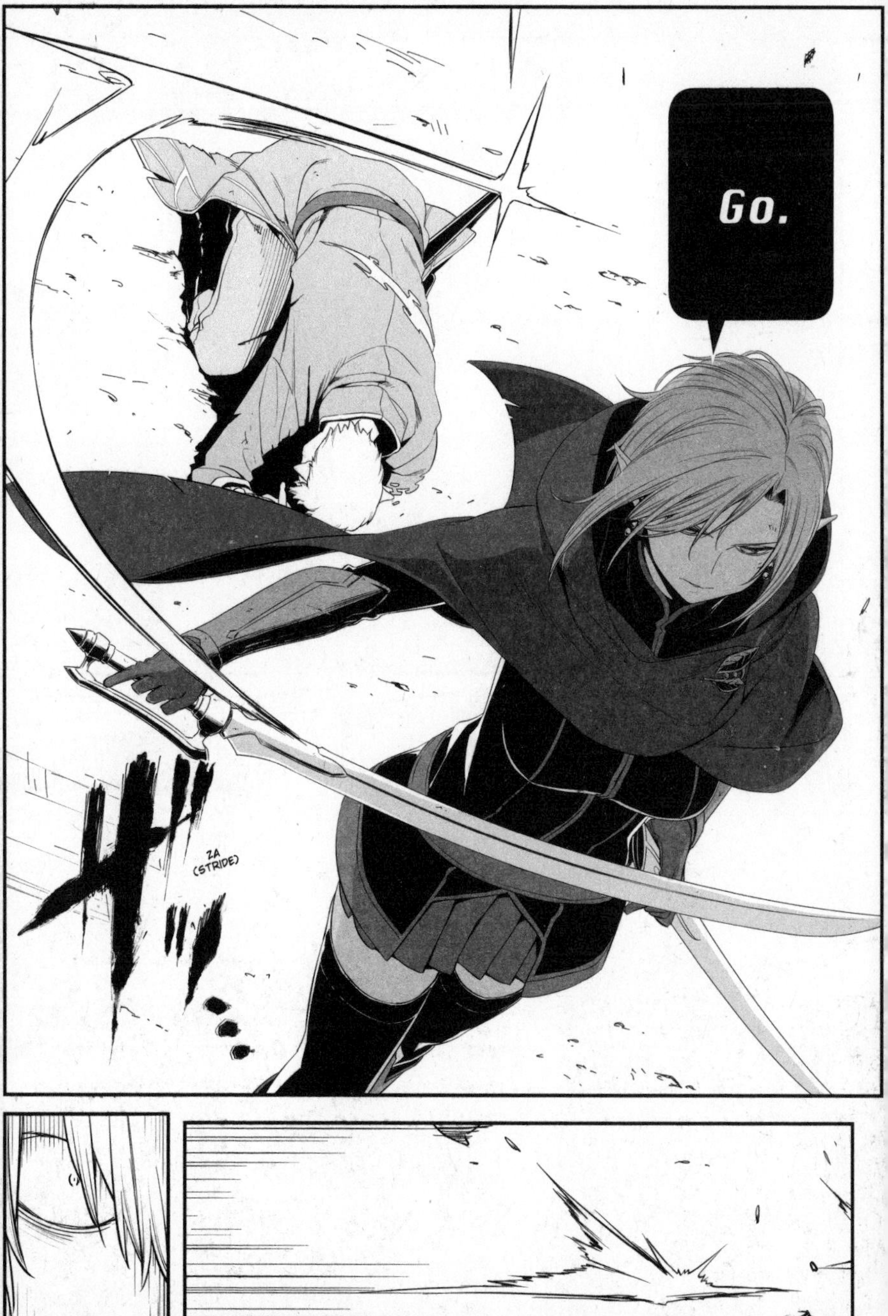
Go.
ZA
(STRIDE)

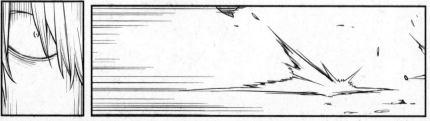

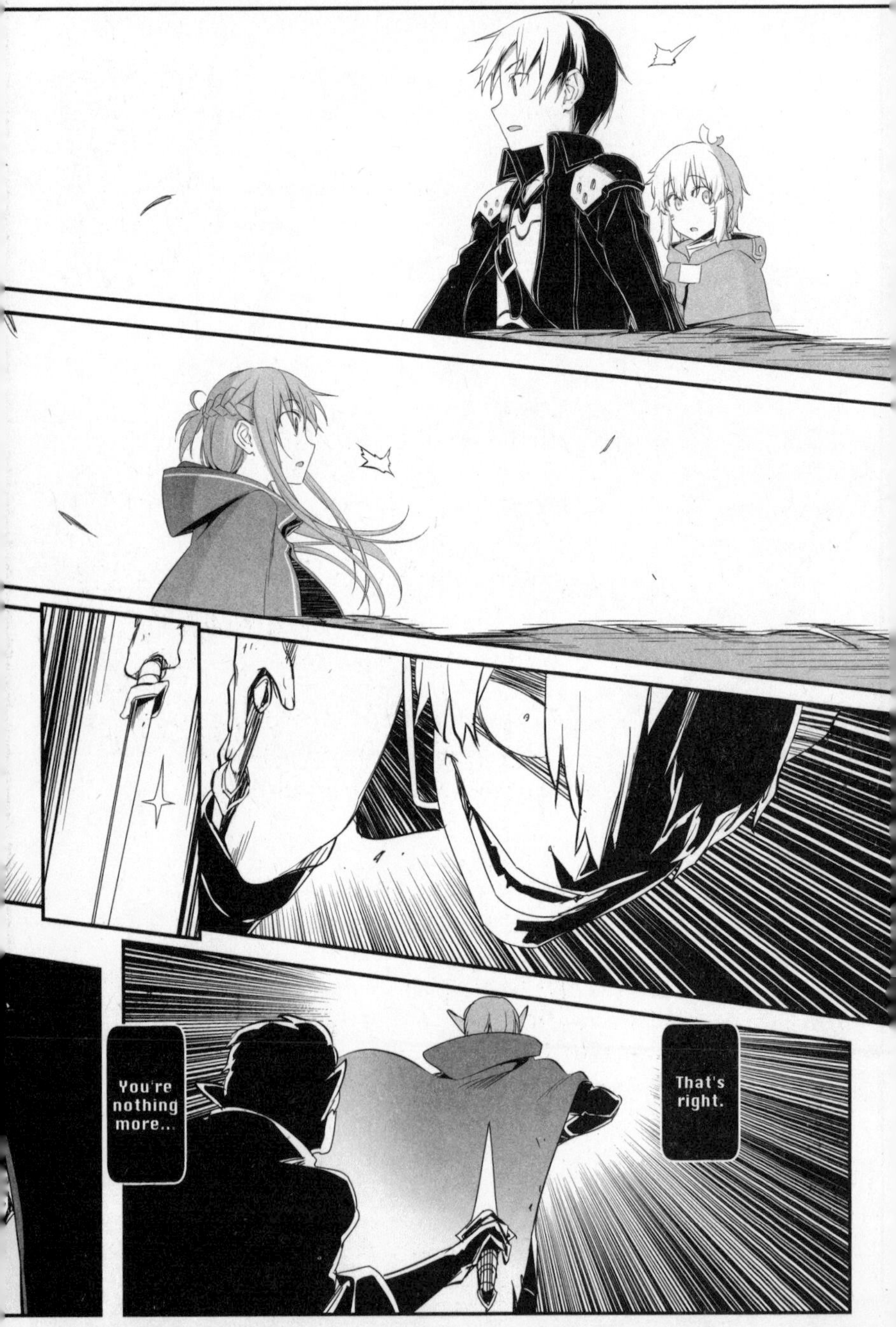
That's right.
You're nothing more...

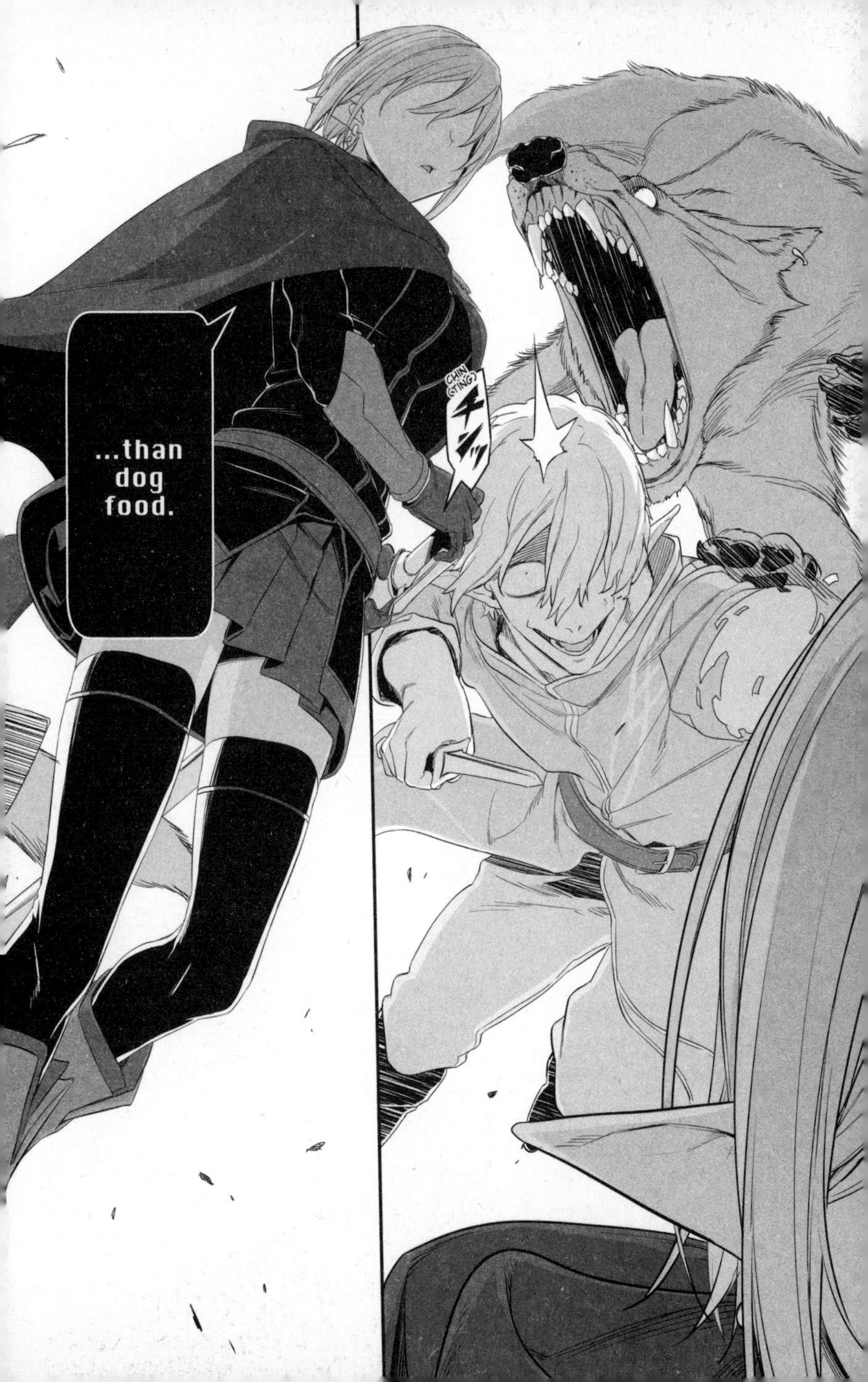
CHIN (STING)
...than dog food.

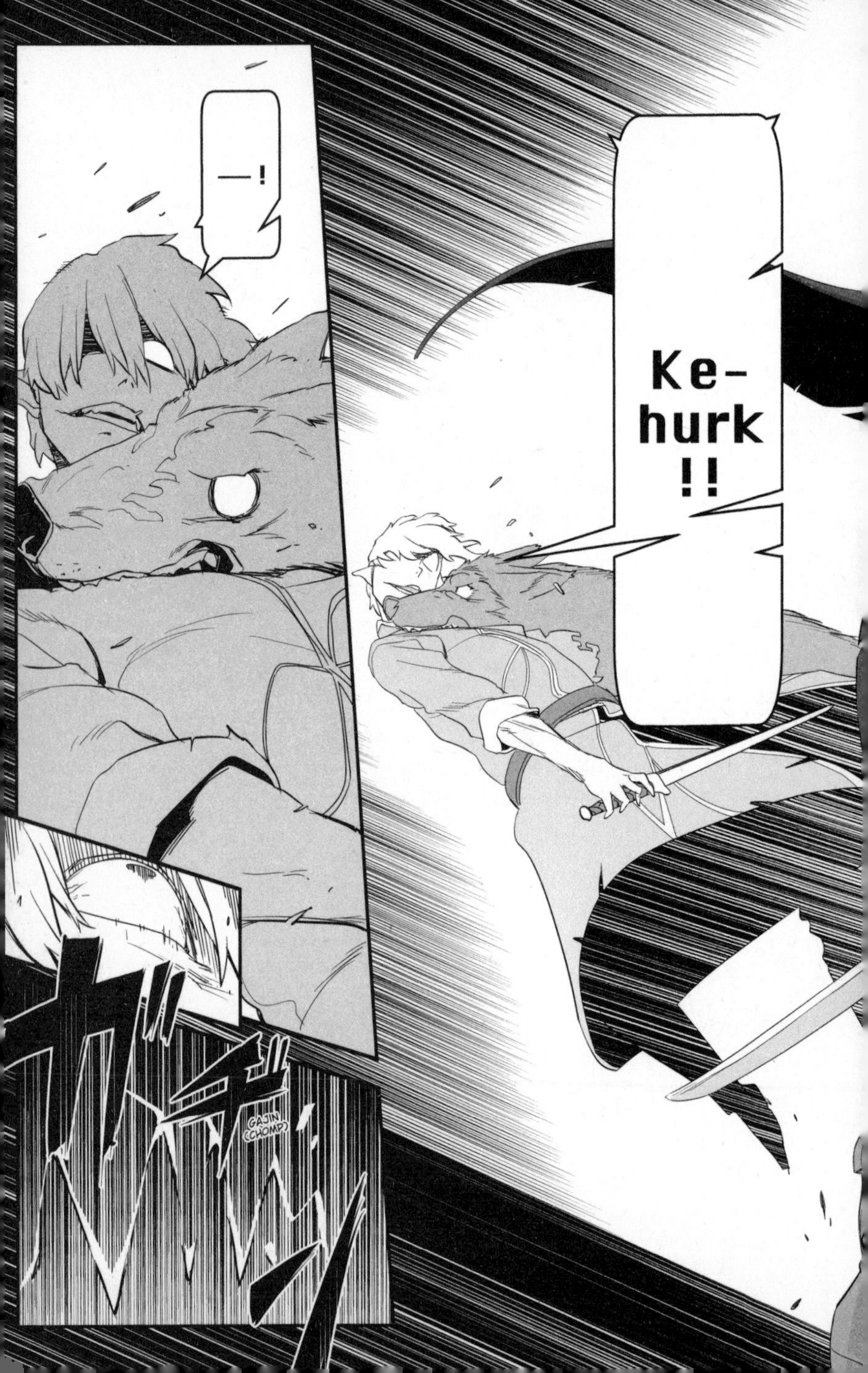
Ke-hurk!!
—!
GAJIN (CHOMP)

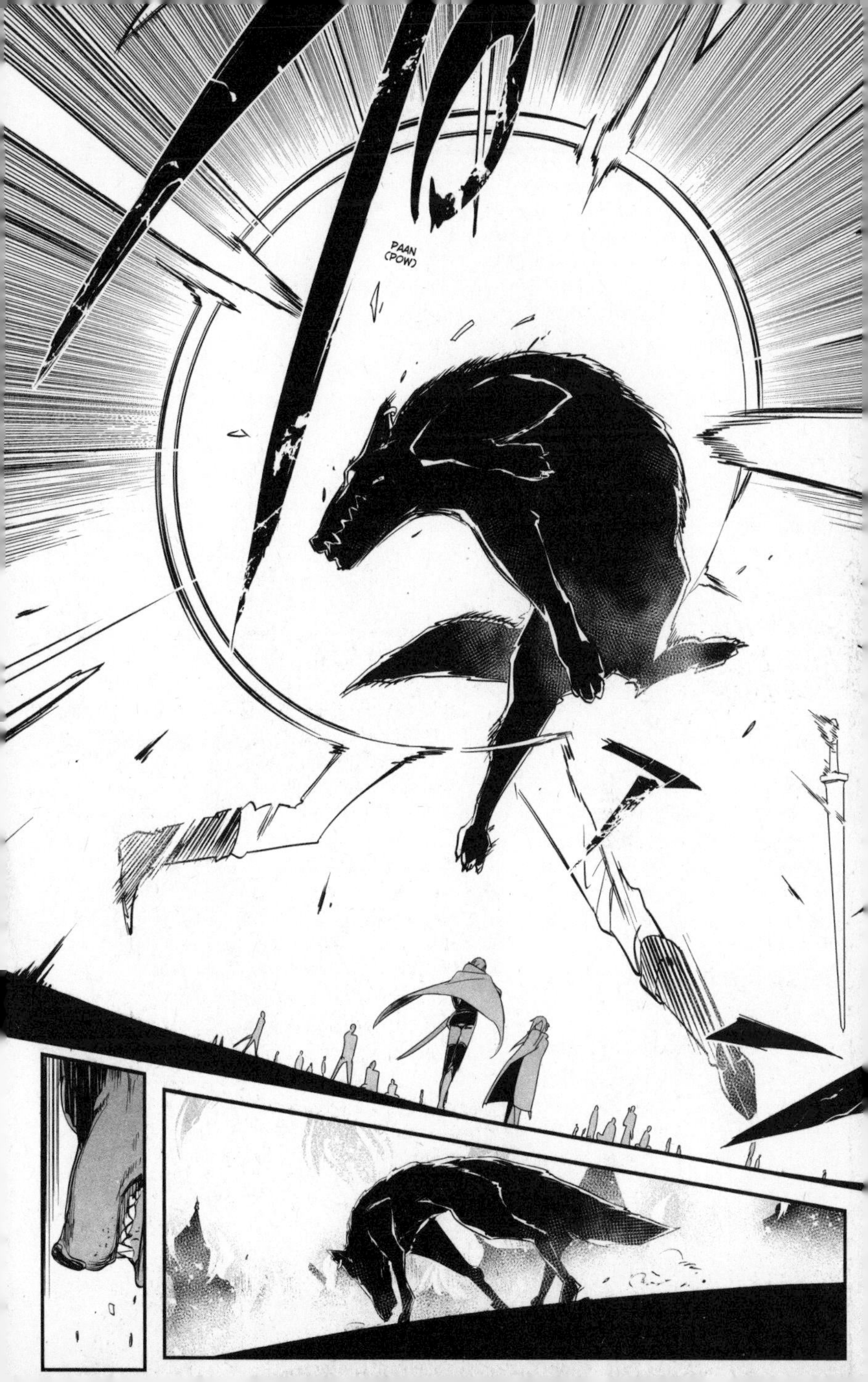
PAAN
(POW)

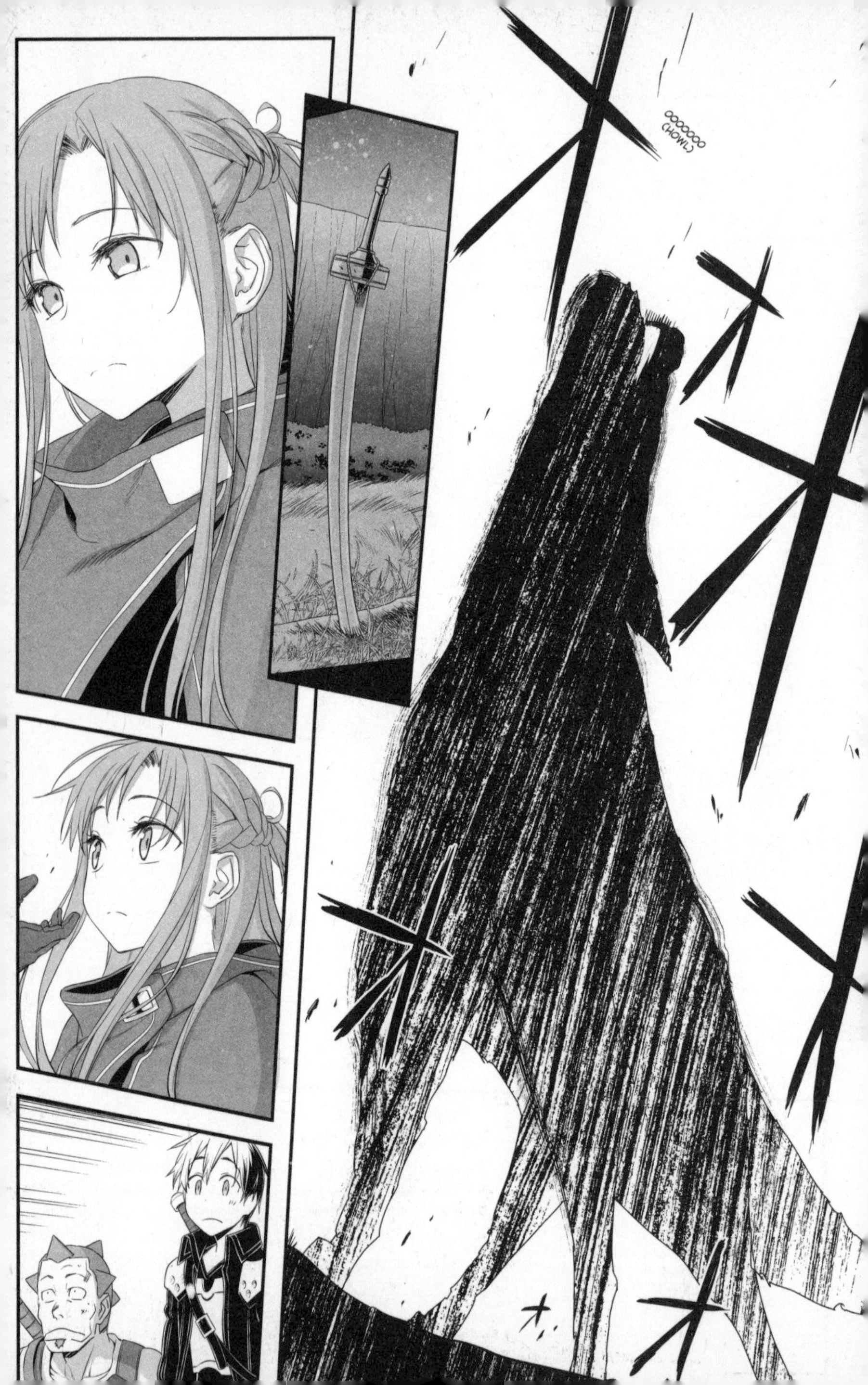
OOOOOOO
(HOWL)

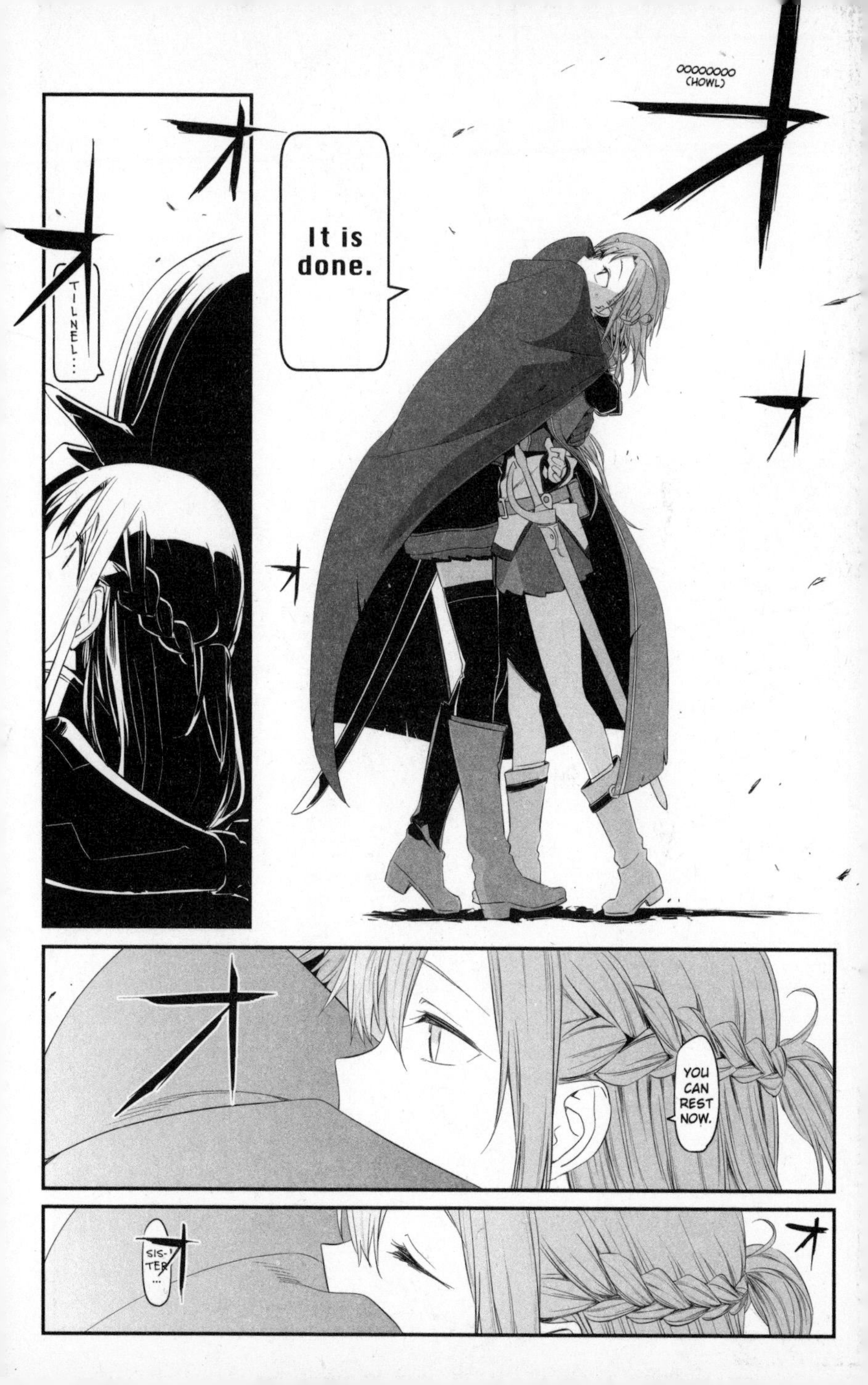
OOOOOOOO
(HOWL)
It is done.
TILNEL...
YOU CAN REST NOW.
SIS-TER...

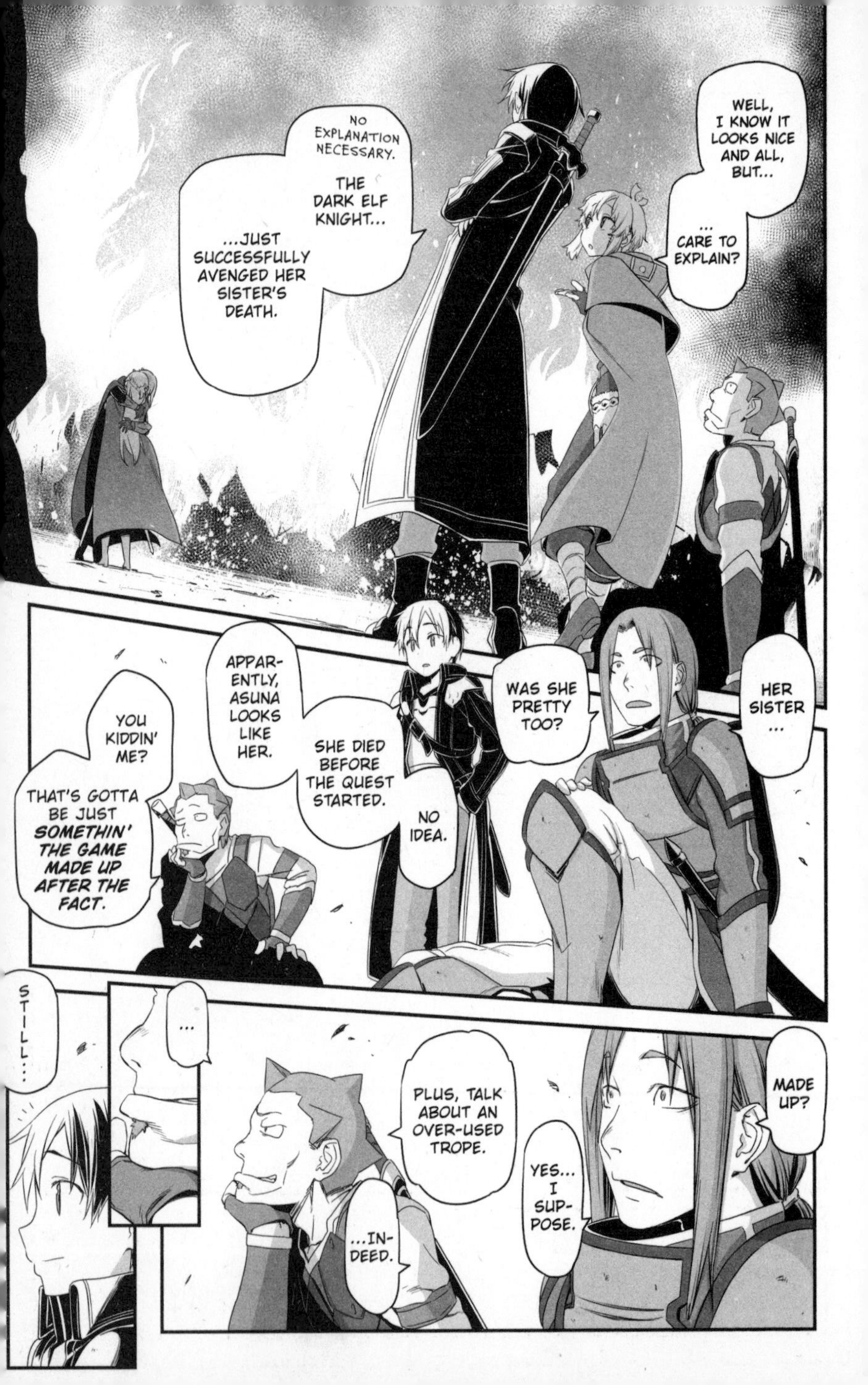
WELL, I KNOW IT LOOKS NICE AND ALL, BUT...
... CARE TO EXPLAIN?
NO EXPLANATION NECESSARY.
THE DARK ELF KNIGHT...
...JUST SUCCESSFULLY AVENGED HER SISTER'S DEATH.
HER SISTER...
WAS SHE PRETTY TOO?
SHE DIED BEFORE THE QUEST STARTED.
NO IDEA.
APPARENTLY, ASUNA LOOKS LIKE HER.
YOU KIDDIN' ME?
THAT'S GOTTA BE JUST ***SOMETHIN' THE GAME MADE UP AFTER THE FACT***.
MADE UP?
YES... I SUPPOSE.
PLUS, TALK ABOUT AN OVER-USED TROPE.
...INDEED.
...
STILL...

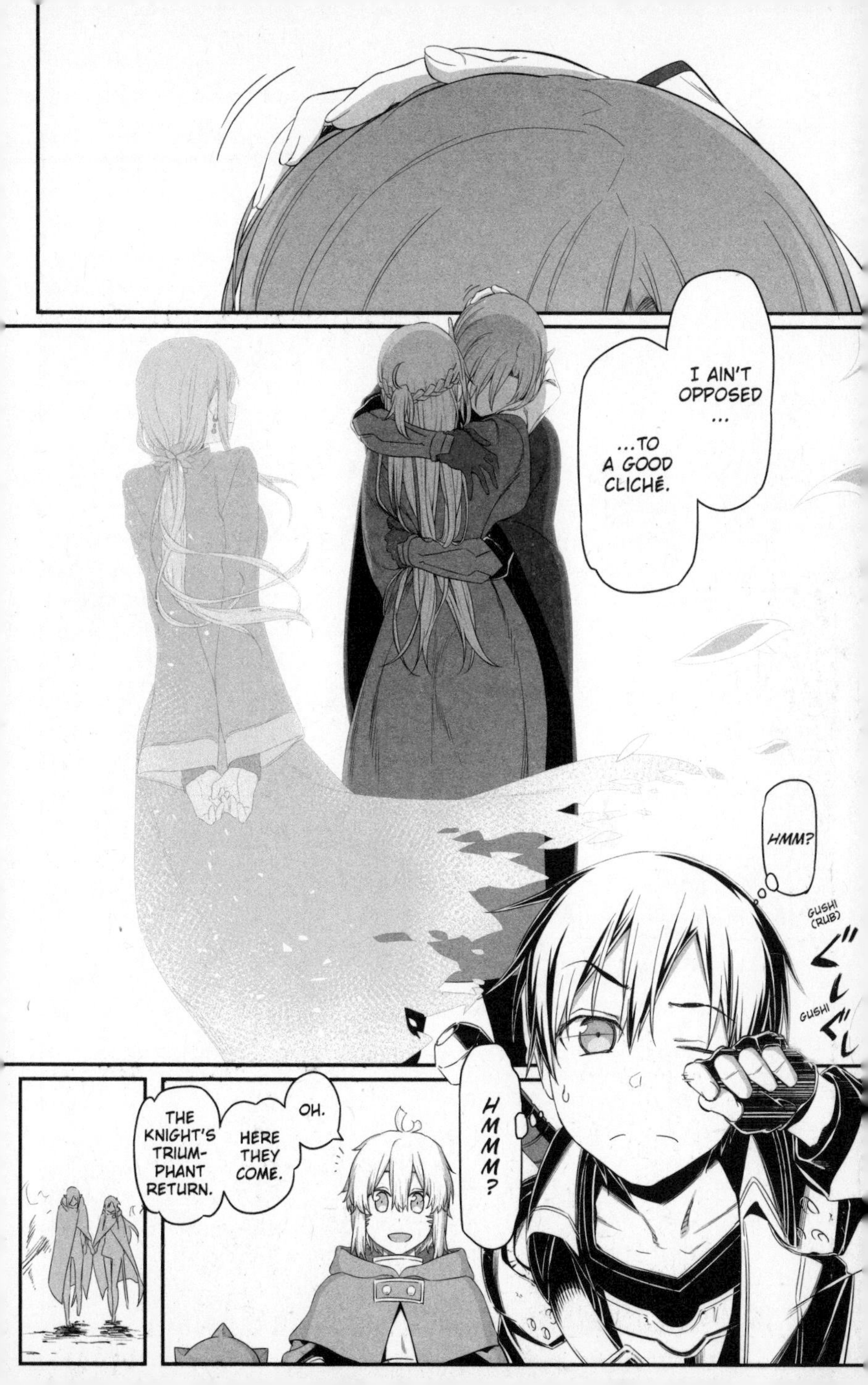
I AIN'T OPPOSED ...
...TO A GOOD CLICHÉ.
HMM?
GUSHI (RUB)
GUSHI
ぐしぐし
HMMM?
OH.
HERE THEY COME.
THE KNIGHT'S TRIUM-PHANT RETURN.

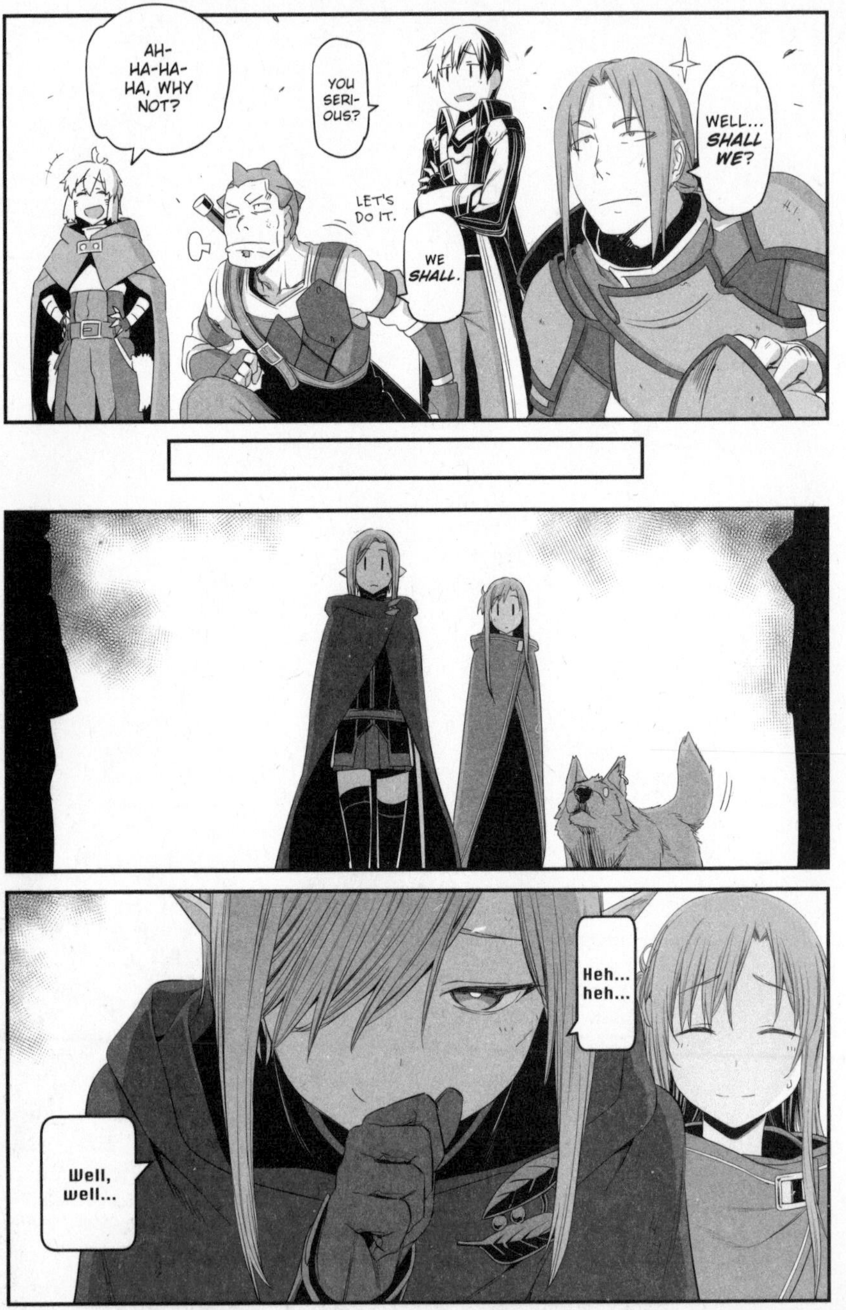
WELL... SHALL WE?
WE SHALL.
LET'S DO IT.
YOU SERIOUS?
AH-HA-HA-HA, WHY NOT?
Heh... heh...
Well, well...

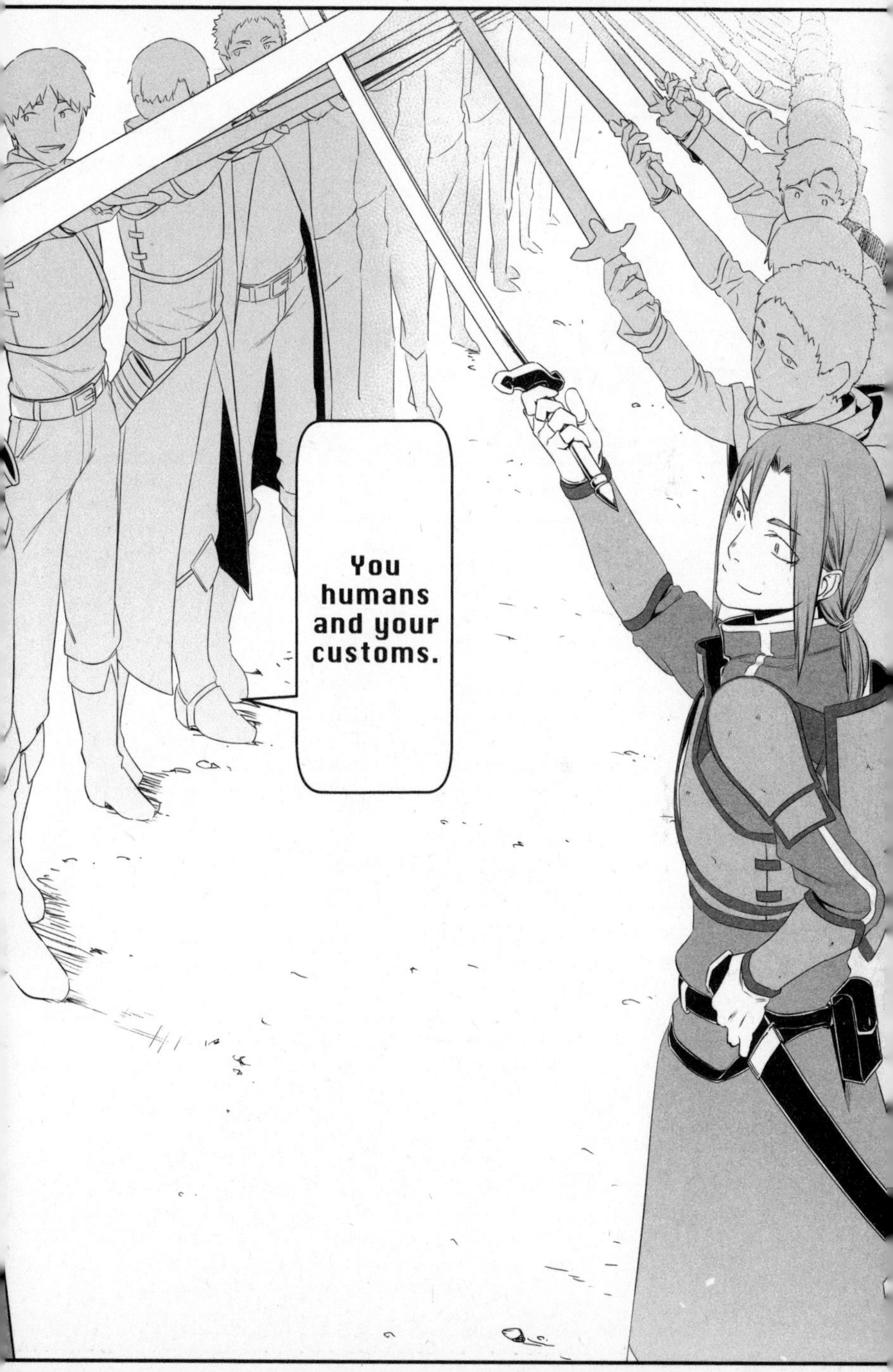
You humans and your customs.

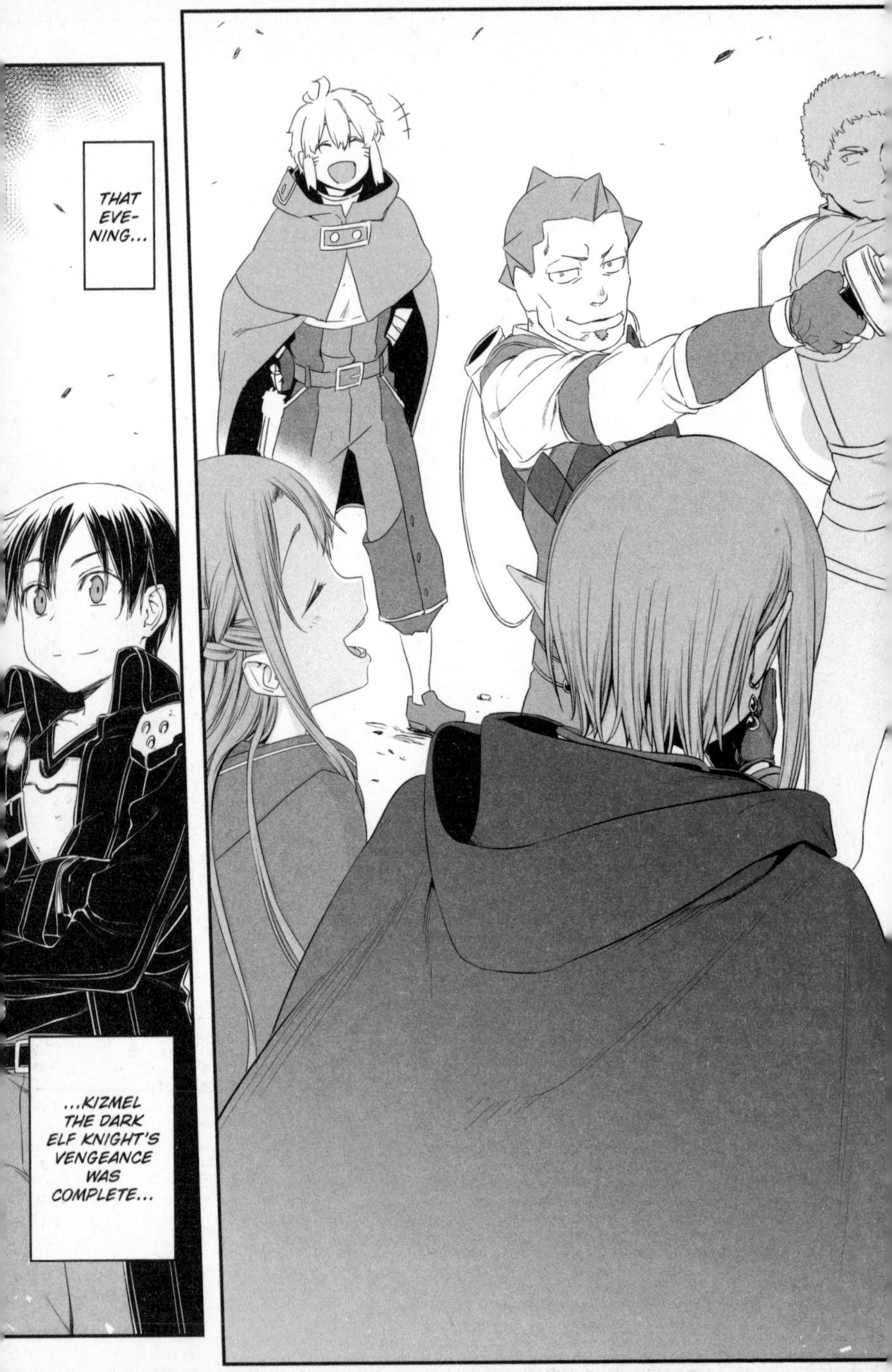
THAT EVENING...
...KIZMEL THE DARK ELF KNIGHT'S VENGEANCE WAS COMPLETE...

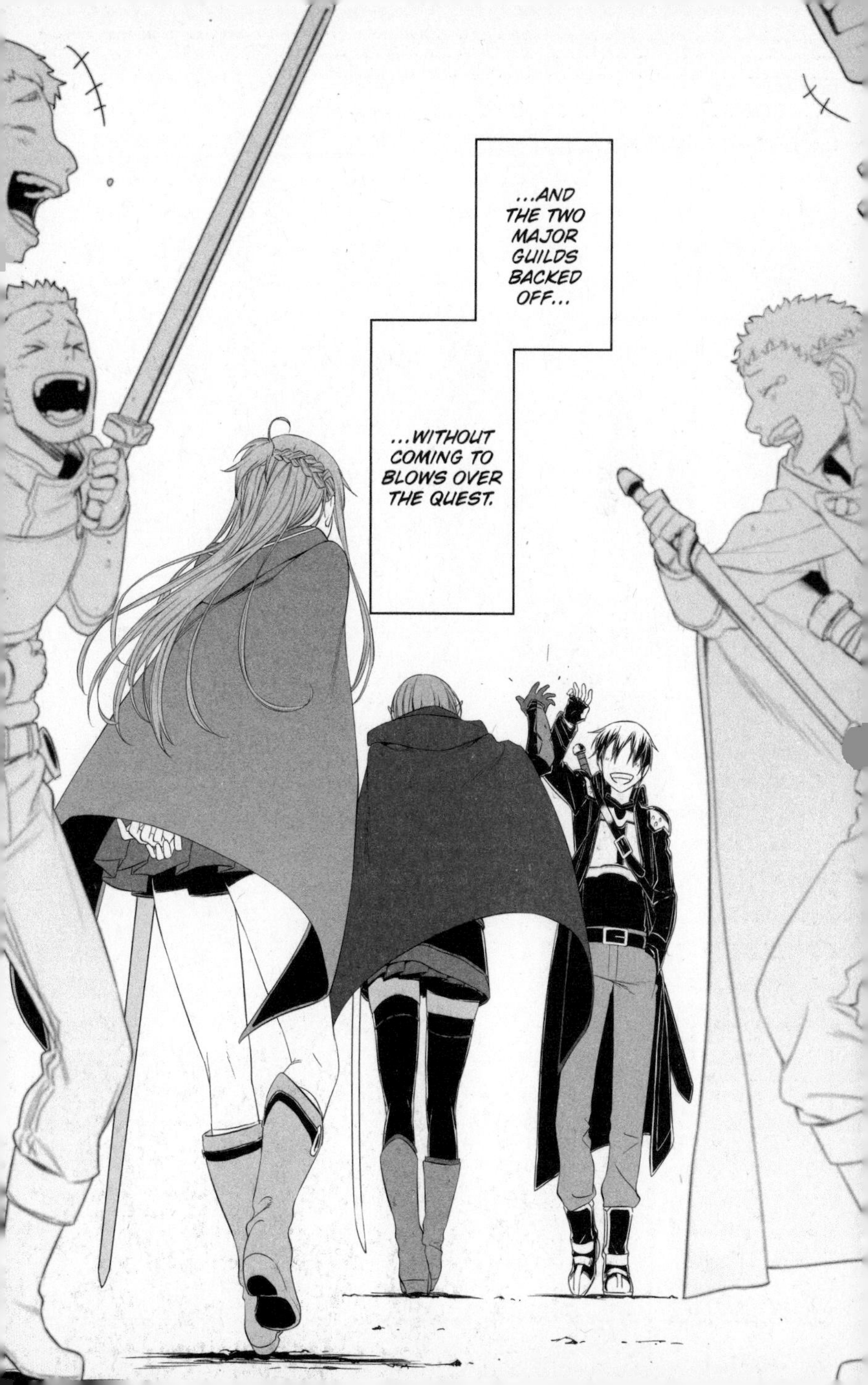
...AND THE TWO MAJOR GUILDS BACKED OFF...
...WITHOUT COMING TO BLOWS OVER THE QUEST.

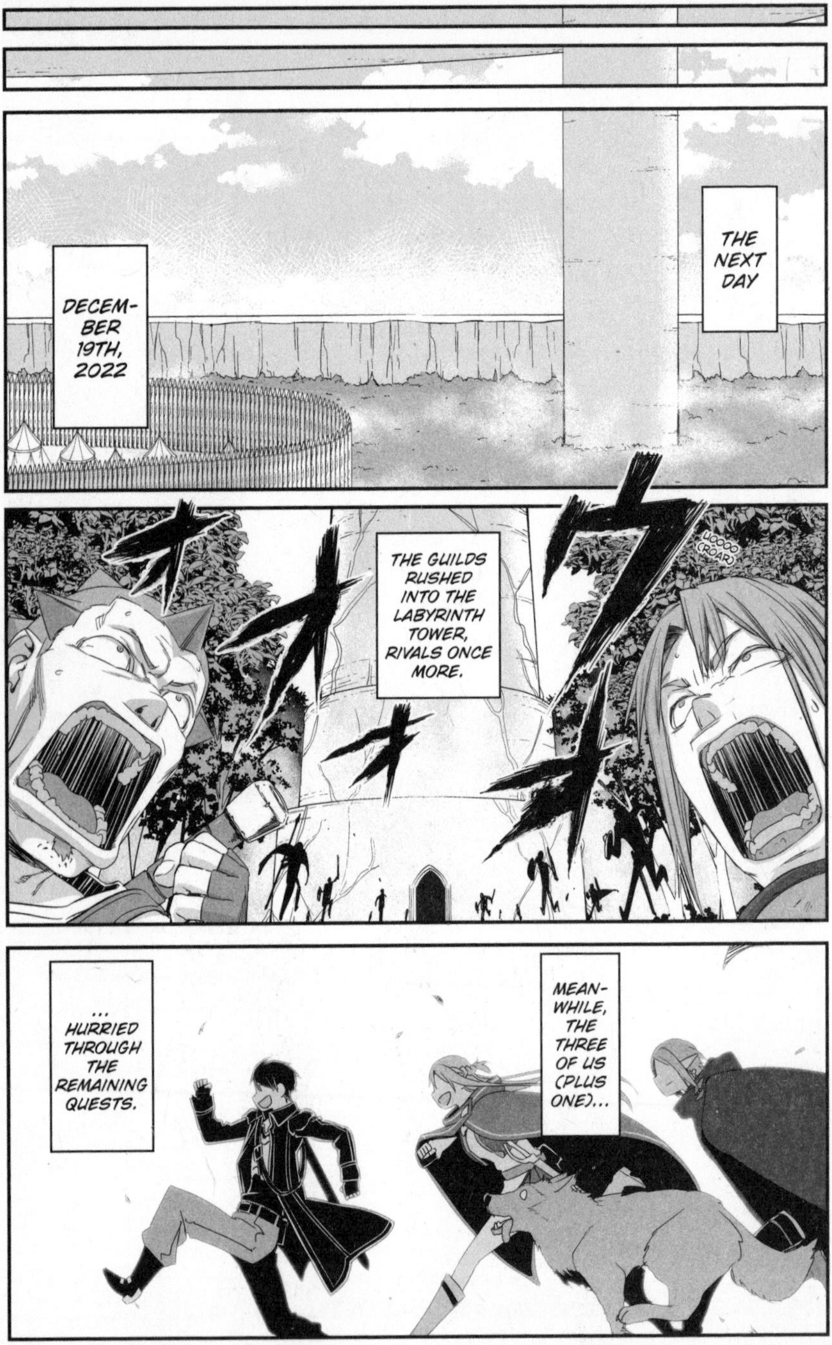
THE NEXT DAY
DECEMBER 19TH, 2022
WOOOO (ROAR)
THE GUILDS RUSHED INTO THE LABYRINTH TOWER, RIVALS ONCE MORE.
MEANWHILE, THE THREE OF US (PLUS ONE)...
...HURRIED THROUGH THE REMAINING QUESTS.

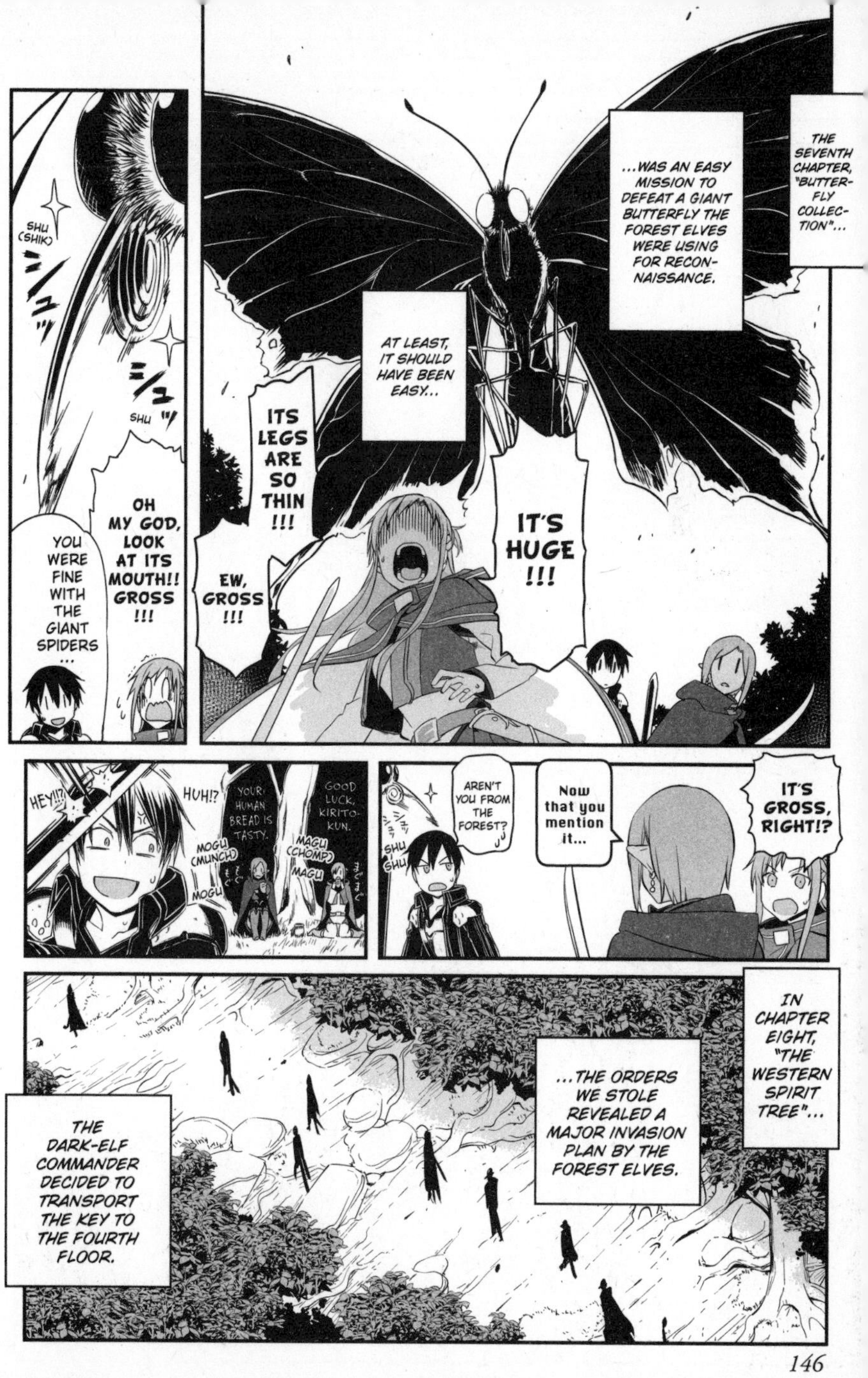
THE SEVENTH CHAPTER, "BUTTERFLY COLLECTION"...
...WAS AN EASY MISSION TO DEFEAT A GIANT BUTTERFLY THE FOREST ELVES WERE USING FOR RECONNAISSANCE.
AT LEAST, IT SHOULD HAVE BEEN EASY...
IT'S HUGE!!!
ITS LEGS ARE SO THIN!!!
EW, GROSS!!!
SHU (SHIK)
SHU
OH MY GOD, LOOK AT ITS MOUTH!! GROSS!!!
YOU WERE FINE WITH THE GIANT SPIDERS...
IT'S GROSS, RIGHT!?
Now that you mention it...
AREN'T YOU FROM THE FOREST?
SHU SHU
GOOD LUCK, KIRITO-KUN.
MAGU (CHOMP) MAGU
YOUR HUMAN BREAD IS TASTY.
HUH!?
HEY!!?
MOGU (MUNCH) MOGU
IN CHAPTER EIGHT, "THE WESTERN SPIRIT TREE"...
...THE ORDERS WE STOLE REVEALED A MAJOR INVASION PLAN BY THE FOREST ELVES.
THE DARK-ELF COMMANDER DECIDED TO TRANSPORT THE KEY TO THE FOURTH FLOOR.

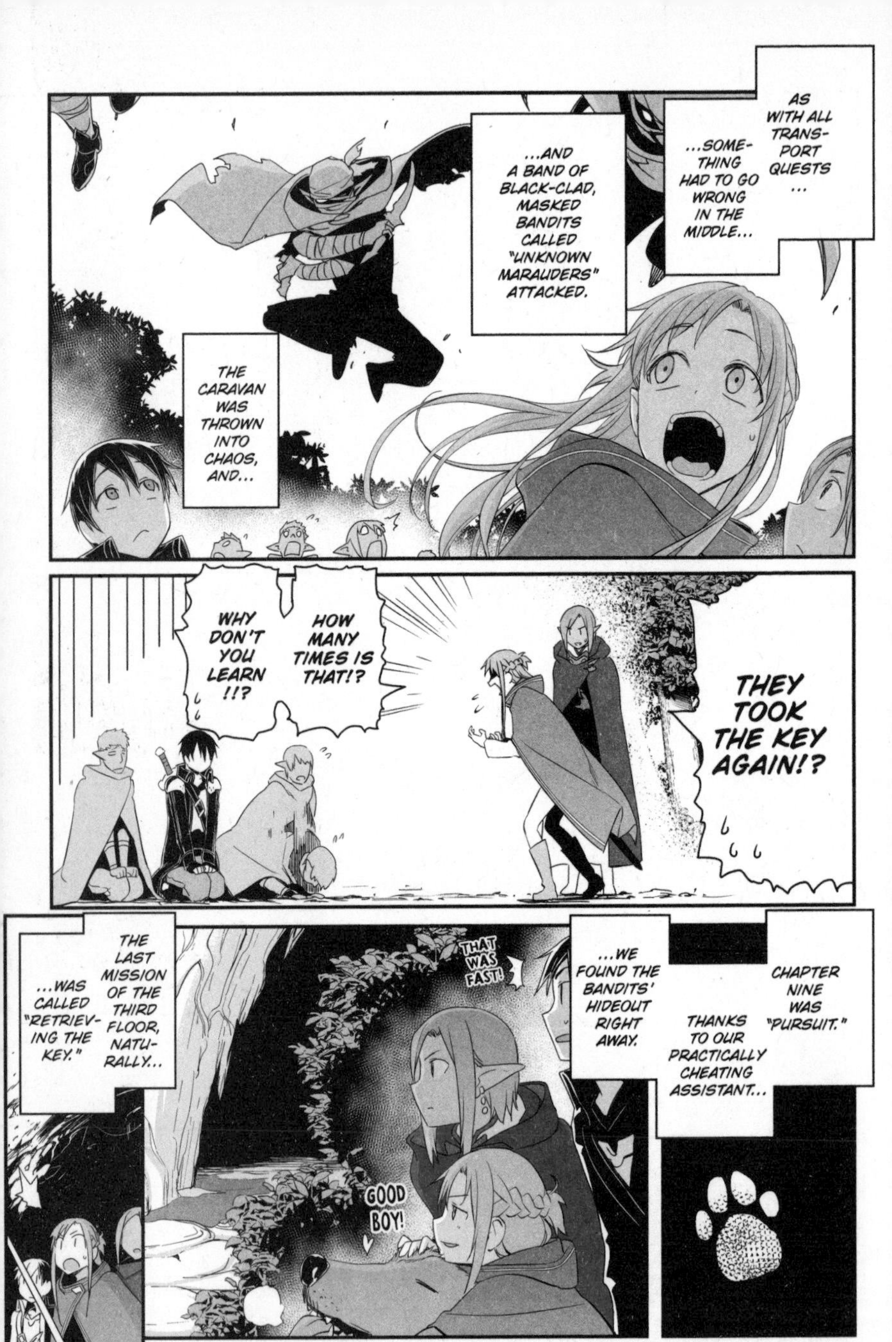
AS WITH ALL TRANSPORT QUESTS...
...SOMETHING HAD TO GO WRONG IN THE MIDDLE...
...AND A BAND OF BLACK-CLAD, MASKED BANDITS CALLED "UNKNOWN MARAUDERS" ATTACKED.
THE CARAVAN WAS THROWN INTO CHAOS, AND...
THEY TOOK THE KEY AGAIN!?
HOW MANY TIMES IS THAT!?
WHY DON'T YOU LEARN!!?
CHAPTER NINE WAS "PURSUIT."
THANKS TO OUR PRACTICALLY CHEATING ASSISTANT...
...WE FOUND THE BANDITS' HIDEOUT RIGHT AWAY.
THAT WAS FAST!
GOOD BOY!
THE LAST MISSION OF THE THIRD FLOOR, NATURALLY...
...WAS CALLED "RETRIEVING THE KEY."

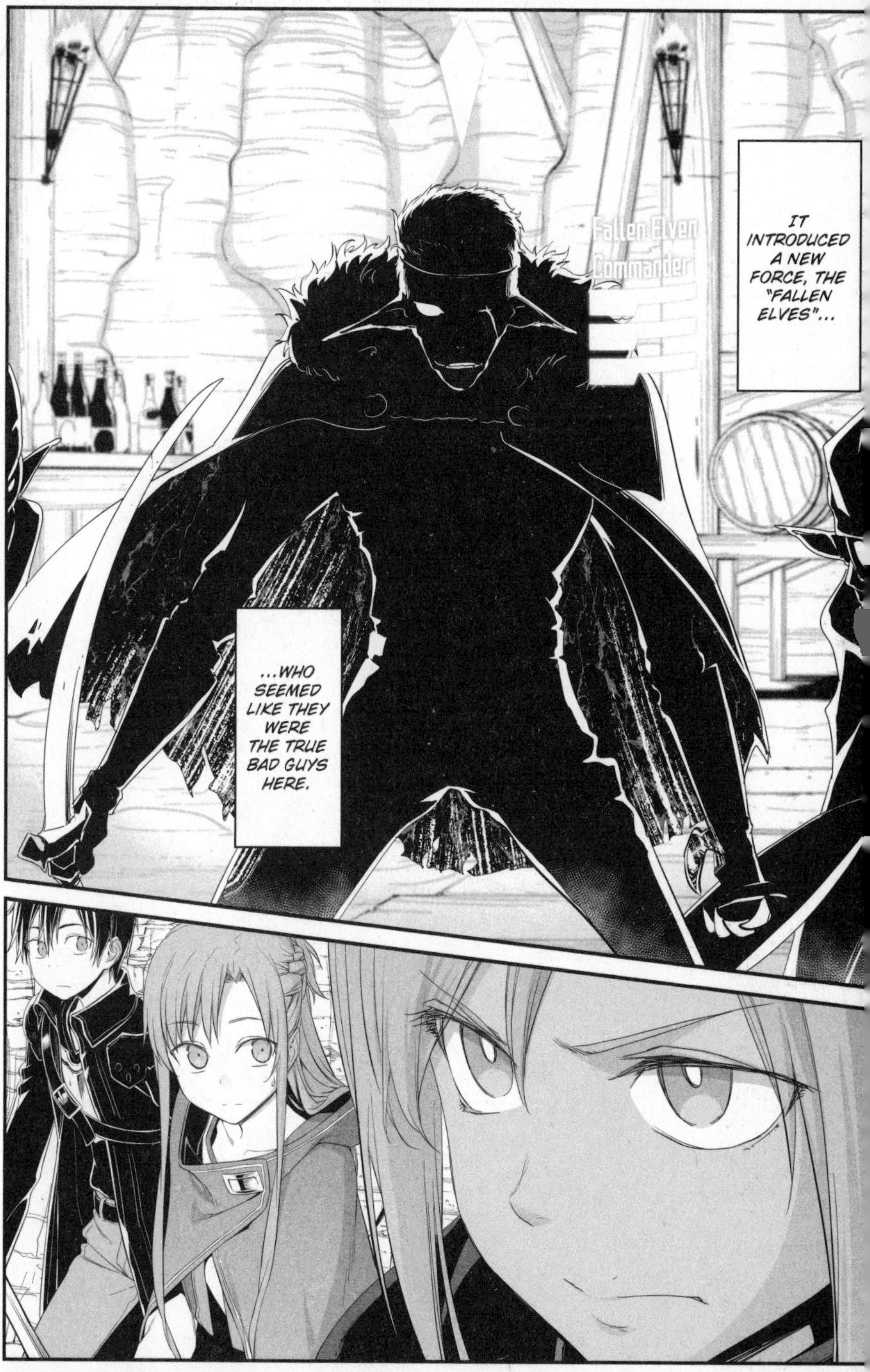
IT INTRODUCED A NEW FORCE, THE "FALLEN ELVES"...
Fallen Elven Commander
...WHO SEEMED LIKE THEY WERE THE TRUE BAD GUYS HERE.

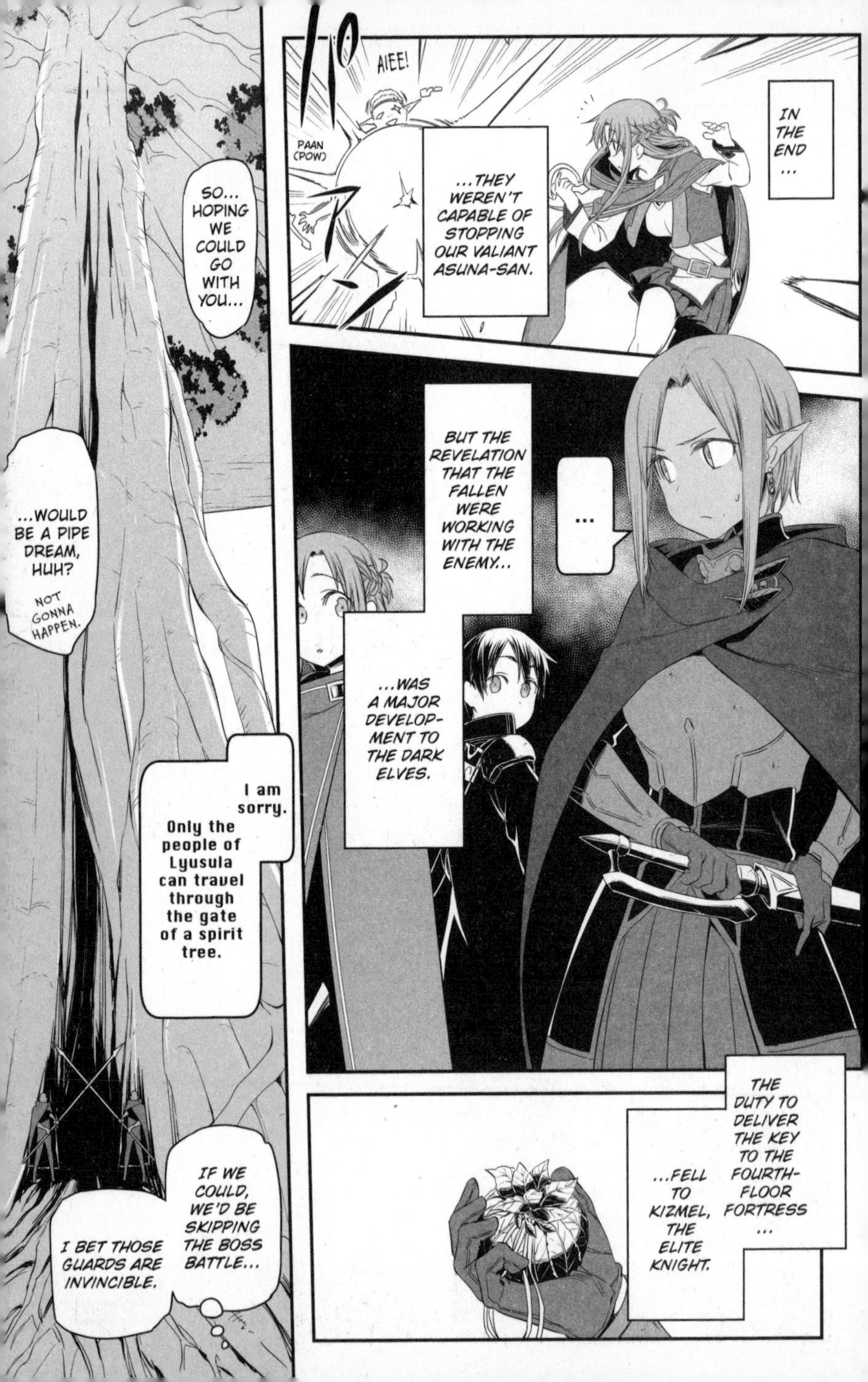
IN THE END...
...THEY WEREN'T CAPABLE OF STOPPING OUR VALIANT ASUNA-SAN.
AIEE!
PAAN (POW)
...
BUT THE REVELATION THAT THE FALLEN WERE WORKING WITH THE ENEMY...
...WAS A MAJOR DEVELOPMENT TO THE DARK ELVES.
THE DUTY TO DELIVER THE KEY TO THE FOURTH-FLOOR FORTRESS...
...FELL TO KIZMEL, THE ELITE KNIGHT.
SO... HOPING WE COULD GO WITH YOU...
...WOULD BE A PIPE DREAM, HUH?
NOT GONNA HAPPEN.
I am sorry. Only the people of Lyusula can travel through the gate of a spirit tree.
IF WE COULD, WE'D BE SKIPPING THE BOSS BATTLE...
I BET THOSE GUARDS ARE INVINCIBLE.

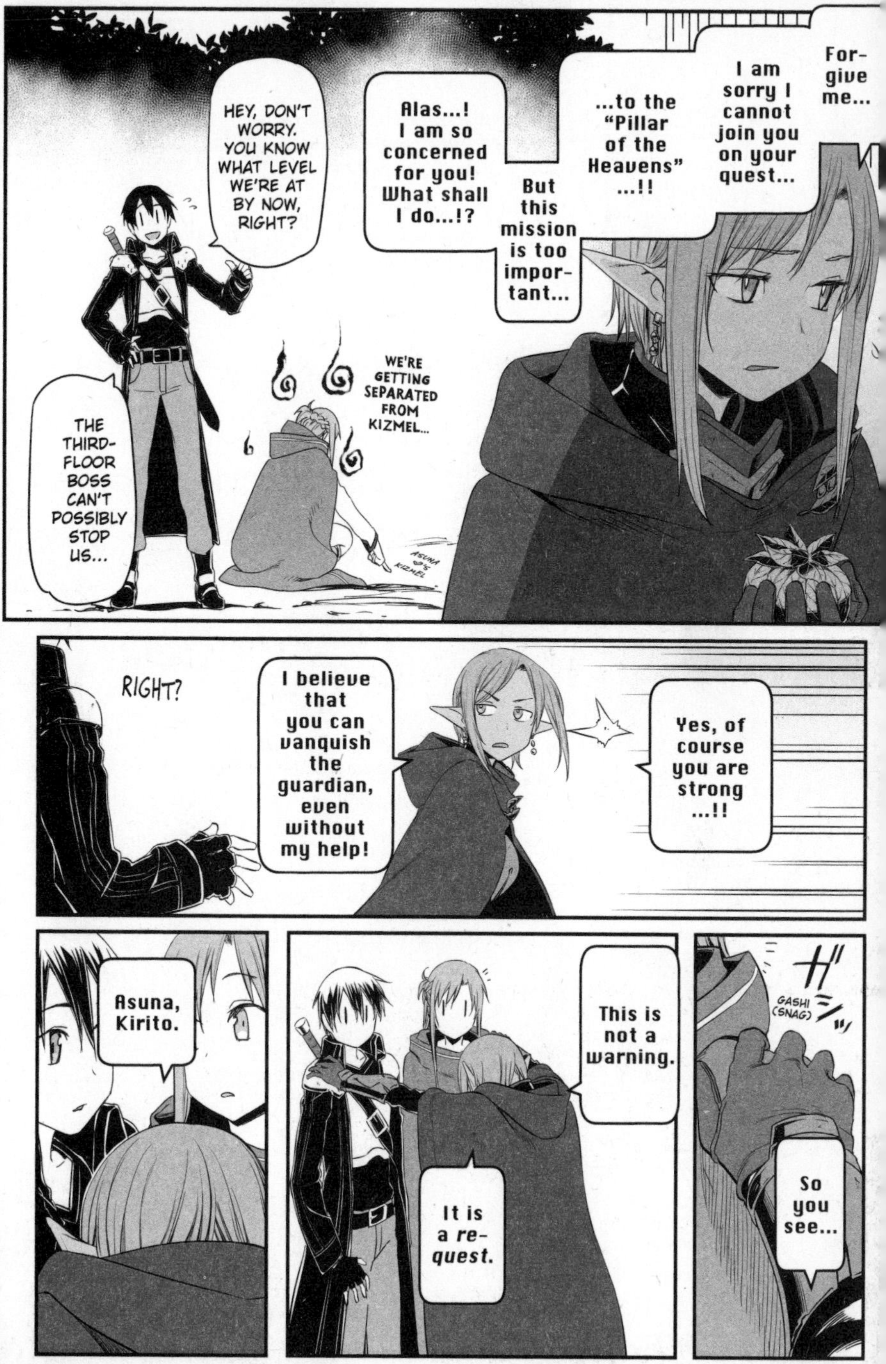
Forgive me...
I am sorry I cannot join you on your quest...
...to the "Pillar of the Heavens" ...!!
But this mission is too important...
Alas...! I am so concerned for you! What shall I do...!?
HEY, DON'T WORRY. YOU KNOW WHAT LEVEL WE'RE AT BY NOW, RIGHT?
WE'RE GETTING SEPARATED FROM KIZMEL...
ASUNA ♡'S KIZMEL
THE THIRD-FLOOR BOSS CAN'T POSSIBLY STOP US...
Yes, of course you are strong ...!!
I believe that you can vanquish the guardian, even without my help!
RIGHT?
GASHI (SNAG)
So you see...
This is not a warning.
It is a *request*.
Asuna, Kirito.

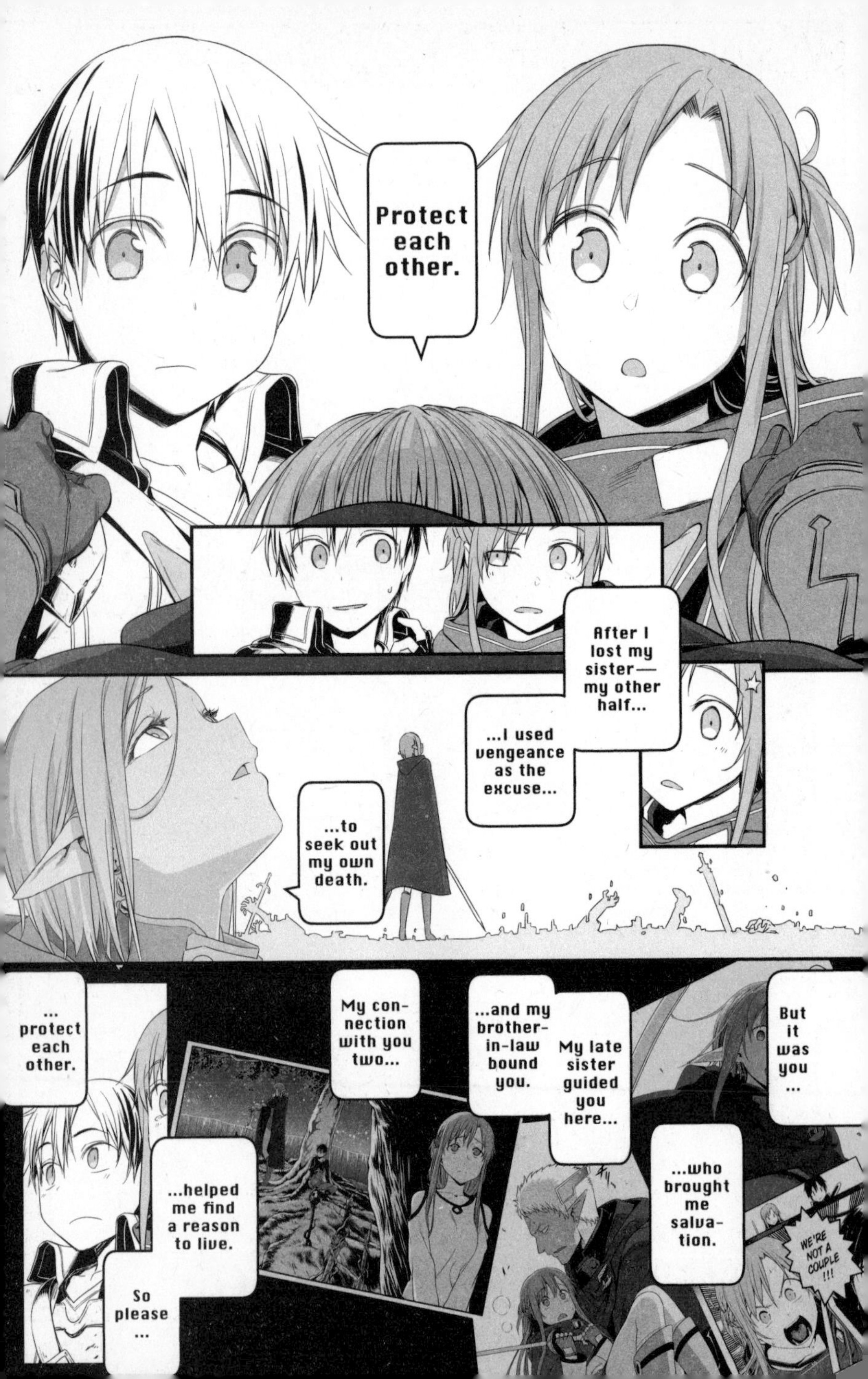
Protect each other.
After I lost my sister— my other half...
...I used vengeance as the excuse...
...to seek out my own death.
But it was you ...
...who brought me salvation.
WE'RE NOT A COUPLE !!!
My late sister guided you here...
...and my brother-in-law bound you.
My con-nection with you two...
...helped me find a reason to live.
So please ...
... protect each other.

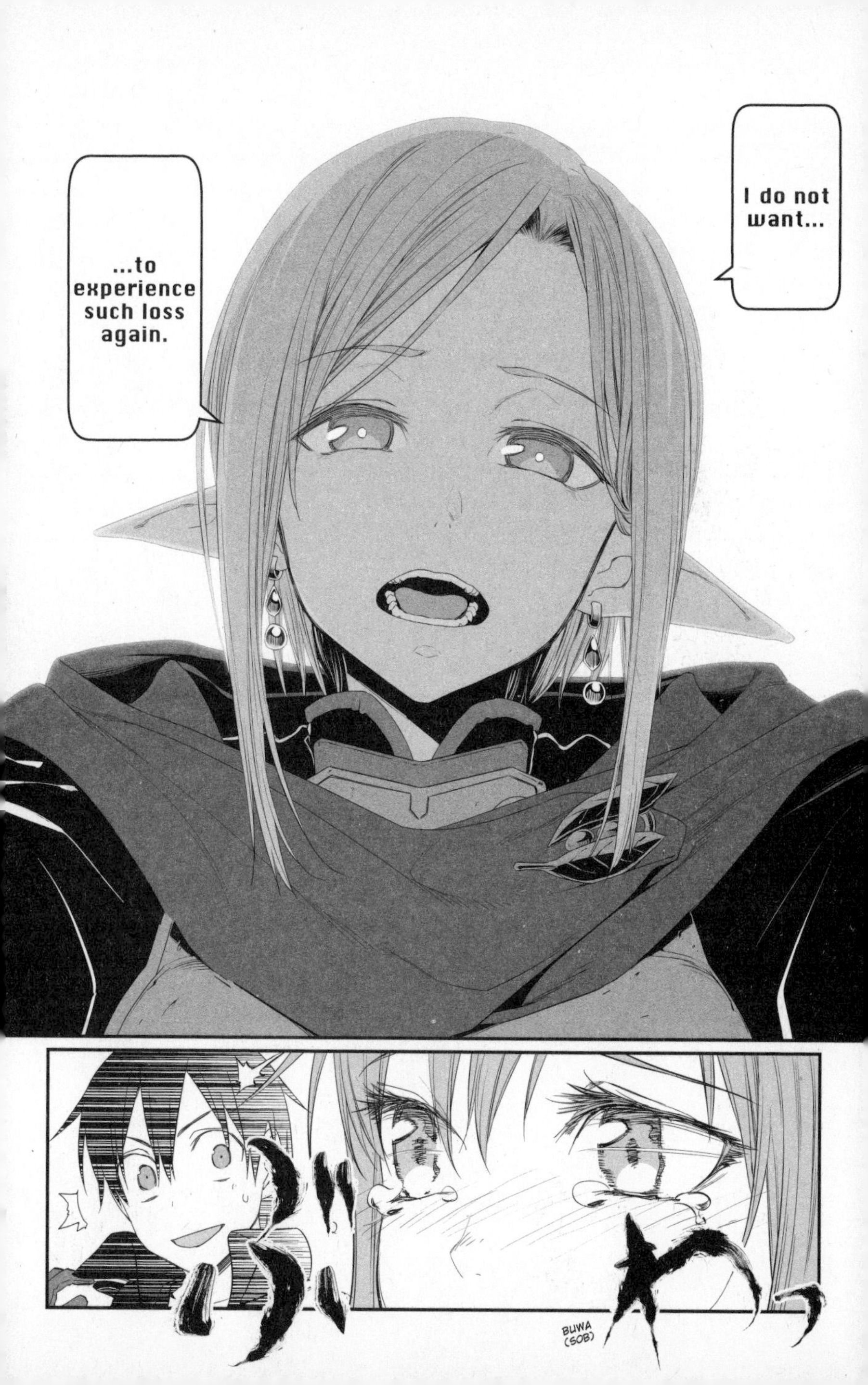
I do not want...
...to experience such loss again.
BUWA (SOB)

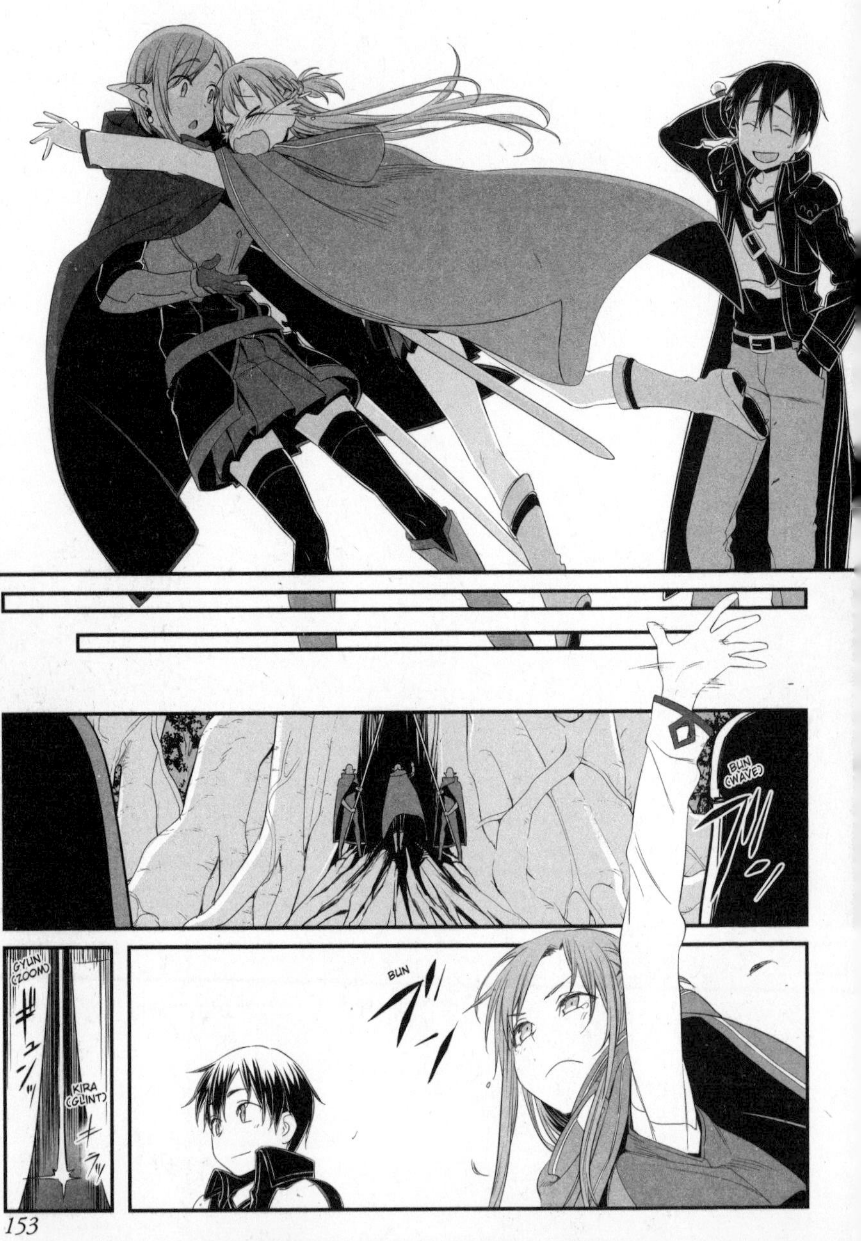
BUN
(WAVE)
BUN
GYUN
(ZOOM)
KIRA
(GLINT)

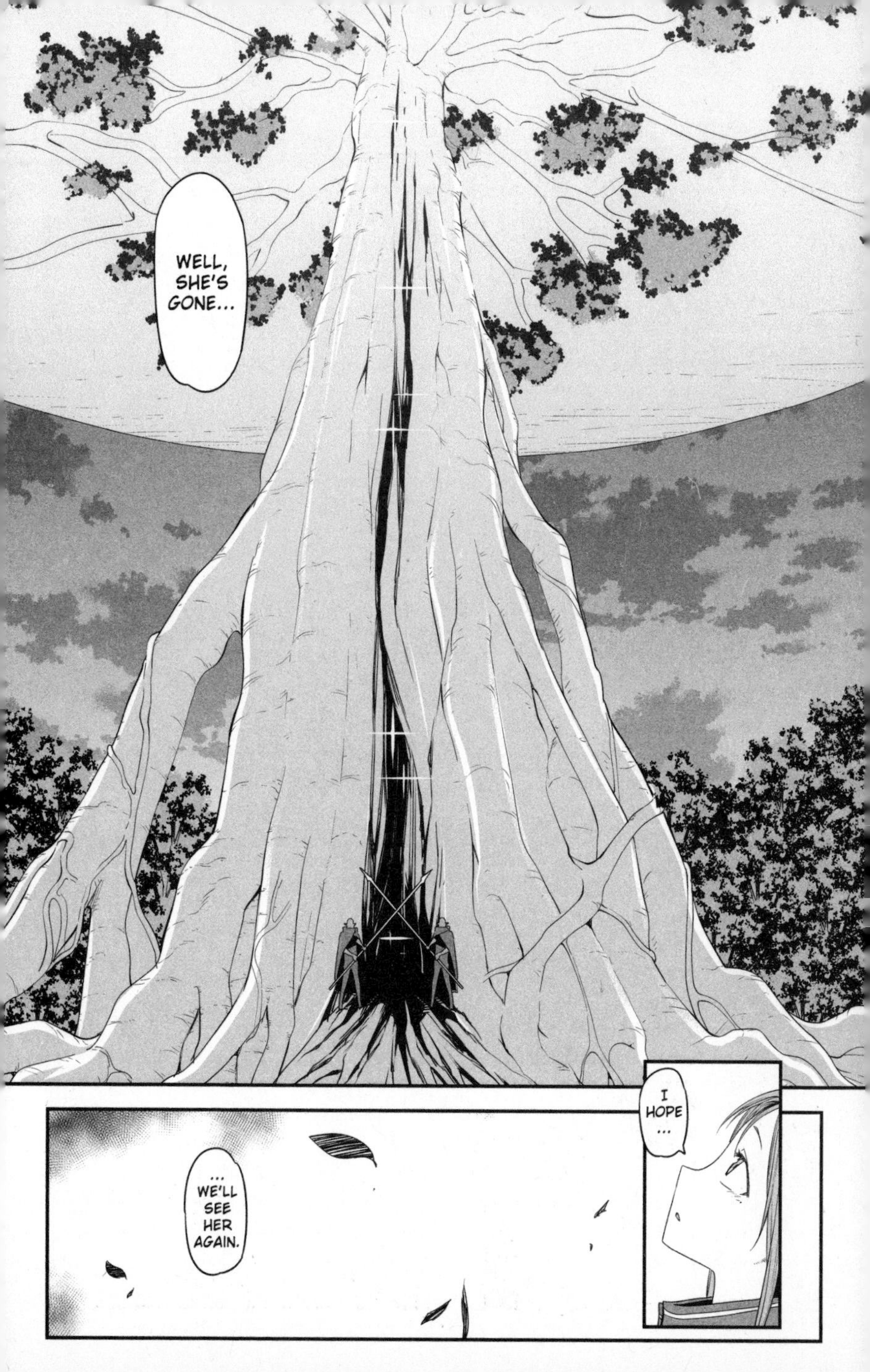
WELL, SHE'S GONE...
I HOPE ...
... WE'LL SEE HER AGAIN.

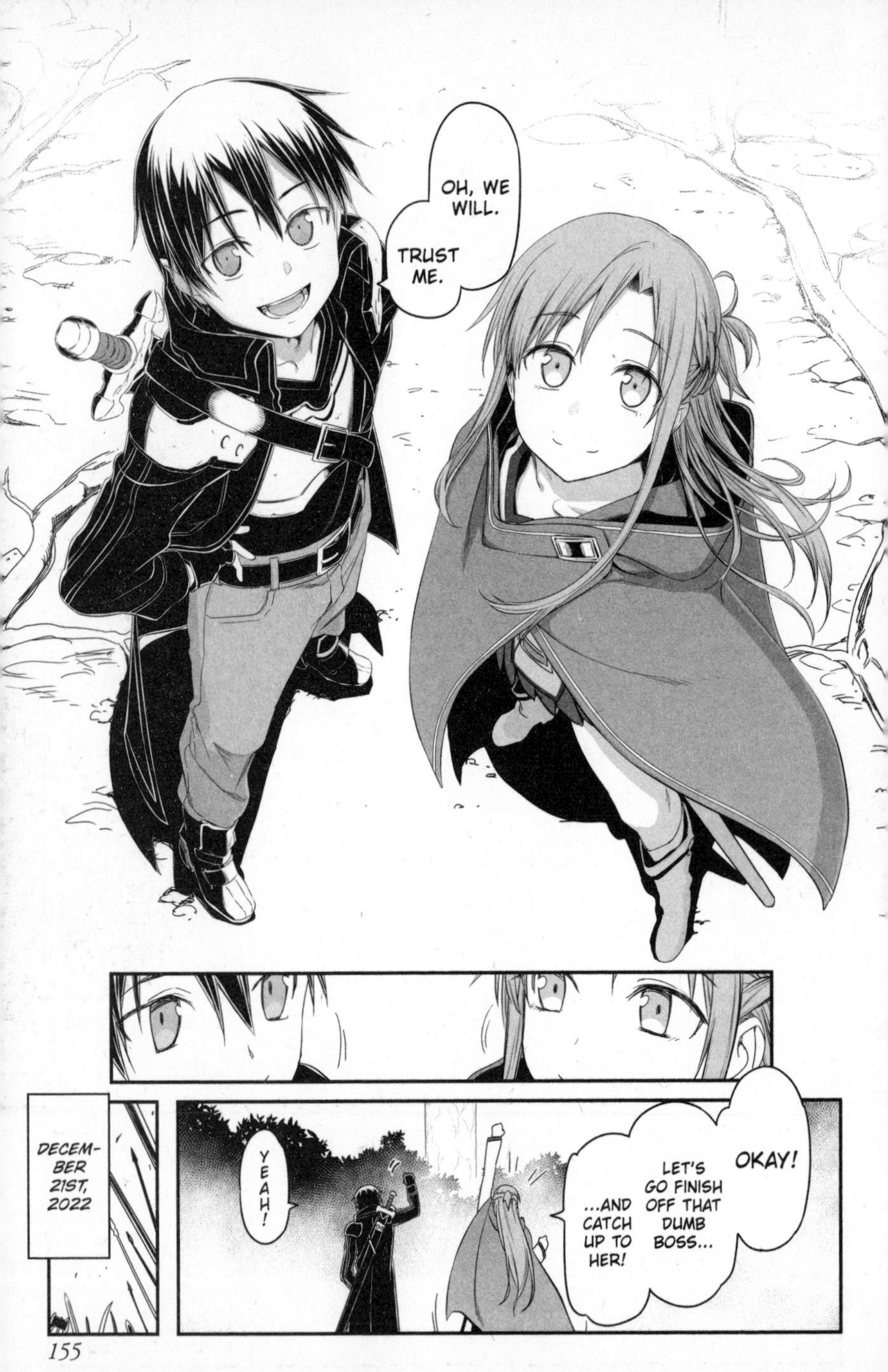
OH, WE WILL.
TRUST ME.
OKAY!
LET'S GO FINISH OFF THAT DUMB BOSS...
...AND CATCH UP TO HER!
YEAH!
DECEMBER 21ST, 2022

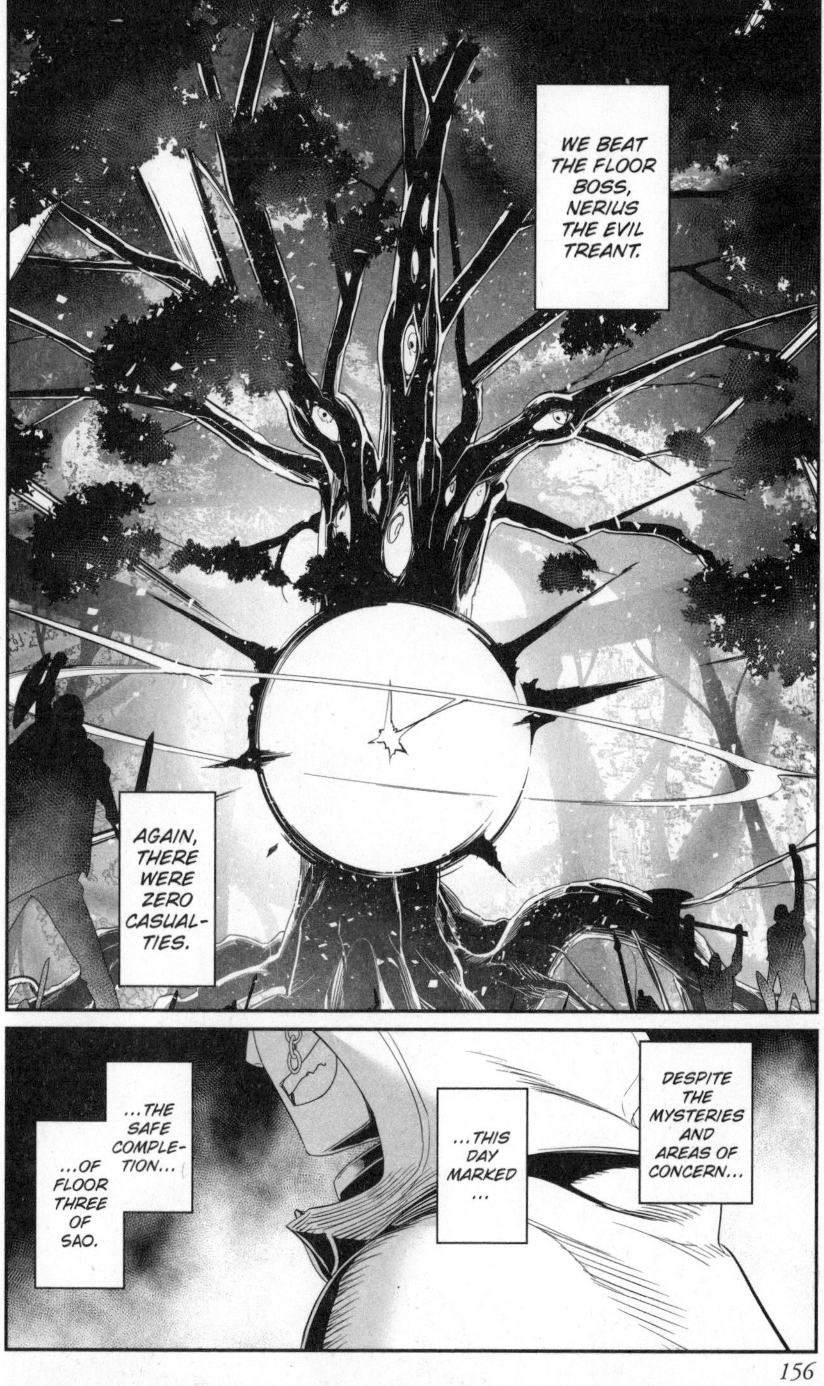
WE BEAT THE FLOOR BOSS, NERIUS THE EVIL TREANT.
AGAIN, THERE WERE ZERO CASUAL-TIES.
DESPITE THE MYSTERIES AND AREAS OF CONCERN...
...THIS DAY MARKED...
...THE SAFE COMPLE-TION...
...OF FLOOR THREE OF SAO.

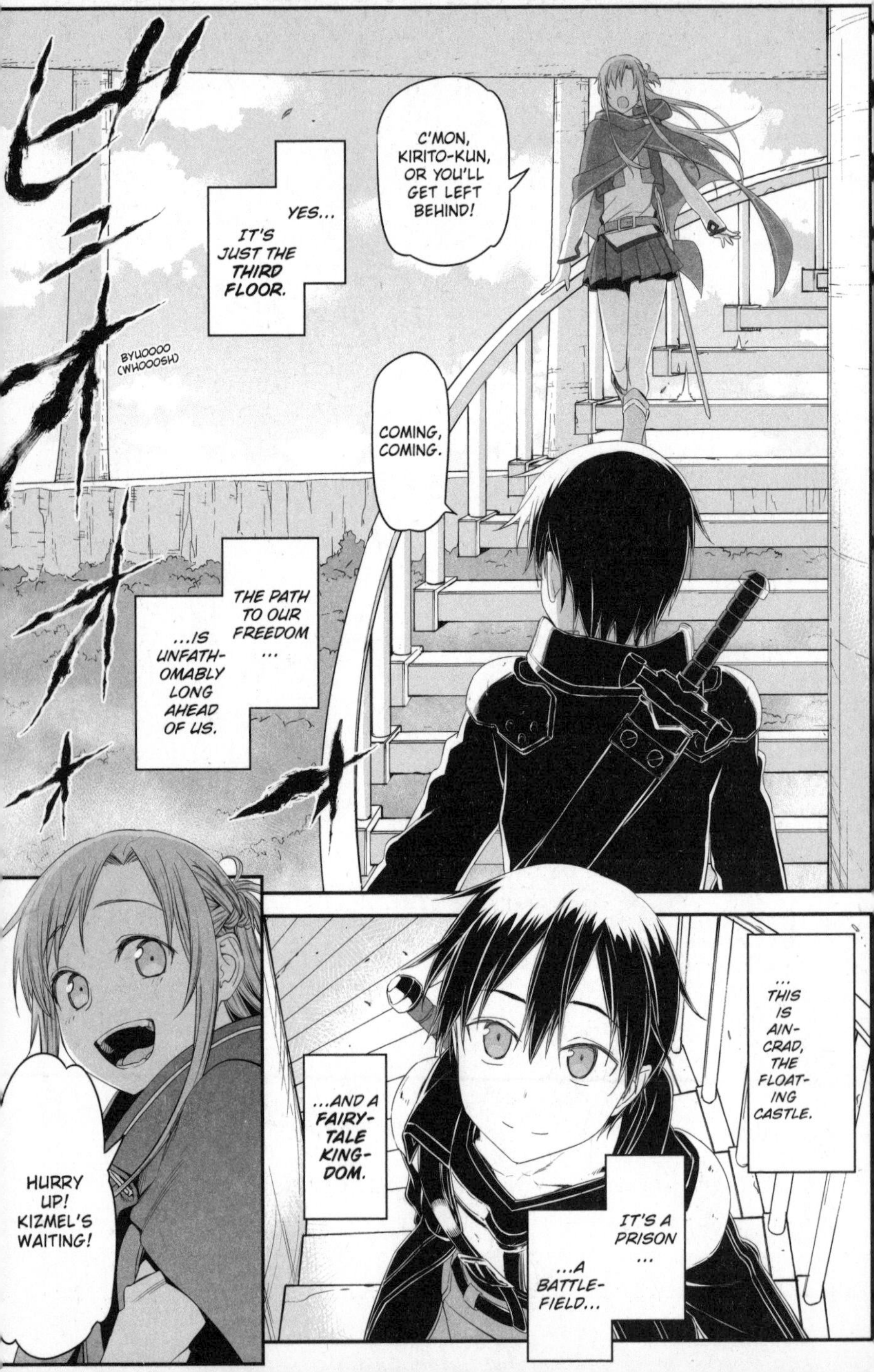
C'MON, KIRITO-KUN, OR YOU'LL GET LEFT BEHIND!
YES... IT'S JUST THE THIRD FLOOR.
BYUOOOO (WHOOOSH)
COMING, COMING.
THE PATH TO OUR FREEDOM ...
...IS UNFATHOMABLY LONG AHEAD OF US.
... THIS IS AINCRAD, THE FLOATING CASTLE.
IT'S A PRISON ...
...A BATTLEFIELD...
...AND A FAIRYTALE KINGDOM.
HURRY UP! KIZMEL'S WAITING!

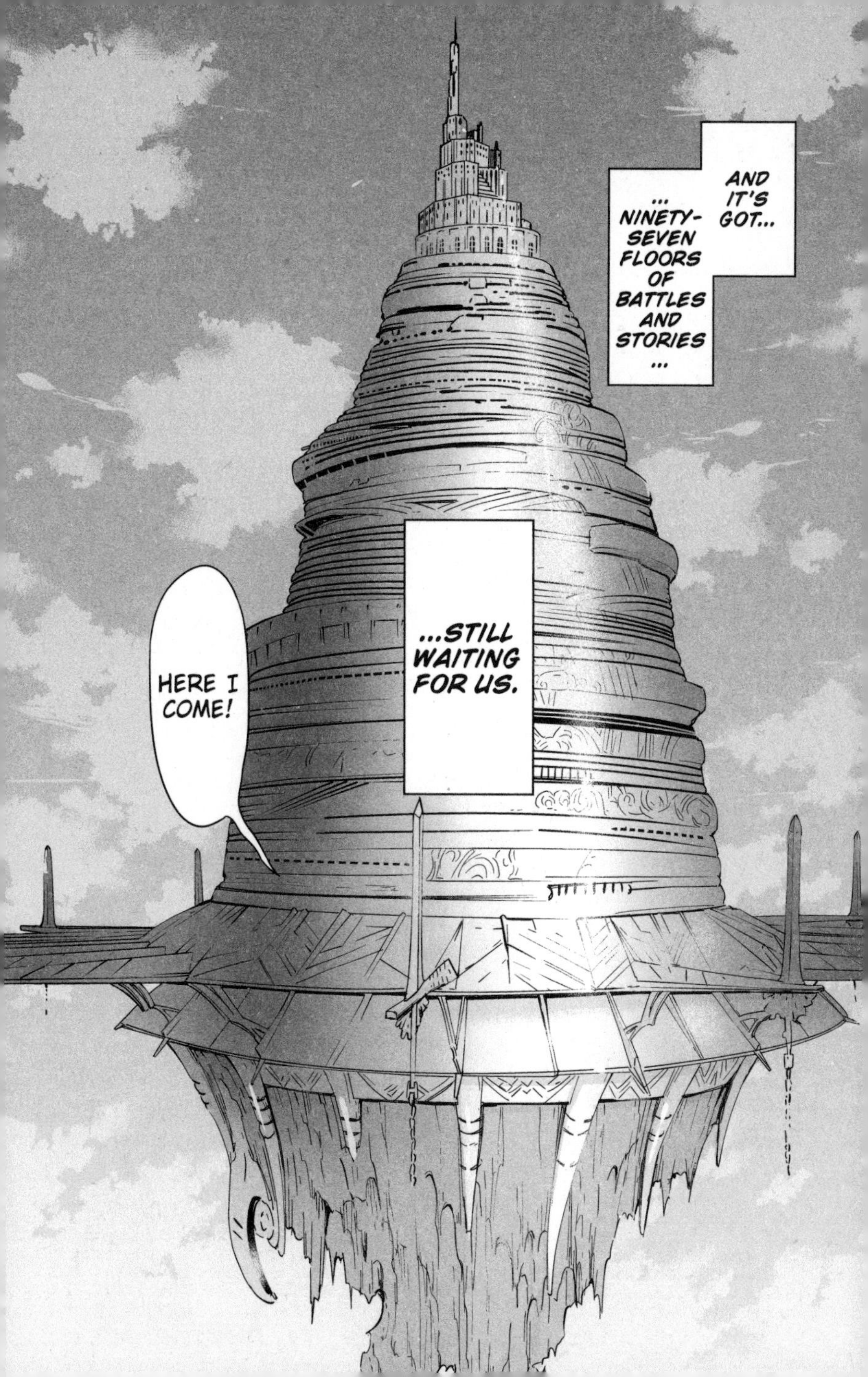
AND IT'S GOT...
...NINETY-SEVEN FLOORS OF BATTLES AND STORIES...
...STILL WAITING FOR US.
HERE I COME!

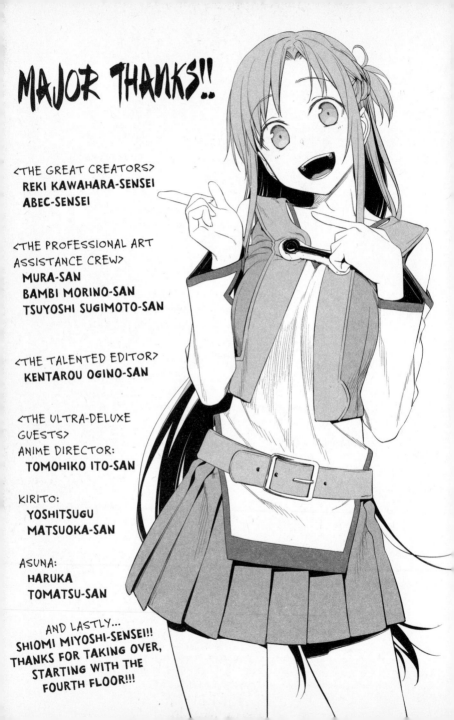

MAJOR THANKS!!

<THE GREAT CREATORS>
REKI KAWAHARA-SENSEI
ABEC-SENSEI

<THE PROFESSIONAL ART ASSISTANCE CREW>
MURA-SAN
BAMBI MORINO-SAN
TSUYOSHI SUGIMOTO-SAN

<THE TALENTED EDITOR>
KENTAROU OGINO-SAN

<THE ULTRA-DELUXE GUESTS>
ANIME DIRECTOR:
TOMOHIKO ITO-SAN

KIRITO:
YOSHITSUGU MATSUOKA-SAN

ASUNA:
HARUKA TOMATSU-SAN

AND LASTLY...
SHIOMI MIYOSHI-SENSEI!!
THANKS FOR TAKING OVER, STARTING WITH THE FOURTH FLOOR!!!

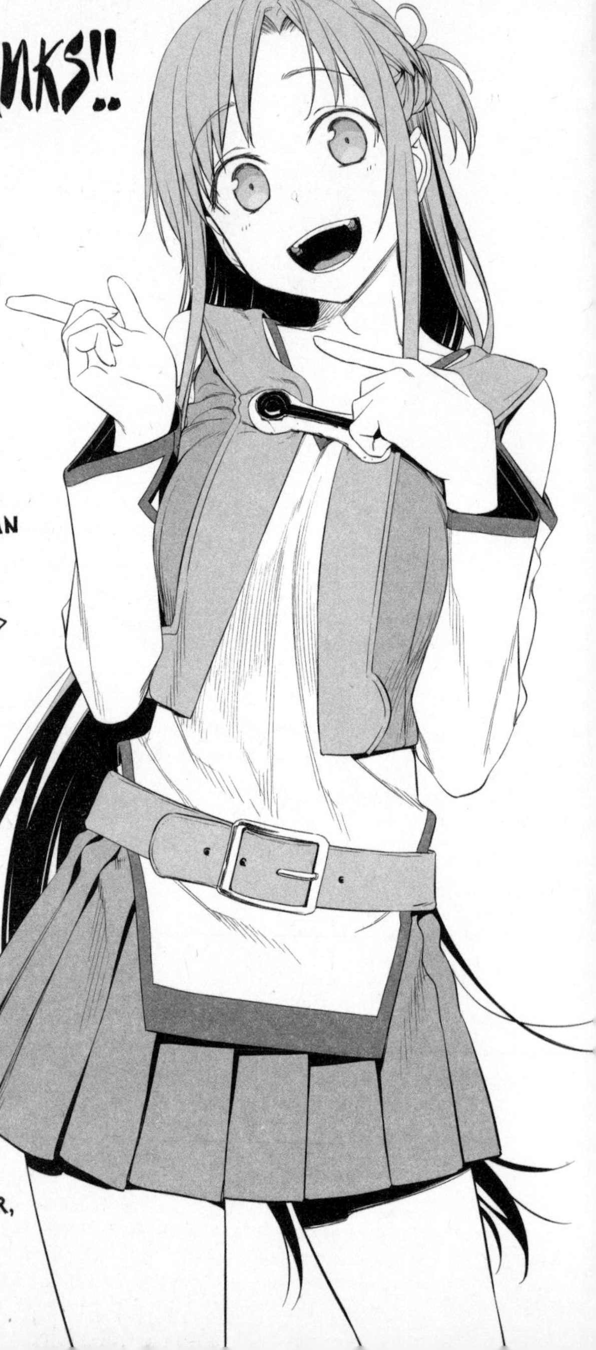

SPECIAL MESSAGE

SWORD ART ONLINE PROGRESSIVE

Here are some messages from people deeply involved in the *Sword Art Online* anime to celebrate the completion of the original run of the *Sword Art Online Progressive* manga!

D0556429

SWORD ART ONLINE

Director: *SAO* season 1 & 2 & movie

TOMOHIKO ITO

I HAD SO MUCH FUN READING THIS VERSION OF SAO AND THE UNIQUE ESSENCE KISEKI HIMURA-SAN BROUGHT TO IT!!

I NEVER REALIZED THERE WAS SO MUCH BARE SKIN IN THIS...

WELL, CONGRATS, AND ENJOY SOME REST!!

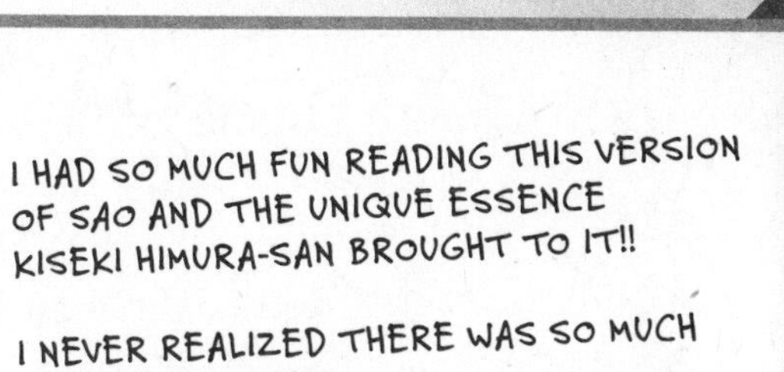

I'M IN THIS SO MUCH...

GEH HEH HEH...

TOMOHIKO ITO